MW01596860

COUSINS

RANGERS, RACISM, AND REDEMPTION IN EARLY TWENTIETH CENTURY TEXAS

ROBERT J. EELLS

authorHOUSE®

AuthorHouse™
1663 Liberty Drive
Bloomington, IN 47403
www.authorhouse.com
Phone: 1 (800) 839-8640

© 2017 Robert J. Eells. All rights reserved.

No part of this book may be reproduced, stored in a retrieval system, or transmitted by any means without the written permission of the author.

Published by AuthorHouse   03/24/2017

ISBN: 978-1-5246-8518-8 (sc)
ISBN: 978-1-5246-8517-1 (e)

Print information available on the last page.

Any people depicted in stock imagery provided by Thinkstock are models, and such images are being used for illustrative purposes only. Certain stock imagery © Thinkstock.

This book is printed on acid-free paper.

Because of the dynamic nature of the Internet, any web addresses or links contained in this book may have changed since publication and may no longer be valid. The views expressed in this work are solely those of the author and do not necessarily reflect the views of the publisher, and the publisher hereby disclaims any responsibility for them.

To the Memory of My Father, Walter E. Eells,
Whose Life in Medicine Inspired Me to Develop
the Central Character and Medical Adventures
in All Three Novels in the *Tex Med* Trilogy

Designed by, Allison Hall

CONTENTS

CHAPTER ONE

ESCAPE AND REFUGE

TOBY WASHINGTON, A THIRTY-SEVEN-YEAR OLD Negro, sat on a bench outside the Lone Star Café in Los Indios, Texas. He was grateful that his boss, Burt Martin, allowed him to take a short break on a bench in late morning after the big rush of locals had mostly subsided. By this time, he'd already been at work for six hours. His feet ached and his arthritic knees throbbed. His break gave him time to reflect on what he had experienced since his unplanned arrival in this small, dusty town in October 1916.

He had been on his way to Brownsville, his last hope, where a friend had been alerted about his imminent arrival. Fleeing in panic from his home in Temple, Texas, he had already failed to relocate to a place among friends or acquaintances at two other previous quests. He didn't blame them. Most colored folks were on edge that summer and early fall. Events in Waco were seared into their minds. A Negro named Jesse Washington, a distant cousin, had been tried and convicted of murdering a white woman in May. Executed not by civil authorities but by a crazed mob that tortured him before hanging and burning his body over a

1

huge fire. Staring at the photograph in the Waco newspaper had chilled him to the bone. Toby sighed heavily thinking how unfair it had been for anyone to link him to the Waco affair. But they had. Apparently, he was just too darn friendly with people, especially with white females in Temple.

He refused to believe it even when some of his colored friends warned him about rumors they had heard involving "teaching him a lesson." His skepticism vanished, however, that night in late August when a firebomb shattered his front window and drove his wife, two daughters, and himself out into the night. They fearfully huddled together in the backyard as several white men, the leader hooded and wearing a flowing white gown, rode around shouting racial slurs and curses warning them to get out of town before even worse things happened. *Worse*?

They raced to a neighbor's where they watched their home, a shack really, burn to the ground. Toby had fled the next morning after much prayer and discussion with his wife and a few close friends. Thankfully, he was able to relocate his family temporarily until a more permanent refuge from this insanity could be found.

A passerby at that moment would have seen Toby's face change from a frown to a smile as the nightmare part of his daydream ended and his mind shifted to his initial experiences with the people of Los Indios. He pictured himself stumbling into town and wandering around, knowing he might have to return and sleep at the depot since the train was only stopping briefly. Would the people be friendly? Would they even let him eat at the local restaurant?

Composed of a main thoroughfare with perhaps three or four parallel streets on both sides, it wasn't much of a town. As he shuffled around, a few locals smiled at him, most ignored. At least they didn't cross to the other side to avoid coming too close for comfort. The Lone Star Café was clearly the only restaurant in town so he inhaled deeply, hiked up his pants, and entered not knowing if segregation was a part of Los Indios. If so, he would be asked to leave, kindly or otherwise.

The combination of a growling stomach and the existence of several inviting empty tables made for an easy decision. He quickly walked to the nearest table and sat down wondering if this would be the "last straw" and his stomach would remain empty a "mite" longer. He waited anxiously for a few seconds with downcast eyes. Nothing happened. He raised his chin and looked around noticing a couple curious glances from surrounding tables. He judged them to be impersonal. *A positive sign?*

There were two waitresses on duty. Both spotted him at the same time and moved in his direction. They comically collided in the center of the room and broke into laughter.

"That's my table," announced the redhead.

"No, it's mine," responded the brunette as the giggling continued.

From the redhead, "Okay, we'll both take it." And they did, marching straight toward him arm in arm.

"I'm Heather and this is my friend, Anne," said the redhead. "We're both pleased to serve you, sir. Would you like to see a menu? Or you can order from the list of today's specials on the blackboard there on the side wall."

Caught up in his reverie on the bench Toby shifted. He was grinning at the memory of his first encounter with these lively (and lovely) young ladies. He recalled how they instantly recognized him as a stranger and asked gentle and appropriate questions about his situation. Never once had they appeared uneasy about the color of his skin. Heather, in fact, seemed mostly concerned about the state of his finances after he confessed he was nearly broke. He remembered saying, "Don't think, Miss Heather, I can even afford to order from the menu," which Anne had just placed before him, "to say nuthin' 'bout those tasty lookin' eats on the wall." Without hesitating, Heather declared they would figure something out with the owner and marched off with Anne to confront the man working behind the counter. The three of them conversed for a bit, then the owner turned in Toby's direction, smiled and waved the ladies away. Returning, Heather said, "According to Mr. Martin it's *'on the house'* today, Mr. Washington, dessert included."

"Thank you kindly, Miss Heather," was all Toby could manage to utter.

"You're very welcome, Mr. Washington," said Anne. She then leaned toward him and whispered, "Heather and I will twist Mr. Martin's arm and try to persuade him to start a new tradition – like offering a free meal to the first stranger who arrives here on Saturday afternoon. Good idea?"

Toby recalled saying, "Yes, ma'am, a wonderful thought," while inwardly thinking perhaps he'd died and gone to heaven. *Was this town for real?*

After finishing a substantial meal, including a huge and delicious piece of apple pie, Toby mentioned he'd better move along and make his way back to the depot to sleep and wait for the next day's train to Brownsville. Heather seemed disturbed at this revelation and said, "Hold on, Mr. Washington. We don't want you sleeping on a hard bench or the floor. We'll try to find a place for you to stay overnight. In fact, our friends, the Townleys, will be arriving shortly for dinner. It's their Saturday habit to eat here. Katherine Townley will know what to do. Have some more coffee and when they arrive I'll make the introductions." Wondering what now lay in store for him, he replied, "Mighty kind of ya, but I don't wanna cause no trouble."

"No trouble at all," replied Heather. "We'll let 'em finish supper and then I'll take you to their table."

The Townleys arrived shortly thereafter, and the Mrs. waved to the other customers, even engaging in an animated conversation with an elderly couple before rejoining her husband. She asked both waitresses to join them, but they declined saying their shift would continue a while longer. The foursome did, however, briefly talk during which a few fingers were pointed toward Toby's table. His nerves were on edge as the minutes dragged.

To Toby the couple appeared to be late middle aged, nicely but casually dressed, neither looking particularly Western or Texan: no cowboy boots, hats, or jeans. His first overall impression was positive. After finishing dessert, cake not pie for them, the couple rose and walked directly toward Toby's table. He remembered standing awkwardly and waiting for a waitress to arrive and introduce them. No one appeared, but it wasn't a problem because the wife took over smoothly by first introducing herself then her husband: Katherine and Brian Townley. Firm handshakes were exchanged.

"Mr. Washington, I understand," said Katherine, taking the lead from her obviously more reserved husband. "Heather has shared a few things with me about your predicament but fill us in with more details. This is a friendly Christian community and we like to be as helpful as possible. We don't want you sleeping in the depot, that's for sure."

At that moment, his daydream was interrupted as the back door creaked open and he heard his boss jokingly say, "Y'all still nappin' out there, Toby? Don't worry, though.

It ain't busy inside so take a few extra minutes." Toby was happy to return to his memories.

He was fairly certain that the real reason for the train trip had not been shared during that initial conversation with the Townleys. He had said something about relocating for a new job opportunity, partly true of course. "I'm a handyman," he had said at one point. "Done many jobs, always willin' to try somethin' new."

"Impressive," interjected Mr. Townley.

"Certainly is," agreed Mrs. Townley. "By the way," she continued, "are you a family man?"

"Yes, ma'am, wife and two young'uns, both girls. Want to have 'em join me as soon as possible." Talking about his family also gave him a chance to say, "I'm also a Christian, ma'am. Baptist, in fact."

"That's wonderful. We're Baptist too. Southern Baptist to be precise."

He knew he wasn't of that brand but decided not to point it out. Rather he said, "We Baptists have much in common, don't we?"

"We do indeed," answered Katherine with conviction. "That gives me even more reason to find a place for you to stay tonight. Let me make a call, then I'll elaborate." She excused herself and went to call from the owner's office in the rear of the restaurant. To Toby's relief, Heather and Anne showed up to help keep the conversation alive.

Katherine returned and quietly summarized the new developments. She had found a place to stay with a Mr. Henderson. She invited Toby to worship with them at their church's early service, and she asked him to join their family and others for coffee and fellowship later that night at their home.

"Just a few people tonight, Mr. Washington. Heather and Anne will be there as well as our daughter, Diane. I've asked Worth Henderson to stop by too. You can come with him after you freshen up a bit at his place. We'll drop you off now, if that's convenient?"

Toby was stunned and could remember only two reactions: slowly easing back onto his chair and somehow managing to croak, "That's way too generous, ma'am. Much more'n I deserve."

"Nonsense!" said Katherine. "I'll take that as a 'yes,'" she added with a wink.

A free dinner, coffee with new friends, a pillow for his weary head, and a place to worship, all experienced within the last three hours. He couldn't make any sense of his luck as they gathered to depart.

In his mind he relived these events during the ride to Mr. Henderson's sitting in the bed of the truck. Katherine had urged him to ride up front in the single seat but he had quickly declined feeling it might not be appreciated by everyone in town, and he realized he was dirty and stank from his long journey.

Worth Henderson seemed relatively at ease with the spur-or-the-moment arrangements and showed Toby to his room where he placed his weathered knapsack filled with his meager belongings on the bed. Worth gave him a brief tour of the house then they walked toward the Rio Grande to kill time before their scheduled appearance at the Townley's. The shallow and placid river stretched before them and Toby made note of its appearance to Worth.

"Usually wider and more powerful but we've had a bad drought lately. Kinda unusual for this part of Texas 'cause we're closer to the Gulf which gives us a bit more rain and humidity."

Toby said, "Most folks believe all of Texas is hot and dry like west Texas. Ain't the case, I guess."

"True," replied Henderson who then paused and glanced south toward Mexico. "Say, see that there island in the middle of the river? Lots of crazy things been happenin' there this past summer." Toby looked puzzled so Worth described the audacious raid by the Mexican bandits into Texas and the courageous response of the citizens led by the Rangers. Worth continued, "In fact, several incursions took place along the border at the same time. Damn fools were tryin' to steal Texas from America and force it back under the Mexican flag. We taught 'em a lesson, though. Won't be makin' that mistake again, I bet."

"Ain't heard a whisper 'bout it up north," said Toby, shaking his head in disbelief. "Great tale, though, and worthy of the Texas fightin' spirit."

"Not just a tale, it's true. Worthy of braggin' 'bout, in my opinion. Heroes should be praised and remembered. Someone should write a book or make a movie 'bout 'em."

A little more wandering and a few more stories followed until Worth announced, "Sun's goin' down. Better head back so we can wash up 'fore walkin' to the Townley's. They're close. Only take a few minutes."

As he washed off the Texas dust, Toby decided that the trip over would be a good opportunity to raise the awkward question about race relations in Los Indios. He hardly knew Mr. Henderson, so this was risky but necessary. He simply had to know if his experience with the three ladies at the restaurant was a good example or rare indeed.

After walking the first block, and with a dry mouth, Toby found the courage to make his inquiry. Worth paused then said, "There are many good Christians in town, Toby, and some fine people who aren't particularly religious. But 'no,' the acceptance you felt from these special women would not be typical. Friendliness, yes, but not the type of love displayed at the restaurant. I think in part it's 'cause we don't have that many colored folks in town. We aren't very experienced dealin' with 'em. And it's the South, ya know, even the deep South. No need to remind y'all of that fact I figure." *No need at all* Toby thought as they reached their destination.

As they anticipated, he was warmly greeted at the Townley home.

Their daughter, Diane, smiled her way into his heart and it almost seemed as if she wanted to turn her handshake into a hug. After all the formalities had ended, they all were escorted into the dining room where the table was adorned with a chocolate cake and a big pot of steaming coffee. A pitcher of lemonade was available for those who preferred a cool drink. Once seated, Toby made sure to let everyone else be seated first, then more friendly questions were directed his way. He quietly answered all to everyone's satisfaction.

Katherine then regaled the company with an exciting telling of many of the events of the past summer in Los Indios. Toby learned even more details about the bandit raid Worth had previously mentioned. She let Diane relate the story of the dramatic rescue of Heather and her cousin, Sarah, by Sarah's brother, John McFarland, and the Rangers. Sarah and Heather had been kidnapped during that very same raid. Diane didn't forget to mention the helpful role Heather had played in the rescue efforts.

Diane's mom regained the floor and breathlessly recounted how John and Heather had listened to her pleas and soon after returning from Mexico agreed to travel to Midland to save her son, Ted, from a life of danger and debauchery in the oilfields of west Texas. Glancing at

Heather, she said, "I can't thank you enough for saving my son. And glory be, Ted's coming home soon, a changed man, I believe. Anne's excited about that too. Aren't you, my dear?"

Anne blushed and reached out to place her hand on Heather's which rested on the table. Their eyes met briefly before Heather's dropped to her lap. An embarrassing silence followed before Katherine cleared her throat and added, "And John also will be returning soon from his adventures out West, won't he, Heather?"

A clearly disappointed Heather sighed, "He will if our prayers are answered."

"And they will be," declared a confident Anne.

"Praise God!" Katherine nearly shouted. "With everyone finally back together, some big decisions will need to be made. Brian and I want Ted to finish college. The bigger question involves John's future. We hope he stays in Texas but he needs to finish medical school in Michigan. He and Heather got some plannin' to do."

Sensing some uneasiness, Toby asked Heather and Anne to describe their normal activities. Surely they were more than weekend waitresses. He was astonished to discover how busy they actually were. Heather, being a teacher, also volunteered with Anne at the clinic while Anne worked part-time as an elementary aide at the school. Both co-taught Sunday school in the morning and took aid and comfort to the Indians at the nearby village Sunday afternoons.

"I'm surprised ya have any energy left to bump into each other on Saturdays at the café," Toby said humorously. Though few knew the background to this remark, laughter broke out around the table.

"Why is everyone surprised?" asked a slightly annoyed Diane. "These two women are my heroes. I wanna grow up to be just like 'em. Oh, and like you too, Mom," she hastily added to the amusement of the whole room.

Small talk ensued while cake, coffee, and lemonade were enjoyed. Toby noticed suddenly that the talkative host hadn't spoken for a while and looked pensive like she was thinking about something. He didn't have to wait long.

"I've just had an interesting thought,' she declared, reasserting her lead in the table talk. "Earlier Brian had asked our guest about his employment history. I'd like you, Mr. Washington, to comment further on what you mean by 'handyman.'" All eyes turned to Toby as he coughed nervously and began to speak.

"Well, colored folks like me gonna have to be a 'jack-of-all-trades' to make do. We learn right quick that most jobs will be part-time and many different skills will be needed. So, as a handyman, there's little I ain't done."

He then listed everything he could remember doing in recent years. He'd worked as a church and school janitor, a day laborer on construction projects, been a painter, a field worker picking cotton and vegetables, been a gas station car mechanic, a restaurant dishwasher and cook, as well as a laborer at a hardware store. Toby's work history seemed to impress everyone around the table.

"Just as I had hoped," said Katherine grinning broadly. "Now I'm even more convinced that my idea, or proposition, makes sense. Toby, here it is: Why not end your wanderings and settle in Los Indios? There are several jobs around town, mostly part-time I'm afraid, but perhaps more permanent as you prove your worth." Silence followed as everyone seemed initially taken aback by her words. The silence was quickly broken when all three young women answered affirmatively and almost simultaneously. Then Worth and Brian nodded their assent.

Heather summarized it best saying, "We'd love to have you here in the community, Mr. Washington. And I bet it won't be long before you'll be sending for your family to join you. By that time, we'll have located a place for the whole family to reside, won't we, Mrs. Townley?"

"You can count on it, Mr. Washington," answered Katherine. "What do ya think of my proposal?"

Toby was speechless. After pausing to collect his thoughts, he stammered, "That's too much to take in, Mrs. Townley. I'll have to think on it overnight. Do a heap o' prayin' on my knees. I guess, though, I should ask 'bout what jobs in particular, ma'am, to help with the prayin' and thinkin', I mean."

"Thought you might ask that question," Katherine replied. "I have two in mind. Clerkin' at the Townley general store and helpin' out at the café. I know we need help and Helen Martin recently brought up they're a bit short-handed too. I've also heard that our gas station needs a worker. Their main helper is a mite accident prone and is laid up again. That's a good start for ya, I do believe."

For Toby everything after that moment was a blur. He did remember waking up at Worth's with aching knees, proof that many prayers had been sent heavenward. At least the prayers put him in the right mood for Sunday worship. On the way to church, he said to Worth that after the service he'd make his decision known. *Accept and stay or leave?* He asked himself for the nth time as he and Worth entered the sanctuary.

Most congregants greeted him warmly though a few passed by with only brief eye contact. Pastor Dan spent several minutes welcoming Toby in the back before the service. "Glad you're here," said the Pastor with obvious sincerity.

Already leaning toward staying in Los Indios, the sermon itself was the tipping point. The topic was Christian equality based primarily on Galatians 3:28. At one point, the Pastor looked directly at Toby and boldly added racial equality to the text. His exact words were: "Perhaps if Paul was writin' today he'd expand the 'neithers' by including 'there is neither white nor colored.' All of us are one in Christ." Toby could hardly believe his ears. As if this weren't sufficient confirmation, at that exact moment, he felt a hand on his shoulder coming from directly behind him. He turned and stared into the smiling face of Miss Heather Benson. A great sense of relief washed over him as he realized his decision had just been made. He would stay! He knew he'd have to "test" the waters for a time to prove that his first impressions were accurate – this could be a place of refuge for him and his family!

Toby remembered how delighted his friends were after church when he announced his decision. To celebrate, Katherine invited him and several other members to the Townley's for food and fellowship. Anne whispered that Katherine had stayed up half the night preparing for the "settled" decision. He wasn't surprised.

As his group started to leave, Pastor Dan rushed up, grabbed his arm and said, "I hear you're stayin'. Wonderful! I 'spect to see you here on Sundays, Mr. Washington. No colored church around these parts, so make this your worship home."

"I will indeed, Pastor." He meant it.

Toby's reverie was interrupted again, bringing him back to the present when the backdoor was flung open and Burt yelled out, "Break's over, Toby. Back to work. A small group's just arrived."

Today he was serving as a waiter. As he went among the tables taking orders listening in on several conversations, he was again reminded of the fact that Mrs. Townley's two selections, the café and the store, were the ideal locations to discover more information about the town and its inhabitants. Especially in the morning hours, locals arrived eager to discuss everything under the sun. News, rumors, gossip – he overheard it all. As a believer, he had mixed feelings about the rumors and gossip parts but it sure was entertaining and informative. In less than a month he'd learned enough to send for his family. Hopefully, it would be their new permanent home. Toby had become the town's number one listener. This would prove to be important for him and the town in the near future.

CHAPTER TWO

SCUTTLEBUTT

THE LONE STAR CAFÉ PROVED to be slightly better than the general store for learning everything "under the sun" about this new town. Toby figured it was the strong black coffee that helped loosen tongues in the early morning hours. Also loosened were belts due to the ample portions of pancakes, eggs, bacon, and inch-thick slabs of steaks that he kept cooking or serving to the locals. Today he was mostly serving, at least until Anne showed up in late morning to help with the lunch crowd. After lunch Anne would head to the school or clinic and Toby to the store, and Helen Martin and one other older waitress, a Mexican lady named Rosita, did the serving.

As usual, weather was the first topic to be introduced on this Wednesday dawn. Dallas Young, a retired cotton farmer, complained that if the drought didn't end soon, he'd be "spittin' cotton" himself. "It's so dry," he humorously whined, "that the trees are bribin' the dogs." Most customers, clustered around two tables, chuckled at his description, but Toby was caught off guard and laughed so hard he almost dropped a plate piled six inches high with pancakes. Another regular, Travis Robinson, piped in, "Easy there, Toby. Be a shame to feed Burt's cakes to the rats out by the trash bin. Y'all should be used to our jokes by now."

"Workin' on it, Mr. Robinson, but I ain't heard that one 'fore and it nearly made me double over." He probably shouldn't have said that because it produced a torrent of weather jokes, some old, some new, some inappropriate for the younger crowd or Baptists for that matter. "So dry the catfish are carryin' canteens," he'd heard before. "So dry and hot my ducks don't know how to swim" was original to him, and two more risqué efforts were shared that compared the weather to certain parts of the female anatomy. The latter came, as usual, from Wesley Bartlett, and it resulted in another familiar reaction — an elbow in the ribs from his wife, Renee.

Lucas Harper, a retired cattle rancher, turned serious with a sour expression on his face and said he was getting a bit weary of weather jokes. "My son Don, who y'all know runs my ranch, is havin' a terrible time findin' enough feed for his cattle. He's lost twenty per cent of the herd already. Things don't end soon, our only hope will be to hang on 'til we join the war in Europe." Mentioning the war paused the conversation.

Fannie Walker, a retired teacher, broke the silence by admonishing Lucas. "A good Christian like you, Mr. Harper, shouldn't be hoping for war. Already we've been reading about how awfully destructive the European conflict has become. Seems like people are dying by the thousands on a regular basis. God have mercy!"

Looking a bit pale, Lucas' wife, Janice, added, "I agree, Fannie, Lucas here seems to forget that our grandson is only twenty-two and might get drafted to fight if we join the war effort."

"Now, honey," Lucas responded, "we've discussed this before. They ain't gonna draft farmers and ranchers. No way. But when we do join up, our guys will need beef to eat and cotton for uniforms, that's for sure."

Trying to get the men's backing, Lucas turned to Scott Hunter, a retired Army officer, and asked him to join the conversation. Pausing briefly to collect his thoughts, Hunter said, "Y'all know I fought against the Spanish in '98. War is sometimes necessary but it's still a horrible experience. General Sherman called war 'hell' and he's right. It should be avoided if at all possible. Even Colonel Roosevelt discovered that ugly truth when he witnessed so many of his friends killed or wounded all 'round him as they charged up that hill in Cuba. And I don't think President Wilson can keep us out either. He's just been re-elected and he'll be under a whole lot of pressure to join the fightin' in Europe. Sorry, Lucas, there's money to be made but the price will be high, very high."

Silence again as everyone thought about Hunter's grim forecast. Toby had been listening closely off to one side still holding an empty tray. *What did the possibility of war mean for him?* He finally found the courage to say, "What 'bout us colored folks? Will we be drafted? Got me a family an' I need to look after 'em."

Hunter responded, "Be draftin' everyone, Toby, all men between eighteen and forty or so. Includes you, don't it?"

"Yessir. Be thirty-eight right soon. Don't wanna kill nobody though."

"Ain't gonna put y'all in the infantry, Toby. Y'all be behind the lines supportin' the troops. Make ya a cook or truck driver or somethin'. No dodgin' bullets for you, Toby."

"Still rather stay and be with my family," Toby sighed. *Ain't got no luck, no how.*

Attempting to shift away from the war talk, Julia Hunter said, "I hear y'all have a nice place of your own now, Toby. Tell us all 'bout it."

"Yes, ma'am. Mrs. Townley found me a nice little house on the town's outskirts. Martha, my wife, is pleased and right quick she's makin' it real homey. We sure are beholden to y'all fer bein' so kind."

"Well, y'all deserve it," Julia concluded. "Hard work should be rewarded."

"Thank you, ma'am. I do find a way to keep busy 'round here. I'm real blessed."

All heads turned as Anne Yoder burst into the café slightly out of breath. "I think I'm late," she said guiltily. "Nurse Nancy kept me longer than usual at the clinic. People are showing up with cold and flu symptoms and she's overwhelmed. I'm afraid that when I'm finished with the noon rush, I'll have to return to the clinic. Doc Miller's pretty much out of the picture now, as most of you know. Sure wish Heather's John were here to help out."

Everyone watched as she quickly put on her apron and cheerfully became a waitress. This gave Toby a chance to work briefly with Burt who was training him in the mysteries of cooking for Texans, Texas white folks that is. Burt seemed pleased, however, when Toby occasionally shared with him a secret or two about how colored folks did their cooking.

Toby switched to serving when the lunch rush began. A busy time, but Anne still found a moment to ask Toby to run over to the school after work with a message for Heather: no Anne today; it was back to the clinic for her in the afternoon.

"She'll understand," whispered Anne. "In fact, knowing her, she'll probably offer to join us when her school day ends."

"Yes, ma'am. Be happy to take the message fer ya. School's right on my way to the store."

Anne paused then added, "Say, Toby, why don't you stop by also when you're finished with your clerking. We need all the help we can get."

"Right kind of ya, Miss Anne. Bet Martha can hold back supper a bit fer a good cause." He wondered, as he returned to work, how many more jobs the good people of Los Indios could line up for him. *Pleased to stay busy but couldn't they pay a bit more?* Feeling sorry for himself seemed ungrateful, so he quickly pushed these thoughts from his mind.

During lunch, Alice Davis entered and was a little peeved that her favorite two-person table in the corner was already occupied. Recently widowed, she had decided she couldn't live without a daily helping of Burt's tasty and nourishing black bean soup. Anne noticed her frustration and personally escorted her to the counter with a pledge to grab her special location as soon as it became available. Promptly the table became available and Anne made a beeline to the counter, picked up the still steaming bowl of soup, and led Alice to her favorite spot.

"Awfully nice of you, sweetie," said a grateful Alice.

"My pleasure. I know how much you hate sitting at the counter on those uncomfortable stools." Anne turned to leave but was stopped by a tug on her sleeve.

"What's the news about Ted?" asked Alice. "I know how excited you are for his return."

"I am. I'm also anxious to see if he's as changed as his mother believes."

"She tries to see him in the best possible light," offered Alice. Perhaps a bit naïve because of his history of youthful shenanigans. A mother never really gives up on a child, I guess."

Anne said, "Katherine never will, that's for sure." Pausing, she added, "I've received a letter from him recently with another interesting twist: Ted may not be returning alone." Just then Anne was called to another table by Toby and was unable to offer an explanation, much to Alice's disappointment. Alice was a person who didn't miss much from her corner seat and didn't keep much to herself either.

Anne finished the story, however, when the two women met at the door as Alice was leaving. Anne recounted the tale of the Ranger, Captain Decker, who was wounded in Mexico as John, Ted, and others were hunting for the bandit, Pancho Villa.

"Perilous times, I do believe," said Alice, shaking her head. "Heard the part 'bout Villa from Katherine herself. She broke down tellin' me 'bout it. Can't recall her referrin' to a Ranger captain though."

"According to Ted," Anne said, "the captain was badly wounded and Ted decided to stay behind in El Paso a few days to see if he'd recover. Seems like they became good friends having those adventures. Heather and I also knew him from that time. At any rate, the captain may return with Ted when he's well enough to travel."

"Why Los Indios?"

"Apparently he has no family and had just quit the Rangers. Rather sad when you think about it."

"Quite a story, young lady. Indeed, it's right sad 'bout that Ranger fella, no family and out of a job. Perhaps, though, it casts Ted in a good light; ready to stand up for a friend and work through hard times." It warmed Anne's heart to hear those last words about Ted. As she watched Alice depart, Anne smiled as she realized Mrs. Davis would spread the story far and wide.

Relieved when the last of the lunch crowd finally disappeared, Toby and Anne went their separate ways. Toby stopped by the school and informed Heather of Anne's predicament. Not bothered at all, Heather, as predicted, declared she'd pitch in at the clinic as soon as her school day ended.

"Amazing ladies," Toby muttered to himself as he made his way over to the store.

That's when it happened: something unexpected and troubling! Three young men headed toward him on his side of the street, strutting and jostling, plainly in high spirits. Just young white folks having some fun, Toby prayed as they came closer. Everything changed when they spotted him. They abruptly halted, gave him the evil eye, glanced at one another for support, and then spread out — three abreast — leaving no room to get by on either side. Hoping for a peaceful outcome, Toby slowed down but kept moving forward. Familiar images from events in Temple flashed through his mind. *Would Los Indios be any different?* Seconds later Toby stopped but they kept coming, pulling up inches from his face. Their obvious leader was in the middle with hatred contorting his face. First uttering a racial slur, he then ordered Toby to get off the elevated boardwalk and down into the street.

"This sidewalk belongs to Americans, white people," he shouted with a face twisted into a haughty sneer. "Get off a here 'fore we throw ya off," he hissed through clenched, rotten teeth.

Toby's heart pounded and his knees started to shake. *Should he stand firm?* He wanted to but it was three against one and the street was otherwise empty. No one to give him a hand even if they dared to defy these ruffians. Toby stepped back just as the leader's hand shot forward intending to push Toby down. It missed but the message was delivered nonetheless. Toby meekly stepped down into the dusty street right into a pile of horse manure — which he had not seen until the last second. The ruffians broke out into loud guffaws.

"Perfect endin'," said the leader flashing a wicked grin. To add insult to injury, he then let fly a big blob of spit toward Toby's feet. It landed right on top of Toby's clean shoe. "Y'all ain't welcome 'round here, boy," he said angrily. "Got us two other Negro families in town as it is. Two's 'nuff, actually more'n 'nuff. Y'all better leave if ya know what's good fer ya."

Toby stood there feeling helpless and humiliated as the assailants swaggered away peering over their shoulders with obvious amusement at the plight of their hapless victim.

Still shaking and emotionally battered, Toby sat down wearily on the bench outside the store to clean his shoes and calm his racing heart. One arriving customer noticed his situation and mood and asked why he was "down in the dumps." Toby smiled weakly and said he was just fine, wanting to avoid discussing with a stranger what had just happened to him. Once inside though, Brian Townley recognized something was different and said," Where's that smilin' face, Toby? Somethin' eatin' at ya?"

Toby wouldn't make eye contact, so Brian pulled him aside and demanded an answer. Toby sighed and told him what had occurred.

"Describe the leader to me," demanded Brian.

"Tall, droopy mustache, dirty clothes, rumpled Western hat, beat up cowboy boots, a small scar on his left cheek."

"I knew it!" snapped Brian. "That's Wade King, local troublemaker. He's got several other young thugs hangin' on his every word. They're the cause of half of the two-bit crime in these parts, in my opinion. Our good-for-nothin' sheriff is too scared to make a case against 'em, and the Rangers have too much on their plate and way too much territory to cover. Need to have a sit down with Captain Springer soon, I believe. Things are reachin' a boilin' point."

"I'll try to avoid 'em in the future, Mr. Townley, now that I know who they be. Maybe things'll quiet down anyway."

"Not likely, Toby, probably get worse. Racial scares been risin' lately I'm 'fraid. Been readin' 'bout it in the San Antonio paper. Things got hot up in Waco last year. Y'all hear 'bout it, Toby?" Toby shrugged his answer.

"There are some rumors of a new Negro-hatin' organization up north somewhere. Movin' south, too, accordin' to some reports. I'll let ya know if I hear anythin' else. Best to be prepared." *New organization?* Toby remembered the one robed and hooded rider in Temple who had driven them from their home. And he knew well the horror stories from the post-war South. *Could it be happening again?*

"'Preciate yer concern fer me and my family, Mr. Townley," he managed to say as he tried clearing his mind to focus on his work.

Concentration proved difficult, and he made several silly mistakes with customers as the minutes dragged on. Even his skill for listening suffered as the normal conversations around him seemed to fly in one ear and out the other, little stored for later reference. Toby promised himself he'd do better when taking his mid-afternoon break, this time a casual walk around the block. Thankfully, his frame of mind had settled down by late afternoon, so much so that Burt even ushered him behind the cash register to show him how to ring up customers.

"Thought it was time ya learned the ropes, Toby," said his grinning boss. "Won't be long 'fore y'all will be in charge of everythin' in the store. Maybe not the orderin' of supplies and such but everythin' up front here at least."

Maybe Brian was saying all this to make Toby feel better in light of their earlier racial discussion. Whatever the reason, he felt honored and said, "I'll live up to yer trust, Mr. Townley. Won't never let ya down."

"I know y'all won't, Toby. Ya keep makin' progress and it won't be long 'fore Katherine and I can take off a day or two and leave y'all in charge."

That praise changed everything for Toby, and within minutes he was back to his old self: smiling broadly at the customers, providing first-class service to all, and mentally storing every bit of news and advice picked up while helping.

One customer in particular seemed worthy of remembering: Carlos Sanchez. Carlos was known by all as being the best handyman in town. He had entered the store just before closing and was busy buying a few items to finish his present job. Noticing Toby, he came directly over and said, "Listen, neighbor (they lived a few houses apart) you know what I do for work, 'bout anything people need. Brian mentioned you're a handyman like me. I know that two jobs keep ya pretty busy already. But I'm swamped this fall. If ya can spare a few hours, after work or weekends, I sure could use some help. Interested?"

"Have to think on it, Mr. Sanchez, but 'preciate the offer." And he would mull it over, he thought, for two good reasons. One, it would be great to work with his hands again. Tearing apart and building things were second nature to him. Two, he could use the extra money to save up to buy the house he was presently renting. Taking in all his recent blessings, he knew fortune was breaking his way. *God be praised!*

Halfway home, Toby suddenly remembered his promise to spend some time at the clinic. He increased his pace the rest of the way home and reaching there he informed Martha of his pledge, hoping for the best. Thankfully, she sent him on his way with a kiss on the cheek, though he did detect a hint of disappointment on her face. "Be back soon," he yelled to his daughters who were playing out back, then started for the clinic, his third job for the day.

The clinic was jammed with people. A few were standing around outside waiting to be seen. Toby inched his way between mothers who were holding infants and children until he reached Anne on the far side of the waiting room.

Anne was pleased to see him and immediately introduced him to Nurse Nancy who stood close by.

"Thanks for coming, Toby," Nancy said, looking tired from her long hours working at the clinic. "Lots of sick people here, mostly children. All six beds in the other room are full. Just a few cots here to catch the overload. We believe it's the flu or a nasty cold. Either way it's rough on the kids. First we wipe 'em down with cold compresses and give 'em little sips of water. If that works, great, if not, we empty the vomit bowls and start to introduce a method Doc John taught us this past summer, one that deals best with dehydration — a serious condition in the young."

"Y'all mean, Miss Heather's John, Miss Nancy?"

"He's the one. He taught us to squirt a little water up the rectum with a syringe then squeeze the cheeks together tightly so no liquid leaks out. Amazin' how fast it works. John says it gets absorbed right through the walls of the large intestine." Pausing briefly, she then said, "I even added a touch myself: a sprinkle of salt to the water. Read somewhere that dehydration depletes the body of salt. Can't hurt and everybody needs salt in their diet. It's common knowledge."

"Well, if that don't beat all," Toby said, shaking his head. Taking in the whole sea of misery, he rolled up his sleeves and said, "Well, ladies, what can I be helpin' y'all with?"

"Two jobs and they're both nasty," Anne chimed in. Before she could explain, Toby interrupted, "It be okay with me, Miss Anne. I ain't no stranger to nasty work. My little ones is sick sometimes too."

Nancy gave Toby instructions by outlining two jobs in particular: first, emptying vomit bowls when necessary and second, regular washing of the syringe, which Toby discovered resembled a baster for cooking.

"Works better for me," Nancy said when Toby looked puzzled. "Careful – we only got one."

Toby began immediately. He soon discovered it wasn't so bad, as long as he regularly washed his own hands. The smell was the worst part; it was overpowering. Pinching his nose gave some relief from the stench, but frequent trips outside to breathe fresh air was the better answer. He felt sorry for the little ones and prayed he wouldn't take the sickness with him when he finally went home.

Heather burst in at suppertime waving a small piece of paper in her hand. Toby saw her pull Anne aside and above the commotion heard her say, "I got held over at school by a concerned parent. Took more time than I expected. Then on my way over here the telegraph operator saw me and asked me to give you this message. Guess he figured I'd find you faster. He was right and here I am. 'Yes,' I did read it because it isn't even in an envelope. I didn't think you'd mind. You're my best friend, Anne. Take it outside and read it now. I'll cover for you here."

Toby went to the window and watched Anne read the telegram. Anne turned back toward the clinic grinning from ear to ear. She raised both hands to the sky as if praying and celebrating at the same time. He guessed the reason for her joy but wanted to find out for sure. He did when Anne skipped back inside and shared the good news. Mr. Ted was coming home next week! Heather and Nancy elbowed their way over and wrapped her in a big hug leaving Toby in charge of the clinic for a few moments. They seemed unmindful of the misery around them. Nancy was the first to break away and return to her duties leaving two very happy young ladies, still embracing, with tears streaming down their faces.

The foul smells snapped them back to the reality around them. As they turned in Toby's direction, he thought he saw a flicker of pain or sadness on Heather's face. Anne must have seen it, too, because she put her arm around Heather's shoulder and whispered in her ear. Toby imagined it was about Heather's still missing friend, John. This hunch proved correct when Anne spoke again as they drew nearer, this time loud enough for everyone to hear. "John's next, Heather. Trust me. I can feel it in my bones."

When their work for the day had slowed down, Toby heard Anne tell Nancy that Ted was bringing someone with him, a fellow she called Captain Decker, a Texas Ranger. She was worried that he might need further medical attention due to a recent gunshot wound. Nancy urged her not to fret, he'd be looked after.

"In fact," said the nurse, "I bet there'll be an extra bed here for him soon. He's welcome to get back on his feet here if necessary. We'll all take good care of him."

"Yes we will," said Heather with sureness. She now put her hand on Anne's shoulder and added, "We'll relieve the burden on Ted, giving him more time to spend with you, Anne Yoder. Do you like my scheme?" They embraced and finished their volunteer work in great spirits. Hard not to be infected by their optimism for the near future, Toby felt, as they all saw the last recovering patients leave.

After the three volunteers were washed up and prepared to go home, Heather called everyone together for a final announcement. "I've been mulling this over and here's my idea. I think we should celebrate Ted's return with a big party. I suggest combining it with Thanksgiving. I know Katherine will jump at the opportunity. She'll offer her home and will want to invite lots of people. And you, Toby, with your whole family." Scanning three faces, she finished with, "First-rate notion, isn't it?"

The two women instantly agreed. Toby was uncomfortable but nodded. Los Indios, not a perfect place but special nonetheless, thought Toby, as he set off for home and a very late supper. Halfway there, the "not perfect" part returned as a bad memory and he picked up his pace, glancing nervously in all directions praying his earlier nightmare wouldn't be repeated.

CHAPTER THREE

THE PRODIGAL RETURNS

Toby listened as Janice Harper talked about Ted Townley's return. "He's been quite a handful over the years for Katherine and Brian. Drinkin' and partyin', have caused his mom many sleepless nights. John and Heather say he's startin' to change. Hope that's true, also for Anne's sake. We all adore her." Toby hoped to meet him soon so he could judge for himself.

I WAS DRIFTING IN AND OUT of a snooze on the train when a disturbance broke out from the rear of my car. The noise brought me back totally alert. The man beside me, Captain Decker, put a hand on my shoulder and said, "Been watchin' those youngsters fer a while. Gettin' drunker and rowdier by the minute. Weren't fer my cane and sittin' by the window I'd have ordered 'em to pipe down or suffer the consequences."

"Y'all ain't a Ranger no more, Captain."

"What the hell difference does that make," Decker answered with irritation. "Reckon I'm a grownup who speaks with authority, and I'm packin' a six-shooter. That's more'n 'nuff."

"Shall I come with ya?"

"No need but y'all can trail me if ya like. Best not to stay too close."

Somewhat nervously, I rose, stepped into the aisle, and made room for him to march toward the troublemakers. Despite using a cane, he reached them quickly, though with all the ruckus they didn't notice his approach. Peeking from behind his shoulders, I could see four men clawing and swinging at each other, like a tipsy free-for-all. So drunk, I guessed, that everyone was a target. Decker shouted but to no avail. He merely shrugged, then pulled out his pistol, and clobbered the first two men he could reach. Both immediately collapsed unconscious to the floor.

Sadly, the second blow also smashed a whiskey bottle which was being wielded as a club. It shattered and its remaining contents splashed over Decker and myself. Dismissing my shower for the time being, I watched the captain stare down the two other wavering louts who both looked befuddled.

In a commanding voice he ordered them to sit down and hand over all their contraband. They gazed at the man and the gun, then at each other, and slid down into their seats. I heard some grumbling over being robbed of their personal property, but Decker's intimidating presence won the day. Over came several more bottles of whiskey and beer which were handed to me for safe keeping.

"And the rest, fellas? Give it to me."

"What d'ya mean?"

"Y'all know what I mean. The bag, give me the bag."

A small bag appeared from a back pocket and was also transferred to my possession. I had to hold it briefly between my teeth because my hands were full of bottles. I quickly put one bottle down on the floor and placed the bag into my own back pocket. I was familiar with its lingering odor: marihuana!

Some of the roustabouts in Midland had started using it recently. As a co-worker on a summer break from Texas A & M, I wanted to be accepted, to fit in. So I had tried smoking it myself. I didn't like it. It made me a little too relaxed and being relaxed is dangerous when working around oil rigs. I needed to talk to Decker about the subject of marihuana, sooner or later.

The captain ordered the conscious men to care for their hapless buddies when they came to. He also told them to get off the train at the next stop, the one just before Los Indios. "I don't care what ya paid fer," he said with a smirk. "Y'all ain't ridin' further 'til ya sober up." I figured they would obey though they sure didn't look happy about it.

All the way back to our seats we received many thanks from the rest of the passengers. I promptly gave all the goods to Decker once we were reseated. Passing over the bottles, I recognized one brand, *Jim Beam*. It had been my favorite. I decided not to share this information with my friend. I did say, "That was marihuana, right?"

"Yup. *Mary Jane, weed,* lots of names fer it."

"Some of the roustabouts, 'specially the Mexicans, use it. Y'all ever tried it?"

"Once or twice. Take it or leave it. Ya know, though, that it ain't legal. You're 'sposed to get a doctor's script fer it."

"Think it oughta be legal?"

"Don't know. Becomin' a bigger problem lately 'cause of all the Mexicans fleein' the Revolution and lookin' fer work. How 'bout you?" asked Decker.

"Same as y'all, Captain. Once or twice. Didn't like what it did to me."

"Some Rangers think we should put a stop to all the weed comin' in now. Affectin' too many Americans. Probly right but I ain't a Ranger no more."

"But if ya find work as a deputy sheriff in a border county, same situation might apply."

"Good point. If y'all join me on the force, it'll be a problem fer both of us, won't it?"

"Damn, sure hadn't given that a thought. It might just turn up in the future."

Two other troubling ideas suddenly occurred to me. I turned to Decker and said, "Captain, I have a favor to ask, actually two favors."

"Shoot, son, I can always say 'no,'" he said, grinning.

Returning the same, I replied, "Hope ya don't fire away, Captain. The most pressin' issue is how I or we smell. I smell like I've been on a bender. In an hour or so, we'll arrive at our destination. My parents will be there on the platform along with my gal, Anne. Would y'all help me explain why we smell like booze?"

"Glad to. It's the truth. I'll even lasso a couple of passengers fer support if need be."

"Thanks. They might come in handy. The second favor will come later. If we end up with an offer from the county commissioners to join the sheriff's department, I'm gonna need some big time help convincin' my parents, 'pecially my mom. Maybe even the four of us can meet together fer a confab."

"Since I really would like y'all to join me on the force, it'd be my pleasure. We'll convince 'em." *I wasn't so sure.* I was grateful for his backup, though.

"Remind me agin, son, 'bout that no good sheriff y'all have to put up with."

"Well, most of what I've heard is second hand but it's pretty discouragin'. He drinks too much which makes him miss a lot of work, and even when he shows up, not much gets done. Many people are fed up, includin' my parents."

"What's the low down on his deputies?"

"He hired 'em and they mostly follow his lead."

"County officials fed up too?"

"Yup. Dad says they're ready to act. Just need a little more encouragement from the good citizens."

"Sounds like it's made fer us, Ted. I plan to meet with 'em soon and make my offer: me, a full-time deputy, y'all my part-time helper. Who knows, maybe they'll even make me a temporary sheriff."

"Let's not get 'head of ourselves," I hesitantly replied. "First, you get mended all the way. I'm still recommendin' a couple days healin' at the clinic. Then we talk to county officials and my parents."

He groused about the clinic for a while but began to waver a bit at my persistence and, in the end, agreed. "Listen, a few days with Anne and Heather hoverin' over ya couldn't be that awful, right?"

"Guess not. But my limit's two days," he added. Breathing a sigh of relief out of the corner of my mouth, I knew that was it.

We soon made our last stop before Los Indios. Decker and I escorted the cowed drunkards off the train and voiced a second warning to sober up. I closed my eyes and pictured Anne waiting for me at our next stop. I couldn't wait for the next chapter of my life to begin.

Decker elbowed me back to reality and pointed out the window to a big sign. "Look at that," he said enthusiastically.

"A circus comin' to Brownsville next week. Not familiar with the name, but they have a Wild West show and elephants. Why don't ya take Anne? I know the two of ya have lots to discuss. Maybe this would be a good break amid all the serious stuff."

"That's actually a good notion, Captain. I'll mention it right quick. Bet she'll jump at the chance."

With a concerned expression Decker said, "I know 'bout yer past drinkin' problem and it bein' a matter of contention. I'll do my best to keep a sharp eye out fer ya. Don't want y'all to lose that pretty lady."

"Thanks, you're a real friend. That first favor starts on the platform in a few minutes. That alcohol still smells despite us cleanin' up in the train's water closet."

"Don't worry. I got ya covered."

He better, I thought, as we pulled into Los Indios. As expected, I could see a fairly big group waiting for us: my parents and sister up front with Anne at their side, Heather next to Anne, plus some familiar faces from the town, mostly from the Baptist church. *Was that a colored man standing off to one side? Who's he wating for?*

I knew mom would be the first greeter. With a slightly fake smile, I surrendered to my fate and stepped forward into her massive hug. It turned out, of course, to be the shortest embrace she'd ever given me. As she abruptly broke contact, I motioned to Anne, who was ready to leap in, to stand back. She held back but looked baffled.

My mom stood open mouthed wearing a shocked expression. Thankfully, as she struggled to find the right words, Decker chose that moment to step forward. "Ma'am, let me introduce myself. I'm Captain Ken Decker of the Texas Rangers, a good friend of Ted, here. We had a little altercation on the train awhile back which is the reason fer our condition. Sorry fer the smell, but I can explain." He did and they accepted his explanation. I was proud of him, knowing I couldn't have spoken more convincingly.

With relief I saw mom's smile return and Anne's confusion disappear. I quickly hugged Anne knowing more intimacy would soon be coming my way. Before stepping back, I whispered how lovely she looked. She blushed making her even lovelier.

I turned my attention to the other greeters. I received a firm hug from dad, a hug and a kiss from Diane, a brief embrace from Heather, who was "almost" as pretty as Anne, and handshakes from everyone else. Two men stood awkwardly apart from the group, a somewhat familiar-looking Ranger and the Negro I had seen from a distance. The Ranger was eyeing Decker. As he passed by me, he said, "Any friend of Ken's is a friend of mine." He introduced himself as Captain Springer. He met up with Decker and they stepped aside in all appearances for a genuine reunion.

That left me momentarily opposite the Negro. Neither of us made a move. I'm sure we both seemed slightly embarrassed. The tension was eased when my mom came to my side and made the introductions. Though a bit awkward, I did manage to shake the man's hand. Mom rattled on about this Toby fella, though I missed most of it. I figured I'd find out more later – much more!

The crowd disbanded and we made plans to accompany Decker to the clinic. Springer offered to drive. Decker climbed into the front of the pickup and the rest of us piled into the bed, including Diane. My parents declined a ride, mom indicating she needed to finish preparing the evening meal. Nurse Nancy greeted us at the clinic with the announcement that an extra bed was available, one at the end of the room completely separated by a sheet from the other patients. As Decker was settling in, I could still hear him whining about his confinement and vowing to stay only two days.

I overheard Decker explain to Springer his reason for quitting the Rangers and his hope to become a deputy sheriff. Springer seemed disappointed about Decker's departure from the Rangers but was encouraged when the deputy idea surfaced. "Sheriff ain't been doin' his job, Ken. Skunk far as I'm concerned. Deputies worthless too. I even complained to the commissioners and they sounded like they agreed."

"Then there's hope fer me?" asked Decker.

"Real hope."

"What 'bout Ted? He wants to join me as a part-time deputy."

"Knew him a bit growin' up. Is he reliable?" *I grimaced but kept listening.*

"Good 'nuff fer me. Proved himself many times this summer."

"County sure could use yer help, Ken. Crimes on the upswing, mostly small stuff but the sergeant and I can't deal with all of it."

"Swell," said Decker. "I plan to meet with the commissioners soon as I bolt from this here confinement." Decker spotted me and said, "Pretty much sums it up fer us, right, Ted?"

"Yup, as long as y'all keep yer promise 'bout goin' to bat fer me with my parents."

"Then it's settled, Ted. Go 'head and arrange the meetin'. Make it three days from now. We'll appeal to yer parents after the confab. We'll press the commissioners to make a decision on the spot. That should prove to yer parents how serious y'all are."

I happily agreed. But it was time to talk with Anne who was heading my way with a face that said "time to get down to business." *I knew it was the first of many talks and many serious faces.*

She led me by the hand outside to the back of the building. Alone, she hugged me again and unexpectedly planted a moist, lingering kiss on my willing lips. I was done for, knowing I'd be unable to resist. I wanted to be the object of her heart's desire.

She pushed away and said, "I have a feeling you know what's coming." I did.

She laid it out for me, gently but firmly, as we made and held eye contact. I had to: one, quit drinking; two, recommit myself to my Lord and Savior; and three, either get a job or return to college and finish my degree. Pure and simple, right to the point, just what I had expected from this determined Christian lady. Finishing, she said, "I can't be engaged or married to a drinker and a lackluster Christian, Ted. Can you promise me that you'll do everything in your power to complete this transformation?"

I had heard her refer to "marriage," causing me to pause and swallow audibly before answering, "I promise. That's what I want too, Anne Yoder."

"Wonderful, Ted Townley. A couple more conditions, though. We'll be talking frequently, and two other ladies who care for you will be keeping an eye on you: your mom and Heather. Hope you don't feel this is too tough on you. Agreed?"

She had me cornered, so I answered, "Agreed. All this increases my chances of stayin' on the 'straight and narrow.'" *I wondered if the scrutiny might be a tad irritating but I held my tongue.* Her smile drove any thought of irritation from my mind.

As we rounded the corner to rejoin the others, I stopped abruptly and said, "I have something else I need to bring up. It's related to what we just talked 'bout and it can't be put off any longer." I took a breath and told her of my hopes of becoming, along with Decker, a deputy sheriff. Her eyes widened and she paused before saying, "That's big news! I'll have to think about it for a time. It could be dangerous but I guess Captain Decker is the man to keep you safe. I know, though, your mom will be really disappointed. How will you soften the blow?"

"Captain Decker has agreed to join me when I tell her and dad. Say, why don't you join us, if you're at ease with the idea? We'll gang up on 'em."

"If my prayers lead me to support you, I'll be there as part of the gang."

I grabbed her for another hug and kiss. With my lips on hers, I heard a throat clearing and glanced up to see Heather standing there with hands on hips. "Hey, you love birds, everyone's about to leave. Didn't want you two to miss your ride." We all laughed and headed for Springer's truck. As we bumped along, Heather said a celebration combining Thanksgiving and my coming home was being planned. I thought it was an excellent idea. I wondered who would be attending. Knowing mom, probably half the town.

The next two days proved to be occasionally difficult for the staff at the clinic. At times, Decker was like a caged beast, so restless and noisy that they had to shoo him outside for the sake of the other patients. I tried to calm him down when I showed up on the afternoon of the first day. Nothing seemed to work until I mentioned that I had called the commissioners and arranged for a Friday morning meeting, his day of destiny. Planning strategy for the meeting brought his mind into sharp focus right quick.

"I reckon it would help, Captain, if a few highlights of yer career were written down fer the county officials."

"I like it," he said as he started to rattle off his accomplishments year by year.

"Hold yer horses! I can't keep up, and can't remember all of this. I'll fetch pen and paper from Nancy and we'll do it right." I jogged back inside, returned with the materials, and found him under the shade of a big oak tree still mumbling to himself about his storied career.

We began again, and perhaps ten minutes later I had filled up almost an entire page. He listed service in the army where he rose from private to sergeant, oil company security guard, police officer, chief of police, and two different periods of service with the Texas Rangers. He embellished it with a description of a few awards and honors along the way making special note of his citation as premier army sharpshooter.

"I'm very impressed, Captain. Bet they hire ya on the spot." He nodded. I think he missed the slight hint of humor in my last comment.

"Didn't think it was necessary to mention any of my occasional troubles with the 'higher-ups,' but that ain't none of their business no how." *I hoped they didn't get wind of any for his sake and mine.*

Before leaving the clinic, I told Nancy I'd return after supper and also spend much of the second day with Decker in an effort to keep him out of her hair. She thanked me with a huge look of relief on her face. As it turned out, my help wasn't needed that first night because Anne and Heather arrived and smothered the captain with attention. *Poor man having to suffer such a fate!*

Late the next morning, Springer rode by horseback to spend some time with his friend. Just before lunch I saw them cozied up whispering intently. Decker then pointed to a window that opened to the rear of the clinic. What was that all about?

Before long Nancy walked up with soup and sandwiches for her patient. She had thoughtfully included enough for me as well. Clearly lunch wasn't on Springer's mind because he rose and gazed out the window, nodded to Decker, and walked toward the exit. A few seconds later, I spat out my mouthful of food in reaction to an explosion: the piercing crack of a familiar sound, a Colt .45. Another boom. *What the hell?*

"What's goin' on?" I shouted to Decker.

His garbled response was unintelligible. "Swallow the damn grub, Captain," I ordered, not caring about my tone of voice. Everyone in the room needed to know what was happening before panic set in. Nancy had already dropped to one knee as if covering from an attack.

"Ain't nuthin' really, son," he finally muttered. "Springer's unloadin' on a coyote. Seen him yesterday showin' signs of rabies. Springer offered to do the deed fer me, fer us. Surprised it took two shots, though."

"Couldn't ya have at least warned us?" I said still annoyed. "Look at yer nurse on her knees." I pulled back the sheet that separated his bed from the others and added, "Don't these other patients, 'specially the children seem frightened to you? They do to me. I believe y'all need to offer 'em an apology."

Before he could respond to my demand, I bent to offer assistance to Nancy and, when finished, left quickly to catch up with Springer and his victim. I found him looking at a coyote, a scrawny one with white foam dripping from its open mouth. Decker had been right and perhaps saved us

40

from this serious nuisance. I realized I probably owed *him* an apology but decided to wait to see if his came first.

Springer and I found a shovel and buried the carcass in a ravine about fifty yards behind the clinic. I kept my distance from Decker during the early afternoon. Even took a walk to clear my mind. When I returned, Nancy admitted Decker had offered an apology to her and others, though not entirely sincere in her opinion. Best we would get, I figured, so I approached him with my own confession. He shrugged but seemed pleased with the effort.

What really brightened his mood was Springer's return in late afternoon with important news: the commissioners had just fired the sheriff! And his incompetent deputies had been reduced to part-time status. Springer suggested it was probably related to our upcoming meeting with them next morning. With a satisfied grin he said, "Good sign, don't ya think, Captain Decker?"

"Do indeed, friend, do indeed. They'll be in a shaky position to reject us now. Can't wait to meet 'em and make our case." To celebrate he picked up his cane and broke it over his knee.

All I had to do now was find someone who'd type his list of accomplishments. Thankfully, Anne agreed to do the typing on Thursday night before hustling me out of her apartment. She also said she would pray for my success. This was an even bigger lift to my spirit because it meant she gave her overall support. I stole a final kiss before starting my walk home. I tried not to dwell on my parents' reaction to this possible job offer.

Nine a.m. Friday we met the commissioners. They seemed cordial and eager to hear what we had to say. They were impressed that we had come with a typed document they could examine. Before beginning the interview, they spent a few minutes on the failures of the fired sheriff, a warning they meant for any new hires to be different kind of lawmen.

They aimed many questions at Decker and sounded pretty satisfied with his answers, less so with mine. I was clearly a beginner when it came to law enforcement. Decker, however, came to my rescue by vouching for me to the high heavens. "He's double backboned, gentlemen," he declared with a wink in my direction. I could hardly believe my ears. Even more so when he finished by saying it was a "two-for-one" deal, take both of us or we would look elsewhere. From their expressions, the issue appeared settled. *Did he really believe all he said about me?*

My biggest worry came when one member wanted to see some written recommendations from past employers. The suggestion sounded reasonable and a consensus quickly formed within the assembled group. Decker said okay, though it might take some time before responses came back and time was of the essence. *I doubted his latest Ranger boss would be contacted for support.*

The commissioners left the room to consider Decker's proposal. I was more outwardly anxious than he as we waited their return. It came in less than thirty minutes. We were both hired; Decker as a full-time deputy, myself, to be determined later. They said as a deputy but probably only one or two days a week. Further, and to Decker's delight, he might be promoted to County Sheriff, if he proved his worth.

As a last item of business, they announced that the present two deputies were being retained though reduced in hours. Was this a problem for Decker? He said it wasn't as long as he was in charge. That was fine with them and we all shook hands to seal the deal. Formal contracts would likely be written later. I walked out of the room as a very part-time deputy, one with unsuspecting parents. *Help!*

Before I could even bring up the subject, Decker reminded me of his promise and said to make the arrangements with my parents and he'd be at my side. I mentioned Anne's possible involvement; he loved the idea. "They can't say no to all three of us," he said with confidence. I prayed he was right.

I arranged for lunch on Saturday with my parents and hinted I had something important to discuss. I'd bring along Anne as well as another person for support. They accepted, more intrigued than alarmed.

Alarmed would come soon enough, I feared.

With Decker close behind, Anne and I entered my home precisely at noon. If my parents were surprised at Decker's appearance, they didn't show it. I was too nervous to eat so suggested we sit in the living room and get right to it.

The three of us sat together on the couch opposite my parents. I wasted no time and informed them that I'd just been offered a part-time job as a deputy sheriff and had accepted. I plunged ahead filling in the background for the recent firing of the sheriff as well as Decker's selection as chief deputy and man in charge. I finished and stared across at mom whose mouth had dropped open in shock. Dad's response was a furrowed brow.

"But I don't understand, "she finally stammered. "I thought you wanted to finish college and become the engineer you've always talked about. That's our hope for you too." Silence all around.

I inhaled deeply for the strength to make my final point. "I've already missed the first semester at A & M. Might as well make it a full year and start fresh next September.

Besides, my limited hours as a deputy will give me plenty of time to help out at the store. A good solution all 'round, don't y'all think?" More silence.

I elbowed my supporters on either side and they came to my defense. In her sweet voice Anne said, "This is what he really wants, Mrs. Townley. He also told me about its temporary nature and his reliance on Captain Decker to keep him safe." As she spoke of safety, she had leaned in front of me to meet Decker eye to eye.

Decker horned in and said he needed my help and definitely wouldn't let anything bad happen to me. "Reckon I owe this young man of yers a lot fer all he's done fer me, Mrs. Townley. Time to repay his helpfulness with a watchful eye. He's in good hands, ma'am."

They both offered some more words of encouragement then we all settled back and waited for mom's response. It came slowly and deliberately along with a few tears. "I guess the decision is set in stone. I'm disappointed but I will learn to live with it." Dad sighed and gave his acceptance with a simple nod. Easier than I had ever imagined, I thought, as my racing heart began to slow.

Guessing we needed a distraction, I said. "Listen, folks, why don't we all go to the circus next week in Brownsville. Let's go Monday or Tuesday. I know it's Thanksgiving week but that should give the ladies plenty of time to finish the preparations fer our big party. Let's go, it'll be fun."

"I'm all fer the circus since it was my idea in the first place," said Decker. "That is, if y'all will invite me to join ya."

"Circus for me," chipped in Anne. "Positively time for some fun."

Another nod from dad and another pause from mom. She finally smiled weakly and said, "I hate it when people gang up on me, but it's working this time. Let's go. We need to bring as many people as possible."

Church on Sunday, circus on Monday or Tuesday. Things were looking up. I hoped it stayed that way. *What could go wrong at a circus?*

CHAPTER FOUR

THE BIG TOP

*Toby thought he'd heard all the weather jokes
from the café customers, but when Dallas Young
claimed it was so hot this November that "the
hens were layin' hard-boiled eggs" it did cause
him to chuckle. The main topic today was the
circus next week in Brownsville. Several
were planning to attend. He wanted to go but
lacked the money. Oddly, Janice Harper said
sometimes accidents happen at a circus. He
wondered what she meant but didn't hear her
explanation as he was called back to the counter
by Burt. He really wanted his little girls to see it.*

I GLANCED AROUND AND TRIED FIGURING out how these people
would fit in two vehicles. Mom had invited Helen Martin,
Nancy, Anne, Heather, Decker, Captain Springer, and the
entire Washington family. When combined with the four
Townleys, there were fourteen people. I was curious about
Toby's family but didn't say anything. Anne and Heather
seemed pleased they were included and that was enough for

me. Not true for Springer who made it clear he wasn't happy and objected to the Negro family riding with him. Decker stood off to one side not wanting to be involved. Springer turned a mite sheepish when confronted by Heather and Anne yet held his ground. It was pretty tense for a brief moment when the three of them squared off. Of course, mom sided with the two young women and solved the dilemma by suggesting they ride with her and dad in their car, a tight fit as Helen and Nancy also chose the car. The rest of us climbed into Springer's pick-up, Decker in front and myself and the three ladies in the bed: a big treat for Diane.

A flat tire on the pick-up slowed us down about halfway to Brownsville. Springer switched the flat with the spare as everyone else squatted on the opposite side of the car, the only shade for miles around. The occupants of dad's car did the same a few yards up the road. As Springer worked, I offered to help, though I mostly wanted to discover why he'd made such a fuss about not wanting "certain people" in his truck. He started to answer a bit too loudly, so I motioned for him to lower his voice. After an angry glare, he obeyed. "Listen, son, I ain't got nuthin' 'gainst y'all or anyone else, but I got my reputation to consider. What if it got back to Sergeant Collins and the other Rangers that I let colored folks ride with me?"

"This here can't be the first time Rangers helped out Negroes that way, Captain. Y'all'd give 'em all a ride in an emergency, wouldn't ya?"

"This ain't no emergency, Ted. It's a social event. People find out and there'll be hell to pay."

I wasn't so sure but could only think to say, "I guess y'all won't be sittin' nearby at the circus then."

"Damn right, though it probably won't be a problem anyway since Negroes have to sit in a separate area." *I hadn't thought about that. I wondered how mom would react to segregated seating.*

We easily located the outdoor circus. It seemed awfully small, just one big tent, two smaller ones, and a short midway. It was mid-morning on Monday and hardly anyone had come. The sign out front said, "Bailey and Sons'" which was odd. Perhaps it was a sideline from Ringling Brothers, who had recently purchased the Barnum and Bailey Circus. Was someone trying to cash in on a famous name? At any rate, none of us were impressed at first glance. Anne even said, "Wow, this is puny compared to the one I attended in Philadelphia a few years back. You could put this entire circus in their big tent, if I remember correctly."

The big parade wasn't to start until early afternoon, so we all wandered up and down the midway playing a few games and indulging in some over-priced food. I noticed mom quietly slipping some money to Toby. He showed embarrassment but put it away nonetheless.

We saw some caged animals and several others being rounded up for the big parade. Heather was the first to mention their condition. "Anne, look how thin they are." Pointing to the big cats, she continued, "Some are filthy and have open sores. It makes me sick just lookin' at 'em."

"Me too," said Anne. "These animals are suffering terribly. It's clearly a shoestring operation. I'm going to write a letter of protest to the owners as soon as I get home." I knew she would and probably get Heather and me writing as well.

Walking around, I found some proof of the reality of racial segregation when I noticed all the Negroes, and there weren't many, keeping their distance from the majority of whites. Most of them chose to stay entirely on the other side of the midway. Apparently mom hadn't noticed. Yet.

Further proof came as we entered the big top to watch the opening parade. Negroes were already being directed to sit on the other side of the arena where a small, rickety bleacher had been erected. As Toby was leading his family away from our group, mom finally realized what was happening and called for him to turn around and rejoin us. Toby hesitated and everyone froze in place for a moment. Mom glared at the two security guards. Neither could hold eye contact with her. Resigned to his perhaps familiar fate, Toby responded, "Ain't no matter, Mrs. Townley. We be fine over there." Immediately Anne and Heather were at mom's side and all three started to march toward the guards with determination written on their faces. *Trouble ahead!*

Dad and I made our move, quickly stepping in front of the crusading ladies. Dad took the lead by gently saying, "Now ladies, y'all can fight this battle another time. Might even join ya myself. Let's not embarrass Toby anymore today." I was proud of dad. It wasn't easy to stand in front of that threesome. And it worked. They stepped back, locked arms, and glared again at the guard before rejoining the others in our group. I glanced at the faces in our party and saw support from the women, less so from the somewhat relieved lawmen.

The parade was truly a letdown, taking only ten minutes from start to finish and composed of perhaps seventy-five people. You expected clowns to look sad, but in this assembly everyone seemed depressed or at least weary and merely pretending to enjoy their work. Cowboys shuffled along listlessly as if they'd just come in from a difficult cattle drive. Fake Indians wore ill-fitting costumes that were probably never worn by any historic tribe. A few acrobats tripped attempting the simplest of maneuvers, and the emaciated and sickly animals had to be prodded to move around the circle. The best part of the parade turned out to be the band, whose members were lively and energetic but failed to inspire anyone else.

People were beginning to mumble about how disappointing the opening parade was. Several threatened to demand a refund if things didn't improve. Refusing to be disillusioned, Diane said, "The elephants are comin'. They'll make y'all feel better. Elephants are wonderful. Ya can't have a circus without 'em."

They were at the tail end of the parade, and we could hear their trumpeting outside. Diane's excitement was shared by many, especially the children. None were disappointed as six large elephants appeared. All looked to be in good health and well cared for. Each had a female rider on top and a male handler alongside. These twelve humans displayed more liveliness than all the other non-musical performers combined. Finally, a real circus, I felt, as they made their way around the circle to the delight of the crowd.

As I watched them, something about the last one in line bothered me, an eerie wildness in his eye and fanned out ears. His handler realized his mammoth was becoming dangerous and used skilled moves to calm the beast. Decker was sitting next to me and I got his attention. "Noticed it too, Ted. Not quiet like the rest. Best to be alert, I reckon." *I buried the thought in the back of my mind.*

As the elephants filed out, the clowns and acrobatic acts took over. Anne nudged me and pointed to a man sitting a few rows behind us. "That's Dr. Wilbur," she said excitedly. "He works here in Brownsville and also helps out occasionally at our clinic. You just have to meet him. He's a great doctor and knows John too." Before I could respond, she rose and made her way up to him. They spoke briefly, then she led him down to join the rest of us. She had more than a greeting in mind as she asked everyone to make room for him to sit with us, naturally right next to me.

Anne introduced me by saying I was John's cousin. This gave the Doc an opening to spend the next few minutes telling me about some of the great medical adventures he and John had shared this past summer. I was impressed until I remembered my own recent history with my amazing cousin. Sensing Dr. Wilbur was slowing down a tad, I barged in to recount a few exciting and dangerous episodes John and I had experienced – medical and otherwise – in late summer and fall, both in west Texas and northern Mexico.

It was now his turn to be impressed. "Sounds exactly like him," he said matter-of-factly. "He's gonna be a great doctor, maybe even a surgeon, if he puts his mind to it. One of the nicest young men I've met recently." Leaning forward and eyeing Heather, he nudged me and added, "And he's made the right choice for the future with that pretty redhead."

"He certainly has," I responded as I winked at Anne. I asked him if he'd heard anything about John's adventures in California.

"A few stories have made their way back to me. Got one letter from him where he admitted he was uncertain about his future, regardin' medical school, I mean. Got me to thinkin' and plottin' with a student friend of his up in Michigan, fella named George Beck. Have ya heard of him?"

"Can't say I have."

"Well, George and me, together with other professionals are workin' on a plan to keep him in Texas and speed up his trainin' partly 'cause of the war, of course."

I must have looked really puzzled to him because he abruptly added, "Listen, Ted, I probably shouldn't have said anythin'. Ain't nuthin' finalized yet. Don't say a word to

Heather. If we can work out the details, I know he wants to be the first to tell his gal."

I wanted more details and tried a couple more questions, but he resisted any further revelation. Anne had been listening in but shrugged her shoulders to indicate she, too, was in the dark. *What was going on?*

Dr. Wilbur joined us for a food break during the intermission to sample the goodies. More stories centered on John, with giggling and shaking of heads at all the trouble he'd gotten himself into these past months. The doctor guffawed when I told him John had become expert at stopping internal bleeding by inserting the burning end of a stick into an open wound. "Painful but works 'bout every time," he said. As the others joined in the "John talk," I realized I was getting a mite tired of the topic and was glad when we began to walk back to the big top and the Wild West show. *Was I jealous?*

The Wild West show was rowdier than the earlier acts. Even the horses were galloping and rearing up on command. It was mostly cowboys versus Indians in a fierce battle, using blanks, of course. At the finale, the shooting rose to a noisy and smoky explosion. Through the haze it looked like the cowboys were surrounded and beaten. To the rescue, as expected, came the soldiers who rode in with more guns blazing. Combined with the roar of the crowd, I could hardly hear Diane shout, "Do you think the Indians will win?" I shrugged my answer but knew they wouldn't. They never did.

As the Indian enactors fell or surrendered, the crowd applauded. I was glad to see Diane not joining in. To celebrate the victory, the soldiers and cowboys fired off even more shots into the air, all the way to the exit and beyond. I thought I heard sounds of terrified animals from outside the tent. I hoped all the wild animals were caged or securely tied in some fashion.

They weren't! A few seconds later, an angry bull elephant charged into the arena, a "rogue" elephant completely out of control. I knew instantly it was the same one I had noticed before. Many spectators screamed and tried to flee when they recognized the danger before them. Not everyone was successful. From our secure vantage point in the large bleacher we were out of immediate harm's way and could only watch in horror as the rampage unfolded below us. The smaller bleacher across the floor didn't survive as the elephant slammed into its supports, causing it to partially collapse spilling many people onto the floor right in front of the angry beast. Several people, young and old, were trampled underneath those massive feet. Luckily, I could see the Washington family escaping danger on the far side of the tent.

Nothing could stand in the elephant's way. It was sickening to hear the victims' screams and be unable to do anything. Springer and Decker had drawn their pistols, but were too distant to stop such a huge brute with such limited fire power. And firing away was too dangerous anyway because of the people running back and forth. Dad and I urged the women not to watch. Mom and Diane didn't; Anne and Heather did, though their heads turned away during most of the carnage. I could see their faces pale and eyes moisten as they clung to each other for comfort.

What seemed like an eternity was probably only a minute or so. The elephant tore around the arena and bolted out the main entrance causing more screaming from those who had already escaped. Springer and Decker sprang into action, jumping off the bleacher and running after it. Springer added to his arsenal by yanking a Winchester rifle from a terrified security guard cowering at the entrance. Moments later I heard several pistol shots, then a few rifles, one being the boom from the type used to drop big game, and at last came the distinctive crack of a Winchester. I felt the ground shake when the elephant collapsed. I ran outside and discovered the fallen creature surrounded by several armed men. I quickly glanced around and was relieved to see no one else appeared injured.

I rushed back inside and was not surprised to see Dr. Wilbur already on the arena floor determining the condition of various victims. Nor was I surprised when I spotted Nancy, Anne, and Heather alongside him. Some stouthearted souls quickly joined them. Doc yelled to me to have the circus staff get any available truck and car to the entrance so that the victims could be taken to the Brownsville hospital. It took a few minutes to round them up, and when I returned, the victims were ready to be loaded carefully and moved to better medical care. Helping out, I realized that two people were already dead, including one child. Five or six others had severely smashed arms and legs, twisted in all directions. Several had bone fragments poking outside the skin and were bleeding profusely. Our three helpers were already covered in blood. Adding to the overall misery were the cries and moans of the grieving families and friends whose loved ones had been injured or lost. This was the worst scene I'd ever witnessed, more gruesome than anything I had experienced with John. When the loading was finished, I bumped into Dr. Wilbur, who said with a worried look, "I wish we had your cousin here today. He'd be a great help." Yes, he would, I thought, now ashamed of my feeling jealous.

Wilbur asked our three ladies to accompany him and they readily agreed, though clearly shaken by the horror they were facing around them. I hugged Anne tightly and whispered how proud I was of her. She hugged me back and planted a light kiss on my cheek. I promised we'd follow closely in our two vehicles and stay at the hospital until their work was finished. Gazing back from the bed of my truck, I could see a long line of vehicles following on the trip to the hospital, almost like a funeral procession.

We kept our promise. Some in our group paced back and forth in the hospital waiting room. Others, who couldn't handle the despair of the grieving, preferred the outdoors, under the shade of two large cottonwood trees. I chose the latter along with the two lawmen. Springer was pleased, thinking it was his shot that had downed the rogue elephant. "Nailed 'im right between the eyes," he bragged. Decker, not referring to the boom of the big-game rifle, teased him by saying it was a huge target, even a five-year-old Texan male could have done the same. They both laughed humorlessly.

While waiting, I noticed a man with a camera entering the hospital. I figured it was a reporter from the Brownsville paper wanting to interview the survivors. Finding this idea distasteful, I asked Springer to re-enter the building with me, hunt him down, and remove him, by force if necessary. He was found and cast out, thanks to the iron-like grip of the captain. His name was Jenkins and he was pretty upset. When he discovered my name was Townley, he switched gears and said, "Say, that sounds familiar. Weren't y'all involved with fightin' that bandit invasion last summer? Been tryin' to find out more information for my readers." *Trouble!*

I merely said, "Don't know nuthin' 'bout it. I was in Midland most of the summer." He looked discouraged, but I also had the impression that his investigation might not be over.

Our three nurses came out looking exhausted. Efforts to clean up were only partly successful, with blood splatters remaining on shirts and dresses. Nancy was no doubt more used to this kind of appearance than either Anne or Heather.

We decided to split up with dad driving all the ladies home, in Springer's truck, and the remaining guys stopping by the circus to help with cleanup efforts. Springer wasn't happy about the "loan" of his truck but we outvoted him. Waving goodbye, I figured that most of the passengers would nap much of the way home.

There was no rest for us when we arrived back at the circus. The most glaring problem was how they were going to dispose of the elephant's huge carcass. Surely they'd need a hole much bigger than the one we dug for that coyote. I found out later they carved it up and buried it, at a high price, in a nearby farmer's field. And everyone was astonished at the destruction caused by the elephant. The big tent's interior resembled the aftermath of a tornado. We worked hurriedly due to the tent's splintered main beams. Half of the work crew threw debris outside while the other half loaded it onto waiting trucks for hauling away. Soon after the tent floor was cleared, a heavy gust of wind brought down the whole structure. Fortunately, no one was injured, except perhaps the owner's pocketbook.

I was impressed with Toby's work effort. He pitched in without complaint and his strong help made a difference. In fact, he seemed to accomplish as much as two men. Several other workers remarked about his strength to our group. Though not praising him directly, I'm sure he overheard their comments. As the only Negro present, his skin color seemed unimportant, at least in this kind of emergency. I grinned, thinking how pleased mom and Anne would be.

Helpful Toby made only one mistake, and it wasn't really his fault, just a matter of bad timing. It happened when we were standing around the dead elephant just recapping the day's tragic events. One circus fella was running off at the mouth non-stop. My wildcatter boss, Phil Archer, would have probably accused him of "talkin' the legs off a chair." At any rate, I was so distracted I didn't hear Toby yell out, "Don't step right there, Mr. Ted." Too late! I looked down and saw my foot smack in the middle of a huge pile of elephant droppings, almost up to my ankle.

"Judas priest!" I cried out. Toby seemed startled, as if I'd just used a real profanity. Most of the other witnesses just smirked and turned away to keep from laughing. Still upset, I yelled, "These are my best boots, the new ones I bought in El Paso. Even Anne loves 'em."

"Real sorry I didn't warn ya quicker, Mr. Ted," said Toby, looking sincere, even a bit scared.

I sighed more loudly than intended, then shook away as much crap as possible, and said, "Not yer fault, Toby, I should have been more careful." I limped over to a big water trough and washed away the rest of the filth. The boot made a squishy sound when I walked. I hoped for the best before I met up with Anne or anyone else back home.

Toby tried to cheer me up by telling me about his recent boot incident. It did make me feel better. A little better.

What a day! All the way home I recalled the day's high points as I held my boot out the window to let the Texas sun do its work.

CHAPTER FIVE

THANKSGIVING

Toby listened to Julia Hunter describe Thanksgiving in Los Indios. He agreed with her reckoning that it might be a little less joyful this year because of the recent flu outbreak and the tragic events at the circus in Brownsville. Everyone agreed. In a more upbeat mood, she recounted how nearby towns had begun a new tradition of serving Thanksgiving meals in a town hall or a big church and inviting the whole town, not just the poor. "We should start that practice here," she said. Pausing, she added, "But that will be difficult since Katherine Townley invites half of our town already." That brought laughter from everyone except Toby, whose family had also been invited this year. He felt slightly embarrassed about admitting it. He'd never been to a white family's home for Thanksgiving. He was optimistic, yet a Negro family had to be prepared for anything.

I ARRIVED A FEW MINUTES LATE to Thanksgiving dinner because of walking over to Heather's apartment to escort my two favorite ladies to my house. I decided not to bring up the fact that I had shown up half an hour early precisely to avoid being late. Growing up in a house with two women had already taught me the lesson that women understood "time" differently than men, especially when they needed to pretty up for a special occasion. Besides, a Thanksgiving meal at the Townley's never started on time, anyway, so I said as much to my companions as we reached my front door. They smiled sweetly, and knowingly, as we entered to very warm greetings.

As we made our way across the room shaking hands or receiving hugs, I counted nineteen people including myself. A moment later, I peeked into the dining room and counted twenty-three chairs. Curious, I turned to mom and dad and said, "'Pears we ain't the last to arrive. Who else is comin'?"

I got a scolding smile as she leaned in to answer. "Please don't say 'ain't' today, Ted. Be on your best behavior for our guests." Stepping back, she added, "You're right. I've invited the Washington family. I urged them to be early so they had extra time to get better acquainted with everyone before we sat down to eat. I hope nothing's wrong."

The Washington family? That would be an interesting mix, I thought, as I glanced at three other guests: Betty Marshall, the Ranger secretary, who stood beside Decker and Sergeant Sam Collins, Springer's chief Ranger partner. Betty wasn't a problem but I had my doubts about the other two. Decker had mixed feelings about Negroes, and if Sam's attitude mirrored Springer's, it could get a mite awkward. Anne and Heather, naturally, were thrilled about the Washington family coming. "The two children are adorable," Anne said. "Everyone will love them and their mom." I reckoned we'd find out soon, if and when they arrived.

In customary Texan fashion, after a few minutes of pleasantries, men and women split into two separate groups. The groups stood far enough apart which hampered my overhearing what the ladies were discussing: probably food and children. We men, of course, had three topics in mind: weather, politics, and guns. Too hot and dry summed up the weather talk. However, several good weather jokes were shared, one of which, surprisingly, came from Pastor Dan Willis. "So dry the Baptists are sprinklin', the Methodists are spillin', and the Catholics are givin' rain checks." It was good to see another side of the usually solemn Rev. Willis.

Politics brought out Texan bravado from the exclusively Democratic group. It mostly dealt with our seemingly inescapable entrance into the European war. Most of these red-blooded Texans favored entering; a few of us urged caution, especially Pastor Dan, myself, and Diego Trevino, who worked at the town's only gas station. A few women glanced nervously our way as the disagreement grew louder.

Hoping to avoid my mom's intervening, I abruptly changed the subject to recollections of favorite Thanksgiving meals. They all became startled by this change and became quiet. Finally, Diego described a typical Mexican meal, a mouth-watering collection of "chili with everything": a chili-rubbed turkey, tamales, menudo, and homemade pasteles. It sounded like a great meal. I got a scornful look from Decker, who probably believed a good Texan Thanksgiving should be a juicy steak and mashed potatoes.

Decker horned in and began talking about guns. His jumping off point was the gun or guns used to bring down the rogue elephant at the circus. Just about everyone but the pastor and I claimed their rifles and bullet sizes were the best. It was more "caliber" talk than I had heard in a long time. Soon it became personal as even my dad joined in praising his favorite firearm. People yelled louder to be heard. The fact that the circus had ended in suffering and death seemed to be the last thing considered.

I became aware of approaching doom as mom suddenly appeared with fire in her eyes! She nudged me aside and chastened us all with the stern face of a practiced disciplinarian. "Gentlemen, that's enough talk of guns and killing. We have just experienced great misfortune in this town and county. And this is Thanksgiving! I'm disappointed in y'all, even you, Pastor Dan. Now, I suggest y'all rejoin us ladies and start talkin' in a more appropriate manner and tone." Her tongue-lashing did the trick. No one could even make eye contact with her. Sheepishly, we made our way over to the ladies. Some I could tell, were sympathetic.

Rightly blamed, we made a few feeble attempts at conversation with our newly enlarged circle, but failed miserably. Respectable topics were mostly about food and recipes. I elbowed Diego hoping he'd repeat his description of a Mexican Thanksgiving. He didn't get the hint or couldn't find his voice.

Soon all talk played out, as even the women had been intimidated by mom's outburst. Mom apparently realized what was happening and used the silence to introduce a new topic. "Let's each one of us share one thing we are thankful for," she more or less ordered. *Talk about awkwardness!* Looking across the table, Decker and Collins were pale and fidgety. I worried they'd bolt for the door and skip the Thanksgiving meal entirely. Naturally, no one volunteered anything, so Mom started with, "I'm thankful for God bringing Ted home safely and for Him giving me so many people to love and serve." *The fact that it was more than one thing would never be mentioned by me.* Her sincerity stirred other women to share: Heather was thankful for John's fast-approaching return and Anne for having me in her life, which made me blush. Other ladies related much the same, causing rosy cheeks from their husbands as well.

When it came to the men, however, it was like pulling nails – very long nails from tight wood. Again, silence all around. Wishing to end my agony quickly and knowing what was required of me, I said that having Anne in my life made me a very lucky man. Knowing what was good for them, other husbands copied my statement almost word for word. While not being very original, these statements were acceptable to their partners. Only three males remained: Hank Brady, a rarely employed handyman, and the two lawmen. Mom intervened by singling out Hank. This was even more awkward. Hank was practically toothless and when he finally mumbled his answer it was unintelligible. "That's wonderful, Hank, and so true," said my Mom, who probably didn't understand it either but graciously sought to avoid any further embarrassment for her guest.

The lawmen endured a few more seconds of excruciating agony before Collins found the courage to say he was thankful for the honor of being a Texas Ranger. That was Decker's cue to say the same thing about being a new deputy sheriff. You could feel the tension ease when our group therapy session ended. I promised myself to plead with mom never to do this exercise again.

Dad took over and asked Pastor Dan to say grace. Mom started to interrupt but was silenced by the reverend's prompt response to dad's request. Pastors always showed a readiness for prayer. And they could cover a whole range of subjects, which he did for what had to be nearly three minutes: families recovering from the flu, the deaths and injuries at the circus, the town's misfortunes, and so on. When the final blessing came, I sensed (guilty?) relief from almost everyone present.

Mom unexpectedly stopped everyone from entering the dining room by saying, "Could y'all wait a few more minutes for Toby Washington and his family to get here." Everyone halted in place not knowing what to do or say.

"But our food will be gettin' cold, dear," said my Dad a bit nervously.

"It'll hold a little longer, dear," said Mom, emphasizing the word "dear."

I straightaway offered to go over to the Washington home and make sure they were coming. "It's only four blocks. I'll be back with 'em in a jiffy."

Anne said, "Heather and I will join him, Katherine. Our presence might help convince Toby's wife, Martha, if she's the reason for the delay."

Mom smiled her answer and we took off, casually because of the presence of the gals. When we reached Toby's home, Martha greeted us at the door. She seemed surprised and reluctant for us enter. I started to explain our presence when she suddenly motioned me to stop, stepped aside, and waved us in. "Toby needs to explain hisself to ya, Mr. Ted. Maybe words won't be necessary, come to think of it." *What could she possibly mean?*

Martha asked her daughters to go and fetch their father from the bedroom. He soon stepped out, slightly bent forward at first, but then straightening to his full height. We were shocked by his battered appearance! A torn and swollen lip along with a prominent black and blue bruise on his left cheek made him clearly uneasy as he approached us.

"What the heck happened to y'all?" I demanded a bit too forcefully. My companions were speechless, hands covering their open mouths.

In a barely audible voice he said, "Fell down and hit my head, Mr. Ted. Ain't no cause fer ya to come here. Go back an' enjoy yer Thanksgivin' meal. Please."

"Wasn't no fall that caused those scrapes, Toby. Y'all need to tell what really happened."

He remained mute with downcast eyes. Finally, Martha said, "He was attacked late last night by some brutes. Won't give me any more details. He's too embarrassed now to come to yer momma's home. Says it'll spoil the day fer everyone else."

"Nonsense," Heather uttered before I could speak. "You are all coming and that's the end of it. Isn't that right?"

Anne and I genuinely agreed. "They're holdin' the meal fer us," I added. "It really will be wasted if ya don't hurry up."

"But what will I say 'bout my face?"

"I'll tell 'em it was really was an accident and the fine points are comin' later." I figured few would believe me and I'd have some explaining to do myself in short order.

Toby and Martha relented to the delight of their daughters. After hurriedly getting ready, we all quickened our pace back to my home. Toby's two eager young children running ahead of us shortened the return time. Along the way, Anne quietly mentioned her disliking my fibbing about Toby's visible scrapes.

"I agree," I said, "but cousin John taught me this summer that sometimes a 'white lie' is better when the whole truth will cause more harm, as long as the whole truth comes out in the end. Right, Heather?" I continued, hoping for her support.

It came with some reluctance. "I did hear John utter a couple of 'white lies' in touchy situations. Everything did work out after all, though I was never completely comfortable with it morally speaking."

Well, partial support was better than none, I figured, as I squeezed Anne's hand at my doorstep. No return squeeze but at least she didn't pull hers away as we stepped aside to allow the Washingtons to enter first. I prayed my explanation wouldn't hold up the meal too much because, as I entered the room, my stomach growled so loudly I was sure it was heard by all.

Toby's battered face ended all the small talk. Great uneasiness followed until I offered my not-so-believable explanation. My quick fix for their obvious disbelief was to say, "Listen, now's not the time fer the particulars; it's time to eat. So, let's sit and chow down." That was all anyone needed to hear, as people turned and rushed into the dining room to find their assigned seat. Mom had left nothing to chance. She had thoughtfully placed me between Anne and Heather. More risky was the placing of the lawmen directly across from the Washington family. I knew this was her deliberate attempt at forcing interaction among them. As the meal continued, it became clear as a bell her scheme wasn't working. The Washingtons were being ignored by Decker and Collins. Providentially, mom had placed talkative couples on either side of Toby and Martha.

At one point, I rose and walked over to the lawmen to whisper that the three of us would have to talk in earnest about Toby's condition. I knew they knew he'd been attacked. They agreed, though didn't seem very eager. I was troubled by their attitude. I decided to face them about it after we'd eaten instead of ruining the meal.

Our relatively somber and restrained conversation gradually became more relaxed and happier as the women took over – talking about mom's decorations and her abundant offerings: a huge, smoked turkey with spicy stuffing, sweet potato and squash casseroles, mac and cheese with roasted chiles, collard greens, two versions of cornbread, and plenty of iced tea and lemonade to wash everything down. Dessert would be pumpkin and pecan pies – proudly baked by Diane. Compliments poured forth from the ladies, with a few sincere additions by most males. I think Hank Brady was one of them but it was hard to tell.

As the dishes were being cleared for dessert, a different topic was introduced on our side of the table. It was non-threatening at first, focusing on some details of Decker's assigned duties and first experiences as lead deputy sheriff. I even made several comments having spent a few hours with him the previous day. Several questions were asked by others close to Decker, who answered them all in his quick and confident style.

Decker was cut short when Diane and mom placed the pies before us. They looked scrumptious. After a few bites, nearly everyone joined in praising their creator, making her blush and glow with pride.

Regrettably, Collins seized the moment to return to the topic of policing. With a pie-filled mouth, which made him sound like Hank Brady, he began to offer details relating to the new "wave" of crime sweeping the town and county: like theft, burglary, assault, animal cruelty, and public intoxication. His recitation soured the atmosphere real quick. Decker backed up Collins' comments. Everyone else looked decidedly ill at ease. I knew mom would be upset and wasn't surprised when she intruded a second time with this warning: "Enough of this crime talk, gentlemen. This ain't the time or place for it. Besides, I think we're all talked out. Finish these wonderful pies, then I'll ask Pastor Dan to bless us again as we bring the meal and fellowship to a close. *I decided to tease her about her lapse in grammar another day.*

We finished, the pastor prayed, and most of us moved slowly to the living room for a few last words before departing. I left Anne and Heather and motioned for Collins and Decker to join me in a corner of the room. Betty came along which was fine with me. Her reputation was solid, and rumor had it that she knew as much about rangering as the Rangers themselves. I was pleased to see that the Washington family was surrounded by friendly guests quite a distance from us, and relieved also because I didn't want them to overhear our conversation.

Desiring not to waste any time, I got right to the point. "Reckon y'all have guessed Toby's condition wasn't no accident. He didn't trip and fall and bang his head. He didn't tumble out of bed or receive a thumpin' from his wife. He was bushwhacked, and that beatin' was rotten and cruel." Collins and Decker acknowledged this fact by nodding, though it seemed a tad reluctantly. Only Betty appeared genuinely sympathetic. Continuing I said, "Somethin' oughta be done 'bout it. What d'ya propose?"

"Well, what 'bout Captain Springer snoopin' 'round a little?" said Collins. "Maybe he'll get some leads."

"I'm atakin' to that notion," said Decker. "Meanin' I'll do some snoopin' too."

Irritated, I joined in saying, "Snoopin' 'round may bring up some dirt but y'all know these brutes are likely to be Wade King and his gang of thugs. Burt Martin told my father who told me 'bout an earlier run in Toby had with these no good fellas. Start yer search with these fellas and it'll end there right quick."

"Hold yer horses, Ted," Collins blurted out. "Wade's got some influence in these parts, his dad at least. Hayden King owns a big ranch not far from here and he used to serve on the county commission. He ain't nobody to mess with 'round here."

"I can't believe my ears! Y'all are sworn to uphold the law, and the law covers Negroes not just whites."

Collins obviously didn't care too much for my tone and quickly said, "Settle down, son. Rangers uphold the law. We'll get this done, maybe not as fast as ya prefer, but it'll happen."

"Sorry, Sergeant. I spoke a bit harshly. But I'm upset 'bout the way Toby and his family are bein' treated 'round here. My parents have become quite fond of 'em as have several other people important to me. They need ya to solve this matter."

Betty said she'd keep her ear to the ground and might even be able to turn up some witness to the attack on Toby. "It's a small town and tongues wag. Figure I'll have some news in no time."

"Thanks, Betty and fer both of you makin' yer promises," I said, glancing at the lawmen who turned and said farewell to the Townleys. Betty squeezed my hand indicating her commitment. "Can't wait for your cousin's return, Ted. John and I became good friends this past summer. Hope you and him will work together like brothers."

"Me too," I said as she left. I then turned and saw my dad heading my way.

"Listen, Ted, why not make a full circle and walk the Washington family back home. Have the young ladies join ya. It'll be a fittin' endin' to the day for 'em."

"Good idea. I'll get 'em all away as soon as possible."

It seemed forever before everyone else said their farewells, typical of the Townley home. Anne and Heather were happy to join us for the short walk back to the Washington's. Our conversation focused on how openly they had been accepted by most everyone at the meal. Martha took the lead in expressing her thanks. "I've been doubtin' Toby's claims 'bout this town bein' so friendly, but after today, I'm movin' his way. I know it ain't everyone," she said with a glance at Toby's face. "But it's most folks and I'm real happy."

That was a great way to sum up everything, I thought, as we said goodbye at their door. We started for Heather's apartment when Anne suddenly announced, "Ted, I forgot to tell you. Heather received a short telegram from John late yesterday. He says he's coming home soon, probably in a week or two. Isn't that good news?"

"Yes, of course," I said, seeing Heather's smiling face. "Y'all must be countin' down the days."

"Hard not to," Heather admitted with a sigh of relief. "Been a long time since that aspiring doctor left me."

Overly long, I felt, hearing the "heartache" in her voice. He'd finally be back for a future that held promise. *What would be in my future?*

CHAPTER SIX

THE DOCTOR IS IN

Toby was at the store when Janice Harper came in to buy some supplies. He heard her talking with Mr. Brian about how happy she was about John McFarland's return to town. "I hope he stays," she said. "He's such a good doctor. He fixed my son's leg he broke fallin' from that darn horse. It's healin' right proper and he should be able to play baseball in spring. John made it possible." Two other customers joined in praising John's medical skills and also eagerly awaited his return. So was Toby, who wanted to discover the truth for himself.

A NNE RUSHED INTO THE CAFÉ and found Decker and me finishing up an early lunch. After laboring all morning at the store, I had returned home to change into my new deputy's uniform for Decker's appraisal. He liked it, especially the addition of a shiny-holstered pistol. Anne, however, was so excited about something that she failed to comment on my appearance. Quickly sliding lady-like into a chair, still smiling from ear to ear, she said, "Heather just received a letter from John. He's probably already on a train heading home. Could be arriving any day. Isn't that great news?"

"Yes, of course," I replied sincerely, excited by her enthusiasm. "And I bet Heather's fit to be tied. She probly knows the train schedule by heart and jumps at the sound of every toot."

"She does. I'm happy for her. She's the most patient woman I've ever known."

I couldn't argue with that, I thought, as Decker quickly added how eager he also was for my cousin's return. "Damn good doctor and a fine young man. I'll mention it to our Ranger friends who'll be glad to have him 'round agin."

"And that's not all," said Anne enthusiastically. "Remember John's hint that someone may be coming with him?" She teased us with a pause before declaring, "It's Chief Parker!"

"Parker!" I responded happily. "Can't wait to hear the reason. Don't believe he's got any family or friends 'round here."

Anne said, "John thinks it's his growing friendship with himself and you, Ted. And there is a nearby Indian reservation. Perhaps Chief can give those poor souls a helping hand."

"That's an interestin' idea," I said, "but he'll find it hard to make much money 'round there. I'll bend dad's ear and see if we can find him some paid work if he's afixin' to stay."

"Well, you two crime fighters, Heather has even more news: John's been working on a plan to keep him in Texas somehow for the immediate future. He wouldn't give her any details. Says he wants to tell her in person."

"Reckon she'll want that news outta him right quick," said a grinning Decker.

Anne had brought up John's dilemma which gave me a chance to tell them about Dr. Wilbur's recent mysterious comments on the same subject. They were both intrigued, especially when I revealed his not wanting me to mention anything to Heather.

"'Pears Doc Wilbur's been hard at work in east Texas on behalf of my cousin. Wonder what's goin' on? If John tells Heather and she stays mum, Wilbur better open up right away."

"If she don't," said Decker, "we'll all be hogtyin' 'im and doin' our own yankin'."

Another day and a half went by before Heather heard the toot that brought John home. John had shrewdly stopped in Laredo to call and tell us the approximate time of his arrival. The advance notice helped. We finished work and cleaned up before heading for the depot. Arriving an hour early, our welcoming committee included: Heather, my parents and sister, myself and Anne, Decker, Springer, Collins, Betty, Nurse Nancy, and numerous friends from the town and church. There must have been more than thirty people anxious for his arrival. I even noticed Toby standing at the back of the crowd. *Had mom invited him?*

Tears of joy and relief were flowing down Heather's face as the train pulled in. John and Chief were the only two passengers stepping off at our little town. John came first, taking only three steps before Heather threw her arms around his neck. She held him tightly for a few seconds then kissed him on his cheeks and lips. Neither Anne nor I were uneasy about their open display of affection, but I wondered how mom and a few others might react. They finally separated and John made the rounds with Heather glued to his side.

He naturally greeted the Townley family just before Anne and me, receiving a hug from Anne and a firm handshake from his cousin. We did exchange a knowing glance that said something like, "It's been a heck of a summer and fall for both of us, right?" Then they slowly made their way through the crowd, many wanting to exchange a few words with him or Heather before they were hailed by another greeter. Looking like the perfect couple as the greetings continued, I was thinking the scene was kinda like a wedding reception. *Should I mention this image to Anne?*

John spent a fair amount of time with his Ranger buddies and Betty, plus Decker and Nancy. I knew they had many memories to share. Some of those memories included adventures I'd shared with him, making the envy bug bite again. Anne sensed my mood. She looked at me and said, "You two will have lots of exciting things happening together in the near future. You can count on it."

I released her hand and put an arm around her shoulder saying, "Thanks. I sure needed to hear that. I believe we will." *Adventure being John's middle name.*

As the crowd cleared, John turned and noticed Chief standing alone to one side. No one, except Anne and I, had apparently spoken to him. It probably didn't bother Chief, but it did John, who asked me to bring him over so that John could introduce Chief to those remaining. I did and it was interesting to see how people reacted: no antagonism but not open friendliness either. Decker shook his hand having known Chief in west Texas and northern Mexico and developed a grudging respect for him. But Springer and Collins did not shake hands with Chief. Instead, they gave a faint nod, before turning away from him. I felt none of the three would be insulted by this restrained greeting. Other Texans appeared bewildered by a Shakespeare quote made by Chief as he walked among them.

I saw Toby leave before meeting John. This was odd because my parents usually made introductions for our family. But I suddenly realized they had left early, probably to make final preparations for the evening meal. John, Heather, and Anne had been invited to join us for a cozier get-together. Toby's introduction would no doubt come later since mom had practically adopted the Washington family.

Dinner was lively with good-humored remarks but with no new information about John's plans for his immediate future. Neither Anne nor I brought up the subject, nor did anyone else. Better left unspoken until plans were decided. *We could always follow Decker's suggestion.*

The highpoint of the evening was when John entertained us with stories about Jim Thorpe, Wyatt Earp, and his job as a medic on the set of a Hollywood Western movie. Having only heard a few tidbits from John's letters to Heather, we were fascinated by the run-down of deeds. *I suffered another attack from the envy bug as I listened. Why hadn't I gone with him? It was Decker, of course, and my duty to stay with him in El Paso while he recovered from his gunshot wound suffered chasing Pancho Villa. But I sure had missed some great fun in California!*

I knew I'd hear more stories as time passed, from Chief Parker, who had turned down an invitation to dinner. Chief had gone straight off to the Indian reservation to meet the council members and offer his help to the tribe. Getting this "man of few words" to recap tales wouldn't be easy, but I was set on hearing them.

While waiting for dessert, John and Heather invited Anne and I to join them for breakfast at the café. "Got some private information for you two special people," he said, as he leaned toward me and whispered, "Heather will be the first to know when I walk her home tonight." I figured that might be "the moment" a secret was disclosed. We'd sure be at the café to celebrate the news.

The next morning, there were no more stories of adventures in Hollywood, just John getting right to the point: there was a real possibility he could stay in Texas and finish his training at the medical school in Houston! Heather glowed and John began speaking so excitedly and rapidly that I knew I'd miss something important. "Whoa there, cousin. Slow down and give us the big points one at a time."

"Sorry, got ahead of myself. Here it is: one, Dr. Wilbur and others, together with my med school friend, George Beck, have been working on a plan for me to transfer from Michigan to Houston; two, it's an accelerated program letting me begin in January and be completed by December of 1917; three, my work this past summer would shorten up my internship a lot, thanks to letters of reference from Dr. Wilbur and other doctors I've worked alongside; and four, George is applying for a similar program at Michigan. He says it's happening all over the country."

John hesitated, glancing at Heather, then added, "There's a catch. These programs intend to push students to finish their studies more rapidly so they'll be ready to join the war effort in Europe. Medical schools are pretty sure it'll happen soon, and lots of doctors will have to be ready to go with the troops when war is declared."

"Wow!" I said, looking briefly at Heather. Her previous smile had been replaced with a face marked by sadness, even a hint of pain. I asked her what she thought of the plan.

"I don't much like the idea of John going off to war, but at least he'll be closer to me for a while. A lot closer than

Michigan, that's for sure. And John hopes to be able to hop a train in Houston and spend weekends here with me and working at the clinic. I'll sure hold him to that part of the plan."

Anne offered some words of comfort, then John said, "Let's take it easy. It's not a done deal yet, according to Dr. Wilbur. But he's working hard and gotten some encouragement. Believes there'll be an answer by Christmas. Guess we'll all be on 'pins and needles' 'til then."

"Want us to keep it all hush-hush for now?" Anne asked.

"You bet," John answered, "except I owe my parents in Michigan a 'heads up' and Uncle Brian and Aunt Katherine here in Texas should be told. Only hope Diane doesn't find out. She won't be able to keep quiet and within no time at all the whole town will know."

Anne and I sat there speechless about what we'd just heard. I saw Toby standing perhaps ten feet away holding a tray of dirty dishes. Had he overheard any part of our conversation? I felt I'd better find out real quick. As we stood to go to our separate jobs, I pulled Toby aside and point-blank asked him. He claimed he hadn't heard anything, but just in case, I asked him not to let anyone know anything of our talk. To my relief, he agreed and promised not to say a word. From the look on his face, I believed him.

On the way out, John grabbed my arm adding he had a favor to ask of me. "Listen, cousin," he began, "I know you're busy doing a few jobs already, but would you be willing to help Nancy and me at the clinic from time to time? It's good to have a second man in the room in certain situations. You've already proven your worth helping me this past summer."

"Glad to, cousin. Hunt me down and I'll sure do what I can. Probly be a mite later in the day, if'n that's okay."

"All right by me, Ted."

Little did I know he'd need my help that very afternoon. Following my work at the store, Decker and I had been on some deputy duties around the town when Sergeant Collins rode up on horseback saying John needed a hand at the clinic.

"What's goin' on?" I said.

"Me and the captain was keepin' an eye on a young man who was actin' funny like and carryin' suspicious lookin' loot. Chased 'im down and sure 'nuff, the loot was stolen. Sad to say, our chasin' caused the youngster to break his damn leg. Took 'im over to the clinic. Doc John says he and Nancy are alone and would be pleased if y'all showed yer face."

Decker and I followed Collins to the clinic where we found Springer man-handling the prisoner on the examining room table. The prisoner clearly didn't appreciate the captain restraining him. He was crying out and cursing up a storm. An exasperated John immediately ordered the three lawmen out of the room. Noticing my pistol, Nancy suggested I have one of the Rangers hold my weapon to keep it out of the prisoner's reach. Embarrassed at my oversight, I gave it to Springer. He smirked saying he wouldn't let anything bad happen to it.

I took over holding him down, and the patient quieted enough to let Nancy to give him some ether. Having his patient under its effect, John said, "Whew! This might just be a case of 'Ranger justice.' Prisoner keeps swearing he fell off his horse but the damage to his leg came from the captain stomping on it while he was on the ground. Springer just shrugged and grinned when I charged him with it."

"His word against a Ranger, actually two," I said. "Guess he loses."

"But I'm not tickled pink," John said. "He's also got a nasty cut on his temple. I spotted a small blood smear on Springer when he dragged the man in. More 'justice' I guess."

"I hate the thought of havin' to confront him right now," I remarked.

"Maybe we'll have to someday," said John. "Better several of us do so, includin' Decker, when it comes to that."

After getting his frustration off his chest, John returned his attention to the patient. "Not much we can do about the leg," he sighed. "Just clean it up a bit and let the swelling go down before setting it properly. Cut, though, is deep enough to require several stitches. That's why I asked Nancy to use the anesthetic. Having multiple pain sources might make him way too jittery. Be prepared to hold him down if he suddenly wakes up."

"Sure will," I said, watching in admiration as he went to work.

As John was finishing, we heard a commotion in the waiting room and I went to see the cause. Entering, I found the three lawmen trying to calm down an angry Chief Parker. He was striding around speaking more loudly than I had ever heard before.

"What the blue blazes is goin' on?" I asked carefully.

"Chief here claims the reservation's been robbed and believes this here loot belongs to the tribe," said Springer, holding up several items in his hand. "A few coins and cheap trinkets which look to be Injun made."

"This is fine Indian jewelry," Chief protested. "They sell for good prices throughout Texas. It's how they make a living." Looking in my direction, Chief stopped pacing, scowled at Springer, and added, "Ted knows these good people aren't trying to cheat anyone. Calling the jewelry 'cheap' is just plain ignorant." *Uh-oh!*

Wanting to avoid an angry Ranger response, I said, "Should be easy to prove Chief's charge, Captain Springer. Just check in at the reservation and y'all will have the answer. If the goods are recognized, that prisoner is in a heap of trouble."

Noticeably annoyed, Springer barked, "Been a Ranger more'n twenty years, Ted. I know how to do my job."

"Of course ya do, Captain," butted in Collins as he stepped between Springer and me. "We'll put a guard on that fella fer now, and if the tribe identifies the loot, he goes straight to our jail after Doc John releases 'im."

"Dandy idea," I quickly said. "By the way, he looks kinda familiar to me. Anyone know 'im?"

"Yeah, think he's one of Wade King's gang," Springer answered. Wouldn't surprise me if the robbery was a King operation. We'll pressure the rascal to rat out his buddies, then we'll have more arrests to make."

"Well, won't that cause trouble with Big Daddy?"

"Hope so," said Springer with a wicked grin. "'Bout time."

Tempers cooled. After pausing briefly to admire his handsome cowboy boots, Springer assigned Collins to stay and guard the prisoner. As we began to go our separate ways, Chief interrupted one last time and said, "If these robberies continue, I wish to offer my services as a tracker."

Without hesitating, Decker said, "I'll vouch fer him. He's the best, fellas. If y'all don't want him, the sheriff's department sure wants him and his skills." I flat out agreed with Decker's judgment.

A couple days later at the café, as I was finishing a second cup of coffee, Toby appeared at the counter with a worried look on his face. Not waiting for me to ask why, he said, "Mr. Ted, my daughter, Emma, is sickly. Can't keep nuthin' down. Terrible pain in her side. We're real worried 'bout her. Should we take her to the clinic?"

"Absolutely. Y'all can bet John will know what to do."

"Best I go now. Think Mr. Burt will mind?"

"Y'all git goin'. I'll take care of Burt."

Toby smiled weakly, stopped what he was doing, and left with only a slightly guilty peek over his shoulder toward the rear of the café.

I spoke with Burt, who didn't object whatsoever to Toby's abrupt departure. I knew I would worry all morning myself about Emma's condition.

At noon, Anne rushed into the store with a message from John; he needed my help with Emma and to get to the clinic without delay. Anne offered to join me because Nancy wasn't available and knew John would need at least two others to help him. "What's the matter?" I asked.

"I'll let him tell you. But it appears Emma might need an operation."

We arrived to find the other three members of the Washington family huddled together praying in the waiting room. I knew Anne would be silently praying herself. We tiptoed past them into the examining room. John was standing beside Emma, who was lying on her back on the examining table. The smell of ether meant John was ready to begin.

John said, "Martha held her while I examined her and then put her to sleep. But she was so upset that I asked her to wait outside. You two are just in time."

"In time fer what?" I asked nervously.

"For an operation," he answered with a grimace.

"You're going to operate alone?" Anne said uncomfortably.

"Have to. I'm convinced it's her appendix and it might burst at any moment."

"What 'bout Doc Wilbur?" I said. "Shouldn't ya call and have him come over?"

"Been done and he's tied up 'til later tonight. Says no other surgeon is handy right now."

"Sure 'bout yer dicision to operate?" I continued.

"Talked with Wilbur and he agrees. Gave me a few tips and said he was confident in my abilities."

"What happens if it bursts?" Anne asked.

"It spills lots of nasty contents into the surrounding tissue and infection rapidly sets in. Many people, and almost all children, don't survive."

"Damn!" I uttered, forgetting for a moment the lady at my side. Thankfully, she didn't react to my swearing.

Without hesitating, she did say, "No drugs available to help out?"

"Not really, at least not yet. We clean the surface thoroughly with soap and an antiseptic, wash up ourselves and put on surgical gloves, clean the internal areas as best we can, and hope for a positive outcome. Prayer is our best medicine," he concluded after a brief pause.

"Let's get started," he said. We took our turns preparing at the sink with one person always watching the patient. John asked Anne to stand at Emma's head and be in charge of the ether drip through the covering filter. I tried to breathe normally hoping to avoid fainting and falling forward onto the patient.

That would not be good.

"I sure wish Nancy was here in my place," I said as John applied the antiseptic to the surface area.

"She's making rounds on house calls, including the reservation," he replied. "Couldn't reach her, though I sent out one of Uncle Brian's friends to track her down."

"Maybe she'll get here soon," I said, hoping she'd walk in at that moment.

"Maybe," he said offhandedly as I saw him make the first incision. Blood began to flow and I focused again on my breathing.

"Use those pieces of sterile gauze to stop the bleeding with wiping and pressure," he ordered like a practiced doctor. "And keep the area open as much as possible with your hands. I'll do my best to tie off the bigger bleeders with the silk and catgut threads on the stand to your right."

We somehow managed to keep the bleeding under control as he went deeper. He finally found the area of the appendix saying with relief, "This is it. I can feel it. A couple more careful cuts and it'll be exposed." He made the cuts.

"That ain't normal, huh?" I asked, forgetting he was hardly an expert at removing an appendix.

"Don't think so," he replied as he gently squeezed the organ between his thumb and forefinger. "Wow! It's as hard as a rock. Ready to rupture at any moment I guess."

"Now what?" asked Anne as she saw Emma twitch a little as the anesthetic began to wear off. Anne responded by releasing a couple more drops of ether onto the mask.

"Now I cut it free and close the opening it created, followed by additional stitches as I work my way back to the surface. Keep dabbing and applying pressure, Ted, and I'll be as quick as possible."

I dabbed and swiped and he used the needle and thread until he reached the outer layer, sooner than I had expected.

"Now what?" Anne and I asked at the same time.

"Now we wait and pray." Glancing at Anne, he invited her to pray that very moment. She did and it was heartwarming to listen to her faithful voice turned heavenward.

After cleaning ourselves and covering up the patient, John asked me to let the family back in so they could be present when she woke up. We left John with the family and sat down wearily in the other room, holding hands, talking quietly about what we'd just experienced.

"Pretty incredible, don't you think?" said Anne.

"I do. John's quite the doctor. More impressed with him every day."

"You're kind of impressive yourself, 'Dr. Ted,'" she said, prodding my shoulder.

"Just followin' orders, ma'am," I said, gently caressing her shoulder in return.

That's how the Washington family, except Emma, found us, nearly asleep, leaning against each other. They were overjoyed at the outwardly successful operation and kept praising us until were both uncomfortable. Martha said she'd be back later in the evening and would be honored if we would also visit her daughter from time to time. Anne made a promise I knew she would keep.

Wanting to change the subject, I asked Anne to stay with the ladies for a bit so I could talk with Toby outside. Once outside and out of earshot, I brought up Wade King's name and his gang. "Any sign of 'em, Toby? Are they leavin' y'all alone?"

"Sometimes they pass me on the street and give the evil eye and spit out some hurtful words."

"That's gonna stop soon if I have anythin' to do with it," I said forcefully. "Here's somethin' I'm afixin' to do. When y'all finish workin' at the store, I'll show up and walk ya home. If they give me the same look, they'll wish they hadn't."

"Y'all don't have to do that, Mr. Ted."

"It'd be my pleasure, Toby. I'll start this minute by walkin' the three of ya back home." Anne joined me as we escorted them along the route. I was itching for a run-in with the hateful King gang. No showdown came to pass. But I knew it was only a matter of time.

Had I suddenly adopted my mother's mindset or Anne's regarding Negroes? Was this part of my transformation? These thoughts did give me a new sense of purpose as the Christmas season approached.

CHAPTER SEVEN

CHRISTMAS

Toby heard many stories from customers about how families spent Christmas in this part of Texas. It was another special family holiday, and he wasn't afraid this time telling people that he and his family were again invited to the Townley home. According to everyone, there would be more great food, games to play, and carols to sing. There was, however, a concern from a few locals, who worked at the feed store. "Many of us spend Christmas with faraway relatives. Now that we have so many break-ins and burglaries in this county, it's scary to leave our homes. We don't have much, but what we own we've worked hard for." Toby wondered about his own home and scant belongings. Robbing his home wouldn't take very long at all.

I T WAS WEDNESDAY MORNING AT the store, and I was anxious about next Monday's Christmas party: I hadn't yet bought gifts for anyone, even Anne. That's when it happened, the stabbing pain when I bit down on a piece of hardtack during a break. "Ouch!" I cried out loud enough for dad to hear.

"What's the matter, son?"

"Just bit my tongue, Dad," I lied. I couldn't quite face him or particularly mom, who had nagged me for years to make brushing a daily habit. Occasional brushing had already caused me to have one tooth pulled, and I dreaded making it two. And this pain came from a lower molar, the type used by Texas males to grind up those inch-thick steaks. A second painful bite convinced me to join Anne and Heather for lunch at school and get their advice.

They were pleased to see me, of course, and began babbling away before I could present my sorry case to them. Noticing my silence, Anne finally said, "Cat got your tongue, Mr. Townley?"

"Not funny," I replied with a fake smile. "Ain't feelin' so hot right now. It's my tooth. Think I'm in trouble with a big one on my lower right. Not gettin' it yanked if there's somethin' else to be done."

"Well, we aren't dentists," said Anne, "but I can at least spot tooth decay. Let me get a magnifying glass and I'll have a look."

Heather and I shared a few words before Anne returned. "Move over by the windows where the light is better." I did, she examined my mouth, and then pulled back with a frown, yet said nothing. Handing the glass to Heather, she asked for a second opinion. Same reaction from her as she glanced at Anne, obviously waiting for my gal to give me the bad news.

Inhaling then grimacing, Anne said, "I have good news and bad. First, your breath is improving. It appears you're taking my advice about gargling frequently."

"I have. Found the bottle of Listerine I misplaced earlier. Now, what's the bad news?"

"Both of us see a fairly large cavity on a lower tooth in the back. It won't get any better, Ted, even with daily brushing."

"Figured as much. What do y'all recommend?"

"A dentist, Ted," scolded Heather. "It has to be filled or removed. Sorry, but it looks bad to me, with swelling in the surrounding area."

Discouraged, I caught myself from swearing and said, "Well, son of a gun! Ain't goin' to Brownsville fer no dentist. There's no one but a barber who yanks 'em out here. I wouldn't trust him to yank a nail outta a piece of cheese."

"What about John?" offered Heather. "He knows anatomy. Maybe he can suggest some other dentist or procedure."

"I'll ask him. Ain't really got a choice. 'Cause I'd prefer not to miss out on all that great food at Christmas." And everything between now and then, I thought, as I thanked the ladies and left – without enjoying their kind offers to share in their lunchtime fares.

Slightly warm coffee became my lunch before I met up with Decker for some routine deputy work. Unfortunately, he chose horses for transportation, and I winced at every bounce. *Could the damn thing be jarred lose by accident?*

I stabled my horse in late afternoon and walked over to the clinic hoping John wasn't too busy. Sadly, I had to wait about twenty throbbing minutes before he could wedge me in between patients. He briefly examined me and agreed with Anne and Heather: a cavity so deep the tooth had to be removed.

"Let's get it over with," I gasped as a sharp pain shot through my nerve endings.

"Ease off, Deputy. I can't do it now with all that inflammation. It's clearly infected. You'll have to wait 'til it calms down before I can pull it." Seeing my disappointment, he added, "Maybe in a couple of days. In the meantime, gargle several times a day with sodium peroxide. That'll clean the surface area and give your body time to fight off the infection."

"Pull it on Saturday, regardless."

"Risky, Ted."

"I'll take the chance. It's killin' me!"

"Saturday it is, then. I'll clean it as best I can and pack the hole with sterile gauze."

I shook his hand and started to leave, only to bump into Chief in the waiting room: an angry Chief once again.

"Been another robbery at the reservation, Ted. They snuck into a hut during a spiritual ceremony and swiped weapons: two rifles, several pistols, and some ammunition. 'Double toil and trouble,' if you ask me."

"Forget the Shakespeare, Chief, this is serious."

"I aim to do somethin' about it."

"What 'xactly?"

"Aim to track 'em down myself and bring 'em to justice."

"Not all that good a plan, Chief. They'll be huntin' y'all down too."

"Time for action, Deputy."

"True, but give me forty-eight hours. They're probly local thieves who won't go far. That'll give me time to meet with Decker and the Rangers and figure out a plan of action. Just give us two days, Chief."

"That's a mighty long time."

"I'll get everyone together Friday morning at the Ranger station, and you can join us."

"Friday morning at dawn. I'll be there."

"Not sure 'bout the dawn part, but I'll let ya know."

My crime-fighting friends weren't too pleased with their junior partner taking the lead, but agreed to hash over the problem at a café breakfast meeting. They would also let Chief be present as long as he kept silent, hardly a problem for him under "normal" circumstances.

Surprisingly, at the meeting there was agreement on taking action. Summing up, Springer said, "The threat of stolen weapons alone means we gotta get on top of this." Chief was pleased and seemed ready to begin the hunt before the last bite of syrup-drenched pancake was swallowed. A holdup in acting swiftly developed as we argued about jurisdiction: whose responsibility was it when it involved an Indian reservation? Collins felt it was mainly a federal concern and Marshals should be called in. An irritated Springer countered that they rarely showed up and usually did a rotten job anyway. "It's also the state's affair," he said with a confident Ranger smile, "and *we* represent Texas." Decker made a case that since the reservation was in our county it was also a responsibility for the sheriff's department.

As the squabbling increased among the three lawmen, I cut in and said, "Federalism is a wonderful topic fer discussion, men, but probly fer some other time. Look, several days ago we were talkin' 'bout the subject of drug smugglin', right? It's really the same point, one of overlappin' jurisdictions. Two things are clear as all git out: the feds ain't gonna be able to handle it right this minute, and both the Rangers and sheriff's department have a claim and are ready to act. It's simple as pie, we join forces and forget 'bout who's the 'top dog.'"

Further grumbling arose before they gave in to the wisdom of my proposal and agreed to cooperate with each other. Chief, who had fidgeted uncomfortably during the whole argument, spoke for the first time. "We all know it's the Wade King gang. Let's bring 'em in right now and get it over with." His comment nipped conversation right quick.

Eager to please the Rangers and, at the same time calming Chief, Decker said, "Chief, other criminals are active 'round here too. We shouldn't jump to conclusions. Besides, tomorrow's Christmas Eve. Let's hold off 'til Tuesday mornin' and we'll all get a fresh start then." *A second delay for Chief?*

My friend's face stayed unreadable, but his eyes were anything but calm. Acting as "Mr. Compromise" again, I hurriedly spoke before he could mess up his chances of working with us. "Chief, fella lawmen, I suggest that early Tuesday mornin' we locate Wade and his bunch and bring 'em in fer serious interrogation. Somethin' might break if we put pressure on 'em."

It was a relief to see everyone nodding in agreement, everyone but Chief, that is. Shaking his head, he said, "Pressure hasn't worked so far, I hear, with the robber caught earlier. Can't break him or anyone, better to charge them."

"He'll break," hissed Collins, "and some of the others."

"Maybe, maybe not," replied the skeptical Indian.

A few more details were covered before we non-Indians settled on the meeting early Tuesday morning. Chief simply got up and left without a further word. Knowing he was still upset, I hustled and reached him as he was mounting his horse. Warily taking hold of his horse's bridle, I said, "Chief, don't do anythin' rash. Stay with us. We need ya on our side." Right at that moment, I thought of a way to distract him. "Listen, y'all can do me a favor Saturday mornin'. Meet me at the clinic, please. John's gonna pull my achin' tooth. Y'all can help by holdin' me down." Grinning, I added, "Y'all can squeeze my arm real hard if it suits ya. And how 'bout another favor: why not take me out to the reservation and help me select some fine Indian jewelry fer everyone, 'specially Anne? Figure y'all are more of an expert on those items than me."

My plea worked. Looking down at me with a sigh of resignation, he said, "I will do this for you and John. But on Tuesday morning I may go on the warpath if justice isn't carried out."

"They'll get it done. I give ya my word." *I prayed I could keep it and his friendship.*

I headed to the clinic Saturday morning for the extraction. Anne came along for additional support. Chief and John were already there. My "dentist" sat me in a chair that he had fixed up as a dental chair. His handcrafted neck support seemed a bit flimsy as I leaned back and tried to relax. Chief strongly held one arm. Anne stroked the other. John ordered me to open up wide and close my eyes. Here it comes, I knew, as I peeked and spotted the object in his hand. *Was it a carpenter's pliers?* He pushed back my head and grasped my tooth with it, then applied pinching pressure until I gasped in pain and my eyes watered. Then, with his left arm around my shoulders for support, he yanked out the offending tooth with one big pull. Pain shot from head to foot.

His exertion caused him to stagger backward and almost end up on his butt. My opposing reaction was to slam my head into John's makeshift contraption, causing it to break and me to pitch backward. Had it not been for my arms being held, my head would have collided with the floor with considerable force. Through watery eyes, I gazed up from a forty-five-degree angle and thanked my saviors. They sat me upright while John proudly held my tooth in the bloody pliers.

"Got the sucker!" he declared.

Attempting to smile, I gargled out, "Great, now what?"

"Now I have to clean the area with antiseptics and pack the hole tightly with gauze to stop the bleeding." He cleaned and packed as I squirmed and moaned some more. Finished, he asked Anne to pray for me. She prayed and I did feel a teeny bit better. His parting words were, "Sorry, cousin, it's gonna be sore as the devil a while."

"How can I fix that?"

"Well, rinse and gargle with hydrogen peroxide several times a day. Use aspirin for pain, and put some ice on your cheek to keep the swelling down."

"Thanks, John, what do I owe ya?"

"Payment is full recovery."

I remembered to thank my "helpers" as we walked back outside. With her arm around me, Anne tenderly said, "Let me tag along, Ted. I'd be happy to be your nurse for the next few hours."

I planted a very light kiss on her cheek before saying, "I need to go with Chief to the reservation to check on somethin'." *Which was true.* "It won't take long. Then y'all can nurse me when I get back." I was glad when she agreed to my suggestion: I wanted my shopping spree to be a secret.

At the reservation, I was astonished at the variety and quality of the jewelry. I loved anything with turquoise in it, so Chief helped me pick out the best-for-the-price items: a big squash blossom for Anne, a necklace for my mom, earrings for Diane, and a belt buckle for dad. I had taken what I thought was enough money with me, yet I left with a nearly empty wallet. Oh well, it *was* Christmas after all. I praised Chief for his savvy advice, and we parted, grateful that the subject of Tuesday morning hadn't come up.

Christmas, like Thanksgiving, was a big event for my parents. When I counted eighteen in the living room early Monday afternoon, it was no surprise. Mom's guest list for Christmas included singles: bachelors, widows, or widowers. Therefore, in addition to the usual family and friends, plus the Washingtons and Carlos and Lola Sanchez, she had invited Alice Davis, Fannie Walker, Travis Robinson, Chief, Decker, and naturally, Hank Brady. Apart from Chief, everyone was in a festive mood. John and Heather seemed almost to glow. *What was going on with them?*

We always played games prior to eating, and the highlight this year was mom handing out paper and pencil and asking all present to create as many words as possible from "Christmas Party." "The winner gets a special gift after dinner," she said as added inducement. We were supposed to work alone, but I peeked over Anne's shoulder at her growing list. She caught me and pretended to be annoyed. My ultimate list had fourteen, Anne and Heather had sixteen, John seventeen, all pretty good in my opinion. The winner, however, was no surprise: retired teacher, Fannie Walker, with twenty.

As usual, the table was overflowing with food: smoked ham and pork ribs, mashed as well as sweet potatoes, green beans and other vegetables, and tamales. Dessert, mom declared, would be spiced cake with raisins and pecans and banana pudding. Two of the ladies had also brought along ample supplies of sugar and chocolate cookies for those whose stomachs had any leftover room. To *my* great anguish, I was forced to chew gingerly on my left side and focused mainly on slivers of ribs, the potatoes, and the cake. Thankfully, I was also able to melt several cookies into mush in my mouth before swallowing them. Sipping tea and water helped everything to slide to its destination.

Following dinner, we sang quite a few carols, with mom accompanying us on the piano. I was surprised how well we sounded, especially Decker whose deep baritone added a nice touch. The only "sour note" came from Hank Brady, who couldn't carry a tune if his life depended on it. I hoped he didn't realize people were inching away from his presence as the singing progressed. *Silent Night* was everyone's favorite and it sounded heavenly. The crowning point of our singing, though, was a rendition of *O Come All Ye Faithful* in Spanish by Carlos and Lola Sanchez; its beauty gave us all a few moments to reflect on grace in general and Grace in particular: the Christ child. Earlier mom had agreed not to repeat her Thanksgiving "exercise" at the party. Had it been repeated, however, this would have been the perfect time for it. I almost volunteered to speak. Almost.

I had given my gifts to family and friends earlier in the day. Anne was thrilled with hers, though uneasy about its costing too much. She gifted me with a handcrafted holster from a famous Brownsville merchant. I loved it and forgot to ask how much it set her back. All my other family members seemed to share my love for turquoise and proved it, along with Anne, by wearing the gifts as soon as the boxes and bags were opened.

We hung around for a while exchanging pleasantries and enjoying the warm companionship. During this relaxed period, mom presented Fannie Walker with her gift: a cookbook. Later I would have to ask if a more "masculine" gift had also been bought, just in case.

We all at once realized John and Heather were trying to gain our attention. John finally resorted to a loud whistle that did the trick. "Friends, I have two special announcements to make. First, I received a call Saturday from Dr. Wilbur who informed me that I have been accepted as a transfer student in a special medical program in Houston. It starts in January and Heather and I couldn't be more pleased."

Even Chief looked happy and applauded with the group after John's announcement. John and Heather were quickly surrounded and received hearty handshakes and congratulatory hugs. After a short while, Mom broke in saying, "John, you had two announcements to make. What is the second?"

Clearing his throat and pulling Heather close to his side, he replied, "Yes, in fact there is. Last night after church I asked this beautiful lady to marry me and she accepted. We are engaged and hope to have a summer wedding." Another round of cheers erupted followed by more handshakes and backslapping for John and hugs for Heather. Tears of joy soon marked the cheeks of all the ladies present, as well as a few men, who naturally tried to wipe them away without being noticed.

I stole a quick kiss – on the lips – from my gal, just before she ran over to Heather for a sisterly embrace. I heard her say with pretend anger that she was mad at Heather for keeping this a secret from her. Heather responded, "I'm so sorry, Anne. John wanted to let everyone know at the same time. I desperately wanted to tell you, though, because you're going to be my maid of honor, if you're willing?"

Anne shrieked and embraced Heather again. "I accept and I'm the one who's honored. I can't wait to begin planning."

As the excitement died down John said, "I must confess I told this lady a tiny white lie last night. I promised her we'd pick out a ring soon." Turning to face Heather, he continued, "Sweetie, I have already purchased the ring for you, in California a while ago. I hope you like it." He then reached into a pocket and retrieved a small box and handed it to her. Visibly shaken, she eased it open, appraised it ever so briefly, and simply nodded. I reckoned this meant approval. She proved me right when she allowed John to remove it from the box and slide it on the appropriate finger. Time seemed to stand still as they embraced again, so completely that it felt like there was one body in front of my eyes rather than two.

Anne seized that moment to draw me close, and with her head next to mine whispered, "I love you, Ted." Since this was the first time I'd heard those words from her, I tightened my hold on her and responded in kind. Pushing away, she said playfully, "But you don't have to present me with a ring right away, Mr. Deputy Sheriff." *That was a relief since I was nearly broke.*

I wanted us to be like John and Heather, but I hadn't forgotten about the "conditions" imposed on me earlier. I was making progress. Would it continue? *God give me the strength!*

Mom asked dad to conclude the festivity in prayer. He did with a special request for God to bless the new couple, a fitting end to a wonderful Christmas celebration.

As farewells were being exchanged, I noticed the Washingtons were to one side waiting their turn to meet my parents at the door. With Anne at my side, I went over to them and said, "Toby, despite my earlier promise, I've only walked ya home once. Let me and Anne accompany y'all now. How 'bout it?"

"Ain't no need. Never had no trouble with family beside me. We'll be fine."

"Okay, but the offer still stands, 'specially after yer work is done."

As I watched them walk away, it made me reflect again on what might happen when morning arrived. Trouble ahead? I hoped not, but I had to admit I was anxious about the darkness that sometimes follows the dawn.

CHAPTER EIGHT

DEPUTY SHERIFF

Toby grew increasingly uneasy as he listened to reports from café customers about the slew of burglaries during Christmas. Previous predictions had been accurate: vacant homes became perfect targets. He had also been a victim, yet was anxious because he didn't know what to do. Other owners were confident in approaching law enforcement. He wasn't too sure since Texas officers, in his experience, weren't very aggressive in pursuing criminals who targeted colored folks. Yet, maybe this town would be different because Mr. Ted now wore a badge. He was mulling this over when the door burst open and two Rangers strode in, followed closely by the object of his hope, Deputy Sheriff, Ted Townley.

D ECKER AND I ARRIVED AT the café at eight a.m. just as
the Rangers drove up. I had spotted Chief pacing in
front, clearly frustrated with the decision to meet at such
a "late" hour. His habit was to rise at at five a.m., so his

day was already well under way. Somewhat reluctantly, he agreed to join us for a working breakfast. I smiled to myself, thinking if he owned a watch, he'd probably check it every few minutes to see how much time had been wasted before we finally set out to arrest the Wade gang.

We had barely sat down at a corner table when two men approached and loudly complained that their properties had been burgled the previous night. Diego Trevino claimed the robbers had stolen his prized shotgun as well as an ornate crucifix, which wasn't expensive but had special religious value to his family. Another man, unfamiliar to me, grumbled about his corral being breached and his best breeding bull taken. This last item, I knew, would be easy to identify and link to the culprits. These men also gave us the names of several other victims of break-ins and robberies during the past forty-eight hours. We calmed them down by promising swift action, but what was our game plan?

Springer began to outline a strategy only to have Toby cut him off and take command of the conversation. Where he found the courage I couldn't guess, but the captain surprisingly allowed the interference. Toby's story was similar: another break-in, more stolen items. "Took Martha's silverware," he said gravely. "She got 'em from her own momma who had been a slave herself as a child. Real broken up 'bout it. And they found our hidden stash of money in the kitchen. Weren't much, but it was all we had. Ain't got nuthin' now." No one spoke so he turned and left. I was amazed at my colleagues' indifference.

"That's an outrage!" I exclaimed before Springer could seize the floor. "It ain't right. They've lost way too much."

"Simmer down, son," said Decker. "We'll get the robbers and the loot. Right, Captain?"

"Sure 'nuff," answered Springer, though he didn't refer specifically to Toby's situation.

Decker seemed to sense I wasn't ready to drop Toby's case and gave me a cautionary look. "Captain, I have an idea fer my deputy here. Let's have Ted make a list of all the stolen items from the last couple days. It'd make our work a lot easier and help with any future court action."

"Excellent point. You're a college boy, ain't ya, Ted? Writin' up a list shouldn't be a problem fer ya, right?" replied Springer with more than a hint of sarcasm.

Settling down somewhat, I returned his sarcasm with, "Happy to, Captain. I'll give the list to Betty, yer secretary. She's probly the best reader among you Rangers, right?"

Springer's face reddened and he started to speak but Collins jumped in and said, "Hey, men, we're all in this together. Let's stop the bickerin' and get to work." Springer glared at me briefly before shrugging and returning to figuring out our course of action.

Decker took the lead in this planning session and everyone except Chief made a suggestion or two before our overall plan became clear. Since this was an interrogation not an arrest per se, and we had no warrant, Decker and I argued that we first call ahead to the King residence and tell them we were on our way. The Rangers raised some objections to this, but finally backed off, perhaps out of deference to Decker. *Or maybe they had a longer history with Wade's pappy and wanted to avoid any conflict at the house?* Then we decided to split our approaching force, one going by car and the other by horseback. If one or more members of the King gang were intercepted, they would be taken immediately to the Ranger station for questioning – to avoid interference from Wade's parents, especially Big Daddy.

What seemed like a practical plan, at least to Decker and me, wasn't for Chief, who now spoke and strongly objected to alerting Wade with a phone call. He spoke with so much emotion that it startled everyone. I could see by their faces that the Rangers would side with him.

At any rate, Chief took their momentary silence as an opening to push even harder and said, "Calling ahead is a crazy idea! Even a 'blinking idiot' can see that. It would lead to a 'wild goose chase' and everyone might escape."

Uh-oh! He sure was worked up. Probably more Shakespeare. I reckoned nothing good could come from his latest oddities so I jumped in saying, "Now just simmer down, Chief. However, gentlemen, my Indian friend might have a point about calling ahead. I move we discuss it a bit longer."

Thankfully, Decker came to the rescue by agreeing with me to re-introduce the subject of the call. It didn't take long for five active participants to drop the idea of phoning ahead. *Barging in was more of a Ranger stunt.*

Chief said his offer to track the scoundrels was still good. The Rangers chose the truck for transportation, leaving horseback for the rest of us. We got back to the Ranger station and retrieved our rides. Then it was on to the King ranch for our unannounced visit.

As we neared the enormous ranch-style King house, I noticed dust rising off to one side. I feared someone had been tipped off and was fleeing the scene. *Who had alerted them?* I reckoned Springer was confident we could catch them, if need be, since he didn't call out orders to chase after the riders. We simply joined him as he stomped onto the porch and pounded on the door. Waiting impatiently, an angry woman finally flung open the door. "What y'all doin' here?"

she barked. "Ain't got no time for no nonsense, 'specially from no high and mighty Rangers."

Springer looked mad enough to just haul off and slug her, so I started to intervene, but Collins beat me to it by stepping between them. "Reckon y'all are Wade's mama, ma'am. We're here to speak to him. Is he 'round here?"

"Ain't nobody here, so get off my property."

"Need to look 'round, ma'am," said Decker. "Never know what we might find. Been told yer son ain't no stranger to us lawmen."

"Y'all accusin' my son o' bein' a varmint?"

"No, ma'am, just doin' our job."

"Y'all have a search warrant?"

"No, ma'am."

"Then ya ain't comin' in. My ol' man would be madder than a hornet if'n I let ya in."

Springer had had enough and pointed off to the side saying, "Looks to me like someone took off a moment ago, makin' this a case of 'probable cause.' Now step aside!" When she stood her ground, he merely shoved past her and strode into the living room with a hand atop his holstered pistol.

The rest of us filed in as she became more cantankerous. Decker noticed her getting more worked up and immediately ordered me to keep Mrs. King out of everyone's way as the search progressed. I somehow managed to fend her off, though my arms suffered a few scratches as she tried to fight her way past.

The ornery lady stopped fussing when Collins stepped out of a room at the end of the hallway and said, "Lookie here. Bet these are from the wife of that Negro fella." He raised up some kitchen utensils. "Keep searchin', boys. 'Pears they vamoosed 'fore they could take much with 'em."

I took the liberty of asking Wade's mom if her son had been hosting a buddy or two in the house. With hate-filled eyes, she answered, "None of yer damn business." Same as a "yes," I figured.

Our search continued until a rifle was found hidden in a closet. Springer claimed it fit the description of one recently stolen from the reservation. A good start but we needed more evidence by the captain's reasoning. He tried to question the testy mother about other hiding places. She answered with threats that Wade's dad would file lawsuits against everyone in the room, plus the town, county, and the Rangers. Unhappily, I believed her. I hadn't been thinking of lawsuits filed by them!

Though Mrs. King didn't have the pleasure of throwing us out, she sure did slam the door behind us. Being the last to exit, my fanny narrowly escaped serious injury. Had there been any glass in the door, I would also have been showered with shards. *Never happier to leave a house in my life!*

We stood in the front yard a while figuring what to do next. Collins brought up a rumor floating around the county about Wade having a secret hiding place where he stashed his stolen loot. Decker said the dust cloud spotted earlier was no doubt Wade and others fleeing the scene and heading for that rumored place. We all agreed, and Chief was assigned to track down the culprits. I smiled when thinking of Chief's skills as a tracker. We'd have 'em in no time, I reckoned, as we watched him tear off after the Wade gang. The rest of us horsemen mounted up and rode off after Chief, leaving the truck to eat our dust.

We crested a ridge an hour later and gazed down into a gully at a copse of trees that about obscured the outline of something. Springer took out his binoculars for a closer look. He had spotted the shape of a small building. "Found 'em," he called out in triumph. Crowding around the captain, we listened as he outlined our assault. We set out in two groups, one to the front and the other to the side to cover any escape attempt from the rear. I went with Chief and Decker to the side, leaving the Rangers to unload their Winchesters at the front, if the command to surrender was rejected.

Springer shouted out his order. Nothing but silence. We knew someone was around because several horses were tied to nearby trees. He called out again, and this time was answered with a hail of bullets from the front of the rickety structure. It seemed their rifles were pouring lead from between gaps in the boards on either side of the front door. I regarded this foolhardy action as their undoing. The Rangers' volleys quickly smashed through the flimsy front of the building. In no time we could hear screams of pain and surrender from inside. Brashly, one outlaw tried to make a dash for freedom out the rear, and Decker dropped him with a single rifle shot.

When the firing ceased, two men staggered out through the nearly destroyed front door, hands raised, squinting to shield their eyes from the blazing Texas sun. One man's left hand was dripping blood from an obvious splinter gash. The Rangers ran down the embankment, roughly shoved the men to their knees, and hogtied them. Chief and I followed Decker as he jerked his victim up from the ground and pushed him around the side of the building to join his hapless partners. No binding needed for him, as Decker allowed him to press a hand against his bleeding shoulder.

Our biggest letdown: no Wade King. Springer cursed up a storm before ordering Chief and I to guard the prisoners while Collins and Decker joined him to search the building. Springer soon came out smiling, saying he'd found the "motherlode." Decker brought out a blanket and they placed umpteen items on it: rifles, pistols, boxes of ammunition, jewelry, various household items, a bag of cash, and two paintings of Indians in ceremonial garments. I wondered what Chief thought about those portraits.

Springer's main concern was the whereabouts of their leader, Wade King. He fired rapid questions at the three captives to no avail. Springer then applied more forceful Ranger interrogation: kicks to the sides of the two prone bandits and slaps to the face of the one being held upright by Decker. Apart from the groans of the victims, no one spoke. Collins soon joined in, and the "ramped up" interrogation continued for a "long" minute, until I yelled, "Fellas, this ain't workin'! Let's throw 'em in the truck and take the two on the ground to jail and the bleedin' one needs John to patch him up. Maybe someone will talk, 'specially the one Decker plugged when the shock wears off." I had my doubts about the talking part. But they reluctantly agreed, taking great pleasure in the "throwing in" part.

Just before we left, Chief approached claiming he'd found fresh tracks behind the building and felt they might belong to Wade King. He offered to trail them and report back if he was successful. "Good idea," said Decker.

"If ya find anythin', don't do nuthin' stupid. We'll deal with him later." Chief nodded, gave us a wry smile, and rode off. *I was pretty sure the word "stupid" had gone in one ear and out the other.*

At the Ranger station, Decker kept prodding Springer into letting us take the wounded man over to see John. Springer laughed it off saying the wound was nothing and he'd wrap it up himself. I whispered for Betty to take charge and she nodded she understood. Finally, Decker was allowed to borrow the truck to move our man to the clinic.

Luckily, John was on hand to tend to our prisoner. It didn't take long since his shoulder had both clean entrance and exit wounds and no major blood vessel had been affected. As John worked, Decker asked about the gang, its dealings, and Wade King. An icy stare was the prisoner's only response. I had to admit I was impressed by his – their – stubbornness in not talking. *Were they afraid of some payback for squealing from Wade or Big Daddy?* When John wasn't looking, a frustrated Decker copied Springer's violence by firmly squeezing the man's injured shoulder. "That's 'bout 'nuff, Captain," I called out. The patient's yelp of pain also caused John to quickly turn back around.

"I agree with Ted, Captain," said my annoyed cousin. "Ted spoke about that earlier Ranger technique when you arrived at the clinic. Aside from the fact that it's wrong, it's worthless. This gang appears to have an arrangement to keep quiet under any and all circumstances. I'm guessing things will become clearer in the very near future." Decker mumbled something but didn't challenge John. We were soon heading back to the jail with our surly prisoner in tow, now with a bandaged arm.

Entering the jail, we noticed more signs of bruising on the other two prisoners. I decided not to say anything unless more beatings happened in my presence. Collins let on that the miserable pair had not been forthcoming with anything since we last saw them. We talked for a time about the day's events, including the strength of our case against the three men scowling at us from behind the bars a few feet away. "Open and shut," claimed Springer with conviction. "Even the best lawyer in Texas can't get 'em off." Each of us felt pretty much the same when our conversation was cut short by the sound of approaching horses. I peeked through the window and couldn't believe my eyes.

"Y'all won't believe this!" I exclaimed. "It's Chief and he has Wade King with him! My three companions all rushed outside where we watched Chief yank his bound prisoner off his horse and deposit him roughly on the ground.

"Snuck up on him a few miles from the shack hiding like a coward behind some bushes. Didn't hear me coming and didn't put up a fight. Maybe he's scared of Indians," he finished as he smirked at his prisoner.

Laughing, Decker said, "Y'all may just be right 'bout that, Chief. Let's make sure to rat him out to his buddies."

With an unnerving grin of confidence, the grounded prisoner said, "Ain't scared of no Injun or any of y'all either. My dad knows how to handle Rangers. Been doin' it all his life. Damn sure y'all will find out 'cause he'll be here 'fore ya can count to ten. If ya can count that high."

Springer cussed a blue streak as he and Collins dragged Wade into the jail. Even under these circumstances, he kept his cocky attitude, sneering at Springer as if he pitied the Ranger captain. Without warning, Springer delivered a whopping kick into Wade's side. Wade gasped and tried to regain his breath while curling into a fetal position. For a moment everyone froze in place. Winding up for a second blow, everyone – except Chief – lunged forward to stop him.

"Easy there, Captain," Collins warned. "I think we done 'nuff of that today. 'Sides," he said in a lowered voice, "y'all have some witnesses yonder who might just break their silence once they appear in a courtroom."

"I agree with Collins," said Decker. "Let's just toss him in with the other no-accounts and have 'em lick their wounds fer a day or two." When Springer didn't answer back, Decker and I hustled Wade over to the cell, unlocked it, and tossed him in.

Betty stepped in quickly to help calm Springer down, giving me a chance to ask Chief to fill us in on details of his hunt for Wade. He did, though with irritating briefness. He had just reached the point where he was ready to leap out from his hiding place and face the suspect, when we heard the screech of brakes, followed by the scream of horses tied to the hitching post, then the sound of two crashes. We bolted out the door and discovered that a big ol' Cadillac had demolished the post – thankfully not the horses – and even slid into the front of the station. Through a cloud of dust, out stepped – it had to be – Hayden King, Big Daddy himself. The driver followed and came around to meet his passenger where they stood brushing off dust and sand from their fancy Western suits. Boss-man seemed mightily displeased with the inconvenience.

Pretty soon everyone but Chief and I were shouting threats and cussing. I reckoned they all had reason to be upset, though the uproar got annoying real quick. I whistled loudly – twice – before the noise subsided.

Staring at Springer, Big Daddy hissed, "Y'all holdin' my son in that stinkin' jail, Captain? If so, bring him out right now."

"He's my prisoner and he stays put," replied Springer with obvious pleasure. "He and his worthless gang have been caught red-handed with stolen goods. They'll all be facin' a trial and prison."

"Don't know 'bout no gang, but my son's innocent. The missus swears up and down he was home most of the day."

"I'm sure she does, but it don't change a thing. He stays put."

King sneered, then pushed his driver forward and nodded for him to speak. The driver pulled out a document from an inside suit pocket, nervously cleared his throat, and said, "I have here an order from county Judge Colson for the release of a Mr. Wade King into the custody of his father, Mr. Hayden King, pending any future judicial hearing. It was signed by the judge before myself and two other witnesses. It's a lawful order and it's your duty to release him."

Collins snatched the paper from the driver, read it and gave it to Decker, who glanced at it and handed it to Springer. *Wrong move.* Springer, whose face had reddened noticeably, angrily tossed the document on the ground without so much as a glance at it. He then stepped on it and ground it into the dirt with his boot.

Big Daddy responded to Springer's sign of disrespect by calmly saying, "As y'all know, Captain, this doesn't change a thing. If ya persist, I'll ask my friend, Judge Colson, to write out a contempt order against ya, meanin' he'll have *you* thrown in that cell along with those other hooligans, except my son, of course. He'll be with me on the outside lookin' in."

Springer had reached his limit and sprang at King, grabbing his lapels and pushing him back against the car. Luckily, Collins had anticipated his move and was on Springer in a flash yanking him back before any real damage could be done.

"I couldn't have planned this any better, Captain," announced King as he smoothed his rumpled suit and motioned for his driver, also apparently his lawyer, to speak.

"Mr. King is exactly right, gentlemen. What I witnessed is an assault. We'll add this charge, plus wrongful arrest and several others, to our countersuit against your baseless allegations against my client, Mr. Wade King. Now, deliver the prisoner to us and we'll be on our way. We'll meet y'all in court mighty quick, gentlemen."

We strode off to one side to hash over our predicament. Shortly, even the fuming captain accepted the hopelessness of our situation, and he stomped away, found one of the frightened horses, and rode off.

I was glad Springer wasn't around to watch Wade swagger past us to receive his dad's bear hug. The captain probably would have tried to punch Wade's sneering face, placing himself in even more legal jeopardy. I felt like punching him myself. At the last moment, to save face, Collins called out to Big Daddy that he'd be getting a bill from the Rangers for damages done to the station by the out-of-control Cadillac. All three passengers pretended not to hear him as they sped away.

Before going our separate ways, we discussed what might happen at the upcoming trial. We had plenty of evidence, yet there was a bad feeling about the outcome. Hayden King had power and influence in the county. Collins summed it up by saying the three prisoners inside would probably get handed light sentences; maybe two years, meaning with good behavior they'd be back on the streets in a year or so. The fancy lawyer would get Wade off scot free, and we'd get a slap on our wrists for wrongful imprisonment. Chief couldn't stomach such negative thinking and walked out the door, no doubt to find his horse and ride back to the reservation. I still worried about his earlier threat to take matters into his own hands, and even more concerned when Decker said, "That bastard Wade will probly start recruitin' a new gang of thieves 'fore the sun goes down." A bad ending all around, I realized, as my head began to ache.

Changing the subject, I said, "How 'bout givin' back Toby's stolen kitchen pieces?"

"Can't do that," said Collins. "Have to keep everythin' together fer the trial. Won't be too long, though, 'cause

Wade's lawyer is gonna make all this move forward right quick."

Frustrated, I sighed and replied, "Well, at least I can tell 'em we found Martha's items. That should cheer 'em up a bit."

We heard another horse rein in outside and I wondered "What now?" as Deputy Tex Morgan strode in like he owned the Ranger station. Just looking at him you had a hunch he wasn't much of a lawman: dirty, sweat-stained hat, wrinkled and torn shirt, pants so dirty they might never have been washed. I had patrolled for a bit with him and already formed two impressions: He smelled almost as bad as my oil-rig friend from Midland, "Stinky" Clyde, and he didn't seem to know the law or care much about enforcing it, at least not regularly. It was a mystery to me how he'd escaped being fired long ago. Further, he smelled of booze, beer most of the time. I planned to stay upwind of him as much as possible.

Decker introduced Morgan without enthusiasm and brief handshakes were exchanged before everyone, but Betty, made a beeline for the door. "Hey," he called out, "I hear y'all had an interestin' day. Who's gonna fill me in?"

"Betty," yelled Collins over his shoulder.

"Hell, she won't tell me nuthin'. I'll just get the scoop from Ted. We're 'sposed to ride together tomorrow afternoon."

I groaned when I heard his last comment. *The dangerous idea that I needed a beer entered my mind which made my head pound even harder!*

CHAPTER NINE

PERILOUS PARTNER

"Sure am glad the county finally fired that terrible Sheriff Hopkins," said Travis Robinson. "Happy that one deputy is gone too," added Scott Hunter. "Other one should also be given the boot. I almost filed last time to run against the sheriff, but I'll hold off this time and give this fella Decker a chance to prove hisself. And Ted Townley is a fine young man, as long as he can stay on the 'straight and narrow,' if ya know what I mean." Toby wasn't quite sure about the last comment but was sure Mr. Ted was already doing a good job in light of the recent information about Martha's cutlery because it had been found. He was hopeful the law in these parts would finally treat everyone equally.

I MET WITH DECKER AT THE café early in the morning on December 30 to discuss something important: Tex Morgan's clothes, including his body odor, and his overall scraggly look. "Can't stand the sight of him and his smell makes me gag. We'll be ridin' together today with y'all bein' tied up with paper work. What outta a guy do?"

"Order him to clean up, Ted. Tell him the order comes from me. Here, I'll write a note which y'all can hand him if he refuses." He jotted down a note and slid it to me, clearly written and signed. I had to admit it did place me in a stronger position when I confronted Tex. As we got up, Decker winced slightly at the effort. *What was that about? Arthritis?* I was determined to find out if it continued.

I had suggested meeting Tex at the stables behind the Ranger station where, thanks to the new spirit of cooperation between the Rangers and deputies, all our horses were now kept. I had chosen the stable because the Rangers couldn't stand Tex's presence either. With the stables and Tex in sight as I rode up, I called out, "Y'all didn't stop first at the station, did ya?"

"Damn right I did," he answered, clearly annoyed. "But the secretary said the Rangers weren't there. Lyin' though, 'cause I heard 'em talkin' 'fore I knocked. What's goin' on?"

Building up my courage, I said, "Listen, Tex, they agree with me and Decker that yer appearance is a 'bit unprofessional.'"

"What the hell does that mean?"

Swallowing nervously, I said, "That yer clothes are dirty and ya stink to high heaven!"

"Ain't nobody's business 'cept my own. Let's get ridin'. Got work to do."

"No, Tex," I shot back. "Order comes right from Decker." I handed him the note and waited. He read it, mumbled some profanities, then looking a tad sheepish said, "I ain't got but one set of clothes."

"Well, it's yer lucky day, Tex. I've got some extra clothes fer ya up at the house. After we pick 'em up, there's a tub waitin' fer ya where my cousin rents a room. We got time fer everythin' and still make our usual patrol rounds."

"Had this all planned out, didn't ya?"

"Yup, and ya don't really have a choice. So, get a move on!"

He cussed some more and glared at me with pure hatred but eventually calmed down and followed orders. An hour later we rode away from John's house, Tex looking fresher than me. How long before the old Tex returned?

As we rode west I noticed sullen stares and scowls from several business owners on both sides of Main Street. *Were they at me or Tex?* I asked him if he had noticed. He said to pay it no mind.

"But why are they upset?" I asked.

"Always bitchin' 'bout the sheriff."

"Previous sheriff not doin' his job?"

"So they say."

High school age males were a different story, however. Several were hanging around on each street corner, and at first I didn't think much of it, being Christmas break. A few of them even seemed familiar to me. Probably they were freshmen when I was a senior. It wasn't at me, though, that they were directing their friendly smiles and waves. It was Tex. Strange. He was at least a half dozen years beyond high school and wouldn't normally be hanging around with these youngsters.

"You're pretty popular with these fellas," I said nonchalantly, hoping he'd offer an explanation.

"What d'ya mean?"

"Well, lot of 'em are wavin' and I don't think at me."

"Ain't nuthin'. Probly 'cause I went to school with some of their brothers and sisters. Even dated a few of the older sisters," he added with a wink.

Suddenly recalling a recent comment by my father, I said, "Y'all ever have to arrest any of 'em fer petty crimes? My dad says it's a problem in town. He has to keep a sharp eye on 'em in the store."

"Ain't that big a deal, Ted. Owners are just makin' excuses. They're mostly good kids."

I wasn't so sure. I remembered some of the stunts I pulled with some buddies in high school. Languished a few hours in jail myself until my dad bailed me out. However, I wasn't going to pressure Tex without more backup information.

More reasons became evident as we rode past a business selling farm equipment. Mr. Clark, the owner, was sweeping up debris on his porch when he spotted us. Pausing, he waved to us to come closer.

"Y'all see the slivers of glass scattered all over this porch?" he yelled, looking directly at me. "That's the second time in a month. Damn kids. Somethin' oughta to be done 'bout it. Maybe I'll stop up at night and use some buckshot on 'em. How 'bout that?"

"Not a good idea," I said, trying to calm him down. "Know who done it? Got a description?"

"Could be any one of several hooligans. They run in a pack."

"Have ya described 'em to the sheriff or his deputies?"

Glancing at Tex, he answered with a hearty laugh. "Many times. Nuthin' gets done. Not even a single arrest. Sheriff's department ain't worth spit."

Tex scoffed at that and rode away. This gave me the chance to remind him there was a new sheriff and deputy in town. "Listen, sir, I'll stop by the next day or two. Any new leads y'all can think of I'll share with the sheriff and the high school principal. Maybe we can fix this problem fer ya."

He paused, watched Tex move out of hearing range, then said, "Guess I ain't got no choice but to trust ya. Takin' a big chance though."

"And why's that?"

"'Cause as a youngster, Ted, y'all swiped a thing or two from my store yourself. Or don't ya remember?" *Ouch!* My mind flashed to the look of disappointment on my dad's face after one particular misbehavior. Snapping back to the present, I said, "I'm a man now and a deputy too. Y'all can rely on Ted Townley." I quickly turned and spurred my horse toward Tex's trailing dust not wanting to continue the conversation.

I caught up with Tex outside the last house on the block. The front yard was completely fenced in to protect a vegetable garden, mostly harvested this late in the season.

"Best garden in town," Tex said with a smirk.

"Impressive," I added. "The owner must have laid up enough to keep 'em supplied with canned goods fer months."

Just as we were turning our horses away, the door burst open and an elderly woman stormed out marching right up to us. "Spent most of the fall chasin' away kids who stole my fruits and vegetables, officers," she wailed. "Robbed me blind one night. Gave a description to the sheriff but nuthin' come of it. Gettin' too old to keep this place goin' much longer. Damn shame."

"Yes it is, ma'am," I replied sympathetically. I then repeated my promise to return and follow through with neighbors and the school. She shrugged and went back inside.

"Crazy ol' bird," snorted Tex. "See the vines closest to the fence? Them's tomatoes. Half of 'em hang right over into the road. Awful temptin' fer a passerby. Might have grabbed a few myself in past years," he finished with a sly grin. *That I could believe!*

"Sure, but it's still stealin'."

Tex pulled his horse close to mine and said, "Well, ain't y'all the do-gooder." He leaned in so closely that I almost gagged at his breath. Reining my horse back a couple of paces, I said, "Tex, yer breath reeks of alcohol. Ain't no drinkin' on the job. It's 'gainst the regulations."

"Never do, Deputy," he shot back. "Just had one or two beers 'fore headin' out with ya. Got some serious drinkin' to do tomorrow night, though. It's New Year's Eve and time to paint the town. Hey, why not join us? A bunch of us fellas are gettin' together at my place to bring the New Year in right. Plan to get 'drunk as a skunk.' Y'all could use some juggin' and jawin' yerself."

"I don't cotton to that. My parents are hostin' a few people tomorrow night. I'm bringin' my gal, Anne. There'll be games, singin', and food without the booze."

He snorted, "Seriously? That ain't no real party. Well, if'n y'all change yer mind, stop by. Lot's of whiskey and plenty of cold Lone Star beer, my favorite." *Trouble! It was my favorite, too. I tried to repress the memory of how good that tasted.*

We didn't do our usual patrols New Year's Eve. Instead, in late afternoon I took Anne for a long walk along the bank of the Rio Grande. It was a perfect day to turn my attention to her: gentle breeze, temperature in the mid-seventies. At one point I pretended to do some fishing. No luck with the fishing, better luck with the kissing. When we weren't smooching, Anne talked excitedly about her role in Heather's wedding. I played along when she dropped repeated hints about how wonderful weddings could be. I knew she was dreaming of her own future nuptials: with me, hopefully, if I lived up to her quite reasonable expectations.

New Year's celebration at my parent's home was not as special or elaborate as Thanksgiving or Christmas: mainly snacks and punch would be served to our smaller gathering. Apart from Anne and my family, only nine others were invited: John and Heather, Pastor Dan and his wife, the Washingtons, and Hank Brady.

This evening was also a farewell to John who was departing for Houston on January 2. John talked briefly about his possible near future, based mostly on Dr. Wilbur's knowledge of a few of his instructors at the medical school. Despite his promise to return on weekends, Heather had teardrops glistening in her eyes before he finished speaking.

Mom lightened the mood by playing the piano and leading us in singing. We also played several games, especially mom's new favorite, *The Landlord's Game*, based on the buying, selling, and development of land and property. Much to mom's —pretended – dismay, I won that particular board game.

Mom, together with dad and Hank Brady, then carried out the punch bowls from the kitchen. There were three and I sampled them all. The first two were sweet and familiar, the last one sweet and oddly familiar but not in a good way. I sipped it again and the recognition hit me like a bolt of lightning: It was spiked with alcohol! Probably tequila. I motioned John over to the bowl and asked him to try it out. He tasted and agreed. I picked up the bowl and hauled it back to the kitchen, followed closely by my flustered mom. When I told her the reason, she became really upset. She paced back and forth for a few seconds before turning and saying, "It must have been Hank Brady! He offered to help Brian and me. He was all by himself in here for a spell. He'll get an ear full from me," she announced as she marched out to find him.

She promptly returned with Hank who was trembling and getting paler by the second. He stammered something after a sharp tongue-lashing from mom, probably a confession, though it was hard to make out what he was saying because of his mangled words. Mom proved he was the culprit by pulling a nearly empty bottle from his back pocket. She scolded him a second or two longer and he seemed to shrink at every word. He could finish the night, she said, but his future visits to her home were quite uncertain. He slunk away a chastened man.

Mom asked me not to tell anyone else about this humiliation. I made a promise I immediately broke when Anne came and asked what was going on. I gave her a short version and when I finished, she smiled and threw her arms around my neck for a big hug. "I'm so proud of you. You're sure heading in the right direction, Ted." I prayed she was right for both our sakes.

When the clock struck twelve we all cheered and exchanged friendly hugs and kisses. I noticed that mom stayed clear of Hank Brady. We sang a few verses of *Auld Lang Syne,* and Pastor Dan ended the evening with a prayer of invitation for God's blessings for the New Year. Except for the spiking episode, a mostly pleasant evening for all.

I devoted the first morning of the New Year helping John prepare for his trip to Houston. Actually, Heather was also present and I was the "awkward" third person. So I said my goodbyes and went hunting for Anne. I found her at the clinic assisting Nancy and eventually persuaded her to leave and spend her day with me. Inviting her to dine with me at home helped to add to my pleasant day that, sadly, ended at mid-meal. I bit down on a piece of meat and felt another jolt of pain. *Uh-oh!* I decided to wait another day or two to see if it would go away. And I didn't tell Anne because I knew she'd want me to visit a "real" dentist.

My breakfast with Decker the next morning brought another surprise: Decker's appearance. He looked pale and weak, very unusual for him. I mentioned this and, of course, he denied he was feeling poorly. "Nuthin' to worry 'bout, Ted. Been worse off plenty of times. Just need a cup of coffee and some grub. Y'all know I'm as tough as a nickel steak." Nonetheless, I didn't think he'd be able to do a full day on patrol, even a few hours, in his state.

Even he had to admit he was in trouble when he attempted to stand after finishing his meal, took a step, and started to pitch forward. Luckily, I caught him before he collapsed onto the floor. I tried to cover for his embarrassment by easing him back into his chair and blocking anyone's view by standing in front of him. "Okay, Captain?" I whispered. "What's wrong?"

"Reckon it's the bullet wound. Pain's comin' from that region. Comes and goes, but when it hits, it's like bein' stabbed."

"We could take ya to the clinic, but John's leavin' shortly fer Houston and Nancy wouldn't be much help. I think it's time to have Doc Wilbur in Brownsville see ya."

"Nah, I'll be fine. Just let me rest fer a while."

I doubted he was right but said, "I'll walk ya over to the Ranger station where y'all can lie down." He came around enough to walk with me, but I had to hold him upright as the pain struck several more times.

We placed him in an open cell where he could rest on a cot. The Rangers were also uneasy about his condition and agreed that Brownsville was the next step. Springer gave me permission to borrow his car if Decker didn't soon rally. I made them aware that Tex Morgan would be the only deputy on patrol if we went to Brownsville. Starting to explain my concern about Tex, Springer interrupted and said, "We're familiar with Morgan, Ted. Ain't no need to go on. We'll keep an eye on 'im best we can. Probly should have been fired with the rest of 'em."

By mid-morning it was clear we had to make the trip. I took a few minutes to gas up the car and stop by the clinic and my house to inform everyone of our plans. Back at the station, the Rangers helped me move Decker to the car. We told him to lie down on the backseat but he refused and gingerly sat in the passenger's seat. Our journey took less than an hour, though it probably felt longer to him. The partially paved road still had its share of holes and ruts. I swore he thought I hit most of them. I tried to cheer him up by saying the jarring ride even bothered my persisting toothache. "Ya don't say," he hissed through his clenched teeth. As the road smoothed out, he seemed more sympathetic and said, "Maybe y'all should drop me off and stop by a dentist." Perfect, I thought, and replied, "That's what my dad had in store fer me."

At Wilbur's office Decker told me not to wait but find my dentist and deal with my own pain. "Just don't forget to pick me up when you're done," he said. "I'm sure the Doc can fix me up and I'll be champin' at the bit to head back with ya." I wasn't so sure.

Even with a map, it still took nearly a half-hour to locate the dentist. Once inside and signed in, it took another hour to be seen, stewing the whole time about my ordeal to come. After probing a bit and not fazed at all by my constant jerking and wincing, the dentist said, "I see you've had some work done already. The tooth's been pulled along with a bit of infection carved out. The thing is, he done a poor job. It's still all festered up. Gotta do more diggin' and cleanin' and it's gonna hurt some. Y'all ready?"

I nodded through my tears as he began his scraping and drilling until I thought I was a goner. After repacking the new, larger hole, he handed me a few pain pills. "These have some cocaine in 'em," he stated. "Lot better than aspirin. Y'all should feel better in a day or two. Think I got all the infection this time. Remove that packin' swab yerself this go 'round and tell yer friend he done a lousy job." *Probably not. John had done his best. No point to it.*

I swallowed a pill with a glass of water he handed me and returned to the waiting room hoping the pain would swiftly fade away. After a few minutes, the pain did let up a little. I stood up, only to sit right back down. I felt woozy and drowsy, perhaps side effects of the cocaine. The clock on the wall looked to be down the road a piece. Finally feeling steady enough to stand up again, I slow walked to the window and looked out at the traffic going by: cars, trucks, men on horseback, and horse-drawn wagons. Directly across the street was a bank which was plenty busy in mid-afternoon following the New Year's break. I watched a car pull up right in front of the bank, odd because it was a no-parking zone. Three men jumped out and entered the bank. The driver remained in the idling car.

I instantly sized up what was going on: a robbery! Despite some lingering dizziness, I ran to the door, threw it open, and got to my car that I had parked at the side of the building. I unlocked the glove box and took my gun out of its holster. Gun in hand, I kept my eye on the bank. By now my head and legs were working better. Using the car as a shield and prop, I waited, breathing deeply to calm my nerves and steady my hand. The bank door suddenly swung open and out came three masked men all carrying a bag of money in one hand, a gun in the other.

With my pistol pointing out the open car window, I yelled, "Stop right there. I'm a deputy sheriff and all of ya are under arrest!" *Arrest? Was I kidding?*

At any rate, my yelling had startled them and they stopped. Well, the two closest to the car halted, the other one paused in mid-stride, faltered a little, then kept going down the front steps. Misjudging the distance, he stumbled forward tumbling. As he rolled his gun misfired. The sound startled his partners who turned toward me, raised their pistols, and squeezed off several shots. Some went over my head, others were buried in the door. I fired back but also missed. Both men dove into the car and it sped away leaving the last man behind. He got to his feet and chased them screaming "Whoa!" The car didn't stop. The unlucky man stood in the middle of the street staring at the speeding getaway car. He wasn't aware that I was running over to him. I called out for him to drop his weapon and get down on his knees. He seemed to give up, then turned slowly toward me raising his gun at the same time. I shot him in the side before he fully faced me. He fell over, dropping his gun and the moneybag. The bag split open spilling money into the street. The street was suddenly alive with people, one being a bank guard, who pushed me aside and rushed to grab some cash before anyone else had the same idea.

I was still in a befuddled state when a policeman appeared at my side, relieved me of my pistol, and arrested me on the spot. He then escorted me handcuffed to the police station around the corner. I figured Decker might have to wait a little longer to be picked up.

They checked me in with suspicion: no badge, only a card, which the desk sergeant said could easily be phony.

Fortunately, I wasn't that discombobulated and gave the phone number for the Ranger station. Betty quickly described and identified me as a true-blue deputy sheriff. Her intervention changed everything, and I made fast work to answer all their questions. Twice: once for the sergeant and again for the chief who arrived as I was finishing up my first narration. The chief seemed pleased with my second go-round and said if more details were needed, he'd phone me. However, if the gunshot victim didn't admit his part in the robbery and a trial was held, I'd probably be called as a witness.

Hoping my part was done, they dilly-dallied a bit longer as the chief heaped praise on me for my plugging the robber. "Damn fine shot, son," he said, smiling broadly. "Y'all sure were a calm one, given the circumstances." Yeah, I reckoned, especially for just recovering from a dose of cocaine!

But I modestly replied, "Thanks, though I believe it was mostly luck."

We shook hands and he ordered the sergeant to return my pistol. As I took possession, the door opened and in stepped a man who had "trouble" written all over him. It took me only a few seconds to peg him as that newspaperman, Jenkins, the one who had tried to question me earlier at the circus. Unfortunately, he recognized me at the same time and immediately began firing off questions as he rushed to reach me. He backed me into a corner and even started jabbing my chest with his finger, demanding answers. That was the "last straw" for me. I snatched his wrist and pulled him over to the front desk. He protested loudly to the sergeant thinking he'd find support. The sergeant, however, glanced at me with a face that said "Don't worry sir, I'll take care of this 'pain in the ass' fella." Jenkins was ushered into a side room with the promise of a prompt visit from the chief. The sergeant locked the door and motioned for me to vamoose, which I did with a grateful nod of thanks. I heard angry yelling from the side room as I left to retrieve my car and return to the doctor's office to pick up Decker. I had a feeling the reporter and I would meet again.

To my relief, the doctor was just finishing up with Decker when I arrived. *A grave sign?* Decker cleared it up, explaining Wilbur had been interrupted twice with emergencies. "What's the deal 'bout yer condition?" I asked nervously.

"Unclear," he answered calmly. "Doc gave me some pain medication as I waited and it's kickin' in. Says I may have internal bleedin' and if the pains come back agin, I'll probly need to be opened up." *That sounded serious!*

"Well, my cousin claims he's the best, so go along with what he tells ya."

"Will do, Ted. Don't wanna feel that kinda pain again."

Decker really perked up on the ride home when I filled him in on my "heroic" attempt to stop a bank robbery. In fact, he grumbled as I finished, "I wish I'd been beside ya. We'd have taken 'em all down." *Probably could have considering his skill with a six-shooter.*

Not wanting to boast any further, I again mentioned my distrust of Tex Morgan. "Ya know," I said, "y'all will have to rest fer a day or two, meanin' I'll be alone with Tex in the afternoons. Need to act 'fore he causes more trouble fer the county and beats up the reputation of the sheriff's department."

"Yup. Be talkin' with the Rangers and, if they're on our side, I'll meet soon with the commissioners. Reckon Tex has a few supporters but his character and drinkin' problems oughta get 'im fired."

"I'm bettin' Tex won't even return the clothes I loaned him," I concluded snidely.

"Oh, he'll probly hand 'em over – unwashed of course."

Pulling into the Ranger station, I spoke up about the bullet holes in Springer's car. "I'll take care of that," said a grinning Decker. "Least I can do fer a man of action like yerself." *Had I overplayed the "hero" part?*

The remainder of the week unfolded as predicted: mornings at the store, afternoons on patrol with Tex. At least my toothache had mostly gone away, making my days and especially the evenings with Anne much more pleasant. A rancher showed up Friday afternoon with the news that someone had been digging and probably burying something on the edge of his property. That sounded fishy, so we followed him back to the site where shovels and picks were lined up for us. We dismounted, rolled up our sleeves, and got to work. Despite the January date, we were soon sweating like pigs when we finally unearthed several bags labeled "flour." Laughing, the rancher said, "Bet that's not what's in 'em."

We hauled out ten bags and laid them in front of us for inspection. Tex split them open with a nasty looking hunting knife that he always carried with him on patrol. All were stuffed with green leaves. "Cannabis," declared Tex knowingly. "Some people are now callin' it "marahuana" thanks to the Mexican connection."

"What connection?" I asked innocently.

"Fill ya in later. Let's ask this rancher to guard the bags fer us 'till we can pick 'em up later with a truck or wagon."

That seemed sensible to me. As I mounted my horse, I watched Tex tie one bag to his saddle horn. Before I could speak, he said, "Need to take one back to the sheriff's department and the commissioners fer evidence, Ted. Can't have the Rangers snatchin' the whole kit and caboodle." I had my doubts about where it might end up but I clammed up. Tex smiled all the way back to town.

Nearing town, I recognized Toby's house in the distance. We could also see Toby heading home from work. He suddenly glanced back over his shoulder and began running toward the house. Chasing him were a bunch of young men, yelling and throwing stones at him. I spurred my horse to cut them off, calling back to Tex to follow my lead. He did so, though holding on to his precious bag of leaves clearly slowed him down.

The pursuers saw us coming. Once they recognized me, however, they turned and ran in different directions, probably a practiced action. I caught up to the slowest one and knocked him down with my horse. By the time he got back up, I was on him with pistol in hand. I arrested him on the spot and waited for Tex and Toby to make their way to me.

"Know this rascal?" I asked both of them.

"Not his name, Mr. Ted, but he's done this 'fore," answered Toby.

Pausing briefly to look at my prisoner, Tex said, "Actually I do know him.

Name's Luke Harper, Lucas' grandson. Went to school with his older brother. Doggone it, Ted, what's this all 'bout? They were just playin' with this here Negro. No harm done."

"Plenty of harm done, Tex," I said, trying to curb my growing anger. "This is harassment and its gotta stop. I'm takin' him in. Charges oughta be brought 'gainst him. Neither Toby nor his family should have to stomach this anymore."

Ignoring my tone and words, Tex pulled me aside for a chat. He got right to the point. "Lucas Harper is a big man in town, Ted. Long time rancher, y'all probly see him in the café most days. Good man, 'sides he's in close with Hayden King lately. King's 'numero uno' in these parts as ya know."

So that's it, I thought – connections! Lucas and Hayden. Was that the reason for the King ranch having advance notice of our visit? Had Lucas overheard part of our planning session? It didn't really matter, though, because I wasn't going to be stopped. I held up my hand and said, "Ain't arrestin' anyone's daddy, just this miserable youngster right here." *Would Tex challenge me?* Thankfully not, as he slowly backed off with a shrug meaning "You're makin' a big mistake, fella."

I tied the youngster's hands behind his back and wrapped the end around my saddle horn, mounted up, and nodded to Toby, a gesture he seemed to appreciate.

As I rode off toward the Ranger station with my hogtied rascal trailing behind, I heard Tex yell, "Y'all need to relax, Deputy. Wired a mite too tight in my book. Do my best to help you out a bit," I thought I heard him finish as the distance faded his voice. *Meaning What?*

The Rangers weren't too keen about my arresting Luke Harper yet allowed me to toss him in an empty cell. They figured his dad or Hayden King would bail him out in the morning and any court action against my prisoner was a longshot. I argued that point for a spell. Then we turned to the topic of "marihuana." They granted that problems were growing in the county by smoking this "weed" and something had to be done about it. I wanted to continue the conversation but weariness was overtaking me. They saw I wasn't my usual self. Instead, we all agreed to talk it over real soon. It was a worn-out deputy who shuffled to the stables to brush down and feed his horse.

Finished with my chores, I collapsed on my butt and leaned against the gate exhausted. I hadn't felt this "done for" in a long time. In all the excitement I had forgotten about my tooth. Resting more or less comfortably, it "chose" to remind me of its aching absence. I popped another pill and rose to get a drink from the nearby pump.

On the way back to check my horse one last time, my foot struck something on the floor and I stumbled forward falling to one knee. *What the hell!* I looked to one side and noticed a box partially covered with canvas. On top of the canvas was a note that I picked up. It read, "Thought this might help to relax ya. Leftovers from New Year's. Enjoy, Tex." Guessing what was hidden, I knew I should turn and leave. I didn't. I threw off the canvas and stared at a case of Lone Star beer. I closed my eyes and right away the memory of its smooth, soothing taste came back. That memory was overpowering, and I knew my struggling conscience might lose out. Pretending to myself I would only drink one or two, I sat back down, popped one open, and …

When I awoke it was blacker than the ace of spades. I groaned and rose to light the lantern directly above me. My head ached worse than my tooth. I gazed down at the case and groaned again. Scattered around were six empty bottles! What a fool I had been! Shakily, I made my way to the horse trough where I dunked my head. The dousing helped me walk back home with only a little staggering.

I pussyfooted into the kitchen where I opened the cupboard. Taking out a jar of peanut butter, I spread a heaping glob on some bread and gulped it down. I think it was John who first mentioned that peanut butter covered up the beer smell on your breath. I was praying he was right. Stopping in the bathroom to take a leak, I also stealthily removed some hydrogen peroxide and gargled softly. Couldn't hurt.

Naturally, as I tiptoed down the hallway mom cracked open her door and asked if I was okay. I covered my mouth and whispered, "Fine, Mom, just a busy day. Lots of excitement. Tell ya 'bout it tomorrow." *Well, probably not everything.*

I flopped down on the bed and stared at the ceiling thinking about the way the day had ended. There was bound to be trouble ahead. I knew I couldn't hide my setback from Anne. She'd see it in my eyes. Would she forgive me, ever trust me again? The phrase "confession is good for the soul," came to mind, so perhaps I should start with John for his counsel. *Better to go directly to Anne?* I knew my first confession was to God. I fell asleep praying.

CHAPTER TEN

CONFRONTATIONS

"It's a shame what's been happenin' with our youth at school. The drinkin' and all," sighed Fannie Walker to her friend Alice Davis. They were at the general store and didn't realize that Toby was nearby in the next aisle. "Don't know what's gotten into our young people," Alice said. "They seem outta control." "They do," agreed Fannie. "Mighty sad. I had many of 'em in primary school and feel some of it's my fault." "It's not, y'all did your best," responded Alice. "I blame the Brownsville High School. Youngsters come back different even after one year. We all hear 'bout drinkin' parties 'round town. I fear for the future, Fannie." "As do I," Fannie agreed. And as I do, too, thought Toby, pleased he was a non-drinker and even more determined that abstinence would be taught to his daughters as they grew into adulthood.

I AWOKE REALIZING I HAD WRESTLED with God and God had won. My confession had been sincere as well as my promise to become a changed man. I felt relief and a growing sense of confidence that God would give me the strength to follow through as I reached out to others. Anne was my priority, but somewhere during the night I had decided to first to get John's advice. He had previously called from Houston to alert us he was returning for a quick visit this weekend, arriving early Saturday afternoon. Since I usually treated Anne to breakfast at the café on Saturday, it meant contacting her and begging off. Wanting to avoid a face-to-face meeting, I phoned her apartment and excused myself, claiming Friday had been a crazy day and I needed more time to recover. She wanted some details, but I told her I would get family and friends together after dinner and retell my adventures for everyone at once. She said she was sorry about missing breakfast. Truth was I felt she sensed there was more going on. She was right!

Mom offered to help with the meeting as I hurriedly gulped down one of her big breakfasts – eggs, bacon, oatmeal, cereal, toast, and coffee. I avoided all questions until later saying I had to check on Decker and fill out forms for the Rangers related to Friday's events which was partially true. As I got up to leave, Mom called out, "Son, I found a nearly empty jar of peanut butter on the table this morning. Know anything 'bout it?"

Ouch! "I may have had some when I came in last night. Sorry if I took too much. I'll bring ya another jar from the store. Pay fer it myself."

"Not necessary. I just wondered. I know it's not one of your favorite snacks, that's all."

Had mom smelled anything on my breath last night? I mulled this over all the way to the Ranger station. Betty and Decker were present there when I arrived. My favorite secretary did, indeed, have some forms I had to complete. For the next hour or so I did my best to answer the questions with Betty and Decker pitching in when I got bogged down.

Almost immediately after finishing, the phone rang and Betty said Tex wanted to talk to me. "Tell him I'm busy," I yelled, loud enough for him to hear. Betty relayed my message, listened again, then held the phone in my direction.

"Claims it's urgent, Ted."

I reluctantly took the phone and said, "This better be good, Tex."

"Hey, buddy," he laughed. "A commissioner called me and said a bunch of kids just stole some liquor from a store in Brownsville. Owner saw 'em drivin' off, claims they were headed west, toward Los Indios. Commissioner hopes we can catch 'em. Time to mount up, Ted."

"Maybe the Rangers can handle it," I answered hopefully. Betty shook her head whispering they were out of town. *Great!* Just what I needed: more time with Tex and more alcohol.

Groaning softly, I said to Tex, "Where should we meet?"

"Meet at the Negro's house on the edge of town. We can ride east from there and set a trap fer 'em. Good to be workin' again with ya, buddy."

What was all the "buddy" talk about? He certainly wasn't *my* buddy. Thinking his voice had sounded a bit strange, I rode off toward Toby's. At least I'd have a chance to tell him off about yesterday's disgusting prank. He'd pushed me to the limit and it was time to get everything out in the open.

We met up, but Tex raced off before I could begin my lecture and lecture it would be. We rode east for three miles or so and reined in behind some tall bushes on a rise that provided a good view of the road from Brownsville. Several cars and horse-drawn wagons passed by with nothing being of suspicious nature. After a while the traffic died down giving me a chance to speak. "Listen, Tex, I don't appreciate that trick ya pulled on me last night, leavin' the beer and all. I'm sure I've told ya 'bout my problem with alcohol. Gotta quit, totally. It's important to me." At the end I was shouting and he inched back with a nitwitted look on his face.

"Bring it down a notch or two," he smirked. "Didn't mean nuthin' by it. Just thought ya needed some relaxin'."

"I got more'n relaxed, Tex," I yelled. "Y'all got me drunk. Don't ever do that agin or I'll put ya on the ground right quick," I added, raising my closed fist. "That'll wipe that stupid grin from yer face."

"Hey, don't get yer pants in a wad," he snorted still wearing that same expression.

"I think ya meant to say 'panties,'" I said, smiling broadly. He paused looking confused. I suddenly remembered Friday's bag he'd carefully tied to the saddle. "Hey, buddy," I said sarcastically. "Are ya drunk or have y'all been smokin' some of those green leaves we dug up yesterday?"

"More'n one way to relax," he answered with his own addled attempt at sarcasm. "Come on over to my place and try some. Bet ya like it more'n Lone Star." I closed my fist and was preparing to punch him right there when we both turned to the sound of tires squealing.

"Damn!" I called out to the four winds. "Ain't no way we're gonna stop 'em or catch 'em on horseback."

"Worth a try," he yelled as he mounted and galloped after them. I jumped on my horse in hot pursuit of both him and the car. Peering through a cloud of dust, I soon heard the sound of gunshots. A few seconds later I found Tex and his horse on the side of the road.

"Damn fools shot at me," he said angrily. "Got off a couple myself, though. I was aimin' fer the tires. Thought I heard one hit home."

I said, "Y'all okay? That was a dangerous stunt ya pulled. Wild shootin' rarely gets anything done right."

"I'm fine, partner. We'll let the dust settle and pick up the trail from here."

It was then I noticed that his horse was bleeding from a shoulder wound. A pool of blood was forming on the ground around his hoof. "Damn it, Tex, they hit yer horse," I exclaimed as I shoved him. He fell backwards on his butt – right into a nice steaming pile of "road apples." What pleased me infuriated him and he leaped up to even the score. Without thinking I drew on him.

With a face displaying shock and disbelief he hissed, "Bad mistake, Deputy. Last person who pointed a gun at me is six feet under now." After glaring at each other for a few seconds, I holstered my pistol.

He threatened to report me to Decker and the Rangers. Laughing, I said, "Go ahead. When I tell 'em yer actions were reckless and caused injury to yer horse, they'll probly take my side, throw ya in a cell, and give me the key."

It seemed he believed me because he quickly changed the subject to the getaway and suggested we ride together on my horse and catch up or at least guess where they were headed.

I answered by mounting up and said, "First-rate notion 'cept fer the part 'bout ridin' together." From the saddle I reached over and grabbed his horse's reins and rode away. Over my shoulder I shouted back, "Those are my duds you're wearin'. 'Spect to have ya return 'em soon, all cleaned up, of course." I turned in my saddle and watched him throw his hat on the ground and hurl profanities in my direction. Didn't like the swearin'. Smiled anyway.

Lo and behold I found the car after riding for another five minutes. Tex had, indeed, put a bullet in a tire causing it to slide out of control and tip over on its side. The delinquents had fled; the liquor – at least most of it – was left behind. Cases of beer and whiskey were scattered all around the car, some smashed, others intact. I knew exactly what to do and went right to work. I dismounted, pulled a small shovel from behind my saddle, and proceeded to smash the remaining bottles to smithereens. Very satisfying work! After swinging away for a while, one box remained: a case of Lone Star beer. All but four of the bottles were already broken. I stared at them briefly thinking about my wrestling with God, then lined them up on the side of the road, drew my pistol, and shot three of them. I fixed the fourth one upright with some stones and, using a stick, carved a message in the dirt: "Thought this might help ya relax, buddy. Cheers, Ted." My smile returned and stayed with me all the way home.

At the station, I reported everything to the Rangers and Decker, including a description of the car and its license number. I even mentioned drawing on Tex. The Rangers seemed more concerned about the horse and quickly went to check on its condition.

Decker slapped me on the back approving my actions. "Damned if y'all ain't havin' some excitin' adventures without me, Ted. Feelin' better, though, should be able to join ya tomorrow."

I was happy to hear the news, though I quickly reminded him that tomorrow was Sunday and I wouldn't be working. "'Sides," I said, "I got some people to meet on some personal matters, bridges to rebuild, if ya get my meanin'. Hope to have things worked out by Monday."

"Can I help?"

I sighed heavily and replied, "Maybe, let's go outside and I'll share somethin' with ya."

Behind the station, I unburdened myself about my drinking problem, especially my recent binge. He'd known about my weakness but not the latest bender. Like a good friend he restated his support for me and agreed with my decision to meet with John and perhaps others before seeing Anne.

"I'm on yer side. Bet ya everythin' will be patched up this weekend and we'll start fresh on Monday. A new beginnin' fer both of us."

"Thanks. By the way, come on over tonight so I have a pal on my side when I retell these adventures to some family and friends." He accepted, we shook hands, and I went in search of my cousin.

I found John and Heather together in Worth's living room. Heather's presence unnerved me a bit. "I need to talk with y'all about somethin' real personal, John," I began, glancing at Heather and back to John with a look that said "alone."

He didn't bite and replied, "I don't keep anything from Heather, Ted, so unless it's a medical matter for a doctor's ears only, start talking."

He had me there, so I glanced awkwardly at Heather, who smiled sweetly, and told them of my Friday's adventures: all the pain, the thrilling action, the trouble with Tex, everything I could recall that put "heroic" me at the center of the story. My goal, of course, was to create a sympathetic audience when confession time arrived.

Believing I was finished, John said, "That's a great story for anyone. So why the hesitation in sharing it beyond us?"

"'Cause there's more," I said with a grimace. "And y'all won't like how Friday ended."

"Did the poor man die, the one you shot, Ted? That would be very sad."

"Not to my knowledge."

"Well, then," John said, "spill the beans. What's the bad part?"

I told them. They didn't interrupt, but I could tell from their faces how disappointed they were to hear of my relapse. After a painful silence, I added a few words about my late night wrestling with God and my sense of peace and renewed commitment in the morning. Heather's face showed compassion at this addition to my story. John, too, seemed relieved.

"That's exactly the way to start, Ted," he said. "Now you have to follow through, especially with Anne. How will you approach her?"

"That's why I started with y'all. I need yer backin' and advice. What should I do?"

"Tell her soon, the whole story," Heather said. "I'll do my best to step in for you but the heavy load is yours, Ted. She'll be crushed but I love you both."

"Same here, cousin. However, I have a further suggestion: meet with Pastor Dan. He's a good counselor and is no stranger to the damage done by alcohol in this community."

"I'm willin' to meet with him. How can it all be arranged?"

"I'll set up a meeting for you after the morning church service," John answered. "Perhaps he can meet with you in mid-afternoon. I'll let you know."

"Anything else?"

"I think you should bring some friends together soon, including Anne, and retell your story for them, everything except the drinking part, of course."

"Already in the works," I interrupted. "Fer tonight. Please come, if you can."

"We'll be there," Heather said. "Anne will probably sense something is missing from your story. You'll have to decide to break the news directly to her after the meeting or wait till you've spoken with the pastor."

"I reckon you're right 'bout her sensin' somethin'. Have to 'play it by ear.'"

"Yes, you will," said Heather. "Everything depends on your tone and your honesty."

My story and confession had brought our spirits down. I thanked them for their support, slipped out, and walked home to help my parents set up the evening's big meeting. Naturally, my parents had already done their share, making calls and preparing a few snacks. Knowing my mom, there would be plenty of goodies.

I reached out to Anne by phone and said I'd pick her up, promising to give her a rundown along the way. She was excited. I knew it would be short-lived.

I crossed paths with John and Heather as I made my way to Anne's apartment. They were heading out early to allow me a few extra moments to lay the groundwork for my presentation. Their encouraging smiles boosted my self-confidence. Anne greeted me warmly as usual. Our return walk was so short, however, that I had time for only one topic: my tooth. I chose this topic, somewhat guiltily, to soften her heart and it worked as she squeezed my hand tightly when hearing what I had endured.

Everyone was already enjoying mom's food when we arrived – pie and cookies, coffee and tea. In addition to my family and John and Heather, Chief, Decker, Springer, Pastor Dan, Alice Davis, and Toby had shown up. I wondered about Toby until I remembered mom's fondness for him.

After the usual small talk, I told them the reason for the meeting: wanting to make known my past two days' adventures. I apologized to several individuals, who had already heard some of the story, then plunged right in. It was a short version, with a genuine attempt to downplay the hero part. Thankfully, no one interrupted, and the Friday portion ended at the stable where I dutifully cared for my horse before returning home. I passed over only two actions: Friday's unfortunate relapse and leaving one beer for Tex on Saturday. I feared mom would fail to see the humor in the latter.

Surprisingly, only a few questions or comments followed, coming mostly from the ladies who felt I had foolishly placed myself in harm's way on both days. I had the impression I would hear an earful later from both Anne and mom.

At one point I saw John and Heather huddled with Pastor Dan, talking quietly and occasionally glancing in my direction. As they parted, John caught my eye and raised a hand displaying three fingers. He mouthed "o 'clock" if I was too thickheaded to figure out what the fingers had meant. I mouthed "thanks" in return knowing what I'd be doing Sunday afternoon.

Before taking off, the lawmen again commended me for my actions – loud enough for others to hear. Even Toby was impressed saying, "You a good man, Mr. Ted. Follow yer adventures most days at the café and store. People gab a lot, ya know, and I pick out things. A bright future is ahead fer ya." *I hoped so.*

As I walked Anne back to her apartment, she confirmed Heather's prediction when she stopped and said, "I had a feeling you didn't tell the whole story, Mr. Deputy. Is there more?" *Got me!*

Taking a deep breath, I plunged in, "Well, yes. Maybe a couple of things. I'll give ya one now and one tomorrow night after the evening service. How's that?"

"Okay, man of mystery. What's the first?"

She broke out laughing when I told her how I'd left one beer in the road for Tex after destroying everything else.

"I don't think your mom would appreciate that gesture," she said still laughing.

I covered my lips with a finger and said, "Let's keep it a secret. Y'all sure are gettin' to know my mom," I added with a grin.

"I figure the second revelation won't be so funny. True?"

"We'll see. Whatever it is, it'll be better shared after a good night's sleep and following two sermons from our good preacher."

"Should I be worried?"

"No, sweetie. God is in control and we love each other. Tomorrow night we'll bundle up and take a walk along the river where we do our best talkin'."

We embraced at the front door. It felt less romantic than usual. As I set out for home, I turned back and saw her standing in place. Even in the dim light of the moon I could tell she wasn't smiling. That was unusual. I had a hunch it would be a restless night for both of us.

Anne and I sat together at the morning service. Things were pretty much the same until the sermon text was announced: 1 Corinthians 6: 9-10. *Uh-oh!* I knew that text, knew what was coming, and guessed it wasn't a coincidence. In the text, individuals will not inherit God's Kingdom if not living virtuously. As Pastor Dan read the familiar list of sins – the sexually immoral, idolaters, thieves, slanderers, swindlers, and so on – he seemed to pause before pronouncing the last: drunkards. Looking directly at me, he said this word more loudly than the others. His piercing eyes sent a chill up my spine. Soon beads of sweat were rolling down my neck and my hands were turning cold. I carefully released Anne's hand. The rest of the thirty-minute sermon was just plain misery for me as the pastor ranted against alcohol, not just in the biblical context but also the destruction caused by heavy drinking in our community. How could Anne not make the connection? And was this a hint of what my upcoming counseling session would be like?

I could barely look in Anne's direction during the entire sermon. I think I saw compassion in her eyes but couldn't be sure. Following the sermon, I quickly excused myself saying I had some paper work to complete at the Ranger station. *Another white lie?* At any rate, I needed to be alone. I walked to the riverbank and wandered aimlessly trying to prepare for what was coming.

Suddenly realizing what time it was, I rushed back to the church to avoid being late for my meeting with Pastor Dan: no lunch, stomach growling, and sweating in fear of being admonished. Thankfully, my worst fears didn't materialize. Pastor Dan greeted me warmly and was friendly, even understanding, during the whole session. He listened like a true-blue friend and encouraged me to follow through with my commitments, gave me some literature to read, and prayed with me promising to add me to his daily prayer list. Just before I left he said, "This isn't a one-time deal, Ted. I recommend meeting twice a month this winter. Acceptable to you?"

"Darn tootin'. I'll be here. Thanks fer yer support." And that was it. Now all that remained was the evening service and my walk and talk with Anne. Church that night turned out to be a prayer meeting. Many burdens were lifted heavenward, including alcohol's power over members within our small congregation. I thought we were finished with "demon rum" when suddenly Anne began her plea for God's deliverance from this curse. She remained seated while praying and squeezed my hand the whole time. I knew then she had made the connection. It was actually a relief to realize she had already been preparing for our "talking."

It was chilly that night as we walked beside the river. Anne did allow me to hold her gloved hand which I took as a good sign. Before walking very far, she said, "I think I know what you're going to say, Ted, so give it to me straight. Hold nothing back."

I made my confession, gave her all the details, held nothing back. I didn't even try to shift the blame to Tex for tempting me in such an obvious way. Much of the time I was able to keep eye contact with her. She reacted calmly, though there was clearly disappointment on her face. I tried not to show my real feelings, but on the inside my heart was racing, my lips were dry, and my breathing was labored. I reckoned that was what happened to a guilty lover. It hurt.

We walked for a few moments in silence before I finally added, "I love you, Anne. I need you to forgive me, to give me another chance. I realize it's a last, last chance in my case. Can you find it in yer heart to do that fer me, fer us?"

She tugged me to a stop, took off her gloves, reached into her pocket, and retrieved what appeared to be a piece of fabric. She held it up in the moonlight and said, "Know where this came from, this cloth?" Before I could answer, she added, "It's a small piece of my slip which I tore off before you arrived at my front door. Now, give me your hand, deputy." I offered her my right hand and she wrapped it around my wrist and tied it off with a double knot. Though I could guess its meaning, I still asked her to explain. "This is to remind you of your promise to God and to me about abstinence. Do not take it off! When it gets dirty or falls off by accident, I'll get you another. Every time you look at it you'll know what it means. Understand?"

"Yes, ma'am."

"I know you're trying very hard, Ted Townley, and you deserve another chance. But this really is the very last one."

Then without warning she yanked off my gloves, brought my hands to her face, kissed them, and cupped them around her cheeks. She wrapped her arms around my waist and waited with a flirtatious smile. Not for long because I leaned down and found her lips for one of the best kisses ever. A million times better than my favorite beer. Maybe a billion.

Experiencing a new different kind of "intoxication," I somehow managed to escort her back to her apartment. On my own way back home I raised my arm to give me a better view of my new bracelet. I stumbled only once.

I was at the café Monday morning when Decker walked in, sat down, and placed his breakfast order with Toby. Anticipating what I was about to ask, he said, "Feelin' fine, Ted. Time to get back to ridin' the county."

"Great, but I'm 'sposed to ride with Tex and three's company on patrol."

"Nary a problem. Gave him another assignment."

"What's up?"

"One of the commissioners phoned me last night and told me to arrest two high schoolers fer drinkin' and destroyin' private property. Gave me their names. Trouble is, Tex has a connection to one of 'em. Thought it best *I* bring 'em in."

He gave me their names and we talked briefly about the suspicious connections between Tex and several others including Wade King. "We need to face him with all this," I said.

"Sure 'nuff," Decker said with teeth grinding.

We set off for the high school figuring that was our best bet to find the youngsters. And we were right; found them sleeping in history class. Their initial nervousness changed to smugness when the teacher announced, loud enough for everyone to hear, that one of the fellows was a nephew of Hayden King. "Better be prepared for fireworks, men," he offered as his final remark.

This obvious "warning" so angered Decker that he immediately cuffed both youngsters, something he'd previously declared wasn't necessary. They whined all the way out the door and in the bed of the borrowed Ranger truck as it bounced back to town. Decker shoved them roughly into a cell at the station, turned to me and said, "Had 'nuff, Ted. When this day ends, we're havin' it out with Tex. First with that no-account, then with the county commission. It's either him or me. Can't have both." I figured all kinds of fireworks were soon to explode.

"Him or us," I said. "It's long overdue."

The rest of the day was spent patrolling and planning how to deal with Tex Morgan.

CHAPTER ELEVEN

INVASION

Toby listened at the store as two cowboys discussed border crossings near town. The one from the Wilson ranch said his property went right to the river and Mexicans came across all the time. "Mostly just headin' north fer work pickin' cotton or vegetables. Been doin' it for years. Some of 'em haulin' new stuff with 'em now, though." The second cowboy asked, "What kind of stuff?" The Wilson man responded, "Found some bags last fall. Must have been dropped by accident. Filled with white powder, not sugar, that's for sure. Turned everythin' over to the sheriff's department but never got a report." "No surprise there," replied the other cowboy. "Rumor is the deputies use all kinds of 'stimulants' to get 'em through the workday." This last comment made them both laugh so hard, in fact, that the Wilson rancher sprayed tobacco juice all over the counter. An irritated Toby wiped up the counter wondering what was meant by "stimulants."

By the middle of the following week, Decker and I had developed a plan to deal with Tex Morgan. We knew Tex had taken a bag of marihuana with him earlier, that he'd probably stashed it at his home, where we reckoned more drugs were likely hidden. So our plan was simple: raid his home, find the evidence, and arrest him. At the last minute, however, I worried something was being overlooked. "Maybe we should get the Rangers in on this. I suggest Wednesday at the café. Ya know, another opinion might be good to have."

Decker was peeved at my suggestion. "No need fer 'em, Ted. Just need to get that damn Tex outta our hair. Our plan's good."

"I want that too. But what if there's a bigger picture?"

"Meanin'?"

"Well, maybe Tex ain't workin' alone. Wouldn't it be nice to lasso a whole bunch of 'em?"

Decker paused briefly scratching his stubble, then said, "Maybe yer right. Just don't want the Rangers takin' the lead or gettin' the credit."

"Look, it's our idea and we'll insist on leadership. And if'n it works, Tex'll be gone."

"All right, I guess. Let's find the Rangers at their station and run our plan past 'em."

We did find them at the station where Decker quickly outlined our plan. I added only one point: the possibility of a "bigger picture." "Got any ideas?" I asked, hoping Decker was still with me.

Springer glanced at Collins before saying, "Funny thing 'bout yer plans, men. What y'all are really fightin' is the smugglin' problem, drug smugglin' in particular. Collins here, in fact, just got back from Austin where the Ferguson government had a meetin' on that. Seems everyone's doin' it now. In 1908 Teddy Roosevelt even called fer an international congress to talk 'bout this problem. One was held in 1909. Anyway, governments are followin' through. All kinds of drugs are flowin' in: opium, cocaine, marihuana, and booze, of course, more every month. I'll let Collins add some details."

Collins snorted and said, "That governor's meeting was boring as hell. But I did get to read some handouts as I rode the train back home. Far as I can figure, opium and marihuana are the biggest problems, both sneakin' across from Mexico. Course, Mexicans grow their own marihuana and bring it to smoke and sell it fer a profit too. Opium comes from the Philippines and China. They say Chinamen are the main users and dealers of that nasty drug."

"What 'bout cocaine?" I nervously interrupted before Collins could continue. "Is it legal? My dentist just gave me some pain pills that got cocaine in 'em."

"Far as I can nail down," said Collins, "most these drugs are still legal in Texas. Governments are gettin' worried, though, and regulatin' 'em with a heavier hand cause of their bad side effects. Hard core users are goin' crazy, 'specially Mexicans and Chinamen. Anyway, that's what I've read."

Decker said, "What's the whole story on drug laws?"

Collins answered, "Well, they started with the Pure Food and Drug Act of 1906 under Teddy. And then in 1915, other parts were tacked on with the Harrison Anti-Drug Act under Wilson. Both dealt mostly with stronger labelin' and limitin' distribution and use through doctors' prescriptions."

"My pills were just handed to me," I said, again thinking of the Brownsville dentist.

"Well, it'll take time, I guess," said Collins. "And this is Texas after all. We do things a tad differently here, as y'all know."

"Damn right!" added Springer proudly.

Collins continued, "Listen fellas, I don't think Congress is in any hurry since there's nary a dollar goin' to carry out their laws. Seems a bit strange but that's politicians fer ya. 'Bout the only thing I remember from Austin is that they want to set up a new force of "Mounted Guards" to patrol all along the river, 'sposedly to keep the Chinese out. Started in 1915, and there's only 'bout 100 of 'em patrollin'. Ain't never seen one myself."

"Me either," said Springer. Laughing, he added, "Sure could spot a Chinaman tryin' to sneak across the river. Bet y'all could too."

"These drugs are trouble, no doubt 'bout it," declared Collins. Pausing and changing his tone, the Ranger then said, "But the thing that bothers me most is the Puritans are after my whiskey and beer. I'm talkin' prohibition, men. The Women's Christian Temperance Union and the Anti-Saloon League are gainin' more of a foothold every year. More'n half of our counties are dry already. Can y'all imagine Texas without beer?"

"End of the world, fellas!" shouted Springer without a hint of sarcasm or humor.

Being a college man and knowing a little about the recent past, I said, "It's a natural shiftin', men. The whole country might be dry in a few years."

"Well, damn!" yelled Collins. "I know one thing fer sure: no beer means no Texas Rangers!" We all laughed at his prediction. *Why was I laughing? Had Decker shared my problem with the Rangers?*

"Let's get back on track," I said. "Right now, what are y'all afixin' to do to get the 'bigger picture' linked to Tex? We all want one thing: Tex gone."

Springer said, "My 'pinion is Tex is somehow tied to the Wade King gang. Problem is, we gotta make that hookup stick legal wise."

"That's fer sure!" agreed Decker. "'Specially if this leads to Big Daddy hisself."

"Sure would shake up the county," said Springer.

"Let's all think on it," I said, "and come back here tonight and not leave 'til we work out a plan." We agreed and shook on it.

That night a two-part plan was developed. First, we'd raid Tex's residence and document everything we found – on paper and with Collins' new Kodak camera. We would carry on the raid during the day when Tex was absent. Decker agreed to assign Tex to duties at the far end of the county to make that a reality. Second, we knew we had to catch Tex and others in the act of smuggling. That would be the most damning evidence. So we chose the Wilson ranch as the best location for snaring the bunch. Earlier the Rangers had been told that strange things were happening there: voices and the neighing of horses at the riverbank in the middle of the night. Witnesses held that Wednesday or Thursday nights were the best for catching smugglers. We would take turns lying in wait, hoping surprise would make up for our "small army."

Decker sent Tex on a mission to the edge of the county for Saturday. Though annoyed he would be going alone, and unclear about the details of his patrol, he finally came around. To sweeten the deal, we gave him a fresh horse and saddlebags full of food. But we also endured his babblings during breakfast before he finally rode off. We hurriedly joined up with the Rangers and left to carry through part one of our plan.

Tex lived in an old shack that had recently been expanded by a second room. There was a shed out back as well as an outhouse. Rather humble living conditions for a friend of Wade King, I thought. Was he thinking about adding indoor plumbing and other improvements by certain "illegal activities?"

We first searched the shack. We found nothing in either room; cupboards were mostly bare as well as the dresser. Our disappointment was short-lived, though, once Collins noticed a squeak in a floorboard. He bent down, carefully loosened it with his pocketknife, and finally pried it off completely. Below, partially buried in the dirt, were several sacks. Springer held a lantern over the hole and Collins snapped a few pictures. We gently lifted out the sacks and opened them. Of the six, two contained cannabis leaves and four some sort of white powder.

"Y'all were right," Springer declared as he glanced at Decker and me. "Marihuana and what's probly heroin or cocaine. No doubt ya can sell plenty 'round here."

"I hope it's not meant fer doctors and dentists," I said. "They're 'sposed to get their drugs by legal ways."

"Right ya are, deputy," Collins said. "This stuff's probly fer the black market. Who knows where it'll end up? Most likely with Mexicans and Negroes," he added.

"That's a bit slanted, Sergeant," I said. "Ain't just those two groups abusin' drugs. Know of a few roustabouts in the west Texas oil fields who were usin'."

"Maybe so," Collins answered defensively. "But that's what I learned from the experts in Austin."

Cutting off our argument, Decker said, "Probly all kinds of folks wrapped up in that stuff by now. We're gettin' a peek of the future and it won't be pretty."

We all seemed depressed at such a possibility before Springer brought us back to the present by suggesting we search the shed. As Collins was replacing the items and the plank, we followed Springer outside. The dilapidated shed proved to be a "gold mine": We found more bags of drugs, and under several dirty canvas coverings, cases of booze – liquor and beer. All of the latter were labeled as coming from Mexico.

"Good stuff," Springer laughed. "Collins sure as shootin' will take a couple samples home with him. Probly never be missed."

Duty bound, I said, "Y'all are jokin', ain't ya? Let's at least get the sergeant in here to snap a few pictures." So I fetched the cameraman who eagerly snapped away.

Outside we talked about what the contraband meant for any future prosecution. "Solid evidence," said Springer, "though I reckon Tex could claim it was all planted and he knew nuthin' 'bout it."

"Seriously?" I said.

"Really," said Springer. "If he's tied to Wade King, he might get some powerful legal help. Hate to see that situation repeat itself."

"None of us would," I said. "What 'bout the warrant issue? We don't have one. Gonna be trouble fer us?"

"Would be with our local judge," said Springer. "Got us an ace in the hole, though. Rangers have an understandin' judge at the county seat. We push fer a change of venue. If it works, not havin' a warrant won't be a problem. 'Specially if we catch 'em red-handed."

I felt a little better about our chances as we rode away. At the station, we decided the Rangers would lie in wait at the Wilson ranch next Wednesday, Decker and I on Thursday. I worried about springing a trap with only two lawmen. Asking Chief for help wasn't possible, I told the Rangers, because he was busy working for the tribal council outside of the county. Springer snorted, saying he and Collins could handle anything but promised to find extra help for us poor sheriff's deputies. Decker smarted at his tone and seemed about to reply we'd be fine, but I poked him with my elbow and he got the message, remaining silent.

John came home on the weekend, and I decided to run everything by him. I figured it was a good idea to keep Anne in the dark about our plans knowing she'd fear for my safety. I met John early Sunday morning for breakfast at his apartment. We mostly filled up on cold cereal and milk, Grape Nuts for him and Corn Flakes for me. He entertained me with a brief history of the Kellogg Company of Battle Creek, Michigan before I got down to business.

John agreed with my decision about Anne and also approved my reasoning: it might be dangerous. In fact, if the smugglers showed up, they'd likely be well armed. "Keep your head down, cousin, if bullets start flyin'."

"Will do, John. Decker'll probly shove me down anyway. He's a much better shot to boot."

I asked if drug smuggling and banning of alcohol ever came up in his med school classes. He admitted they both caused contention. "Is there any consensus in Houston?" I continued.

"Seems so," he answered. "Drugs are becoming more common, and national prohibition is right around the corner. Even the vote in Austin gets closer every year. There's some disagreement on whether prohibition will come by way of a national law or a constitutional amendment, but either way, it's on the horizon."

We talked about the difficulty of enforcing something like prohibition, especially in big cities and in a big state like Texas. Shaking his head, he said, "How many Rangers do you think will be ready and willing to enforce it?"

"Less than one," I said. Our laughter was feeble and humorless.

Going our separate ways, me to Anne's then to church, John to the clinic – he again urged me to be careful, and he brought up another point. "Anne will eventually find out about any trouble on the border, Ted. Begin to think of a response."

I said, "I will," and I would.

The first Wednesday night was a bust: no action at the Rio Grande. Springer acknowledged it might take several weeks before another shipment arrived and took it in stride. Collins said it had given him time to test a new brand of chewing tobacco, so it was mostly a successful night for him.

On Thursday afternoon, Springer introduced us to our new addition: "Special Ranger," Todd Stevens. Todd was tall, lanky, and youthful in appearance. So young, in fact, he could have passed as a high school student. I was all nerves, knowing the Rangers had a low opinion of these new, Governor Ferguson-appointed additions to the force. I cornered Springer privately and he admitted it was the best he could do; no regular Rangers were on hand. "I think he'll be okay," he said. "Though I can't vouch fer his shootin' skill." Hardly encouraging but three was better than two, I figured.

No smugglers Thursday night either. It was hardly uneventful, however. Close to dawn Todd proved Springer's assessment to be an accurate one when he accidently discharged his pistol startling all of us. Unfortunately, it also caused a stampede of Wilson's cattle in the southern corral. They knocked down the fences and bolted in panic in all directions. It took us nearly two hours to round them up and herd them into the northern corral. We couldn't have done it without the help of several very angry cowboys. They glared at us the whole time and sure didn't invite us to join them for breakfast.

The second Wednesday was a repeat: no smugglers and another tobacco selection for Collins to try out. On Thursday afternoon, he graciously offered to share his latest chew with me. Just as graciously, I refused. I instantly realized that was a mistake when he began lecturing me about what real Texan men do and what women accept. I countered, "Anne wouldn't appreciate kissin' me with a mouthful of chaw."

With a look of astonishment, he replied, "None of my gals ever kicked up a fuss." I didn't believe him, and from Springer's facial expression, neither did he.

Thursday night was downright cold, it being late January. A half-moon gave enough light to make things out dimly. The stars twinkled and I hoped it stayed that way. If clouds rolled in, we'd be in big trouble. The three of us were hidden behind some bushes on a ridge overlooking the river. I guessed the water was thirty yards distant and we sensed it more by sound than sight. After perhaps two hours of surveillance, I needed to relieve my cramped muscles. I also thought it might be a good opportunity to check out the surrounding area in more detail. Crouching low, I got close enough to the river's edge to see the outline of the fence the rancher had built last summer to keep out rustlers. It already had holes in several spots and had collapsed in others. Not much blockage to anyone, I reckoned. I found nothing heading east but circling back to the west, I heard horses neighing. Stealthily getting nearer, I came upon five horses tied to stakes. Nearby was a wagon hitched to two more. Bulls-eye! I knew what this meant and rushed back to fill in my comrades, holding my pistol in a sure grip to prevent another "accident."

"Sounds like tonight fer sure," Decker said calmly. Todd, though, appeared a mite nervous after hearing my report. Decker ordered us to get our rifles, so we'd be well armed when the action began.

Around three a.m. we heard voices coming from mid-stream. Unfortunately, a few clouds had blocked the half-moon making things even more difficult to see. Soon the voices grew louder and I heard the sound of oars striking water. Decker remained cool and calm; my heart was pounding so loudly I feared my partners could hear it. Todd's nervousness had caused sweat to trickle down the side of his face. *Would he be a "help" or a "hindrance" if fighting broke out?*

In short order, men were jumping out of three boats and dragging them up onto the beach. Decker did a quick count and whispered, "There's twelve of 'em, fellas. Hold yer fire 'til I call fer their surrender. No surrender, let 'em have it." We watched them unload scads of cases and bags. They arranged everything into two big piles. Brief remarks were spoken in both English and Spanish. I thought I could recognize two voices: Tex and Wade King! "Gotcha!" I mouthed to myself as Decker cocked his rifle.

"Stop right there!" yelled Decker. "Sheriff's department. Yer under arrest. Drop to yer knees and put yer hands behind yer heads." Silence for a moment as everyone froze in place. Then all hell broke loose as they drew their weapons and fired wildly in our general direction. I blinked rapidly so I could see better after the bright yellow flames of gunfire in the night's blackness. Seemingly unaffected, Decker quickly returned fire, very accurately, which produced several screams when targets were hit. Todd and I joined in and poured lead down from our elevated position.

The Mexicans promptly realized they couldn't stick it out. While some still returned sporadic fire, others picked up their wounded, dumped them in the boats, and pushed off into the river. With everyone aboard, the able-bodied smugglers rowed swiftly back to friendly territory.

"I see four of 'em still by the river," Decker shouted. "Better get 'em to surrender 'fore they bolt fer the horses." He yelled another command that caused three men to drop to their knees and cast their weapons aside. I could dimly see one still upright and inching west in the direction of the horses. Decker also saw this movement and fired off two rounds into the sand at the man's feet. He got the message and went along with Decker's order.

Decker and I charged down to make arrests with Todd trailing behind. Decker ordered the wanderer to join the party. When he ambled over, Tex Morgan stood before us!

"Look what the cat dragged in," I said sarcastically. "Probly claim ya was just out fer a late night stroll, huh?"

"That's right, buddy," he said with his usual sneer.

"I ain't yer buddy, but Wade sure is yers," I barked. "Heard his voice too." I scanned the other three to confirm Wade wasn't present, then added, "I see the bird has flown the coop. Did he go back to Mexico with his friends, Tex?"

Tex shrugged and said, "Y'all must be dreamin', Ted. Wade was never here."

Decker had had enough and punched Tex in the side, causing him to fall to his knees. Tex spent several moments moaning and trying to catch his breath.

I figured we'd hogtie all of them but Decker had a better idea. He told Todd to retrieve the wagon and saddled horses, and when everything arrived, he made the prisoners load the two piles into the wagon.

One man was having trouble lifting the heavy cases. I saw why: blood spotted his shirt. I examined the wound, decided it wasn't much, and told him to go on working. He hollered and carried on like a stuck pig as the loading continued. When finished, we finally did hogtie them and shoved them on their horses that Todd had tied to the back of the wagon.

Checking over the loaded wagon, Decker said, "I'll take everything to the county seat later in the morning. We're staring at lots of drugs and booze, fellas. Rangers will be pleased with all of the new evidence we show 'em."

It was nearly dawn when we reached the Ranger station. Decker tossed all the prisoners into a single cell. When they bellyached, he simply smiled and said, "Y'all can also share the cots if ya like."

I felt a pang of guilt when I noticed the wounded man doubled over in pain. "Captain," I said, "let me take the bleeder to the clinic. Bet Nancy will soon be there. I'll guard him while she fixes him up."

"Suit yerself, Ted. I'm goin' fer a hearty breakfast."

Tex was still sneering when I entered the cell. Showing contempt for the law seemed to suit him. And he was bold as brass. This boldness came out when threatening to take legal action against us for false imprisonment. "I have important friends on the commission and in the community," he announced. "I'll be outta here in hours and y'all will soon be hearin' from me."

"I can assure ya of one thing," hissed Decker. "Y'all won't be workin' fer the sheriff's department no more."

"Yer the one who'll be outta a job," Tex yelled. "And that college boy too," were the last words I could make out as I led the wounded man out the door. Shuffling along, we passed the just-opening café, and I realized my stomach was grumbling. I was jealous of Decker as I envisioned him devouring a manly Texas breakfast.

Nancy hadn't yet arrived when we showed up. Since I knew where the key was hidden, I let myself in. I guided the patient into the examining room and put a compress over the still bleeding area. As we waited, I looked down at my wrist and saw blood on my newly supplied bracelet. I hoped Anne wouldn't notice.

Nancy entered perhaps twenty minutes later. I told her what had happened as she examined the bullet wound. Frowning, she said that the bullet was still lodged in his abdomen and he'd have to be moved to Brownsville. She said she knew someone who could take him to the hospital; I offered to have Todd Stevens guard him on the trip. We both made our calls, and the car and "Special Ranger" showed up shortly later. Todd didn't seem too thrilled about his new assignment and said he'd expect extra pay for his work. I shrugged and told him to take it up with the Rangers. He left in a sour mood.

I tried to wash the blood from my bracelet before leaving the clinic. My efforts were only partly successful, so I slid the spot under my wrist to hide it from you-know-who.

It was past nine when I entered the café. Thankfully, Anne wasn't working that morning. Surprisingly, Decker was still there. "Y'all must have been real hungry," I said as I sat down at his table.

"Lots of good food and coffee and a chance to jaw with the Rangers," he said. "They just left."

"Told 'em everything?"

"Yup."

"Anything new?"

"Yup. Hayden's lawyer showed up and they're out on bail."

"I'll be damned."

"Me too."

"What's next?"

"I ain't waitin' fer no trial," he said. "Takin' the bull by the horns and callin' the commissioners and demandin' a meetin'. My deadline's this afternoon, tomorrow at the latest."

"Them or us?"

"Damn right."

"What are our chances?"

"Close vote. Good y'all have other work."

"I can't make a livin' at the store."

"You'll find somethin', me too. Maybe I'll run fer sheriff. Election's comin' up. That'll be sweet revenge."

"Sure will if ya win," I said as we both started laughing.

Leaving the café, Decker yanked my arm and said, "Lookie here. I'd know that Caddie anywhere."

It was, indeed, Big Daddy's Cadillac driving by: chauffeur behind the wheel, a smiling Hayden in the passenger seat, a wickedly smiling Wade in the backseat.

I responded with a stony face. Turning to Decker, I pleaded, "This all is gonna end someday, ain't it?"

"Sure thing. Me and the Rangers guarantee it."

"I hope you're right," I sighed. Twice.

CHAPTER TWELVE

TRIALS

Late Friday afternoon at the store Toby listened as Ted apologized again for rarely walking him home. Toby said it wasn't necessary because he knew Ted was busy and nothing really bad had happened. "Martha's silverware was returned, though, Mr. Ted, and that's good news." Ted agreed and said he also had good news. "The man shot is recovering and has confessed, so there won't be a trial." "Thank God fer that news," said Toby. He paused then continued, "Y'all know that Misses Heather and Anne are orderin' fancy cloth and other doodads fer the wedding. I think they're the happiest ladies I've seen in ages." At this, both laughed. Ted added, "I forgot to tell ya John has also asked me to be his best man. Of course I agreed on the spot." "Figured he would," replied Toby. "You two are real close." "Yes, we are. Now, put down that broom and let me walk ya back home. Ain't no one gonna cause ya no trouble with a fearless deputy at yer side."

I HAD ARRANGED TO MEET ANNE on Friday after dinner for a little "one-on-one." When I arrived at her door, however, I knew instantly that romance was far from her mind. "Ted Townley! What am I going to do with you?" she said like a stern schoolteacher catching a boy pulling a girl's pigtails. "I served lunch to some cowboys who were talking about some excitement at the Wilson ranch last night. Claimed some deputies fought a grim battle at the river and captured some smugglers. I knew it had to be you. What do you have to say for yourself?"

I told her my story, making sure to put Decker and the new Ranger in the forefront. "It weren't nuthin' and was over right quick," I said meekly. She stepped back to eye me clearly frustrated. Her survey stopped at my wrist. *Uh-oh. I knew what was coming.*

"Let me see that bracelet," she ordered. I stuck out my hand, like a student readying for a ruler spanking. "I suppose you're going to say this smudge isn't blood, Mr. Townley?"

I started a white lie, thought better of it, and said, "Honey, it's blood, but not mine. One criminal got shot and I took care of him. Couldn't do anythin' less, could I?"

Softening, she replied, "I guess not, but I'm worried that you're taking too many risks. What do I have to do to keep you from the line of fire?"

"I'll be fine, sweetie. Decker's takin' good care of me."

"He'd better or he'll get an earful from me."

Knowing I'd have to alert Decker about her fear, I "honeyed" her and the evening ended better than it had begun.

I met at the café with Decker and the Rangers on Saturday morning to get ready for our afternoon hearing with the county commissioners. Decker had informed me Friday that they had agreed to gather, though a couple had strongly resisted. Normally the Rangers wouldn't be involved, but Decker felt they would strengthen our case against Tex. I asked if laying out all the evidence now would make a conviction at the upcoming trial more difficult. Springer said it wouldn't because Tex would probably get a high-priced lawyer provided by Hayden King, one who'd know every trick in the book, anyway. "Sounds 'bout right," Decker said. "Even if we lose the criminal trial, at least we'll get rid of Tex."

We all felt that getting rid of Tex was the main goal. Then we hashed over what could be brought in as evidence. We decided that Decker would go first, followed by the two Rangers and finally me.

When we arrived at the four p.m. hearing, all seven commissioners were sitting behind the big table up front, already arguing among themselves. *A bad sign?* Seated in a chair in the front row on the right was Tex and beside him was King's lawyer, Garret Winston! This wasn't a legal procedure, and I wondered what Decker would do about it. I found out soon enough. "Commissioners," Decker called out, "this ain't no place fer lawyers. What reason is there fer Mr. Morgan bringin' legal counsel?"

The seven argued back and forth for a time before the chairman slapped the table and called for order. "This has already been decided, gentlemen. By a majority vote, Mr. Winston will be allowed to speak for Mr. Morgan, but the normal rules of a courtroom don't apply here. He is aware of these conditions, right, Mr. Winston?"

"I do, your honor... I mean, Mr. Chairman."

"Very well, let's get underway."

As the ground rules were being set, I tried to size up the seven men. It was, after all, a hearing that might lead to an end of Tex's deputy career. I concluded that three were on our side, two were uncertain, and two were strongly in Tex's camp. A little too close for comfort, I thought, as the testimony began.

Decker did a good job of running through all the evidence against Tex, starting with written complaints from mad citizens about Tex's improper and, perhaps illegal, activities. Moving on, he brought up the items found at Tex's home – photos and samples of drugs seized – and finally the dealings on the border where smugglers were arrested and more drugs taken. Winston objected to each point and was overruled each time by an increasingly irritated chairman. As Decker sat down, the chairman said, "One more interruption on legal grounds, Mr. Winston, and y'all will be asked to leave. Understood?" Winston glared but said nothing.

Just as Springer rose to speak, the door opened and in strode Hayden King. I saw him nod slightly in the direction of Tex followed by a similar motion at the two supportive commissioners. His arrival caused a commotion in the front that ended only when the chairman frowned and said, "You're welcome, Mr. King, but you are to keep silent."

King smiled smugly and sat down. I was afraid his being there could be a bit hair-raising for our side and whispered as much to my fellow lawmen. Decker whispered back, "Ain't much we can do 'bout it."

Springer snorted, "What 'bout I shoot him now. That should do it."

"Not funny!" I hissed back at Springer. "Best remember why we're here."

Hearing statements from Springer, Collins, and myself, I hoped the commissioners hadn't noticed my shaky voice when speaking. Overall, I felt our evidence was more than ample to make Tex an ex-deputy.

Now it was time for Winston's counter argument. Speaking up for his "client," he rambled on for quite some time before the chairman ordered him to sum up his case. Winston argued that: the so-called evidence from Tex's home was planted and he knew nothing about it; the raid at the river interrupted Tex's efforts to arrest the smugglers himself since he was on a secret night patrol; finally, Tex would be happy to provide written statements from citizens of his splendid work if given more time. Unbelievable! Now I knew why people hated lawyers.

The chairman announced that the commissioners would go into a nearby room to talk it all over and return with their decision. As they left, Springer whispered, "I could shoot that ol' lawyer rascal too, if y'all like." I groaned but avoided saying "very funny" this time.

I wasn't as nervous when I saw the sour expressions on two particular men as the seven returned. The chairman, looking a bit troubled, cleared his throat, thanked the members for considering this difficult issue, then said, "By a vote of four to three we have decided to remove Mr. Morgan from his position as deputy sheriff." Looking at Tex, he added, "You will be given your pay for two more weeks only which you may pick up here on Monday. Please turn in your weapon and badge before leaving today." Striking his gavel on the table, he declared, "This hearing is adjourned."

There was utter silence for a few seconds, followed by a red-faced Tex leaping to his feet and loudly cussing out the commissioners. A stunned Winston hastily wrapped his arms around his client to prevent him from charging the swiftly departing county officials. Hayden King meanwhile was calling out, "This ain't over, gentlemen. Y'all will regret today's decision." I figured a few members might.

Tex tossed his gun and badge on the front table. Luckily, the gun didn't go off. His lawyer promptly pushed him toward the rear to join up with Big Daddy. As he passed, he glared at me with pure hatred. I grinned back and said, "Please return my clothes when ya pick up yer last pay, Tex." I emphasized the word "last." Only his lawyer's unflinching bear hug kept Tex from leaping in my direction. Lucky for him: I was about to throw a punch at his chin.

We four lawmen soberly congratulated each other. This fight wasn't over by a longshot, and the criminal trial would be a whole different rodeo. Though we hardly needed proof of that fact, it came nevertheless, when Hayden King's Cadillac pulled up beside us outside. He slowly wound down the window and gifted us with his arrogant grin. He challenged us with, "I know y'all recognize that fine gentleman in the back seat, my friend, Mr. Winston. He's never lost a civil or a criminal case for me. "Wins-a-ton," is my nickname for him. See y'all in court soon, fellas." They sped off, all laughing, including the chauffeur.

That chance meeting brought back our uneasiness and the ride home was pretty quiet. At least Springer hadn't shot anyone, I thought, smiling to myself.

On Monday Decker told me the trial would be in mid-February at the county seat in Brownsville. We had about two weeks to get our facts ready. To my relief, Decker took charge of this groundwork with occasional help from the Rangers.

Throughout those two weeks, I spent most afternoons on patrol, mostly alone. During these routine patrols, though, I did nab two shoplifters from my dad's store. As I approached on horseback one late afternoon, two young men raced out the front door with my dad close behind. Seeing me start to dismount, he yelled, "Get 'em, son. Caught 'em stealin'." I spurred my horse after them and caught up as they rounded a street corner. Clean forgetting I wasn't a cowboy, I threw my lariat at one of them and it found purchase around a barber's pole! Two real cowhands strolling along the sidewalk burst out laughing as they watched this comedy unfold. Figuring the youngsters would escape, they chased after and tackled them as easy as tripping a steer. Yanking them off the ground and shoving them over to me, the smaller cowpoke cackled again saying, "Guess y'all need a few ropin' lessons, Deputy. At yer service, if ya have a hankerin'."

"Thanks, I just might," I managed to huff, eager to escape their mocking laughter and the stares of several bystanders. "I'll take 'em off yer hands now, fellas. Thanks fer the help."

Looking at the two cowed offenders, I said, "Don't I know you fellas?" They mumbled their names and I did know them, at least their parents. "Hand over the loot, guys." They had two pair of work gloves and two Swiss army knives. "Y'all risk jail fer this piddlin' stuff!" I said in disbelief.

As they kicked around some Texas dirt and mumbled vague excuses, I began to feel sorry for them and decided to just give them a harsh lecture, then escort them straight home. This I did, pronto.

My dad was delighted when I showed up with the stolen items. So happy, in fact, he gave me a raise on the spot before I even had a chance to tell him what had happened. *Awkward.* I closed my eyes, pictured Anne's face, sighed, and told him the whole true story. His laughter was kinder than the cowboys' but it still hurt. My pain was eased, though, when he said he'd keep his promise about the raise. He also winked and said he'd share only part of my story with the family. *Good man, my dad.*

Decker announced on Friday that he was running for sheriff in the fall election. "Reckon I have a plugnickel's chance?" he asked hopefully.

"I do, 'specially if ya keep hittin' the café every mornin' and minglin' with the voters. Suggest ya smile a bit more, though," I added, showing him my best example. Copying my smile exposed several rotten teeth up front, so I coughed, and said to focus on friendly handshakes instead.

"I'm fixin' to look fer a new deputy," he said. "I'd 'preciate yer help if ya aren't too licked."

"Sure, and I ain't upset at all. We both know I'll probly be headin' back to A & M in the fall. Parents might disown me if I didn't."

"Thanks. Listen, Springer and I will be goin' to Brownsville on Monday to meet with this Ranger-friendly judge. Givin' him a heads-up 'bout what to expect. I'll tell ya 'bout it when I get back."

"Well, best to be prepared, 'specially in court."

My weekend wasn't much to squawk about: a few hours patrolling, clerking, and helping John at the clinic. Neither of us saw much of our gals. Bet both were up to their ears fussing with Heather's wedding plans. We did join them briefly on Sunday after church because of something unexpected – snow. A cold front had moved in and left us a three-inch white blanket. John and I made tracks to their apartment and coaxed them to come outside so we could have a snowball fight. We let them win, of course, and they celebrated by planting cold, wet kisses all over our grateful faces. Sometimes snow was a blessing.

Monday afternoon Decker brought me some bad news. Springer's friendly judge wouldn't be handling Morgan's trial. Big Daddy had managed to get one of cronies, the familiar Judge Colson, to be in charge.

"Springer's mad as hell," admitted Decker. "He wants to go back Wednesday and meet with the county prosecutor. Tell him 'bout the 'bigger picture.' I'll give y'all a run-down when we get in town."

"'Preciate it." And trying to add a touch of humor, I said, "Don't let Springer shoot no one 'fore the trial even starts." No laughter from Decker, so I added, "I was only joshin', Captain."

I spent a couple jittery days waiting for what they had to say about the prosecutor. No news on Wednesday night, so I high-tailed it for the café the next morning and found all of the lawmen nursing some coffee at a corner table. "Now, I'm as jumpy as spit on a hot skillet," I said, joining them. "What all happened yesterday?"

They held back while Toby took my order then Springer groused through clenched teeth, "It's a doggone calamity, Ted. The county gave the case to a new assistant, name of Elliot Jameson. It's his first and he's scart just talkin' to us."

Decker added, "Y'all hit the nail on the head, Captain. Seemed a mite squirmy bein' in yer company." *That I could believe!*

Collins nodded his agreement. Springer merely shrugged. Suddenly standing, he headed for the door. Halfway across the room he turned and said, "Got a bad feelin' 'bout this, fellas. Real bad." He left without slamming the door, more down in the dumps than I'd ever seen him.

I looked at Decker and grimaced. He spied Springer's full plate and said, "Ain't never seen him leave chow, Ted, and I was payin'." He paused, looked around, then grabbed Springer's plate and wolfed down the leftovers. That seemed to cheer him up a tad. Finished, he loosened his belt and blessed the café with two loud belches. I reckoned eating and belching were his ways of dealing with today's frustration.

We all met up with Todd Stevens on Monday morning and set off for Brownsville in Springer's car. I had hoped we'd sketch out more of our game plan, but Springer's persistent worry was spreading so little was said. This was a bad omen. We filed into the courtroom and sat down in the front row behind the prosecutor's table. Jameson turned around and smiled weakly at us. Danged if he didn't look like a newly-bought saddle – squeaky clean, yet to be ridden. I began to mentally prepare for the worst.

I noticed the three defendants were already seated at their table. The wounded man apparently wasn't healthy enough to attend. Tex turned around and sneered at me; I answered him back with my best winning smile.

At 8:55 a.m. Hayden and his fancy lawyer paraded in. Winston made a beeline for his table and clapped the back of his client, Tex. Big Daddy sat down in the first row and smiled back at his friends and supporters who nearly filled the left side of the room. Our side was deserted – until 8:59 when in slithered none other than Jenkins, my least favorite reporter! I watched him take out pencil and paper and get ready to take down any crowd-pleasing entertainment that might happen. Was Los Indios that important to him? A familiar dull ache began across my forehead.

We all rose when the bailiff announced Judge Colson's entrance. Dressed in black and sporting an ill-fitting toupee, he breezed in, smiled a big-toothed grin at the defendants, and ignored us entirely. My head started pounding now – our side was in for big-time trouble.

Minute by minute the judge's bias became clearer. In rapid order he threw out the evidence found at Tex's house because of our "warrantless" search. He then denied Jameson's request to have the Rangers – even Todd – testify claiming it was a county, not a state issue. As the fiasco continued, he badgered the young prosecutor and supported the defense attorney from the bench when he felt Winston wasn't doing a good job. He even made the highly unusual recommendation that Tex take the stand. Tex's statement would put the matter "to rest," as the judge termed it. When Winston dithered, Colson motioned Winston to approach the bench. He whispered a few words to him while looking back at Hayden at the same time. Naturally, the big shot lawyer quickly recognized his mistake and told his client to get up there and testify.

All this had taken place in little more than an hour. Jameson had "defeat" written all over him: hangdog face, drooping shoulders, and a profile dripping in sweat. Who could blame him? His every objection had been overruled and every one of Winston's sustained.

Tex swaggered to the witness chair, smiled benignly at the judge, and ran through his "fairy tale" about being on a secret mission to arrest smugglers before being bluntly stopped by Decker and company. Finished, the judge seemed to go out of his way to thank him for "setting the record straight."

We all knew Tex's "facts" had to be challenged but Jameson seemed paralyzed, unable to even speak. Decker cleared his throat to get the prosecutor's attention. Still nothing. Decker repeated his signal, so loudly that I feared he might burst a blood vessel in this throat. Jameson finally turned to see Decker motioning him to stand and speak. Ashen faced, he slowly began to rise. He was halfway up as Colson shouted, "No objection necessary, counselor, I've heard enough." Staring directly at Jameson, he quickly added, "This is one of the weakest cases ever to come before me. The defendant has waived his rights to a jury trial but it wouldn't have mattered. Their verdict and mine would be the same." Turning toward the defendant's table, he said, "I find Mr. Morgan innocent of all charges and the other men guilty of importing goods without proper paperwork in place. The court fines them each fifty dollars and sentences them sixty days in jail. I now declare those sentences suspended. Mr. Morgan, you're free to leave. You other men may leave as soon as payment is received by the bailiff."

The prosecution side sat in stunned silence. Every one of us, except Stevens, stared angrily at the judge. Jumping up, I stepped in front of my fellow lawmen and said, "Time to leave, men. Nuthin' can be done here. We'll talk to Jameson later 'bout appealin'. Let's leave 'fore any of ya takes the law into yer own hands." Looking at them, it sure was a good thing no weapons had been permitted in the courtroom.

I watched the victory celebration on the other side, during which time Big Daddy made a show of paying fines for the other defendants. We single filed out of the courtroom and walked out to our car. On our walk, Decker uttered some foul language unfamiliar even to this former roustabout; Collins picked up a garbage can and slung its contents all over the sidewalk; Springer, meanwhile, was kicking every object in his path: ant piles, stones, empty bottles. All went flying. One stone struck Stevens. He started to protest but wisely clammed up and dropped to a safer position behind the angry Ranger.

Standing beside the car, Springer copied Decker with his own brand of creative cussing, then said, "That whole damn charade didn't last more than two hours. Worst case of injustice I've ever seen." Collins and Decker joined in, declaring that old-time Rangers would never have tolerated such an outrage. With obvious bitterness, Collins declared that in the good old days Rangers would have been judge and jury themselves.

Not having much choice about it, Stevens and I let them rant and rave a while longer before Springer finally settled down and reached into his pocket for his car keys. "Hold on there, Captain," I blurted out, holding up my hand and stepping between him and the car door. "Y'all need to have someone else get behind the wheel. Yer a mite upset."

He glared at me like I was crazy. I held my ground. The Texas standoff took only a few seconds, though it felt like ages. Finally, he went along and dropped the keys at my feet. A victory of sorts.

Complaining and swearing carried on most of the way back home. We did all laugh, however, when Decker mocked Judge Colson's appearance. "Did y'all see his ridiculous toupee? Ya must have seen it move every time he slammed his gavel on his table. Then he'd turn sideways and shift it back, thinkin' we wouldn't notice."

I tried to keep the fellas laughing with a few more funny observations but soon we were all silent. Things got livelier when I pulled over to buy something to eat at a dinky cantina. Having some food in our bellies helped work out the "gut-wrenching" we'd gone through. And telling tales about John's first introductions to Mexican vittles, good and bad, caused everyone to say something. Since Tex-Mex was part and parcel of what it meant to be a real Texan, comments were downright favorable.

The food, laughter, and different topics lessened everyone's frustration and my pounding headache. Returning to the car and soon catching a glimpse of Los Indios on the horizon helped even more. At last, a chance to unwind and spend some time alone with my gal, I thought.

The mood changed all of a sudden when Todd called out from the back seat, "Hey, ain't that smoke off to the left?" Everyone thought we should drive toward the black haze.

"I think it's a house on fire," Springer said. "Last house on the edge of town."

Last house! My heart sank, fearing it was Toby's house. I floored the pedal causing heads to snap backward. Only the "Special Ranger" complained.

We got there just in time to witness a huge tongue of fire shoot upward, then recede, followed quickly by the collapse of the roof. Within minutes nothing remained but the smoldering ruins. Perhaps twenty people were standing around, a few holding water buckets. I frantically looked for signs of the Washington family. At first nothing, then with a sigh of relief I spotted them off to one side huddled together under a big oak tree. Thanking God with every step, I ran over to them.

"Toby, Martha," I called out. "What on earth happened?" Toby seemed too overcome to speak. Still comforting two weeping children, Martha gulped and cried out, "It was men covered in white sheets and hoods, Mr. Ted. They threw rocks first, then burnin' torches. We couldn't do nuthin' but get out. We's lucky to be alive."

I couldn't believe what she was saying! "Men in white sheets," I stammered. "Ya mean like the Klan, the KKK?"

"Uh-huh. We thought we was safe here. Now what we gonna do?"

I was outraged and momentarily at a loss for words. But from somewhere I found the strength to say, "Come hell or high water, you're stayin', Martha. You and yer family. This ain't my first rodeo and I'm fixin' to hunt the bastards down. Y'all will have justice this time 'round. Ya have my word."

By the look on their faces I knew Toby and Martha believed me. By my colleagues' faces that now surrounded me, I reckoned they would join me.

The hunt was on.

CHAPTER THIRTEEN

FINDING BAIT

Toby was overwhelmed by the locals' kindness and good will shown him at the café and store. Customers also seemed upset that there was a "new Klan" in Texas, especially in their county. "Ain't welcome in these parts," said Wesley Bartlett. "Have a cousin up in Dallas says their numbers are growin' there and they're burnin' all kinds of things – their wooden crosses on front lawns. Supposed to be a warnin' 'gainst colored folks and foreigners and Catholics. Strange since most of these people are also Christians." A lot of headshaking followed this statement. Then Shannon Young added, "I can't imagine there's much support 'round here. Welcome as a 'tornado on a trail drive.' Bet it's only a tiny group, Toby, and your friend, Deputy Ted, will root 'em out in no time." "Hope so too, ma'am," Toby said, though he knew that was a heavy weight to put on such a young man.

I WAS DOWN IN THE MOUTH the morning after the fire about not seeing my two Ranger friends and Decker at the café. Figured the straightaway everyone would want to "git workin'" on a plan to single out and catch the members of this "new Klan." A smiling Toby took my order and said none had been in for breakfast. Toby added, "Maybe they's over at the station, Mr. Ted. Bet ya find 'em there."

He seemed a mite cheerful for a man who'd just lost his home, so I said, "What's goin' on happy fella?"

"Ya know, sir, that yer folks got us a place to stay overnight at Mr. Henderson's."

"Uh-huh, and I'm sure glad it worked out fer ya."

"It did but there's even better news. Yer mom came by 'fore the sun came up. Talked with Mr. Henderson and they made a deal to let us stay as long as needed, 'till we find our own place that is."

"Swell, but it's gonna be kinda crowded there with John 'round on weekends."

"Yer mom says Mr. John will stay at their house and share a room with y'all."

"Oh...well, what the heck. A fella can't be too persnickety, 'specially bein' the 'best man' 'n all." It seemed that deal making was easy as pie for my mom.

Anxious to talk with my colleagues, I chowed down breakfast in record time and rushed over to the station. I burst in so abruptly that I plowed into Betty who was leaving, nearly putting her on her backside.

"Easy there, Deputy. My favorite position right now is standin' upright. You're kinda quick outta the chute this mornin', ain't ya?"

"Sorry, Betty, but I wanna hash over somethin' important with the Rangers and Decker."

"Well, you're in luck, young man, 'cause they're in the back room already jawin' 'bout somethin'."

"Thanks. And I won't tip ya over next time."

She snorted, "We'll see," then winked at me and left.

The men were sitting around a table all gabbing at the same time. Conversation ended as they looked up at me almost guiltily, like I had interrupted some sort of secret meeting.

I jokingly said, "Hey, this ain't a meetin' of the Klan. Right, fellas?"

"Not funny," said Springer.

He glanced at Decker who said, "Listen, Ted, we've been jawin' 'bout two things and we're near done. Step back outside fer a spell. We'll call ya back in and spill the beans."
That was odd and a bit unnerving.

I rambled around the other room until they yelled for me. Decker said, "No offense meant, Ted, but we needed to see eye to eye on two points."

"Okay, shoot."

"We're appealin' the judge's decision to a higher court. And we'll stand firm this time that we get a prosecutor with some horse sense. Good idea, ya think?"

"Sure, let's do it."

"Problem is, we ain't got no money. Gotta win over the commissioners that it's worth the effort. Guess I'm the one to carry that load."

Springer coughed and said, "Second point is the Klan. We'll go along and support ya 'bout singlin' 'em out and bringin' 'em to justice." He paused waiting for my response.

"That's why I'm here."

He paused again making me think there was more. He proved me right when he added, "Y'all should know that yer aims and ours don't completely go hand in hand."

"Meanin'?"

"Well, all three of us are pretty much segregationists. We believe the races are better off livin' peacefully but mostly apart. But bein' lawmen we also believe in law and order and property rights. Don't see how a bunch of hooded cowards got the right to burn down the house of a peaceful man like Toby – livin' at the edge of town with his family, botherin' no one. It ain't right and we'll help ya make it right."

I knew it wasn't the right time to explain some of my motives – based on my upbringing in a Christian home – so I merely said, "Fair 'nuff. Let's get to work on a plan to buck this new evil in our town and county." They nodded in agreement and told me to pull up a chair.

My friends knew some key facts about the first Klan that began at the end of the Civil War. "Reconstruction was a bitter pill to swallow fer many white Southerners in the late 1860s," said Springer. "They felt they were losin' control of their way of life and the Klan was a way to get it back by scarin' their victims and usin' violence too, when necessary. They fixed it by keepin' Negroes from votin' and holdin' office. By 1870, most of the elected Negroes were outta office, one way or another."

"But our Congress reacted, right?" I asked, knowing the answer but wanting it to come from him.

"It did, by passin' the Anti-Klan Act of 1871 under President Grant. The Reconstruction Acts then brought in federal troops which drove the KKK chapters even deeper underground 'til they pretty much disappeared in the 1880s."

"So why did things get worse fer Negroes?" Decker asked. Again, knowing part of the answer, I still wanted to have Springer take the lead.

"'Cause by then the North kinda gave up on the whole Reconstruction experience and turned to other national goals, like conquering the West and the growth of business. The federal government pretty much let the South deal with its own race relations."

Knowing they'd have a hard time saying it, I drew the conclusion for them. "Meanin' bad news fer most Negroes, I reckon. 'Mr. Jim Crow' took over, didn't he?" For a moment, painful silence.

Then Springer said, "Not fer everyone or everywhere but fer the larger part, that's pretty much true."

"Well," I said, "it 'pears there's a whole new Klan. What's the low down on this group?" It quickly became clear that we didn't know diddly squat. Collins held it started recently but not in Texas. The other two had heard only rumors.

"Before fixin' to do anythin', I continued, "we'd better brush up on this new Klan. How 'bout I go over to the library in Brownsville and dig up some ol' newspaper pieces and articles?

"Might as well," said Decker. "Rest of us will make inquiries 'round town. Somethin' will turn up. Pastor Dan might prove helpful. He knows everyone in these parts it seems."

"I'll get Chief in on it too," I suggested. "Indians might seem isolated but they may know a lot more 'bout this county than many whites."

I believed that progress had been made as we went our separate ways. Justice couldn't come soon enough.

Decker and I rode patrol for the rest of the morning. As we bounced along, it dawned on me that Anne and Heather might be first-rate partners in searching for information. *Why not include them, too?*

It didn't take much persuasion for the ladies to join me. They got their hours covered at the café for Saturday and off we went in my dad's car. We spent the afternoon poring over magazines and newspapers looking for any mention of the rebirth of the KKK. By the time the head librarian showed us the door at five p.m., we had learned a lot. The new Klan had been started by a man named William Simmons in Georgia in 1915. He considered it a fraternal organization of patriotic men who were opposed to immigrants, Catholics, Jews, Negroes, and unclean living, that is, no alcohol. Finally, this Klan seemed to be growing rapidly in a few southern states including parts of Texas, namely the Dallas area.

"Looks as if they want to return to their idea of a traditional small town America," said Heather. "A white, Protestant America," she added in a troubled voice.

"I can see why this approach would attract many Americans," Anne put in. "And not just Southerners."

"That's sure the truth," I agreed. "And it doesn't show as many signs of violence like the older Klan. Figure that's a good thing." I hoped she got my meaning in light of what might be in my immediate future: action – hopefully non-violent – to nip this movement in the bud before more tragedies took place.

"There's more interestin' news," I said. "My last article referred to Simmons bein' strongly influenced by a movie called *Birth of a Nation*. John told me 'bout the same movie. Evidently, it paints the first Klan as the savior of the South after the Civil War. And Negroes act like they're dumb as dirt, revengeful, lustin' after virtuous white women, not worth spit. John was disgusted by its central message. A big and successful movie, though, so it's havin' a powerful effect in America."

Neither lady could understand how such a movie could be made in twentieth century America. *Not if they were in charge, I thought to myself.* Heather offered to meet with teachers at her school to alert them to the dangers posed by this new movement. "We'll keep their hateful ideas from our precious children," she said with a no-nonsense look.

Anne had a further suggestion. "Why don't we put our warning on paper and take it to the high school in Brownsville. That's where it's clearly threatening."

"Worth a try," Heather allowed. "And I do know a few teachers in the system, fine Christian people. They'd take the lead once we tell them our whole story."

"That's mighty nice of you ladies. Let's get goin'. We'll talk more on the ride back."

As Anne would declare, "God works in mysterious ways." Proof of that came when we bumped into a man on the library steps, the reporter Jenkins! My gut instinct was anger, especially as he smiled at us in recognition. Not again! I thought as I tried to hurry the ladies away before he started down his familiar path of inquiry.

Strangely, it didn't happen. Following awkward greetings during which we learned his first name was Lloyd, he asked why we were at the library. I hesitated only briefly before deciding to tell the truth. *Probably another example of Anne's influence on me.*

After hearing my explanation, he said, "The new Klan, you say. We're on the same path. I've been studying up on them myself. Even had one short article appearing in the paper. What do you folks make of them?"

Truth time again so I told him, holding nothing back. The ladies joined in with a few choice words of their own which were less brutal than mine.

Our comments caused him to smile again, this time a friendly offering. "I'll be damned," he said. "I couldn't have said it any better myself."

"I'm buffaloed," I replied. "Figured y'all might be cheerin' fer 'em."

"Not at all. Ya see, to begin with, I'm not from these parts." He leaned in and whispered, "Came here a few years ago from Ohio. Tryin' to become a good Texan – like droppin' every possible 'g' at the end of a word. See, there's a couple of 'em right there."

"Well, I'll be doggoned!" I said, avoiding the other "d" word for Anne's sake. "So, reckon y'all won't be joinin' the Klan."

"Hate 'em," he spat. "Be the ruin of Texas if we let 'em spread."

Still not quite believing my ears, I took a leap and gave him a heads-up on our hopes of catching them in Los Indios. I finished saying, "Are ya with us?

"Damn right. I've got plenty of sources in every corner of this county, includin' your neck of the woods. Be happy to keep my ear to the ground and holler if anythin' turns up."

"Mysterious ways" popped into my mind before I said, "Thanks. Call the Ranger station if and when that happens."

"You bet. Say, y'all could return the favor by givin' me a call if the Klan does show up again. Sure would like to cover that story. It'll make the front page for sure, maybe above the fold. Here's my card with my number and the paper's." He handed it to me, shook hands all around, and we parted ways.

From a distance he yelled, "I haven't given up on my other stories up your way. Ya know it's my job, Ted. Need to make a livin'." Ouch. He was still a skunk even for all his talk.

I'd been ducking meeting with Toby, so I pulled him aside on Sunday after church. Told him we lawmen were hatching a scheme for catching the Klan in action and arresting them on the spot. "Don't have it all figured out yet. Y'all have any notions?" I asked.

"Sure want 'em caught and punished but hope ya can do it without anyone bein' killed. Martha made that real clear to me more'n once."

"Can't promise anythin' but we'll do our best. Have to lure 'em out somehow and be there to nab 'em. That part won't be easy. Guess that's why I'm pickin' yer brain."

"Mr. Ted, I've been thinkin' 'bout one thing. Good friend of ours, Darius White, been hopin' to move here to this friendly town, mostly 'cause of reports from Martha and me. He's a young Negro with no family, been fightin' racism in Texas past few years. Ain't scart of nuthin'."

"Let me get this straight. Yer sayin' he'd be willin' to move here and pass himself as 'bait' fer the Klan?"

"Yessir. He might say 'no' but I think he'll be ajumpin' at the chance. I'll write tonight. Should hear back in no time flat. Bet he's here by Monday."

"Well, that is amazin'. He's a true Texan if he goes along. That'd also be keepin' yer family away from danger, safe and sound at Worth's."

"Don't wanna put no one else in danger, though," expressed Toby.

"Agreed. Have to find a place off by itself where we can catch 'em 'fore they hurt anyone, includin' yer Darius fella. More work fer us lawmen but somethin' will turn up." Pausing, I added, "Maybe my folks can help. They know this town like the back of their hand."

We parted ways with his promise to post a letter in the morning and my promise to meet with Decker and the Rangers early in the week to set everything in motion.

As a matter of fact, my parents did have an idea about where Darius could reside; with considerable irony they suggested none other than Tex Morgan's old place.

"Y'all kiddin' me?"

"Nope," Dad said. "Seems Mr. Morgan ain't nowhere to be found. Friend of mine passed by his shack the other day and said it was all cleared out. Tex never owned it anyway, just squatted. Bet that Darius fella could squat there, at least long enough for a trap to be set and sprung."

"Great, Dad. Now we just have to figure out how to lure the Klan in that direction and get the word out."

Dad paused, then said, "I bet Anne and Heather can pitch in with that. Why not check with 'em?"

Of course! I thanked dad and raced off to find the ladies. Managing to catch them after Wednesday night's prayer meeting, I laid out all the facts. It took them all of two minutes to come up with an answer. "I know what to do," declared Heather. "Let's have a welcoming party for Mr. White. We'll make it just those who are the friendliest and most open-minded."

"That's a fine idea," I said. "It's mighty amazin' how well Toby and his family have been received, but we don't wanna press our luck. This is Texas after all." I decided not to tell them about Worth admitting he'd gotten a few disapproving looks after granting the Washington family temporary residence.

"Sad but true about Texas," admitted Heather. "But your mom will know which people to invite and no doubt help us set up on Tuesday afternoon, if he's arrived by then."

"And fetch most of the food and drink," I added with conviction.

"It's settled then," said Heather. "A get-together for some "select" few Tuesday. Everyone'll know to head home by dusk, except, of course, the 'real' welcoming party."

"Yer plan just might work," I said, "and if they don't show up on Tuesday night, hopefully it won't mean waitin' fer too many extra more nights."

"What if takes a lot longer," asked the always-worried-about-me Anne.

"Then we've got a real problem," I answered. "Any other schemes ya got in mind?" None were offered. I thanked both girls and left after planting a grateful kiss on Heather's cheek and Anne's lips. *Tough work for a deputy sheriff in these parts.*

All of us lawmen and Chief finally gathered at the Ranger station late Friday afternoon. Fortunately, that delay proved a blessing because Toby had told me at breakfast that Darius had willingly agreed to go along with this "party" and would, indeed, arrive the following Monday. We got down to business and I brought up the whole deal: the welcoming party as bait, having lawmen as guests, and hopefully jailing some KKK. Everyone was silent considering my statement. Thankfully, they all finally responded. Decker admitted he liked the plan, as did the Rangers, though they were a bit doubtful about Darius. Chief remained his usual stoic self.

Heaving a sigh of relief, I continued, "Y'all know that there's still a tough situation. How do we know when to git there and catch these white-robed cowards?"

Chief spoke up, "Young braves from the reservation might be willing to act as lookouts at several locations around the site."

"How would the braves let us know?" asked a skeptical Decker.

"They'll ride 'hell-bent for leather' to the telegraph office which can sound the alarm to the station. Be there in minutes, catch 'em right quick."

The two Rangers scoffed at Chief's suggestion. "Klan will probly see 'em hidin' and go after 'em," Springer said. "A fight 'tween the Klan and one or two Indians would be a slaughter. Bad idea."

With fire in his eyes Chief replied, "Slaughter, maybe, but it would be white sheets dyin', not Indians."

"Easy, fellas. Chief was just offerin' a suggestion. Anyone else have an idea?" Silence. I persuaded them to keep thinking and we all parted to meet again Monday morning at the café. By then maybe a better idea than Chief's would crop up.

On Monday morning no other plan had been worked out. With that in mind, we all waited anxiously for Mr. Darius White's arrival.

CHAPTER FOURTEEN

UNMASKING

Toby was impressed with the preparations being made for Tuesday night's party and hoped people wouldn't be too upset when they found out the true reason for the gathering. Would he and Darius be resented? More importantly, would the Klan show up? He and Martha were praying hard that no violence would come to pass if they did. But everyone knew how trigger-happy the Rangers could be.

OUR SMALL WELCOMING GROUP WAITED anxiously as the train pulled in. A few passengers quickly got off, then nothing. After a few moments, a canvas bag appeared followed by a large, muscled arm, then a big man: a Negro at least six feet tall, close to 200 pounds of muscle with a rugged face that made one tend to their own business. Thankfully, he broke into a broad grin when he saw Toby. As I watched him tower over Toby and smother him in a massive hug, it reminded me of an A& M defensive lineman plugging up a hole against a running back. Of course, both would have been white, but that's the image that flashed through my mind.

I wondered what images others had as Toby introduced him all around. Darius gave me a firm handshake, dad winced when it was his turn, Chief merely nodded, and Decker and the Rangers? Well, a contest was held as to who among them had the strongest grip. I felt it was a tie, yet I smiled when the smaller Collins put his arm behind him and flexed his fingers after his shake.

The ladies were absent as well as Todd, but a few curious locals were milling around and unsure of what to do. *Another Negro in town?* Darius surprisingly marched right over and introduced himself, giving bone-crushing shakes to the men and a tip of the hat to the ladies. Impressive, I thought, as he made his way back to us. Darius put us at ease by saying, "Toby, here, speaks highly of this town. So far it seems a right friendly place to me."

A relieved Toby said, "White folks gave me a chance to prove myself. They'll do the same fer y'all, Darius. Now, let's mosey on over to yer new place. Hope ya ain't too disappointed."

"Sure it'll be fine. Lead the way."

Dad offered to drive Darius and Toby out to the "shack," leaving the rest of us to pile into Springer's car. As we rode, I asked each for his first impression. The Rangers were willing, for now, to give him the "benefit of the doubt." Decker said he was withholding any judgment. Chief was his usual silent self. I challenged them about their lukewarm responses. An awkward silence followed before Springer said, "Regardless of our plan fer catchin' the Klan, Ted, y'all do recognize you're puttin' this Negro fella in a right difficult position."

"Ain't followin' ya."

"Come on, Ted. Y'all ain't that simple. This might be a friendly town, but it's still Texas, still the South. Bringin' an unmarried Negro here is playin' with fire. He starts cozyin' up with white women and it's trouble with a capital T."

Thunderation! I hadn't thought of that. And Toby's lack of foresight also bothered me. "See yer point, Captain. What should we do 'bout it?"

"Keep a close eye on him, I guess," answered Springer. "He'll probly spot the situation."

Decker said, "How 'bout y'all give yer lady friends the job of findin' Darius a girlfriend. Heather is familiar with Brownsville and they have a Negro section over there. Bet there's some young Negro gals itchin' to get hitched. Anyway, worth a try. Bet both Heather and Anne would jump at the chance at matchmakin'."

"Bet they would," I said, grinning from ear to ear. "I'll run it by 'em."

Anne, Heather, and mom were waiting for us at the shack. Darius greeted them with much lighter handshakes than we men had received. The tour of the two-room building took all of three minutes: not much to inspect despite the addition of some basic furniture and kitchen supplies rounded up for Darius. Fortunately, Darius didn't seem bothered by its plainness. "Lived with less," he confessed. "Had three brothers and two sisters and, fer a time, we all lived in a place 'bout this size. Brothers and me slept in the main room on the floor, next to the stove. So, this place'll do fine, long as the roof don't leak."

"We'll be fixin' it if it does," I said. And won't be long 'fore ya find a more fetchin' place, right ladies?"

Mom assured us all that she would be scouting that out. I had a moment alone with Darius and asked him why he'd come to our town. He answered saying he'd been fighting hard for fair treatment and having rights all his adult life. "I saw how my folks were treated and it hurt me. Both of 'em worked hard and didn't get much for it: little respect and stingy pay. Felt the unfairness myself a lot. Spent two years at a mostly white high school. Real excited 'til I weren't allowed in any college prep classes. Breakin' point, though, was when I wanted to play football. Told me football was fer white boys not people like me. Faster and stronger than any one of those white boys, that's fer damn sure." He was getting riled, and he had a right to be. But I was afraid things were fixing to explode, so I cut him short by waving all the men together to go over our unsettled plans for capturing this new KKK chapter.

Decker brought out the particulars. When finished, we waited nervously for Darius' response. It sure was a relief to hear him say he'd be a part of the scheme. "Hate the Klan and everythin' it stands fer. I'm yer man."

"Would ya like to add anythin'?" I asked him. With a glint in his eye, he looked at us and said, "Feel a mite more comfortable if I had a gun. Any chance of gettin' one?" Dadgummit! Hadn't thought of that either.

Knowing the strain of getting ready for a fight, Decker said, "Sure. I've got the best one fer ya: a twelve-gauge shotgun filled with bird seed. Won't know what it's loaded with, so it'll scare the livin' daylights outta 'em." *Would Darius find this acceptable?*

"Thinkin' of somethin' with a bigger kick but if that's all yer offerin', I'll take it." *He knew the right answer.*

The ladies pulled Darius aside to give him some details of the party. Not sure he cared all that much but he pretended interest. That gave the rest of us time to go outside and pick out our hiding posts when the party-goers had left. Pretty easy since there were several large trees in the distance as well as bushes. There was also a gully close by where horses could be hidden. "What 'bout the outhouse?" asked Collins. "It's big enough fer someone to hide behind."

Springer snorted and said, "Let's play another prank on Stevens and put 'im there. Gotta discourage him from becomin' a real Ranger somehow." Laughter all around about that possibility.

We left Darius alone at last. The ladies pledged to return Tuesday to set up for the party. I told Anne there were one or two points we needed to talk over, and she straightaway asked me to have coffee with her and Heather later that evening. With coffee in hand later, Anne spoke her piece before I even took a swallow. "This may be hard for you, Ted, but I want you to promise me to accompany the Rangers and others...unarmed." *Unarmed?* "I realize you carry a pistol on regular patrol but this Klan business is different."

"I thought we'd agreed that fightin' wasn't this new Klan's style. They'll be carryin' torches and be covered in white sheets, probly get all twisted up and fall off their horses tryin' to reach fer their pistols – if they're packin'."

"I know but I need you to do this for me. If there is shooting, other men are armed and will protect you. They're better shots anyway as I see it." Her words stung like a wasp. Seemed like the choice was clear: Anne or my fellow lawmen. I chose Anne, though I knew for certain I'd get some serious ribbing when I arrived unstrapped.

Anne was happy with my decision then asked what was on my mind. I carefully laid out to both ladies the worry the Rangers felt about an unattached young Negro man in a lily-white town. They appeared puzzled at first. This innocence endeared them even more to me. Not getting any response, I pressed on. "Here's a possible solution – includin' ya both. Decker suggests that Heather, with Anne's help, might be able to talk to some of her friends in Brownsville. Meanin' roundin' up a girlfriend fer Darius – a colored girl from the Negro community over yonder. Do y'all accept that kinda challenge?"

Heather said, "Anne and I need to talk with one another about this unusual request." She locked arms with Anne and walked into an adjoining room, closing the door behind them. I hoped they weren't offended. They came back with an answer: They would do their best. Anne mentioned how accepting our town was and that its people were pretty decent.

"Most are but it's best to be realistic," I said. "At some point we oughta give Toby a heads-up on our match-making efforts. Maybe he can find a way to break the news to Darius that doesn't rile his friend. Best to have Toby on our side."

This whole conversation sobered us. To bring back a more lighthearted mood, I brought up John's weekend visits and the stories he'd been sharing with us about his adventures in medical school. They burst out laughing when I recalled my favorite: the absent-minded professor who kept stepping off the raised platform right into the wastebasket where his foot got stuck. This tale telling helped, meaning the evening ended on a better "foot" than it had begun.

My parents closed the store early Tuesday, and we lugged more supplies out to the shack. Several trips were made to fetch of all the goodies mom had prepared. We used dad's truck to haul out tables and chairs as well as decorations made by Anne and Heather. It took all of two hours. That gave us time to take a break. Darius was impressed by everything we were doing and said it was the biggest party goin's on he'd ever seen. "It's a pity the white folks don't know the real reason fer the celebration," he said.

About fifteen "select" adults showed up plus a small number of children. None of the lawmen were happy to see kids running around, but it was too late to do anything about it. People seemed to be having a good time chatting, with an occasional loud guffaw at a joke. And, of course, they were packing away the food, eating being a Texas tradition. Everyone, that is, except the lawmen who came to the table like Gideon, keeping a sharp eye out for the possible early arrival of danger.

Most had left by dusk. We met briefly with Darius repeating our instructions to not shoot unless fired upon and to try to stay calm. That was a mite easier for us, since he was the target.

We went to our assigned positions. Buried in a clump of bushes, I could dimly make out Todd off to my right hiding behind a tree, not quite big enough to conceal his lanky frame. No one had told him to hunker down behind the outhouse: probably better for us because he'd find it difficult to keep quiet, especially if the wind picked up.

We waited all night and nothing happened. Well, no Klan came around, but we were under constant attack from mosquitoes and other blood-sucking insects. My legs cramped up so bad I was rustling the bushes. And, as feared, the wind got stronger, causing the men closest to the outhouse to cough loud enough to be heard by any creature within at least 200 feet. *So much for the element of surprise.*

It was nearly dawn when we abandoned our first attempt to trap the Klan. By that time, I couldn't keep from yawning and my exposed skin was covered with nasty, itching bites. As we said our goodbyes to Darius, he seemed remarkably unaffected by the long, boring watch. Had he been cheating on us and been catnapping during the night?

I struggled out of bed later the next morning and dashed off to the café in hopes of meeting with the other lawmen. Halfway through breakfast, all three straggled in and plopped down at my table, looking weary and mussed up. After joking about my tender age compared to theirs, they found the strength to order some grub, then mostly grumbled about the miseries they'd experienced last night. They even compared the size of welts from bites, size being a big deal to Texans. Decker claimed victory with a whopper, making me feel a little better about my tiny wounds.

Just as we started to leave, Pastor Dan strode in and sat down with us. He had good news: a plan for alerting us to the Klan's arrival. "If it works," he said, "perhaps y'all can leave only one or two men hiding each night."

"Damned if I don't like the sound of that," said Decker, while scratching a large bite mark. "Lay it on us."

"There are two congregants, gentlemen, both with sons in their late teens who are causin' trouble all the time. Dads say the boys have run along with Wade's gang in the past and they fear it's still happenin'. Been talkin' 'gainst Negroes lately. They disappear at night and don't say anythin' in the mornin'. Both are outta control. In short, they're worried that Wade's got his hooks in 'em. Pretty convinced he's one of the leaders of this new Klan chapter."

"What are ya proposin'?" asked an eager Decker.

"They're willin' to call me the next night the boys disappear. Hard choice fer 'em, fellas. They love their sons but are desperate to stop 'em 'fore they get in any deeper and it's too late."

"Yer scheme might work," said Decker. "Have 'em call me first though. It'll save time and I'm the deputy in charge of the sheriff's department. I'll arrange to get the word out."

The rest of us agreed right quick. Pastor Dan left after we thanked him. The plan called for placing two men on guard each evening with no man getting stuck two nights in a row. Decker and I offered to take that very night and a schedule was worked out for the rest of the week. What would he say to his unarmed sidekick in a few hours?

Decker, naturally, brought up my not packing before we even reached the shack. My weak explanation made him snort and question my manhood. "Anne's a wonderful gal, Ted, but y'all gotta show her who's boss." Before I could answer back, he opened his saddlebag, took out a spare pistol and slapped it into my hand. "I ain't gonna rat ya out, but my deputy will be armed at all times. Understand?"

In a barely audible voice, I croaked, "I do." Then I meekly tucked the gun, a big .45 caliber, in my waistband. *Please, God, keep me from using it.* We then went to separate hiding places. Again, no Klan showed up, just more cramps and insect bites.

Springer and Collins went out Thursday. I figured they could handle anything coming their way, so I spent a pleasant evening with Anne. After returning home and sharing a late night snack with my parents, I collapsed onto my bed and drifted off into some much needed sleep. Shortly after midnight, I was shaken awake by dad who said he'd just answered a call from Decker. "Tonight's the night accordin' to your deputy friend. Says to get a move on. He'll be callin' others and y'all are to gather at the shack."

With a racing heart and a roiling stomach, I rolled out of bed, threw on my clothes, and hightailed it over to the Ranger station and climbed onto a horse that was already saddled and ready. Guiltily, I packed Decker's pistol in my saddlebag hoping it would remain there all night.

We all arrived pretty much at the same time. Decker tipped off the Rangers to what might be happening tonight. I could see Springer and Collins were looking forward to some action. Chief, Stevens, and I led the horses into the gully and hobbled them. We quickly went to our hiding places to begin our wait for the sound of hoof beats. I had left Decker's pistol in my saddlebag hoping my slipup wouldn't be noticed.

When I heard the familiar sound of approaching horses, I took out my pocket watch: nearly two a.m. This is it, I thought. Time to spring the trap! I looked up into the sky and was grateful for the light cast by a nearly full moon. Good light and the element of surprise: should be a victory for us, yet one never knew for sure. I crouched down behind a boulder and waited for the Klan to ride into the open.

A short time later, the lead horse appeared from a copse of trees, followed by others in single file. Once all were out in the open, they reformed and created a semicircle in front of the shack. It was a shocking sight: riders completely draped in white, hoods with slits for eyeholes. Several riders also wore some sort of cap or helmet over their hoods. These had some odd-looking signs or symbols on them. Most of the riders held unlit torches in one hand. Thankfully, no guns were being waved about. Decker's plan was to let things play out, short of setting torches ablaze, before we made our move. I think we all wanted the memory of this crazy-wild event that was happening before our eyes.

With horses in place, the riders began shouting every foul racist word at the shack. They didn't care that the shack was dark and showed no signs of life. The leader then ordered them to ride their horses all the way around the shack a couple times. They did, cursing and yelling out threats as they rode. To me, this spectacle seemed like a hateful imitation of Joshua circling Jericho.

A light suddenly came on in the shack. All the riders began milling around in front of the door. "Y'all ain't welcome here, boy," yelled the leader. "Git out here, ya varmit. We ain't gonna kill ya, just fixin' to give ya a good ol' Texas thrashin' 'fore we send ya on yer way."

Darius opened the door and calmly stepped out into the open, lantern in his left hand, raised shotgun in his right. Seeing the "varmit" wasn't backing off sure brought an end to the devilry. Everyone froze in place. In a commanding voice, Darius broke the stillness saying, "Get the hell outta here 'fore this shotgun goes off accident-like." He placed the lantern on the ground, cocked both barrels, and took aim at the front rider who'd just spoken.

Regaining a bit of boldness, the leader pointed to his fellow Klansmen. "Yer outnumbered, boy. Better think twice."

This warning was most likely a distraction, I reckoned, because in a split second a rider on his left lit his torch and the leader drew a pistol and started to take aim. Damn it!

I jerked when two shots rang out from somewhere in the dark. The torcher and the leader fell to the ground. Then a call rang out, "Everyone stay put. Yer surrounded by the Sheriff and Rangers. Y'all are under arrest. Drop everythin' and get off yer horses real slow."

Confusion followed before half the riders obeyed. The others spurred their horses making a dash to escape. Taking command, Springer shouted for Decker, Chief, and Todd to grab their horses and hunt them down. Not sure Decker liked losing control, but he obeyed. All three rode off promptly in pursuit. I figured with Chief in the chase, not a one of the Klansmen would get far.

The Rangers and I ran to the shack and joined Darius who had those left behind covered with his shotgun. Five men were standing, looking rather testy. So we rounded up their guns and torches before hogtying them. The others were lying on the ground moaning from being shot. The Rangers and Darius weren't bothered at all by the condition of these guys. Going over by them, I made out that they were losing a lot of blood. They'd be goners soon. Maybe they'd live if.... Only one thing came to mind. It would probably make the Klan curse up a storm, but I tore the bottom of their sheets and used the strips to stop the bleeding as best I could. "Should get 'em to the clinic or the Brownsville hospital soon," I warned. My associates remained indifferent.

"Shall we unmask the bastards now?" Collins asked.

"Nah, let's wait and reveal their sorry faces when the others show up," Springer answered. Sizing me up, the Captain said, "Say, Ted, where the hell's yer pistol? Drop it or somethin'?"

"Must have left it behind," I replied meekly, hoping the subject didn't come up again.

Our wait gave us time to hear from Darius and get his take on the night's ruckus. He was darned grateful it was over, happy he'd joined up with us, and was looking forward to the end of the KKK in these parts. "Amen to that," I said, speaking for all of us.

It wasn't long before our men had captured the escaping Klansmen and handed them back over to us, unarmed and still fully sheeted. A few of the angrier ones continued cussing and chewing us out as we shoved them all together. Decker then ordered the sore as hell bunch to line up for what he called the "unmasking ceremony." He took Darius' shotgun and used it to prod a couple of ornery Klansmen to join the rest in line.

"I suggest we start with the two on the ground," said Springer. "Seems they're in charge. Agreed?" We did and Springer yanked off the hood from the leader. I blinked, thinking my eyes were deceiving me: Hayden King scowled up at us!

"I'll be damned!" Springer declared. "We sure hit the jackpot. It's the ol' man hisself." Sarcastically, he added, "Y'all musta been kidnapped and forced to join this party tonight, huh, *Mr.* King?" More cussing was his answer.

Torch-man was next and his uncovering made us all grin: Tex Morgan! "Too good to be true, almost like we'd set the whole thing up ourselves," laughed Decker.

Joining in the laughter, Springer said, "Reckon now he *and* King'll need that fancy lawyer once more, maybe a whole passel of 'em." Tex had enough energy for another outburst of cussing before he started moaning again.

The unmasking of the rest got on quickly and bared familiar faces to most of us since they were locals. The last three had special meaning: two were the youngsters I had arrested earlier. They were, in fact, the sons of the worried fathers whose homes I had previously visited after those same arrests. Guess our combined warnings had fallen on deaf ears.

The final unveiling was icing on the cake: Wade King! Even in the moon's dim light, I could read pure contempt on his face and he sure was uppity. Looking over at his father, then back to us, he snarled, "Y'all will pay fer this. My pappy owns this hick-town and the whole county. Right quick none of ya will have a job and some of ya will be in jail yerselves." He turned and spat at the feet of both Chief and Darius. *Bad move.* Darius reacted to this defiance with a powerful right cross that knocked Wade horizontal like his dad. There were satisfied grins all around from his captors.

Thanks to Wade's threat, we all understood there was a big problem ahead of us. Springer acted first ordering Chief and Darius to guard the prisoners while motioning the rest of us over for a quick confab. "Listen, we've gotta toe the line 'xactly 'cause we don't need another 'failure of justice.' Wade's right, his pappy has power and influence in these parts. Ain't got much time. What can we do?"

"Move 'em to another county," suggested Decker.

"Ain't sure that'd work," replied Springer. "Hayden's ranch spills over into two other counties fer one thing. And then there's the legal problem. Not sure how tough the law is in Texas on the Klan. Pretty weak, I'm bettin'."

"Gotta do somethin'," I said. "This might be our last chance to get some justice."

"Damn straight," agreed Springer. "Here's what I'm thinkin'. Let's house 'em overnight in jail. We'll take 'em to the train station in the mornin' and escort 'em to the Marshal's office in Laredo."

"Why the Marshal's?" I asked.

"'Cause it'll make this case federal and then a federal prosecutor can throw charges at 'em in their court, under the 1871 Anti-Klan Act."

"Sounds like it might work," I said. "Take it out of local, even state courts. What do the rest of ya think?" Everyone agreed and it was settled.

Rounding up our prisoners, we had to decide what to do with the wounded men. The best solution was to have Decker and me drive them to the clinic and have Nancy get to work. Healthy enough, they'd be joining the others on the train, otherwise off to the hospital. We all knew the latter would give Big Daddy time to rally his forces and cause serious trouble.

"Nancy'll do her best," I said. "Sure wish John was 'round but he ain't comin' back this weekend." John and Nancy were a better combination than Ted and Nancy, I knew, as Decker and I talked over how to move the wounded men to the clinic. Decker ended up riding back to the station to borrow the Rangers' truck.

Decker stood guard later as I helped each man into the examining room. We'd tipped off Nancy by phone that we were coming and she was there waiting for us. Maybe she could come up with another "miracle" to avoid a trip to Brownsville.

Her first words were encouraging: "I found clean entrance and exit wounds on both men. That's good news."

"And the bad news?" I asked, fearing the worst.

"The usual, infection and internal bleedin'. Y'all did nice work stoppin' the bleedin', Ted. And ya had clean, white sheets to bandage 'em. Just let me clean the wounds, close 'em with a few stitches, and apply some new bandages. Y'all know they should visit a hospital real soon, don't ya?"

"I hear ya. I'm sure they have a good one in Laredo."

"Laredo? What's goin' on?"

Decker told her the rest of the story, the part about the best location and court to guarantee a fair trial. She saw the wisdom of our plan, yet still worried about the condition of her patients. "That's a pretty long and bumpy ride to Laredo. Hate to see either of these gentlemen die along the way." *That would not be good.*

Both patients came 'round as I talked to Nancy. I figured it might be the "Laredo" part because as Nancy finished up her patchwork, Big Daddy recovered enough to launch into another blue streak of cussing. Prim and proper Nancy brought it to a close by pinching his ear so hard that he cried out. Her response was to apply more pressure. "Don't cotton to such foul language, mister. Not here, not anywhere." He pulled away leaving blood dripping onto his shoulder.

Unfortunately for us, he soon was complaining about us lawmen taking away his legal rights. Demanding to call his lawyer, he kept going on until Decker stepped forward. "Shut the hell up, King. Y'all can call him in Laredo. Keep this bellyachin' goin' and y'all will need a few more stitches on yer noggin'."

He did shut up at that. So did Tex, who had plainly been watching the whole spectacle only occasionally offering a favorable word for his boss.

"All done, Nancy?" I asked.

"All I can do. Where y'all takin' 'em now?"

"To the Ranger station," Decker answered.

"Try to avoid hittin' bumps along the way."

"You bet. Thanks fer everythin'."

Driving to the station, Decker managed to hit a few bumps. At the jail, we put them in separate cells. Big Daddy commandeered a cot while Tex was forced to rest on his backside on the floor. I stayed around long enough to notice the Rangers were getting real upset with the swearing and threats from their prisoners. As I left, Collins was hoisting a bucket of water and heaving its contents into Tex's cell. The loud protests that followed ended at once when he lifted a second one.

What a day, and what a night! I was exhausted. Late the next morning, I stumbled into the kitchen, wolfed down mom's breakfast, and hurried to the Ranger station to help transfer the prisoners to the depot. To my surprise, they'd already left.

"Rangers and Decker couldn't tolerate the whinin' any longer and they left early," announced Betty "

Springer was threatenin' to shoot one of 'em if they didn't shut up."

"Sounds like the captain, "I replied, running out the door heading for the depot. The lawmen had them herded together in a small side room. The prisoners were surprisingly hushed up. *Had Springer carried out his threat or at least clobbered someone?* Then I saw the real reason: off in a corner Collins was holding a fire hose, one hand on the lever. It wasn't long before I wanted him to use it. The warm, cramped quarters and unwashed men made for some powerful stink, so bad I was forced to leave to get a breath of fresh air. Standing on the platform, I heard a train whistle. Good news: The Laredo train was arriving early. The prisoners were prodded onto the platform, soon loaded, and with three Rangers providing guard duty, the train pulled away. It would be a long day for the weary guards even without "accidents" along the way.

For the next two days, Decker and I would have to carry out our deputy duties as well as cover for the Rangers. Double duty meant not much time for the store, or the clinic, or hanging out with Anne, for that matter. And not much time for sleep, I figured, as we rode off to begin the first day's patrol. Bouncing along, I dreamed I was back in west Texas working on Archer's oil rig. Hard work, but rewarding.... And mostly peaceful. The good ol' days!

CHAPTER FIFTEEN

COMPLICATIONS

Toby listened with interest as customers discussed the lingering effects of the drought on agriculture. "In good years I could even plant some cotton," said Dallas Young. "A bit of rain and some irrigation from the river was enough for a crop. Now, even grain and vegetables are in bad shape. Wish we had other ways to make a livin'." Silence followed until Lucas Harper added, "We have to import cattle feed from Louisiana. Our ranch might not survive much longer." Walking back to the kitchen, Toby heard Travis Robinson say, "Damn shame there ain't no oil bein' discovered in these parts. What a blessin' that would be."

IT WAS EARLY MARCH AND I had been avoiding contact with a very angry reporter for several days. My luck ran out on a Tuesday when Jenkins found me at the Ranger station preparing for the day's patrol. I was alone with Betty. "Finally, the man himself," snorted Jenkins. "Thought we had agreed, Ted, 'bout me helpin' to catch those Klan fellas. Even rustled up a few names for ya, possible members of the local KKK chapter. Then, y'all went and nabbed 'em and sent 'em off without a holler in my direction. Mighty disappointin'."

Trapped! All I could say was, "Listen, Lloyd, it all happened so fast that we didn't muster anyone outside our small inner circle. No other reporters, that's fer sure."

"Well, I'm here now and want my interview. Those King fellas have been paroled and are back in the county. They're eager to tell their side of the story. Thought I should give y'all the first shot. Dog ya all day if ya refuse. And I want some questions answered 'bout that circus tragedy and the bank robbery while we're at it."

"Is that all?" I asked, fearing the worst.

"No, I also want to interview those folks who stopped that bandit raid last year. Perhaps a Ranger or two and your cousin. We've been over this before."

Sighing, I replied, "And I've told ya before it's a longshot. But I'll speak to 'em again. Can't promise anythin'." I decided not to joke about Springer maybe shooting him to avoid his interview. And I was glad he didn't mention Decker, who I knew wouldn't give him the time of day.

I looked out the window and saw the head deputy riding up. Turning to Betty with a pleading expression, I said, "Go outside and tell Captain Decker that I'm with Mr. Jenkins and will be delayed a bit. I'll catch up with him later." Betty knew what was happening and hustled outside to warn Decker away.

"Wait!" said Jenkins. "Wouldn't it be better to include him in the interview?"

"Better let me break the news to him first," I replied, knowing how he'd react.

"Fine for now. Let's get to work." And we did for nearly an hour. I tried to downplay my role in everything and provide few news worthy descriptions of the of others' actions. He was clearly unhappy with my answers and kept probing, trying to squeeze more details from me. He finally sighed and gave up. As he looked over his notes, I was surprised at how many pages he'd actually written.

Hoping for a delay, I said, "Lloyd, why not hold off on writin' yer story 'til ya talk to Decker and the Rangers since they're really the men of action."

"Uh-huh. But I gotta get somethin' fast to my editor. He's been badgerin' me for quite some time." *Dag nab it!* I knew I'd be in trouble with my fellow lawmen when his "expanded" story hit the streets.

I tipped off the three lawmen to Jenkins' intentions later that day. Their answer was an icy stare. At least no one took a shot at *me*. The concocted story appeared on the front page of the Sunday edition. The following week I got the "cold shoulder" from all three. Those were the worst days on patrol since I'd pinned on my badge. At least Betty kept talking to me.

On April 2, a letter arrived for me mailed from Midland. Praying it wasn't bad news about Phil Archer or one of his roustabouts, I tore it open and speed-read it. Nothing bad but was it out of the blue! It *was* from Archer and boiled down to three main points: 1) harsh and heavy debt had forced him to sell most of his equipment, 2) after paying his creditors, he had just enough money to dig one more hole in the ground, and 3) he wanted it to be in my county, in fact, close to Los Indios. I couldn't believe my eyes and re-read the letter several times. This had to be a mistake! There were also two short postscripts. The first one said he'd be around in a few days, the second was a plea for me to work with him again, as one of his foremost roustabouts. *Me, a roustabout again?*

I knew I had a bunch of people to share this news with, starting with Anne. Following Wednesday night's prayer meeting, I pulled her aside. Rather than trying to explain the letter, I let her read it. She did, twice.

"Glory be! This is unexpected. I know you well enough to guess you're probably interested, right?"

"Darn tootin'! But I've got a passel of work already with my deputy duties, workin' at the store, and every now and then supportin' ya at the clinic, of course."

"The clinic can probably survive without you," she laughed. "But I can see some problems coming up with Decker and maybe your parents."

"Me too. Most likely somethin' will work out with Decker, long as I can give him a half-day. And it's not the store hours that's the biggest hitch in all this."

"What is then?"

"If Archer wants a long-term commitment, beyond the summer, I mean, my parents will be all riled up."

"They want you back in college, don't they?"

"Sure do. They have their hearts set on it. Had fits with me takin' two semesters off from A & M."

"What will you do?"

"Well, Archer'll be here soon and John's comin' home this weekend. I'll run everythin' past him. 'Preciate yer prayers, sweetie."

"I'll be sending then up every day, Mr. Townley." Since we were alone, she said one right then and there. It made me feel a whole lot better.

The Rangers and Decker met me for breakfast on Friday. After a few stiff-jawed moments, I shared the news about Archer's plans to drill for oil in our neck of the woods and his wanting me to work for him, at least part-time. Since I didn't really work for the Rangers, they didn't seem concerned about my giving up police work. Decker, though, was a bit more put out. "Went to bat fer ya, son," he said, clearly disappointed. "Ain't got no replacement yet fer Morgan. Now y'all might cut back. Need ya more than ever these days, 'specially since those King rascals are out on bail. 'Spect trouble from 'em at some point."

"I think I can still find the hours fer ya. In fact, that's my promise to ya."

Decker took me at my word and we spent the morning on patrol. We were soon riding partners once again.

All that was on the front burner now was a confab with John. That and finding out what Archer had in mind for work.

After Friday night's dinner, I took Anne along with me to talk with John. Heather was with John, so I suggested they read Archer's letter, and we waited for their reactions. Heather admitted it would be nice to see Archer again but was skeptical about drilling for oil in these parts. "A few holes have been sunk since Spindletop in 1901. So far, no success. They've found water which makes farmers and ranchers happy, but no 'black gold' has sprung up."

John was more encouraging, mostly because he knew I had enjoyed being in the oil fields last summer. "You're pretty busy, cousin. Can you hold something else down at this point?"

"I'm afixin' to ask my parents 'bout not workin' at the store. Haven't been all that steady at it, anyway. How do ya think my parents will take that notion?"

"Anyone else who could help at the store?" John asked.

"I'm hopin' that Toby can take my place. Haven't asked him yet but he's got the know-how and sure would be happy fer the extra money. Bet he jumps at the chance."

"Good idea," said Anne. "Ted and I have also talked over his going back to college. The Townleys will hold him to it."

"I think you're right," Heather joined in. "Can you make such a commitment?"

I said that I could and I meant it. John spoke up again. "I see another problem on the horizon, War in Europe! Got a chance to read a newspaper on the train. Congress just declared war against Germany. President Wilson is asking for volunteers. You gonna be one of them, Ted?"

"Reckon I ain't thinkin' all that much 'bout it. Probly should though. It's been big news fer months."

"How would your parents feel about y'all joining up?" asked John.

"Oh…they'd rather have me back at A & M fer sure."

"I think you're right," John said. "Maybe it won't come to anything for you if enough volunteers step forward."

"That's my prayer," Anne said. "I love my country but I'd rather see Ted stay put."

A thought struck me; what about John's future and his medical training? When confronted, he mentioned changes were already being made to graduate him and others as early as the fall. "Evening classes are being added and some lectures are being dropped. And summer recess will be shortened."

John's outline for what was ahead, especially about summer, made Heather grow pale. She recovered quickly saying, "Actually, John talked to me earlier about these developments. And there's good news – there's a small break in mid-July. We're now planning to have the wedding then."

"I'm just so happy you set a date," said a beaming Anne. "We've made some 'high-priority' decisions about the wedding and we'll be ready for a July date."

I said, "Reckon it's settled. Let's get these two lovebirds hitched in July. And thanks fer meetin' with me. I'll run everythin' by my parents tomorrow. Y'all sure make me realize I'm blessed to have such good friends."

I joined Anne Saturday morning for prayer and a little more support. She gave me the confidence I needed to break the news to my parents. What a gal!

My parents went for practically everything I brought up: letting Toby work in my place at the store, sticking to my work with Decker while giving Archer a few hours a day, and promising to go back to college in the fall. They really went for the last point. That left only the war. They weren't surprised at the war declaration but were troubled about my volunteering, quickly or perhaps ever. Dad summed it up best. "We're all patriots 'round here, yet not everyone needs to be a soldier. We'll need plenty of help on the home front now that America's gotten into the war. Surely they'll make exceptions for people like you, son, don't ya think?"

"Guess we'll have to see. Won't even be needed if a lot of young men sign up. Figure plenty of Texans will be eager to volunteer."

Mom sighed and said, "I know it sounds selfish but that'll be my prayer. Please, God, keep my son here where he can serve you best."

We had a group-hug before I set off to see Toby and find out if he liked my idea. I found him at the café and made my pitch during a brief break in his schedule. He jumped at the opportunity. "This is a big favor to me, Mr. Ted. 'Preciate it. I'll work awful hard fer yer folks. Won't let 'em down."

"I know ya won't, Toby," I said. We shook hands and I watched him return to work.

Whatever I was doing for the rest of the weekend didn't keep me from mentally preparing for Archer's arrival Monday morning: men and supplies showing up before noon, the telegram said. I couldn't wait. *Was I a better roustabout than a deputy sheriff?*

Waiting for Archer's arrival, Decker and I skipped our regular patrol and were having coffee in the café when the caravan pulled into town mid-morning: four banged-up, rusty trucks and perhaps a dozen men, some of whom were familiar: Bud Tyler, Don Evans, Slim Jordan and "Stinky" Clyde. I tried to stay upwind of the latter as I greeted everyone. Archer, of course, greeted me with a bear hug, almost as if I was a long-lost son or something. Archer knew Decker from last summer, so as they shook hands, he said, "Glad to see ya, Captain. Guess your Ranger days are behind ya if that deputy badge is genuine."

"It is, Phil, and Ted here also has a badge, as y'all can see. Need his help most days so y'all better not keep him too busy diggin' that hole."

"I'm sure he'll find some time for y'all too, Deputy. What 'bout yourself?" Decker snorted and turned away.

I said, "Not many men with ya, Mr. Archer. What gives?"

"Money's short so I couldn't bring the whole crew. Even lost some on the trip here."

"Lost?"

"Yup. Several are joinin' up, includin' a couple of my best. Like Joe Taylor and Junior White. Fixin' to kill some Krauts, I reckon. All the more reason to nail ya down, Ted. Y'all made up your mind?"

"Uh-huh. I can work half a day fer ya. At least 'til the fall, then it's back to college fer me."

"'Preciate it. Can ya round up any more for me?"

"I'll spread the word. People need the money, that's fer sure. Y'all *will* be payin' 'em, right?"

"Damn straight," he said with conviction though he wouldn't make eye contact with me, which made me a tad uneasy.

Changing the subject, I asked, "Why here, Mr. Archer? No wildcatters have had any luck here yet."

"Got me a geologist friend who swears it's nearby. Showed me his calculations he did a short while ago. I'm puttin' my trust in him anyways."

"Sure hope he's right. When do y'all plan to start?"

"Today, Ted. Can't have any more grass growin' under us." *Today?*

"But do ya have a site picked out? And what 'bout all the legal papers?"

"Yup, to both your questions. It's a piece of unoccupied land north of town. No one claims it. Squatter's been livin' there in a rundown shack, I hear. Headin' there right now." *A shack north of town on unclaimed land? Sounded awfully familiar.*

"Who arranged it all fer ya?" I asked, hoping to hear an unfamiliar name.

"Hayden King. Big name in these parts, I've been told. Ever heard of the name?"

Hayden King! I knew a headache wasn't far away. Decker had rejoined us and started to speak, but I stopped him with a warning look and said, "Have heard that name from time to time, Mr. Archer. I'll fill ya in later."

"Mr. King wants only one-third of the profits which I think is fair. Promises to advance me some money in the next few days." Don't hold your breath, I thought to myself.

Shifting the conversation away from Hayden King, I pointed out an unfamiliar face in the background and asked who he was. Archer waved him over and introduced us to Thomas Cramer. Smiling broadly, Archer declared, "Reason I'm so all fired up 'bout constructin' our rig in a jiffy is Thomas here. He's the best carpenter I've ever known. Got the wood, the nails, and the master. Rig oughta be up by week's end."

The short and wiry man, with a woodworker's gnarled hands, shook his head slightly and said, "That might be a bit hasty, Boss. Gotta make sure it's sturdy enough to support the weight of the drill 'fore we start poundin' the ground."

"Know ya can do it, Thomas. Let's get on out there and start work. Mr. King has kindly marked off several spots for us to see if they fit. Can ya join us today, Ted?"

"Sure 'nuff, in the afternoon. Right now, I'll ask 'round and see if I can hustle up a few extra men fer ya."

Archer slapped me on the back and ordered everyone back to the trucks. Shortly, all I could see was the dust they'd kicked up as they lumbered out of town.

The rest of the morning I spent rounding up anyone who was interested in picking up some extra hours of manual labor. Two were: Diego Trevino, the gas station attendant, and Pablo Reyes, who had a part-time job at the feed store. I told them to get out to the site Tuesday morning and talk to Phil Archer. I figured I'd done my best and the rest of the hiring was someone else's business.

I caught up with Archer as he was finishing lunch, barking orders with a mouthful of food. Ignoring me at first, he suddenly turned and sprayed food all over me as he shouted, "Glad you're here son. Havin' trouble with a couple of lazy fellas. Maybe they'll listen up better to y'all."

"Not likely but let's talk first 'bout Hayden King." I quickly gave him the lowdown, leaving little to the imagination. Finished, he sighed heavily and said, "I was afeared it might be too good to be true. Sounds like I've been hoodwinked. Reckon ya think he won't come through with the money and try to grab more'n thirty percent if we tap a gusher."

"Has he opened his pockets fer y'all?"

"Not really. Just a few hundred. Probably just to hook me."

"Did y'all sign any papers with him?"

"Yup, through the mail."

"Read 'em closely?"

"Nah, didn't have the time."

"'Fraid y'all are in a heap of trouble then, Mr. Archer. Better have a lawyer look at those. I'll have dad steer ya to one."

"Thanks. Feel kinda foolish right now." He did look pretty embarrassed. Wouldn't meet my gaze. He right quick forgot that crossroad as he grabbed my arm and pulled me toward the crew saying, "Thinkin' of puttin' y'all in charge, son. Kinda like my second-in-command. Interested?"

"Others have done this rodeo a whole lot more'n me, Mr. Archer."

"Not worried 'bout it. Y'all have the energy and the crew learned to like ya last summer. They're tired of me yellin' at 'em. Give it a shot."

"Well, y'all can hang yer hat on me doin' my best." He smiled at my remark, pointed to the slackers in particular, and left me to deal with their laziness.

No one had a bone to pick with my orders, so they knocked off the rig's base in nothing flat. The rig was reaching higher by mid-week, but I was getting spooked. Despite Thomas' top-notch work, mistakes were being made. Too few nails were being used and the planking seemed weaker than required. Compared to the rigs in Midland, this one was flimsy at best. I felt reluctant to bring it up, but by Thursday afternoon I could no longer keep quiet.

"Thomas, can I bend yer ear?" I said soon after the crew had finished lunch. "I have a few issues to raise with y'all."

"Ya don't have to say nuthin', Ted. I've seen how closely you've been watchin' me and the crew pound this rig together. Boss didn't have the money to buy fit materials and he's determined to finish this weekend. Think it'll hold but I ain't spendin' any more time at the top than necessary."

"Sorry that he put ya, and all of us, in this predicament. Is it worth my time to open this can of worms with Archer?"

"Not far as I can see. If you're a prayin' man, though, keep pleadin' up yonder."

"Well... I'll sure pray and have a bunch of others join me."

His words were plainly discouraging. The nightmare of Midland flashed through my mind. A collapsing rig had caused so many injuries, including a few deaths. That tragedy was the result of sabotage. This disaster was clearly made by men – and avoidable.

Before heading back to work, Thomas added, "Guess I should tell ya why some of us are workin' harder than others. Archer left west Texas with some debts not paid and not a whole lot of cash in his pocket. He hasn't been able to pay all of us. Only myself and three others got paid this past month. Men are gettin' angrier every day. Hope y'all can keep the lid on. Sorry to tell ya all this bad news."

"That sure explains a lot. It's serious 'nuff fer me to bring these hitches up to Archer."

It was late Thursday afternoon before that happened. He merely shrugged, told me he'd handle it, and went back to work. More bad news, I feared, leaving at dusk to meet Anne and others – my "whole bunch" of praying friends.

Come Friday afternoon and who should show his face at the rig site: Hayden King. Decker also was around when King arrived in his chauffeur- driven limousine. We all sized up each other with frowns. About then, Archer came out of the shack – his temporary office – and prevented any further fireworks.

With alarm, Archer said, "Guess y'all know each other already. Let's keep the conversation friendly, gentlemen."

Ignoring Archer, Hayden walked over to us and hissed, "You two ain't welcome here. Get out! Now!" Decker tapped his holster. I touched his gun hand to keep him from making a big mistake.

"Settle down, fellas," begged Archer. "Everyone's welcome here. What can I do for ya, Mr. King?"

Again ignoring Archer, King continued, "This is my outfit, Deputies. And this is my land."

"Hang on, Mr. King. Y'all ain't got the majority interest in this rig, and I've been told this land don't belong to no one."

"Not for long," growled King, grinning confidently. "I'll have my attorney make an offer soon as I get back to town."

Decker spat, "I reckon Mr. Archer can invite me anytime, Hayden. And Ted is working fer Mr. Archer. So even ownership won't work fer ya as I see it."

"We'll see 'bout that," shouted King as he set off for the shack waving for Archer to follow him.

Listening from a distance as Hayden yelled at Archer, I asked Decker if maybe we should find someone to buy the land first. That would solve some of our problems.

"Right fine idea," he said. "Maybe yer dad can find someone to help us out."

"I'll ask him tonight." I did, later that evening, and he said he would sound out several other businessmen in the area.

"It might not be an issue, though," said Dad. "Rumor has it that Hayden's got troubles. The drought caused him to borrow money to get his grain from as far away as Louisiana. Besides, he's facin' some hefty legal fees from his future trial in Laredo. He's probly bluffin' 'bout buyin' that land."

"Hope so. Archer don't need any more distractions right now. Thanks, Dad, fer checking everythin' out fer us."

Decker had given me Saturday off for full-time work at the site, so I went out early in the morning to see what everyone hoped would be a completed rig. Coming into sight, it appeared that only a few feet of support beams remained to be put in place. Maybe he'd make it in time, I thought, as I watched Archer gaze up with pride at his nearly finished creation. Thomas started to climb up the scaffold with some last supplies when Archer called out, "Wait, let me do it. I ain't a stranger to hammer and nails."

"You sure?" asked Thomas. "Nearly forty feet to the top. Ain't scared of heights are ya?"

"Nah, gone up plenty of times."

Up he climbed, soon pounding away like a master carpenter. Thomas shook his head and said, "He's bein' a bit careless up there. See how the scaffold is shakin' a little?"

I did and held my breath. Thomas dashed over to the scaffold waving others to join him. They took up positions at all four corners and pushed against the structure to keep it firm. After a few scary moments, Archer shouted down, "That's the last of the nails, men. We did it! Got it up in a week! By next week we'll have the puller, drill and engine ready to go."

Holding up his arms, he waved them in triumph, doing a little jig to show all how happy he was. From the ground I joined several men in giving him three cheers. Taking off his hat, he threw it off with a whoop then started down. He'd made it halfway when we heard a loud, snapping noise. Everyone froze in place. Then came more splintering sounds followed by: the collapse! Not just the scaffold but the entire rig. As it flew apart, some large chunks struck the scaffold, which caused it to teeter and lean, farther and farther, until it fell over on its side. Luckily, Archer had the cool headedness to leap for his life before everything collapsed on top of him. It all happened in a flash yet seemingly in slow motion.

Before the dust had settled, we all rushed to where Archer had landed and disappeared. Thinking that twenty feet was better than forty, I prayed that he wasn't seriously injured.

We found him unconscious on the ground with legs bent in unnatural ways. We carefully rolled him onto his back and checked for any obvious injuries. Removing shoes and socks and cutting away his trousers, we found some: a badly fractured right leg and two shattered ankles. Fearing spinal damage, I told Don Evans to keep his head stock-still. On the whole, Archer's condition wasn't good. Worried glances all around as we tried to deal with our own shock staring down at the broken man. I finally said, "Don, doesn't Archer have a stretcher somewhere?"

"Yessir, over there in the shack."

"Get it right quick and we'll move him by truck to the clinic. My cousin's in town this weekend. He'll know what to do."

The stretcher arrived and we carefully placed Archer on it and lifted it into the bed of the truck. Decker had shown up at some point during all the excitement, and I asked him to join me on the ride to the clinic.

There had been no time to warn John we were coming, so when we arrived, he was up to his neck with patients. Quickly noting Archer's condition, he made him his first concern. John pulled Nancy aside and told her to do her best with the other patients until he could rejoin her. Decker and I carried the stretcher into the examining room, put Archer on the table, and stepped away to watch John work. Observing was only part of my job, I discovered, when John motioned me over to stand across from him and be his "assistant."

"Not much I can do with him," John declared after checking over the mangled wildcatter. "I'll clean the wounds but swelling has already begun and he'll need an experienced doctor to properly set the bones. Further, there may be damage to his pelvis or spinal column. That requires an orthopedic surgeon. Doc Wilbur can find someone to do the job in Brownsville. This man should be moved soon, especially if he doesn't regain consciousness."

I said, "Looks bad, don't it?"

"Yeah, he won't be working on a rig any time in the near future."

"Ain't gotta rig anyway. Whole thing is gone."

At that point some commotion in the waiting room got Decker's attention and he went to investigate. Bursting back in moments later, he growled, "That damn Jenkins is here demandin' an interview 'bout today's incident. I ain't speakin' to him, Ted. Period."

Not again! Making a spur of the moment decision, I said, "Here's what we'll do. I'll talk to him and maybe John too, if he's willin'. Y'all take Archer to Brownsville. How's that sound?"

"Perfect. When can I leave?"

John answered, "In a few minutes. Have someone else drive and you sit by his side. Use your judgment about telling him about his future. Understand?"

"Yup. Won't give him any false hope."

Decker and I carried Archer back to the truck. That left me to deal with the nagging reporter and the cousin who wasn't looking forward to being interviewed. I buttered up Jenkins by telling him he might just swing two interviews.

Before letting in Jenkins, I met briefly with John and he summed it up nicely by saying, "Jenkins will start with the rig but quickly move to other topics – like last summer's bandit raid. You know that, right?"

"Uh-huh, but he'll never give up. Might as well get it over with. Don't want him showin' up in Houston, do ya? Just be as hazy as possible when answerin'."

"Fine!" he said in disgust. "Feel like punching you though. But I don't want my best man showing up with a broken jaw."

"Me either. Let me talk to him first. That'll give ya time to collect yer thoughts."

I led Jenkins outside and gave him the lowdown on the rig collapsing, playing up it was likely an accident. I didn't want to put Thomas Cramer in trouble. It truly wasn't his fault anyway. Jenkins believed it would make a surefire good story, probably even the front page. He thanked me and went back inside to grill my cousin.

I helped Nancy for a while then went back outside to pace back and forth until John's ordeal was over. Jenkins came out as the sun was setting, walked up to me and said,

"Worst interview I ever attempted. Not enough details to fill a shot glass. Look here at my notes."

I glimpsed at his note pad. Two pages of scribbling, pretty slim for all the time they'd spent together. I was holding back a smile when he added, "Your cousin said I'd better check with the Rangers for the complete picture. Told him chances were slim to none since I'd been trying to find 'em and sit 'em down for months."

"Well, write up what ya got. Maybe yer editor will print it."

"Doubt it, but I'll sure give it a try." He left without shaking my hand. I wondered if this was the last time our paths would cross.

John and I met with our gals later that night to talk about what would happen now that Archer's plans had gone up in dust. We decided to draw in others and reach a decision Sunday afternoon. After church and lunch, we met with Decker and the Rangers, together with Bud Tyler, Don Evans, and Thomas. The decision was easy when it came down to it. Archer had to give up the project. "Most of the men have left already," said Bud. "Off to the war or huntin' for work with other wildcatters. Same for me and Don. Boss will be beat but we ain't got no choice."

So that was it. My roustabout days were over. For now, I reckoned, I'd work full-time alongside Decker, if he'd have me. Patrols had more excitement than sweeping and stocking shelves. When approached, Decker liked the idea, even promised to give me a say in picking out one or two future deputies. Getting back to being a lawman would suit me fine.

The next two weeks were mostly routine: catching some thieves, nabbing some vandals, helping some old ladies across the street. Our most rousing activity was following reports of the Klan trial in Laredo. It lasted nearly two weeks, and when the verdict arrived, Decker and the Rangers took it better than I did. I was furious.

Springer said, "Thought that might come to pass, Ted. Didn't bring it up before but even in a federal courtroom, the jury would be average Texans. Combine that with fancy lawyerin' and 'reasonable doubt' is what y'all get. Ain't givin' up yet on bringin' 'em to justice down the road."

I stewed for several days before getting back to normal. Anne helped. Really helped, if you get my drift.

On May 18, we heard some news that didn't bode well. Congress had passed the Selective Service Act, the first draft since the Civil War. It seemed not as many men had signed up as the government had expected. My parents were more worried than I and read any newspaper article down to the fine print. It was college for me, not being hunkered down in a moldy European trench. Dad struck what he thought was pay dirt in Houston's Sunday paper. "There are a few exemptions, 'Essential occupation' is one category. Maybe that's your road back to college, son."

"How so? College ain't an occupation in the usual sense."

"I know but petroleum engineerin' might be. That's your major. Bet A & M will go to bat for its students, at least some of 'em."

"Maybe. How will I find out?"

"Start writin' to 'em. It'll take some time to get it all figured out. It's your best chance far as I can see."

"I'll get a letter off tomorrow." I did and thus began my nervous wait for an answer. How long would it take?

On June 1, Anne and Heather showed up early in the morning, both flushed and out of breath. "Sorry," Heather said, "but we ran over to let you know that John just called with news that he's received a letter from Mexico, from Olivia, a friend from last summer."

"She in some kind of trouble?" I asked.

"I don't think so but he says her letter has some disturbing news. He's arriving tonight and will come straight here from the depot. He wants us all to get together, including your parents, Decker, Darius, and the Rangers."

"He didn't give ya a hint 'bout its contents?"

"No, and I sure did try."

"What d'ya think, Anne?"

"It's a mystery to me. I don't know Olivia, of course, but John's not wanting to let Heather in on the news is unusual. We're both on edge about what it means."

"Me too," I said. "We'll get everyone together and find out soon 'nuff, I reckon."

I wondered what was going on as we went our separate ways for another day of work. *Was it more trouble ahead?*

CHAPTER SIXTEEN

THE LETTER

Toby was sitting at the depot on Friday night waiting for the train to pull in. He loved trains, riding them or even something as simple as watching them pulling in and out of the station. That night was unusual because the Townleys had closed the store and dashed home for a special get-together. Just as the train started to pull in, Mr. Ted arrived with his girlfriend and Miss Heather. Must mean Mr. John's home this weekend. Sure enough, John was the first to step down and greet everyone, in a somewhat serious mood, he thought. Turning to leave, they spotted him, smiled, waved, and walked right past him. Strange. That was the quickest greeting he'd ever received. They seemed distracted. Toby wondered what was going on before setting off for home.

A LL THREE OF US TRIED to pry some news out of John as we walked home. No luck. Said he wanted to wait until later at the get-together. "Come on, sweetie, give us a hint," Heather pleaded. Again, without success. This silent treatment was very unusual since he was putty in her hands. Must really be serious, I reckoned. What was the big secret?

Mom, as always, had some snacks prepared for us. We chowed down as both parents also tried, unsuccessfully, to get John talking. We were all getting spooked because he sure was holding back something.

John tried to take our minds off the mystery by telling some more humorous stories from medical school. One student, he said, fainted when a cadaver was cut open. Not uncommon, but this time it wasn't the sole female, rather, a big muscular male who looked like a Longhorn wrestler. That got a few chuckles. Most of us also laughed, if a bit uneasily, at his second story. This one involved a photograph showing up around campus of a few of last year's graduates celebrating: at a lake, clearly drunk as a skunk, smoking huge cigars, and without a stitch on. Mom didn't laugh at this story. Soon all of our small group had arrived: both Rangers, Decker, Chief, and Darius. Darius had already proved his worth at the Klan fray so he was "on our side" now. The group polished off mom's snacks, and while finishing our drinks John finally turned to my parents and said, "Please ask Diane to leave the room. She shouldn't have to hear what I'm about to say." Diane, of course, was ruffled by her cousin's comment.

"I'm sixteen and can handle anythin'," she nearly shouted.

John wasn't cowed at all, though for a moment it seemed my parents were. Dad finally cleared his throat and said, "Off to your room, young lady. We'll stand behind his request." I feared she wouldn't obey, but she did, knocking over her chair in sulky protest as she stomped away. Glancing down

224

the hallway, however, I noticed her door remained slightly ajar.

Mom found enough chairs to have us all sit around the dining room table where we watched John take some sheets of paper from his pocket. "I received this letter two days ago form Olivia Echeverria, the young Mexican lady we helped last summer. Some of you might remember we 'patched up' her older brother, Eduardo, and later had some trouble with Luis, her younger brother. Both encounters, thankfully, ended up all right. Olivia was very grateful, thus the reason for the letter. I'll pass it around but it would be easier if I summed it up for you. As y'all can probably guess it *is* bad news. The long and short of it, Olivia is genuinely worried another raid is being planned. Her source is Luis, and she believes what he says is accurate. This raid, though, is not like last year's large, two-pronged attempt to return Texas and the Southwest to Mexican control. The 'Plan of San Antonio' was the name given to that failed invasion. This new one, rather, is a small-scale, focused attack. Luis says this is a revenge raid against me and those closest to me for stopping the previous raid. That means they're also after Springer and Collins as well as my uncle and aunt … and Heather."

Both fuming Rangers started to speak, but John cut them short by adding, "Wait a second. Let me finish and then you can speak your piece. According to Luis, a small group of raiders plans to slip across the Rio Grande soon to locate and kill or kidnap everyone on their list. That's why I rushed down here. It's already taken Olivia's letter two weeks to reach me. I know we all would have preferred more time to prepare for battle."

"Y'all done, John?" asked Springer, red-faced, teeth grinding.

"Not quite. Luis also said this group's leader was a survivor of last summer's raid, meaning he's a faithful follower of Pancho Villa and his ilk. Name's Montoya, a rotten hombre who's not afraid of blood being spilled. Olivia believes Montoya has already sent spies to our town to figure out the location of the Ranger station and the Townley home. And where both Heather and I live." John's hoarse voice betrayed his feelings about Heather, his future wife.

Hearing this grim prediction of future events, my mother gasped, Heather's face paled and she began to shake. Anne threw her arm around Heather's shoulder to comfort her. My dad seemed short of breath; the Rangers and Decker looked ready to explode; Chief and Darius acted calm, yet I knew they'd be ready for action when the time came. I sided with my fellow lawmen. No way would anyone be allowed to threaten or hurt my family or friends!

John asked everyone to take a deep, calming breath before speaking. During that brief moment, John also comforted Heather. Then the Rangers quickly jumped in with salty language and specific threats. Springer said it best: "We're gonna kill the bastards, sure as hell!" My mom gasped again at this graphic description.

Decker insisted on the killing and added, "And their horses and bury everythin', includin' saddles and weapons, in their Mexican stompin' grounds." Having second thoughts about one point, he immediately said, "Forget 'bout the horses. Ain't killin' any of them fine animals."

Chief volunteered to provide us with an early tip-off by crossing into Mexico and hiding out, hoping to find their whereabouts. "What if they show up at night?" Dad asked. "They might stumble across ya and y'all will be their first victim."

"I know the most likely spot for entrance where the river is shallow. Sleep light. Hobble my horse and rest with arms over his back. He'll hear 'em first and wake me." A native's savvy skills, I felt, sure would be a great help!

Darius spoke up saying he'd do whatever was necessary to protect his new friends. And we all agreed with my dad's input: move his wife and daughter out of town for a few days. "We have friends in Brownsville who'd be happy to put us up for as long as it takes." All at once the bedroom door was flung open and Diane marched right up to us, declaring, "I'm stayin'. Ain't no coward. I'm a Texan and I know how to shoot!"

I was more proud of my sister right then than I'd ever been. Knew it was foolhardy because my parents would never agree to it. But she did remain with us for the rest of the time, and it didn't feel out of place.

Heather and Anne, voices quivering, made it known they were afraid for everyone's safety, and pleaded with us to avoid violence. "Couldn't Mexican authorities step in on our behalf and cut them off before they come across?" asked a hopeful Anne.

"Ain't no authority over there worth spit," blurted Collins. "If they got mixed up in this at all, it'd probly be to join the raiders."

"Well, there's one thing fer sure," I said with conviction. "You two ladies will be bunkin' somewhere else 'til this is settled." My declaration produced murmurs of agreement around the table.

John then announced, "I'm staying to see this through. I've arranged to take off a few days from school, all week if needed. This is mostly my fault, so I'll head up this fight."

"Since John and I are closer than brothers," I said, "where he goes, I go, what he does, I do." The lump forming in my throat kept me from going on.

Brief silence followed as everyone tried to take in all that John had revealed. He then asked the unstated question, "What can we do to stop them, even before they set foot in Texas?"

The answer came from Springer. "Goin' by our past run-ins, I think I know where they're most likely to cross: at the island directly south of town where we found the bandit's weapons last summer."

"That's my hunch too," agreed Chief. "It's the shallowest point of the river. Easy to cross even on foot."

"That's where we oughta set up our defense," Springer continued. "Island has a few trees and bushes and some fair-sized rocks. We can duck down behind 'em and blast the raiders 'fore they reach mid-stream. Olivia's letter says it's a small raidin' party, meanin' if we lay down heavy lead, it'll be over 'fore the smoke clears."

"Y'all should take stock in that plan," said Decker with a devilish grin. "Seen the island but ain't been out there yet. Several of us can check it out in the mornin' and get back to ya."

"We need to get the details down pat," warned John. "Let's meet here tomorrow morning, say 'bout nine. Get everything out in the open and we'll firm up things then and there."

Thinking ahead, Mom said, "What if they come tonight?"

Chief threw out that he'd start his watch that very night. Darius offered to join him, at least for one night. "I don't need much sleep either," he said, as if it wasn't a big deal.

Heather and Anne stayed behind after everyone left. I could tell from the look on their faces they had more to say. So did John and I.

John and Heather walked to another room, leaving me to deal with my very anxious lady. I did my best to calm her fears, to assure her I'd be extra careful. I reminded her that I was under Decker's protective wing. That seemed to ease her fears a bit. Dropping her chin to her chest, she breathed deeply several times. Then she locked her arms around my neck, almost in desperation. Since we were alone, I wasn't concerned about the length of her squeeze or the kiss that followed. She finally pushed back and said, "Your scary adventures never seem to end, Ted. I can't wait for calm to return to your life and ours."

"I'll be fine. Now stop worryin'." I then made the mistake of adding, "If y'all don't, it might drive me to drink." She didn't laugh.

"I'll be praying constantly for you and the others, Ted. As will Heather and your parents. If we can think of other ways to help you, we will. It's a promise."

I wasn't sure what she meant by "other ways" and I didn't want to ask. What I didn't need was to be more worried and distracted myself. As John and I walked our gals back to their apartment, we both took our "hero" actions seriously. We slept on chairs outside their door until early the next morning. Unknown to them, we both were packing small pistols.

CHAPTER SEVENTEEN

REVENGE

It was hard for Toby to keep this customer's coffee warm because he wouldn't remain seated. Every time new people arrived for breakfast, he'd greet them and stand at their table jawing for several minutes. He was a whirlwind of questions, so Toby wasn't surprised to hear him introduce himself as a reporter, a Mr. Jenkins. He was most curious about some sort of raid that might be occurring in the near future, a raid by Mexican bandits. The customers said they hadn't heard a thing, not even a rumor. Once or twice, people referred to a previous raid, but they didn't want to discuss that with a complete stranger. The reporter seemed frustrated. Why was he asking so many locals? Should Toby mention today's goings-on to Mr. Ted?

NOTHING HAD HAPPENED OVER THE weekend. That was good news; it gave us lawmen time to make more detailed plans about using the island as our defensive stronghold.

We wanted to get the lay of the land, so Decker scouted and had some ideas when we all met together Sunday afternoon. After a brief discussion, we made our way to the island. This time by horse; next time we'd have to wade or row because the horses would be too visible to the raiders.

As we stood on the north shore, Decker said, "Over yonder are some fair sized rocks where a couple of men can hide, in case the raiders make it through that obvious strip up aways. What d'ya think?"

"Reckon that won't be necessary," scoffed Springer. "They ain't gonna get through our rain of lead."

"Let's hear Decker's plan 'fore we get too far along," I suggested, hoping to avoid an argument.

We moved south, maybe forty feet, before Decker stopped and said, "Y'all see that little ridge off to the right? A handful can crouch down behind that rise. It's a good blind and we can fire down on 'em."

"Fixin' to place us Rangers up there," Springer declared, pointing to that exact spot. "Collins and me, along with Stevens, will cut 'em to pieces from that vantage point. Todd's been practicin' and gettin' pretty good with a Winchester."

Clearly irritated, Decker coughed and replied, "Well, fine, y'all dig in there. Rest of us can hide off to the left over in that clump of scrub brush. We'll catch 'em in a crossfire. We ain't bad sharpshooters ourselves. Chief grew up shootin', even from underneath a horse at a full gallop. Been trainin' Ted and he's gettin' better all the time."

John piped in, "I can shoot but I'd prefer to let others do it, if you don't mind. Besides, you'll probably need my medical bag more than my shooting."

"Best idea fer a future doctor," I agreed. "Suggest we put John and Darius behind the rocks in the rear as a last line of defense. Darius can bring that shotgun of his. Ain't no one gettin' past that twelve gauge."

We broke into three groups to sort out positions and do some troubleshooting for the expected attack. I chose the biggest scrub brush and dug a small hole to cut down my visible shape and store extra ammunition. I popped up and down several times taking pretend shots at the imaginary attackers. It was good cover, though useless at stopping any return gunfire. We'd better nail them first, I thought, or there might be injured fellas among the defenders.

John showed up during my playacting and laughingly said, "Hit anyone yet?"

"Very funny, cousin. Just gettin' ready fer the real thing."

"Best to be prepared," he said, still in a lighthearted mood. "Listen," he added, "I've been watching the river shore behind us and there's a handful of youngsters following our every move. Is this gonna be a problem?"

"Hope not, yet I'd better go over and chat with 'em."

This time I waded over through the chilly, waist-deep water. I saw the kids laughing at my struggling. Surprisingly, they didn't run away as they saw me getting closer.

"Ain't y'all 'sposed to be in school?" I managed to ask through chattering teeth.

"It's recess, Deputy," said the biggest fella. "And it's only a half-day anyway since it's the last week."

I made a spur of the moment decision and used another "white lie." "Listen, kids, we've had reports of rattlesnakes showin' up out there. Probly planted by some mean-spirited Mexicans tryin' to scare us. Anyhow, we're clearin' 'em out. Best to stay away, far away, fer the next few weeks. Understand?"

They looked scared enough to stay away, though they *were* Texans, so I couldn't be sure. I waded back over as fast as I could, shared my story with the others, and we took turns blasting away, playacting getting rid of the rattlesnakes.

By mid-afternoon we were all confident that we were tolerably able to ward off any small-scale raid. Everyone returned to the mainland, except Chief who leisurely waded over to the Mexican side where he had left his horse and supplies. Neither the weather nor loneliness seemed to bother him in the slightest.

John and I returned to my house where we'd decided to stay rather than take the coward's way of seeking safety elsewhere. Our girlfriends, however, were a different matter. We'd moved them to Worth Henderson's for safe keeping, as well as their landlady, Mrs. Norton. She had protested loudly and nearly had to be carried away from her ancestral home. Partly to avoid that angry woman, John and I had been eating meals at my home.

That Monday night, two things happened. First, it started to rain, not a heavy downpour though constant. If it kept up, and the raid came to pass on Tuesday, it'd be a mess. Second, Decker arrived at the house with some aggravating news. A cowboy from the Wilson place out west a few miles had ridden to the Ranger station to warn us lawmen that more drugs were crossing from Mexico. The rancher was pretty upset about the situation, had even fired at the smugglers on two nights as they snuck across his property. "Mr. Wilson reckons they're hidin' the stuff some places in our county, 'fore someone else moves everythin' on to a big city. He's demandin' somethin' be done or he'll round up us cowboys and we'll chase 'em away ourselves. Cross over and hunt down the head honchos."

"Ain't got time to deal with this now," I said.

Decker said, "True 'nuff. Better hope it don't happen in the next few days. Would fer sure fool with our plans at the island. Might scare 'em away fer who knows how long."

Decker rode off and we settled in to listen to the rain, dreading the next few hours. We both felt that something bad was brewing. So we threw on our ponchos and dashed off to Worth's to spend a few minutes with our gals. Worth met us at the door with surprising news: the ladies were busy and couldn't meet with us. *What?!*

We were momentarily speechless. Understanding our predicament, Worth whispered, "Listen guys, they're deep into plannin'. Probly weddin' stuff. Y'all would rather skirt that, wouldn't ya?"

"Exactly so," said John emphatically. He promptly turned me around, pushed me off the porch and back into the rain where we then made a mad dash back to my house.

Once inside, I said, "Well, that was peculiar."

"Get used to it," he sighed. "Especially if you're figuring on marriage anytime soon."

"'Spose so," I replied. I was still a tad wounded at our dismissal. But I didn't tell John that.

It rained all night long. We slogged to the café next morning for a quick breakfast. Decker soon showed up grumbling nonstop about the "dang" mud. "We'll sure slew-slide our way out there today, fellas. I'm wearin' my chaps. They're easier to clean. Y'all better have extra guns case ya drop one in the mud. Shoot with a clogged barrel and damn thing's likely to blow up in yer face."

"Not bad advice," I said. "Here's another notion. Let's row out to the island. We'll be wet 'nuff as it is."

"Advise agin it. Most of the island is pretty flat. They might see the boats, just like any horses, and turn back. 'Sides, ain't no Texan 'fraid of wadin' through a little water."

With a bit of sarcasm, John answered, "I'm not a Texan, so perhaps you should carry me, Deputy."

Not sensing any humor Decker said, "Buck up, Doc. Y'all are marryin' one. She'll turn ya into one right quick." John and I shrugged and returned to reviewing our skirmish plans.

It was mid-morning and we were jawing at the Ranger station when I looked out the window and saw Chief's horse galloping our way, full speed, mud splashing in all directions. Something inside me screamed: this is it! Chief reined in his horse so sharply that it slid to a stop mostly on its haunches. My hunch was on the nose. He hollered, "They're coming! Bunching up about a mile on the other side behind a hill out of sight from the island. My guess is they'll cross soon, using the cloud cover and rain to get an upper hand."

Puzzled, I asked, "How can rain help 'em?"

Springer answered, "'Cause folks will stay inside, meanin' no one 'round to sound the alarm."

"Huh, hadn't thought of that."

"Won't be a hitch since they ain't makin' it into Texas, are they, men?"

Everyone shouted agreement. Springer ordered Todd to fetch Darius, and the rest of us ran to the barn where saddled horses waited along with additional supplies. We rode lickety-split to the edge of town and tied our horses behind the southernmost building where they'd be out of sight from the island. We grabbed what we could carry and squished our way to the river, inhaling deeply while taking those first steps into the water one more time. It was soon above my waist and the current was plainly stronger. "Don't slip and fall, fellas," I heard Collins yell. "I ain't goin' in after ya."

Luckily, there was a break in the rain as we struggled on shore. Waiting for Todd and Darius to show up, we scraped mud off our boots and checked our guns and ammo for any water damage. The question on everyone's mind popped out, and I asked, "How many bandits are there, Chief?"

"Counted ten, so we're pretty evenly matched."

Springer snorted, "Twenty, even thirty of 'em wouldn't be 'nuff. Crossfire will take 'em out right quick."

"I hope and pray that killing will be our last resort," pleaded John.

"Ain't here to wound 'em," snapped Springer. "Y'all should know better, Doc."

"Just stating that a life is pretty valuable," came his reply.

Todd and Darius sloshed ashore and we filled them in before everyone moved to their positions. The wait began.

Two anxious hours later we spotted the raiders in the distance slowly riding toward us. They halted on the Mexican side. It was easy to peg their leader, Montoya. He had the finest horse, biggest sombrero, and most colorful clothing. He stayed mounted while his henchmen got off to listen close up to likely last minute instructions. He pointed across the river, and I could barely make out two Spanish words: gringo and *venganza*. Everyone knew what a gringo was, and I reckoned the other meant "revenge." No revenge today, I promised myself, for the gringos are ready for ya.

The heavens opened up without warning and it started raining again. Already smeared in mud, I knew it would only get worse. I gripped my rifle tightly for fear of dropping it in the mud. The driving rain made it difficult to see more than 100 feet. The bandits mounted up and entered the river. I dropped to my knees, (no chaps!) wiped water from my eyes, and waited for the first sounds of gunfire.

I turned my head and caught sight of Darius sliding up to me. He called out, "Mr. Ted, there's a rowboat comin' our way. Almost here. We figurin' on reinforcements?"

"No!" I yelled, probably too loudly as I looked in the direction of the boat. We both crawled our way back to John's covering rocks to greet our "visitors."

"I can't believe my eyes, "said John. "It's Heather and Anne along with that damn reporter. What in blazes are they doing out here?"

Stunned, I stammered, "It's too late to send 'em back. Raiders are makin' their move. Let's get 'em out and find cover fer 'em. Need to hide the boat too."

We quickly pulled the boat ashore. John and I helped the drenched ladies out and led them to shelter behind the nearest big rocks. Jenkins followed, though he was of little concern to us. Darius started disguising the boat as best he could with some branches.

Speaking for both John and myself, I barked at our gals, "What are ya doin'? It's damn dangerous out here. Bullets be flyin' any second." Neither so much as quivered at the sound of my angry voice.

Anne said, "We won't let either of you face this danger alone. We're here and we're staying. We've brought some medical supplies with us, even a stretcher. Figured they might come in handy. Now go and get this over with. And don't offer them a good target. Understand?" I did but continued to mumble to myself at their risky behavior.

I turned to Jenkins, shaking my head in disgust, and said, "And what are *y'all* doin' here?"

"Got ears everywhere, Ted. Heard there might be some action near this island. Couldn't resist, it's my job. Besides, I figured these ladies might need some help in the rowing department."

"Well, I got another job fer ya, Lloyd, and y'all better make it number one. Help John and Darius keep those ladies safe. Pronto!" I hissed as I stepped within inches of his face.

"Consider it done," he said with a false air of bravado.

Kneeling down, I brushed wet strands of hair from Anne's face and said, "Be safe, *Miss Yoder,* and that's a direct order from yer favorite deputy sheriff, okay?" Not waiting for an answer, I ran back to my position next to Decker and Chief. Just as I slid into place, the rain suddenly stopped and a sliver of light broke through the clouds, landing right on the raiders. They were in mid-stream and looked up at the sky, smiling as if this was a sign of good fortune.

It wasn't: Springer took that very moment to open fire. Joined quickly by the two other Rangers, bullets rained down on the startled raiders. Three found their target. Less accurate volleys came from our position. Chaos followed with horses rearing up throwing off their riders. Some fired wildly before disappearing into the water.

So much smoke filled the air that we stopped shooting to wait for it to blow away. When the air cleared, I saw one rider still on his horse, glaring brazenly in our direction. It was their leader, Montoya! He was holding up his rifle as if to shoot. Silence. To my left I saw several bodies floating east. Behind Montoya riderless horses were climbing their way onto the Mexican shoreline. In their midst was one raider swimming for dear life. I figured his life would be measured in seconds and waited for the final shot to come. It never did. We watched the desperate man reach shore, stand up, and dart to cover behind some low scrub brush.

I looked back to the leader. The surging current had swept him to my left, and he was now facing the middle of the island, still scowling and still showing no signs of using the rifle or his fancy pistol. Wise on his part, unless he was foolish enough to take us all on single-handed.

Something weird happened then. He graced us with a wicked sneer, shouted a few curses, and slowly dismounted. He turned his magnificent animal parallel to us so he could move behind it and disappeared from view. "What's goin' on?" I asked Decker.

"Hell if I know."

Since we now had the upper hand, we chose to wait him out. Several of us were now standing to watch the spectacle. He soon appeared holding a huge cigar. He struck a match to light it. Due to the dampness it took several tries before a flame burst forth. His sneer returned. He then took a few puffs and held it out toward us. "*Muy bueno,* thees Mexican cigar," he called out in broken English.

"Toss me one of those damn things," Springer yelled back. "Had one a few years back. Ain't half bad."

"No cigar for you, gringo," Montoya said as he again disappeared behind the horse.

"What's he doin'?" asked Collins as we watched Montoya reach into his saddlebag.

"Maybe he's got a big ol' machine gun in there," Springer wisecracked.

Again moving in front of his horse, he held out what looked like another cigar. Even from a distance, though, I knew something was wrong. It was too long and not quite the right shade of brown. Montoya took several deep draws from his cigar and tried to light this second object. Strange, because the glowing end of the cigar stayed several inches away. We all straightaway saw it was a fuse, a fuse running back to a stick of dynamite!

"Bastard!" yelled Decker as he and the Rangers prepared to fire. Before they could, however, Montoya stepped back behind his horse, using it as a shield. Must have known that Rangers and most Texans would never shoot a horse. We watched hopelessly as smoke from the fuse rose and knew we had only seconds to act. *What could we do?*

Cussing again, Decker dropped face down in the mud, took aim and fired between the horse's lower abdomen and the water. The bullet struck Montoya in his right thigh. Montoya screamed and almost dropped the stick. Reckoning another bullet was headed his way, he grabbed the saddle horn with his left hand, shifted his weight to his left leg and threw the dynamite high in the air toward us. Decker's second shot was heard a split second later hitting the other leg and causing Montoya to roll into the river.

We watched in horror as the dynamite sailed in our direction. In nothing flat I realized it was going to fly past us toward Anne and everyone else hidden, we thought, out of harm's way. *Anne!* My heart sank as I saw it hit the ground and roll even closer to her location. "Dynamite!" I screamed at the top of my lungs. "Cover up, now!" I thought I saw someone move. "God have mercy" I mouthed before Chief yanked me to the ground and covered me with his own body.

The explosion was deafening, shaking the ground and sending mud and debris everywhere. The shockwave drove Chief clean off me. I struggled to get up on my knees but was mired in several inches of mud that caked my entire front. Staggering upright, I spat out filth and wiped my face clearing my eyes. Ears were still ringing. I saw Decker and Chief rising behind me doing the same motions.

I stood shakily for a few seconds trying to recover from the shock of the explosion. *Anne?* I was back to reality in a flash and off and running toward their hiding place. No movement but I heard screams. Panic stricken, I scrambled to the rocks. I jumped over the first and saw everyone still face down on the ground, not separately, but in two piles. The first pile had Heather beneath John with Darius on top of them. Both men were showing signs of recovery so I bolted for the second pile. *Anne?*

There I found Anne covered by Lloyd Jenkins. He was unconscious, but checking him I found a weak pulse. I gently lifted him off to the side and fell to my knees beside Anne. Reaching out to her, I prayed as I had never prayed before, "Please, God, let her live!" She was on her right side with her head resting on her right arm. Thank heaven, her front side was facing away from the blast and her head was slightly elevated to avoid a mud splattering. But she also was unconscious. I stroked her cheek and hair as I softly called out several times, "Anne, open yer eyes. It's Ted, sweetie. You're gonna be fine."

Hearing sloshing sounds, I turned to see Decker and Springer behind me. "How's she doin', partner?" Decker asked quickly and tenderly.

"Don't know, Ken. She ain't respondin'." I'd never used his first name before. He didn't seem to mind.

Continuing my efforts, I asked someone to check on the other three. Springer did so as Decker checked on Jenkins. "Looks like this reporter's got quite a bump on his noggin. Biggest I've ever seen."

Springer reappeared with good news. Everyone in the other group was recovering nicely. Staring down at Anne, he said, "We need to rush Anne and this Jenkins fella to the clinic so John can get to work on 'em."

"Let's get movin'. We'll use the rowboat to move 'em."

I was relieved when I saw John and Heather rushing toward me. "We're both okay," Heather said as they dropped beside Anne. I could see tears streaming down Heather's cheeks as she eased Anne's hand from my grip and began to help John check Anne over. She also was quietly praying. Decker gently pulled me off to one side and put his arm around me for support, figuring I was in a daze. He'd never done anything like that before.

After a brief exam, John thankfully declared he could find no signs of external injury. "Let's get her to the clinic fast, though, for a fuller exam. Darius is preparing the boat right now."

I carefully lifted Anne and carried her over to it. John boarded first, then Heather and I took our seats. Heather sat beside me as I cradled Anne in my arms. Springer and Decker placed Jenkins in the boat's bottom and off we went with John rowing.

My numbness continued. I couldn't imagine my life without Anne. Again I pleaded to God for her recovery, even offered my life in exchange for hers.

After what seemed like an eternity, the boat bumped ashore. I let Heather hold Anne as John and I jumped out to drag it up a few more feet. Turning back to reclaim her, my heart jumped when I saw her open eyes staring back at me. The smiling eyes of recognition. "Praise God!" I shouted to anyone and everyone. "Hey there beautiful, glad to see you're back with us," I said smiling ear to ear.

"What happened?" she asked with a confused look.

"Dynamite exploded near you," I answered. "John's here and says you're fine. We're takin' y'all to the clinic for a better examination."

Once in my arms again, she looked down at Heather and said, "Are you okay?"

"I'm fine. Let's stop talking for now. Plenty of time later."

Anne couldn't keep quiet, though, and said, "I remember someone calling out for everyone to cover up, then something hit me from behind and drove me to the ground. What was that?"

It was Jenkins, of course. I didn't have the time to tell her because John came up and placed his arms under her next to mine. Together we began our trek to the clinic three blocks north.

We carried Anne inside past two startled patients and a concerned nurse. As John and Heather started to undress her, he looked up at me and said, "I think it's time for you to step aside, cousin."

"Oh, uh-huh, sure." I reluctantly let go of her hand but added, "Soon as y'all are decent, Anne, I'll be back at yer side. Never leave ya again, I promise."

"Never," she laughed. "That's probably too much togetherness for me, Deputy."

"Never," I repeated, as Heather pushed me out.

Nancy came up to me and asked if I needed her help. "I'm fine, Nancy. Thanks anyway."

"Y'all need to take a break, son. Why not go outside and get some air? It's stopped rainin' and the Texas sun is shinin' again. And wipe off some of that dried mud while you're out there. I'll call ya when they want ya back inside."

I walked out into a Texas sun that felt like God caressing my upturned face. I scraped off as much mud as possible and was still working on my boots when Darius and Stevens showed up. "What 'bout Montoya? Did he get away?"

"Nope," answered Stevens. "Rangers and Decker got him 'fore he drifted away. Got another one too. Bringin' both here fer the Doc to work on 'em. Can croak fer all I care."

"Better save 'em if we can," I said. "Hope they're afixin' to spill all they know."

"If anyone can rattle their innards, it's the Rangers.'"

As I was thinking about what tack the Rangers might take, they rode up, Rangers and Decker in the lead, three horses trailing behind. Two carried bound raiders bent over in pain, the other, Jenkins, who was thrown over the saddle and anchored with rope to prevent falling off. The raiders looked like drowned rats. Blood was everywhere.

"Y'all didn't try to stop the bleedin'?"

"Too ornery, so I gave up," said Springer with a shrug.

"Lay Jenkins on this here bench and plunk the raiders on the ground at either end. I'll get some things to keep 'em from bleedin' out. Thought y'all were tryin' to get 'em talkin'."

"Yup. Just got too mad to deal with 'em. Though I sure do 'preciate their cryin' out in pain."

The bindings caused the raiders to squirm and groan and my fellow lawmen to smile. Jenkins still wasn't coming around. Maybe he did have some serious brain damage.

Finishing, I asked if the raiders had done any talking. "Well, this fella here sure did. Name's Felix and he ain't really part of Montoya's revenge gang. Seems Montoya needed someone who knew the town's layout and Felix lives right across the border. Been to Los Indios many times. Felix here was the spy checkin' out locations fer Montoya."

"Anythin' else?"

"Plenty," Springer said, eager to tell all. "Found Felix's horse and guess what was in his saddlebag: Drugs! Pound or two of marihuana and some white powder. No doubt it's heroin. 'Fessed up 'bout bein' a damn smuggler too. Gets even better 'cause he admitted to bringin' in drugs to our friend, Tex Morgan."

"Holy cow! That's great!" I said.

"Yessir, and here's the kicker. Felix sneaks across at the Wilson ranch and drops stuff in our neck of the woods.

Those drugs goin' to Morgan are actually fer Morgan's boss, a man named King. Heard that name once or twice, ain't we?"

"Uh-huh. How much pressure did ya use to squeeze out all this information?"

"Just a tad. Volunteered most of it. Between groans said he wasn't too worried 'bout the legal side of things. Claimed King would take care of him. He'd never go to prison. Agin, sound familiar?"

"Damn right. What now?"

"Been givin' it plenty of thought last hour or so. First, Collins and I'll go to Mr. Wilson and tell him to call off that crazy idea of chargin' into Mexico with a bunch of cowhands. Rangers won't join him like we did last summer. Second, Wilson don't have to do nuthin' 'cause we're goin' to the King ranch and lay down the law to father and son – Ranger law."

All this wasn't sitting too well with me. I said, "Hold on. What does that mean? Y'all ain't takin' the law into yer own hands, are ya?"

A mite peeved, Springer thrust out his hands and snorted, "See these hands, Ted. These *are* the hands of the law. 'Specially when the courts fail us. It's all we Texans have left."

"But won't they just use that uppity lawyer like last time?"

"Sure, but this time we remind 'em that all kinda accidents might happen at a big, far-flung ranch like theirs. Fence posts knocked over, barbed wires cut, lightnin' strikes on the dry prairie which can cause cattle to stampede. Risky business bein' a rancher, don't ya agree?"

Collins and Decker laughed. The three of them didn't have many – if any – qualms about taking the law "into their own hands." Squirming a bit, I asked, "What will ya do with those two raiders here, 'sposin' they live?"

"Rot in our jail a while, maybe a long while," said Collins.

"No lawyer fer 'em?"

"Nope. Not citizens, so don't have to give 'em no lawyer."

"Have to spring 'em someday. What then?"

"Probly send 'em to headquarters in Laredo. Wash our hands of 'em, that's fer sure."

Three men hee-hawing, two groaning like stuck pigs, one motionless, one standing with difficulty, and all covered in dried mud. Must have been a strange sight to anyone passing by the clinic. My thoughts were interrupted when John came out smiling broadly. "Anne's feeling much better and is just fine. Probably suffering from a small concussion but she's hankering to see you. Don't keep her waiting."

I charged past him and found her in a chair wearing strange clothes. Same with Heather, both probably came from Nancy. Anne reached out to me. I could see her eyes were clearer and her smile stronger than before. Instead of a hug, I fell to my knees and placed my head on her lap. Never done that before; didn't care how it looked. I liked the feel of her lap against my cheek.

She started to run her fingers through my hair but stopped. Laughing, she said, "Can't tell if it's hair I'm rubbing with all the mud. What you need, Ted, is a long, hot bath. And start with those lovely locks of yours first."

Reaching up, I caressed her cheek then rose and kissed her forehead. "John says you're fine. Tell me he's right."

"My head hurts a little. He says rest is the best medicine for me and Heather."

"Then it's rest you'll be agettin'. And I'm yer nurse every spare minute I have."

"We owe you so much, Ted. First comes my apology for being so rash and putting you and others in all that extra danger. We both are ashamed and ask your forgiveness. And it won't happen again. We promise."

I lifted her off the chair and hugged her, more gently than usual. With her arms around me and hearing her whisper, "I love you" in my ear, I lost my sense of time and place for a short while. John's cough snapped me back to reality and I said, "Anne, you and Heather are forgiven, of course. But it's best to leave the policin' and bullet-dodgin' to me and my fella lawmen." Glancing at Heather, I added, "And John from time to time."

Heather capped it all by saying, "John's future battles will be medical ones." I could see agreement and relief on John's face. Heather hugged John and there we stood, two couples whose lives had crisscrossed and brought deeper meaning to friendship.

Nancy came in and reminded us that we still had three others who required John's attention. I ushered the ladies outside, found Darius, and asked him to walk them back to their regular apartment. Moving away, Anne turned back and said, "We have more to talk about later." I figured as much.

The three patients were brought into the examining room. John quickly determined that little could be done with Jenkins. It was the Brownsville hospital for him. I used the clinic phone and called dad. First I told him we were okay then asked to borrow his car. He was so relieved we were safe that he offered to drive Jenkins himself. That was a big relief. A Ranger "ride" meant the longest and bumpiest possible.

John flattered me for the bindings I'd done on the two bandits. He made sure none had broken bones. All shots had gone clean through. He did have a fair amount of cleaning and sewing to do which took almost two hours. By the time he finished, dad was long gone with Jenkins. The Rangers were provoked to no end by the lost time, hungry, and getting meaner by the minute. When John finally released the prisoners to them, they were tossed roughly onto the horses and led away at a good clip toward the jail. I predicted they'd be the last to be fed. Maybe not even until the next day. And there was no sympathy at all for their fix.

I ran back home to wolf down some food. Between bites I summarized our adventures for mom and Diane between bites. Then, per my orders, dashed upstairs and began scrubbing off layers of mud. Hair first, in the sink, hot bath, clean clothes, and off to Anne's apartment.

Heather greeted me at the door with an index finger to her mouth and whispered," She's sleeping. Might be for a spell. Stay if you like. Use the easy chair in the corner."

Downhearted, I wearily sank into it. And promptly dozed off. I woke to my shoulder being gently shaken. It was Anne, looking revived and as lovely as ever. "It's dark outside. Heather says you've been here for three hours. Let's go to the kitchen, grab a sandwich and coffee, then we'll talk."

We began talking before my first bite. She started with another apology. I cut her off saying it wasn't necessary. "Okay, that's generous but there's something important I still need to say. I don't think you're going to like it, Ted."

Confused, I said, "It can't be that bad. Let me have it."

Biting her upper lip, she said, "When you shouted the alarm, Mr. Jenkins immediately pushed me down and covered me with his body. I think he took the brunt of the blast. I owe him my life, Ted."

"We all owe him a big debt. I have a feelin' y'all have somethin' clear-cut in mind?"

She did and described how, as he'd rowed them to the island, he'd mentioned how interested he was in interviewing our Ranger friends. He said this particular story could be his big break, move him up the ladder, maybe even to San Antonio. "That big city is his dream job. Been corresponding with them. So far, no luck."

I knew I'd stepped on my own noose, so I said, "I'm aimin' to try, and I'll give it all I got." Anne responded in typical fashion: a smile, a hug, and a kiss. How could anyone say no to her? *Should I take her along with me when I met the Rangers?*

Ideas were flying at me thicker than gnats. "Anne, Jenkins once told me that he was a single guy with relatives nearby. If he's to mend proper like, I should bring up his condition to mom. I know she'll open up the house to him, meanin' she'll have both Archer and Jenkins to nurse back to health. Y'all reckon that'd be up her alley?"

"She wouldn't shy from helping them. But is there room at your place?"

"Yup, in Diane's room. She can use the couch, or me, if John's not 'round. She'll kick up a fuss, but I'll figure out a way get 'round her."

"What are you suggesting?"

"Givin' her a chance to help y'all at the clinic. Heard her talkin' to mom 'bout becomin' a nurse. It'd be a great experience fer her."

"Indeed it would. Heather and I would be pleased to get her started. And I bet Nancy would too."

"One more question fer ya. Do y'all want me to stop my deputy work? It *is* dangerous and I know ya worry 'bout me all the time. I'm willin' to do that fer you."

Putting her hands on my chest, she looked up into my eyes and said, "No, it's just for a few more weeks and Decker needs you. Keep both your jobs."

"Thanks, I 'preciate yer faith in me." I reckoned my plate was full for the rest of the summer.

CHAPTER EIGHTEEN

OPTIONS

"Toby, have y'all heard 'bout John's adventures in Hollywood?" asked one of Mr. Brian's customers. He hadn't and was fascinated when the whole story came out about John's help as a medic on a Western movie set where he assisted Wyatt Earp. "Heard of Earp, ain't ya?" Toby had and was eager for more information but the talk was cut short by the needs of other customers. Movies? He'd never been to a movie. Maybe someday, he thought wistfully, as he poured more coffee.

I WAS IN THE CAFÉ ONE morning in mid-June when I spotted a Dallas newspaper left behind by a customer. Decker hadn't come by yet, so I grabbed it, accepted a second cup of coffee, and started reading. A caption below the crease caught my eye, something about Governor Ferguson. The word "impeachment" baffled me and compelled me to read the whole story. It described how Ferguson was having some hard times with the faculty at the University of Texas due to his vetoing their yearly budget. Faculty members from two departments were heading this action: Journalism and History. The professor of journalism's conflict was personal and political since he'd lost the 1914 race to Ferguson. The article didn't reveal a personal reason why the history professor was trying to bring down the governor. Impeachment and removal from office no later than July was, in fact, their goal. Wow! I'd have to tell John and Decker about this if they didn't already know.

Browsing through the paper, my attention was drawn to the movie ads for the upcoming weekend, beginning June 15, 1917. A new movie, *The Patriot,* starred William Hart. That brought back to mind Hart's movie, *The Aryan,* which all four of us had seen last fall in west Texas. I started thinking of a possible Saturday trip to Brownsville, if everyone agreed.

We could catch an early lunch at a good restaurant, then the ladies would need a couple hours to shop for final wedding purchases. After that, we could get to a mid-afternoon showing of the movie and end with a trip to the hospital to collect both Archer and Jenkins to bring them back to my house. Mom, naturally, had agreed to entertain them both and help nurse them back to health. It would be a full day and a crammed car on the return trip, but I reckoned it could all be managed.

Decker finally arrived and I told him about the Ferguson situation. He hadn't heard but figured John would know about it since he was a part of the academic world. I asked his opinion and he replied, "Hope they can do it. Damn fool hates the Rangers, real Rangers anyway." He carried on a while, temper building, before I changed the subject to my ambitious plans for Saturday.

To my relief, he didn't discourage the movie idea. He even hinted he might see the movie himself one day. "Texans are more patriotic than most folk," he said with pride. "And that's a fact."

Hopefully, my other three friends would go for it. I got to John through Heather. She said, "I'll get Nancy to cover for him on Saturday. Short of an emergency at the clinic, he'll come with us. You two men will have to keep an eye on the clock, though, because Anne and I'll lose track of time shopping." I believed her.

Anne was a pushover after hearing about Heather's answer. She had only one misgiving. "Heather and I were a bit troubled about the racism in *The Aryan* movie. That won't be repeated, will it?"

"I don't think so. But if you gals don't like any part of the movie, we'll walk out early. Promise." Her acceptance came with a hug.

How to get to Brownsville was the last hitch. That was worked out when dad agreed to loan me the car. He also felt it was roomy enough for six on the return trip. "Done it many a time, as y'all recall. If Archer has crutches, tie 'em on top. If he's still in a cast, have him poke his leg out the rear window. Seen that 'fore too. A very Texan solution, don't ya think?" Everything was settled.

John arrived late Friday afternoon, listened to my plans, and cottoned to them. We discussed the Ferguson situation for some time. He had heard about it and felt it was good news.

The Saturday ride was pleasant, no problems and the gals monopolized the conversation with wedding talk. John and I faked interest in all but spent most of the trip looking at the passing scenery. We chose a Mexican restaurant for lunch. While enjoying the tasty meal, various subjects came up. I tried to bring up the Ferguson situation. The gals weren't at all interested. Probably a good thing since John and I had hashed over that topic already.

The gals directed us to a new department store and went off by themselves after agreeing to be picked up in time for the movie. We men hung around for a while then went window-shopping for an hour or two. John stopped once to buy medical supplies, and I did the same to purchase a new cowboy-style vest to match Decker's. I hoped he would be impressed rather than offended.

Returning to our ladies, whose arms were filled with packages, we carefully placed everything in the trunk, and made it to the theater as the credits were rolling. We'd missed the previews, a favorite of mine, but I'd survive.

Hart's movie was similar to *The Aryan:* corrupt politics and tragic loss of loved ones. Hanging out with bandits produced lots of violence. But, once again, the hero saw his "foolish ways" and returned to true patriotism at the end. Our companions weren't too comfortable with the fighting scenes and pointed us toward a comedy in the future. Laughter always bucked up a person's spirit.

As we rode to the hospital, I asked what they thought about the chance of "sound" in movies. "Is it even possible?" asked Heather. John piped in, "One of my medical students has a brother working on that matter at Kodak up in Rochester, New York. He says it's only a matter of time."

"Sure would change things," I added. "And it can't come fast enough. It might just cut down some of the overactin'. Hard to watch at times." They all agreed.

We met first with Doc Wilbur to get the lowdown on his two patients. He said Archer was "sore as a boil" because his right leg from foot to knee was in a cast. "He's pretty low-down 'bout losing that last rig. Keep an eye on him. Hate to hear he's done anything foolish."

"Foolish?" I asked.

"Ya know, like bent on endin' his life. Seen it 'fore. "Spect more of it when we begin to treat vets returning from the war."

"We'll look after him," Heather said. "Lots of caring people will tend to him night and day."

When the subject became Jenkins, Wilbur said there was good and bad news. The good was the swelling on his head was nearly gone and no other injuries were discovered after careful examination. X-ray pictures didn't show any broken bones or other problems. "His brain, though, is a different matter. Ya can't see the effects of his major concussion. Mr. Jenkins probably can't remember what happened in the recent past. He doesn't remember the explosion and is confused 'bout why he's here at the hospital. Overall, his earliest recollection goes back five or six years."

"What's the prognosis?" asked John.

"Who knows? Might regain everything over time but there ain't no guarantee. Try to jog his memory 'bout recent happenings. It may help."

I selfishly thought Wilbur's "bad" news might be "good" for a few people in our town, such as me, Decker, and the Rangers. No memory, no interviews, happy lawmen. The ladies could work on his memory recovery. I'd keep my fingers crossed in the meantime.

We crammed into the car and started home. I drove with the gals beside me in front. John rode in the back between Archer and Jenkins. Rather a tight fit in the back and smelly. Wilbur had warned us that the two men had stubbornly refused to wash. Fortunately, the windows were down and the breeze provided some relief. It also helped having Archer put his stinking leg out the rear window, the cast being supported against the windowpane.

Archer was grumpy and said very little. Jenkins kept asking, "Who are you? "Where are we going?" It brought back memories of my grandmother Townley who suffered from senility during her last years. I really didn't want Jenkins to suffer a similar fate.

We dropped off the two men with mom. She'd kept some food warm for them and promptly sat them down at the kitchen table to begin her nursing ministry. She made us all feel humble by her loving care.

We four youngsters were exhausted from our all-day outing. John and I walked our gals to their apartment and went inside to talk about the day's events. Just before leaving, Heather announced that she and John had been thinking of having an outdoor wedding. "It only came up a few days ago," Heather said. "I asked Anne to keep it to herself until we'd firmed it up. We have, so it's time to ask what you think, Ted?"

"Whereabouts is the place?" I asked.

"We found a lovely site at the Wilson ranch. A good place for fishing I'm told."

"I've fished there. Caught some smallmouth bass over the years. It's more of a big pond, though, than a lake."

"Mr. Wilson says it was deepened and enlarged not long ago. And he's added some shade trees and planted grass. Wild flowers grow on two sides. It's all in all lovely."

"Sounds fine to me. I'm guessin' you and Anne are of a like mind 'bout this site."

"We are," said Anne putting her arm around Heather. "It's perfect. Just needs some tables and chairs and special decorations. We'll start a new craze. The Wilson lake, the perfect place for a summer wedding."

"Perfect if it don't rain," I said. "Ya better have a second spot in mind in case that happens."

Heather said, "Already done. Our clergyman, Pastor Dan, has offered the Baptist church as a fallback. We ladies have everything under control." I was sure praying that nothing would spoil my cousin's wedding.

It was late when we left. As we walked along, John apologized for not mentioning the lake idea earlier. I told him it wasn't a problem. He smiled and said the ladies were doing most of the arranging but we still had a few things to finish in the last few days. "Then, it'll all be over," he said with a sigh of relief.

"And all will be beginnin'," I corrected him. We both laughed knowingly. "Where y'all headed fer the honeymoon?"

"Houston. City's getting bigger and better all the time. New restaurants, theaters, and cultural places springing up everywhere. Getting acquainted with a few of 'em myself."

"I 'spect y'all will be livin' there in the fall."

"That's our plan. Might look around for an apartment while we're there. Heather has turned in her resignation at school and is already on the lookout for teaching jobs in Houston."

"Y'all have a lot to do. Don't forget the honeymoon part." My reward for that comment was a punch on the shoulder.

It sure had been a full day. I think I was asleep before my head hit the pillow. I dreamt of Anne and how happy she looked going on about Heather's wedding.

I helped mom prepare breakfast on Monday for her two "guests." They appeared the same: a cranky Archer and a confused Jenkins. I finished eating and went to the café to wait for Decker. Toby was serving but something was different. He refilled my cup using his left hand, again a bit strange for him.

"Somethin' wrong with yer right hand, Toby? Y'all keep tuckin' it behind yer back."

"Hopin' ya wouldn't take note, Mr. Ted," he replied with an embarrassed look. He stuck out his right hand with badly bruised knuckles.

"Been punchin' any cows lately?" I said to lighten the mood.

"No cows, just a hard head."

"Well, tell me 'bout it."

He recounted how he and his family had been approached by young thugs walking home Sunday night. Hateful words were uttered and threats made. They'd been afraid for their lives. At that exact moment, Darius had come out of the shadows and challenged all four of them. They started hitting Darius, and Toby couldn't just stand there and do nothing. So he joined the fracas and injured his hand. During a pause in his explanation, I felt pride in Toby's show of manly courage but wondered how Martha had reacted to his becoming violent.

Continuing, he said, "Darius probly could've handled 'em all by hisself. Hit my target though. Might have done some damage to my hand. Hurts somethin' awful. Should I see Mr. John if it don't get better?"

"I'd say so. Give me a description of those thugs." He did and I was pretty sure I knew two of them. "I'll talk to Decker and we'll face 'em with all this in front of their parents. We'll put a stop to this right quick, I swear."

"Don't want no more trouble, Mr. Ted."

"Ain't no trouble, Toby. Been too much of this already."

After I relayed the story to Decker shortly later, he decided to face them himself. Y'all are a mite too close to this, Ted. 'Fraid ya might say somethin' that will make it worse. I'll handle it."

He was probably right, so I backed off. He promised he'd let me know how his "message" was received and we started our patrol. Nothing unusual happened, and we returned to the café where we ran into the two Rangers. Springer rehashed their meeting with the two Kings. "That was Sunday afternoon. Doubt they rightly got our message. At the end it was just a starin' contest."

"Maybe y'all won it!" I said, hoping for the best.

"Maybe, maybe not. Surprisin' development, though, last night. Learned some so-and-so cut a fence at the King place and must've fired some shots causin' a stampede. Cattle scattered in all directions. Take 'em days to hunt 'em all down and get 'em back to their corral. Most likely just a coincidence, don't ya think?"

I didn't but kept silent. "Now what?"

We wait," Springer answered. "Ya never know when somethin' else is afixin' to crop up."

My three fellow lawmen looked mighty pleased with themselves. To them it was a case of Ranger justice. Getting a mite peeved with their gloating, I asked Springer about Montoya. Springer said he had kept the fancy pistol taken from Montoya. "Know I can't wear it," he grumbled. "But I'm havin' a special case made fer it at home. House is fillin' up with all my 'souvenirs.' Should turn it into a museum when I retire."

"Y'all will never retire, Captain," Collins said. "When it's yer time, y'all will die in the saddle out somewhere in the middle of nowhere."

"Then plant the casket plumb in the middle of my parlor. It'll make my home the best museum in this part of Texas." We all laughed at that image.

Our foursome broke up and as I was leaving for the store, I heard the whistle of a train pulling into the depot. I decided to see if I knew anyone stepping off. Only one passenger stepped down and glanced around. A familiar face – Steve Brundage! What was he doing here? We recognized each other immediately, and he made a beeline for me. While he pumped my hand like it was the kitchen water pump, I said, "Y'all are the last fella I 'spected to see, Steve. What brings ya to our little town?"

"Here to see John. Figure he's here from time to time."

"Yup, shows hisself on weekends. Be here Friday, in fact."

"Great! Tony Milano is coming along soon. Together we have something to show him."

"Comes to my mind him sayin' somethin' 'bout an article or novel. Am I gettin' close?"

"Ballpark close."

"Then what 'xactly is it?"

"Prefer to keep it under wraps 'til he shows up."

That was peculiar. Having an on-the-spot notion, I invited him to dinner. Figured if we had a chance to talk, badgering him with enough questions would cause him to spill his secret. And because it was about John, Heather and Anne should also be there. Maybe Heather could pry something from him. In addition, I told him about mom's two other guests. He admitted to knowing of Jenkins having had an interview with his paper's editor.

"I sat in on it. Didn't go well. Didn't get an offer."

I sure didn't open up about their similar interest: interviewing Rangers. I wanted to see how much, if anything, Jenkins could recall of this burr under the saddle he had with them. Would they join forces? If so, I'd have to warn the Rangers pronto. Not wanting to wait until dinner, I took the chance and said, "Y'all still have a personal interest in huntin' down those Rangers fer that interview?"

"Nah, got other irons in the fire now. Think my reportin' days are over. Not the writin', though. I'm atakin' to somethin' new on the horizon." *That* was a relief!

Brundage left for lunch at the café, whose home cooking he remembered well. I reminded him dinner was at six. Then I scooted to the clinic to invite the gals and stopped by the house to let mom know about her growing number of dinner guests. Naturally, she took the extra work in stride.

Mom's fixings always went down well. But it was a guilty relief to see Jenkins witless of any past meeting with Brundage. Brundage, however, spoke up about his earlier efforts with the Rangers. I held my breath and waited for some memory stirring in Jenkin's mind. Nothing. His foggy memory still persisted. Again, guilty relief, yet a softheartedness as I watched him struggle to make sense of the dinner conversation.

We all ganged up on Brundage afterward. He finally gave in and bared his secret. "Okay, I surrender. It's a screenplay for a movie. Tony is bringin' the completed manuscript with him. The main character is based on John and his adventures as a medic in Texas, Mexico, even in Hollywood. We think it has real potential. We've taken it around to various studios and a couple are interested. Tony has contacted one or two more since I left. In short, we hope to get John's approval to go ahead."

All of us knew this was big but what did John think of it? Heather finally said, "John did mention this possibility to me last fall. I think there's something important you've left out of your report, Mr. Brundage."

Shifting uneasily, Brundage confessed, "Ah... Well, we did suggest that John play the role himself in the movie if other actors weren't available."

"Whoa, there," Mom interrupted. "John's future is set in stone. Marriage to Heather in a few days, then back to medical school. It's out of the question," she finished in a commanding voice.

"That's just one thing we need to discuss with John, Mrs. Townley. We want to present the full concept to him. We're goin' full steam ahead regardless of his assuming the lead role."

Speaking about movies in general was tolerable. Since Brundage had seen them all, he dominated the conversation. His reviews held us spellbound. He thought D.W. Griffith was Hollywood's leading director, and I knew this would meet with John's approval. He also was pretty convincing for talented young men and women to move to California and dive into the whole movie-making business. He finished by saying, "Live theater is dying, folks, trust me. Movies are the future. As soon as sound and color are added, it'll be a billion-dollar game."

Later on, Brundage, in fact, confessed he'd been bitten by the Hollywood "bug" himself. He would soon resign from the San Antonio paper and head west. "I'm going to buy a new typewriter, roll up my sleeves, and start turnin' out new screenplays as fast as I can. I know it's risky, but ya sure can't beat the weather out there!"

As I walked the gals back to their apartment, I continued jawing about Hollywood and moviemaking. We all knew one thing for sure: no way was it in Dr. John McFarland's future. On my way home, I stopped by the café to share the good news about Brundage with the three lawmen. They were pleased yet remained wary. I decided not to tell them that Brundage would be spending a lot of time at the café.

I was stunned Wednesday morning to see all three lawmen sharing a table at the café with that very same reporter. They were all smiles and waved me over. "What's goin' on?" I asked, thinking they were acting like buddies or something.

Collins began, "Steve, here, is tryin' to get us to head out to Hollywood and do some actin' in Western movies." Was *he stringing me along?*

Springer added, "Says workin' as an extra would be a cinch fer us. We all sure know ridin' and shootin'. What d'ya think, Ted?"

Struggling to find my voice, I answered, "Reckon y'all would fit right in. Can ya find the time?"

"We Rangers have some vacation time comin'. Steve says it would only be a week or so. Turn out those Westerns right quick. Might be fun."

Decker said, "Might be but y'all go without this ol' cowpoke. Plenty to do 'round here, 'specially if ya both go all star-struck on me."

Collins and Springer turned their attention back to Brundage and his movie yarns. *Could anyone really picture them as Hollywood stars?*

Brundage and I met Milano at the depot Thursday afternoon. We chatted for a while before the two went off to put together a scheme for putting more pressure on John. Being bitten by the Hollywood "bug" seemed to make men eternally optimistic.

I had arranged for them to meet John and everyone else at my house Friday night. Even Chief would be there. Heather and I met John at the station and walked back home, picking up Anne along the way. We filled him in about the meeting with Brundage. Of course, he was irritated about the whole idea of his acting. He did admit that he'd like to read the finished screenplay. At the front door, he said, "I'll make a fuss if I don't like it. The lead character must be shown in a positive way."

Entering, we said howdy to all though some were a bit offish. After some chitchat about the movies, including a few new adventures Tony had, we got down to business. John asked to see the completed screenplay. Knowing he couldn't read it there, maybe a summary was the best thing. Tony did the talking. Even more elements of John's adventures, in Mexico and Hollywood, came to light. John was silent. Everyone else was clearly impressed.

"You did all that, John?" asked my Mom.

"Most but it's a little exaggerated."

"Not at all," objected Tony. "John's a hero. He was in the thick of everything. Pancho Villa, Thorpe, Wyatt Earp, it's all true."

"Ease off, Tony," cautioned John. "Lots of people were involved. Chief for example. It's too much about me."

"But that's what the audience needs, real heroes in real situations. This is a true story and must be told," Tony added. Most of us put in at least two cents and agreed with Tony. Diane, who was gazing at her cousin, had eyes as wide as saucers. Maybe Tony was right about how an audience would respond to this movie.

"Well, two down-to-earth problems still remain," John said. "One, is there a studio out there willing to take on the project and two, who's playing me?"

Brundage answered, "We have two new studios interested. I'm sure one of 'em will come through for us."

"Big name studios not bitin'?" I asked.

"Sadly no," said Tony. "Gave it our best shot but they're all tied up into the near future. And the big stars, like Bill Hart and Tom Mix, already have contracts."

"Can a new studio handle a project like this?" I asked.

They both answered yes and mentioned a couple of already completed Westerns.

"Who do you want to be the lead actor?" John said. "And my decision still stands, fellas. It won't be me."

His refusal brought reality back to the room. After some awkward silence, Tony and Steve made one last bid to John to change his mind. It failed. Tony cleared his throat and said, "There's one new development I haven't mentioned. It's the main reason we hoped John would accept our offer."

"Must be somethin' bad," I said.

Tony answered, "John, Chief, do you remember Ryan Nolan from last fall?" They both nodded. "Well, he fancies himself an up and coming movie star. Bragging he's on the verge of becoming a new Bill Hart. Thing is he's a terrible actor. He's had a few small roles but he's so awful a couple of directors cut him entirely from the final version. Yet he wants this role, John. Insists on it!"

Shaking his head, John said, "Just tell him no."

"Here's the drawback, John. Ryan's got himself a girlfriend, not just any ol' girlfriend but the daughter of a studio owner. Most likely she's the daughter of the one filming our screenplay. Daddy dotes on his little princess and she's already working on him to choose Ryan. If he does, it'll be his disaster not just Ryan's."

"What can be done?" I asked.

"I think we can still prevail," Steve said. "If we move fast and present the studio with a solid candidate. And we must move fast, real fast."

"Surely there are others in Hollywood who could take on the lead role," Heather said.

"We have a director and together we've interviewed several men. None fit the bill, sadly. Thus, our plea to John." It was a head scratching moment for everyone. No one had an answer to the dilemma.

Tony unexpectedly jumped up and shouted, "I've got it! The perfect lead man! *What was he talking about?*

Tony looked directly at me, "Stand up, Ted," he ordered. I did and he came around to my side of the table and eyed me up and down. "Ted really fits the bill if I'm not mistaken. Look at this fine young man: tall, handsome, strong features gals would swoon over. And he can ride and shoot, and probably even rope a steer. It's you, Ted."

Me! He had to be kidding. "No!" came out of my mouth instantly.

Tony wasn't bothered by my nixing his idea. "Don't be too hasty, Ted. At least take some time to think it over. Get Anne's considered opinion. Remember, we only need a couple of weeks. You'll be back in college in the fall as planned."

Everyone except Brundage seemed as surprised as me. He recovered quickly and gave me a thumbs-up. "Great idea, Tony. Should have thought of that myself."

Anne squeezed my hand and gave me a look that said, *"Not a good idea, young man."* She whispered that we'd discuss it later. I already knew what her final answer would be.

We discussed it at length that night. Pros and cons were examined. Cons won out as I had predicted. With the wedding and other commitments in the next two months, even a two-week break wasn't possible. Besides, I might be in the army soon, thanks to the Selective Service Act. I didn't dare bring up that this Hollywood escapade would be a "hoot" and might lead to other prospects. *Hollywood?* A young man could always dream.

Almost everyone agreed we'd made a smart choice. Only Decker told me privately that it might be a once in a lifetime chance. "I would support ya doin' it, Ted, and send ya off with a slap on the back."

"Maybe y'all should take 'em up on their offer," I said.

"Nah, bein' a lawman is all I know to do."

"Sure hope they find someone. Be a shame if John's story ain't told."

"That's a fact. They'll find someone fer sure," he said, as he turned away.

I met up with Tony and Steve at the café the next morning. They saw my decision on my face and sagged in disappointment. Todd Stevens showed up shortly hunting for the Rangers. He joined us and the Hollywood couple talked up their dilemma. He took it all in without interrupting. All of a sudden a notion struck me. "Wait," I nearly shouted. "What 'bout Todd here? Why not have him do the lead?"

They right quick gave him the once over. "Sure is handsome enough," Tony said. "Manly if we keep him from shaving for a day or two. Or have him grow a mustache. Even a mite taller than you, Ted. I assume he can ride and shoot like the other Rangers, right?"

"Sure 'nuff. Y'all can lay it out fer him and there's a train tomorrow if ya need more time."

Todd was dumbstruck. He agreed to stay, however, and hear their line. Setting out, I glanced back to see "Hollywood" make its pitch. Todd was already crouching forward to catch every word, wide-eyed with a smile beginning to form. I remained a bit jealous. But he didn't have Anne Yoder, so I was an even bigger winner.

Tony and Steve stayed the extra day. Todd sure was gonna ride the gravy train! John, Heather, and I were at the depot to send them off. Springer and Collins were no-shows, though they had been invited. I reckoned they were testy about Todd becoming the new focus for the Hollywood couple. John asked Tony to mail him a copy of the final script. Tony swore he would, shaking hands to seal the deal. I could tell Todd was both excited and nervous. Who wouldn't be? He caught my eye from the window and mouthed "Thank you." His adventure was just beginning.

Heather and Anne spent the next two weeks tying up loose ends for the wedding. We boys helped a little. John's "best" man, along with dad, planned a bachelor's party for Friday night before the wedding. That plus keeping track of the ring were my main responsibilities. John expected a couple of his Michigan medical school buddies would make it south for the wedding. Great guys according to John. I was looking forward to meeting them.

Anne was dropping hints all over the place about how wonderful weddings were. I pretended not to understand, and she became increasingly annoyed at my thick-headedness. I finally realized my "mistake" and pulled her aside for a hug and whispered in her ear, "I get it, sweetie. That's our future too. Let's just get this one out of the way first." She smiled with what someone once called "bedroom eyes." It was hard to break contact with them.

John returned Thursday for the final rush. He had brought along a Houston newspaper. Scanning it that night, I saw the weather forecast on the last page. Not wanting to be blindsided on the "big" day, I read some reports from Gulf shippers that a major storm was brewing. The Coast Guard was busy with distress calls. Forecasters weren't sure which way it was heading – north toward New Orleans or west toward Texas. Showing it to John, I could see the concern on his face. I quietly prayed for a northerly route.

CHAPTER NINETEEN

A WEDDING AND MORE

Toby was in a good mood all Wednesday at the store. He overheard people talking about Saturday's wedding of John and Heather and wondered how many had been invited. Quite a few he figured since the whole Baptist church was included. He, too, was on the list along with his family. He was happy for his wife because she'd been asked to help out as a seamstress making last minute alterations on Miss Heather's dress. It had been her mother's and she was determined to wear this keepsake. Martha was thrilled. She'd never been asked to do anything for a white lady before.

THURSDAY AFTERNOON I SHOWED THE Dallas paper to Anne. With a wrinkled brow, she said, "I think we've got it covered, Ted. We're setting up a big tent which can hold a large crowd, and we'll have the church ready just in case."

I just wanted a plan for the worst and reminded her how quickly things had happened in our recent adventure on the island. Anne promised me she'd have all the other women prepared for anything. But she also didn't want Heather to worry.

That afternoon John and I helped move tables and chairs to the lake. Lots, since the ceremony and reception were in the same place. Mom and Anne were along to make sure no mistakes were made. We also brought along the tent, a platform for the wedding party to stand on, and an arch under which the bride and groom would say their vows. The arch would be decorated with flowers on Saturday morning. Moving this outfit was sure some stunt! We had help from Pastor Dan and several congregants, as well as friends from town, including Toby. And because it was summer, the sun would be up for a while yet. After about two hours, all was fit as a fiddle.

Dad drove the ladies back home while John and I went to our wagon, picked up two fishing poles, and snuck to the northern side of the lake. I just had to relive the experience of bass fishing with my cousin before things got to humming. We hadn't done this in many years. I promised him we wouldn't return home empty handed.

There was a dock on the northern rim where we sat down. Toby's daughters had dug up some night crawlers for us. We cast out; I closed my eyes and ten years vanished. It was a great feeling.

Wasn't long at all before we'd each snagged two bass. We decided that was plenty and got up to leave. Gazing around, a troubling thought came up. "John, look at the layout here. One creek feeds the lake and two empty it. But the south side, the wedding area, it's kinda boxed in 'cause those two southern streams join up. If it rains hard, guests could be trapped. Over to the left is the only bridge, the one we used to deliver the supplies. It's narrow and probly wouldn't handle a heavy downpour. Do ya think there might be a problem?"

"I do. The tent might do in a pinch but if it's heavy rain, we'll need to get everyone to the church. Maybe some wagons and cars could be ready on the other side in case we need to hightail it."

"And a traffic cop or two on the bridge to direct people along. Best to be prepared."

"Heather will be heartbroken if that happens," John said. "She's pretty level headed though."

Walking to the wagon, I noticed the time on my pocket watch. "John, we're runnin' late. No time to go home. Let's head straight to the depot. We can clean up there with 'nuff time 'fore the train pulls in, the one bringin' yer parents, sister, and two buddies from Michigan. I'll call home and ask 'em to bring a car to help get 'em all back to the house. Should be a grand reunion fer ya, cousin."

"It will. Haven't seen my family in months and those two medical school buddies in almost a year."

At the depot we realized that the fishy smell still hung on our clothes. Maybe no one would make any remarks. By happy chance we drew wrinkled noses only from Heather and Anne. Fresh clothes would sure be welcome.

John's family stepped first from the train followed by his friends, Fred Beck and Mike Flynn. After warm greetings all around, especially for the happy couple, John and his buddies had a lot of catching up to do. He made sure they rode with him back to the house. The men, being manly, took the wagon while women rode in the car. John's sister, Susan, sure took to Heather. I remembered how it had been between those two gals who had been kidnapped last summer, then taken to Mexico, and ultimately rescued by John and the Rangers. A special bond had grown up between them. I reckoned looking up to Heather was a good start for Susan who was growing into a young woman herself.

Mom had done her "magic" in the kitchen again for this big gathering. She was also keeping extra servings warm for people who were expected at any moment: Heather's mom, Dorothy, as well as an uncle, two aunts, and several cousins.

Heather was radiant and we all sensed her love for John. Between small talk about the upcoming wedding and joshing John about his "adventures" in medical school in Michigan, we all lost track of time. Mom eventually announced we'd hold off on dessert until Heather's mother and crew had arrived and finished eating. That meant a Texas separation: men gathering in one room the women in another.

Picking up where they'd left off, John's buddies entertained us with more tales about faded romances, botched lab experiments, and strange personalities and quirks of a few professors. My favorite was the absentminded professor who frequently showed up in class with a half-opened fly. "Here's the best part," chuckled Mike. "We made John sit in the front row and assigned him the task of alerting the professor of his predicament, doubly awkward one day because he was sitting next to the only female in class. His face sure did turn beet red!" I glanced at john and spotted a hint of redness emerging as the story ended. He tried to shift the attention away from himself. Failing, he took the ribbing like the man he was. Lucky for John, we heard vehicles pulling up outside indicating the appearance of Heather's family.

I kept saying "howdy" to everyone figuring I wouldn't remember most of the names anyway. The first dinner guests, except Heather and John, remained in the living room as the Benson family enjoyed mom's substantial leftovers. I was pressed into service as a waiter and noted quickly how Heather and John answered her relatives' questions showing mutual love and support. All told, they seemed impressed with him, a good thing since they'd be stuck with this Yankee in-law. "Off to a good start," I whispered to him as I refilled his cup.

Dad and I hauled extra chairs into the living room after dinner so all could eat dessert from their laps, Texas style – informally. Since there weren't enough chairs, Susan, Diane, and two other youngsters had to sit on the floor. They didn't seem to mind.

As the dessert plates were being carried to the kitchen, I pulled John aside and asked a question that had been nagging me. "Don't recall either of you ever mentionin' Heather's dad, right?"

"Right. Passed away a few years ago. She doesn't talk much about him. Think it's painful for her. I don't push." The fact that Heather could hide her pain well wasn't a surprise to me.

John's parents, George and Mary McFarland, wanted to hear more stories about Hollywood. The word "Hollywood" perked up the youngsters as well. Soon everyone was leaning forward with interest. I became the storyteller and did my best to make everything as exciting and truthful as possible. I began with last fall's adventures with Jim Thorpe and Wyatt Earp and finished with John recently being offered a leading role in a Western movie. Seeing their eyes widen, I figured I'd done a bang-up job. Questions flew from every direction at John, and he did his darnedest to answer them one at a time.

I looked around and realized everyone was staring at John with even greater admiration: the man who turned down Hollywood! That made me a tad jealous because I'd failed to include a similar offer made to me. John came to my rescue by telling the crowd of other recent offers. A few shocked faces now turned my way, especially disbelieving stares from Diane and Susan. Those two badgered me with questions. I fumbled around in answering and finally let Anne set the record straight. "Ted has other responsibilities and duties, young ladies. That's the whole story." And that was that.

You could have heard a pin drop. Fred finally offered, "Maybe I should volunteer for the lead role. Gotta be better than that Ryan fellow. I worked here in Texas last summer with John and the Rangers and they taught me how to ride and shoot."

"I can learn too," Mike said. "Can't be all that hard."

Hearty Texas laughter followed. Now the Yankees became the butt of the ensuing jokes. Squirming with reddened cheeks showed they didn't like to be teased either.

The evening wound down with a few wonderful stories about Heather's upbringing. Ending the evening with Heather on everyone's mind was perfect.

Mom had found lodging for everyone at various locations in town. She asked dad and me to show everyone around to their boardings. When we returned, Fred and Mike pulled me aside to ask, they said, a very important question. "You're having a bachelor party for John, aren't you?" asked Fred. "A Texas groom needs one last 'hootin' and hollerin' before he settles down."

"Relax, fellas. Got the whole shebang planned for tomorrow night at the Lone Star Café. Rented it all just for us. We'll have a good time together." They both sighed in mock relief and returned wily grins. As I walked away, I overheard Fred whisper, "Lone Star sounds familiar. Think it's a beer. That's encouraging." *What were they up to?*

Friday morning last minute supplies were taken to the lake. Fred and Mike were a big help when we set up the big tent. Dad asked them if they'd heard any news about the weather brewing in the Gulf. They hadn't, which was good.

That afternoon Anne offered me a unique opportunity: a chance to see Heather in her wedding gown. "Ain't that bad luck or somethin'?" I said.

"No, silly. It's bad luck for the groom not the best man. Besides, as a Christian, I don't believe in luck anyway, good or bad. But promise you won't let on anything to John."

"Promise. Probly wouldn't be any good at describin' it anyhow."

"Anyway, Martha's with her in the bedroom sewing some last pieces of the lace. She's really talented and doing a wonderful job with all the additions and alterations."

"Is Heather fit to be seen?"

"Of course! She's wearing it now. Even has her hair pinned up like she'll have at the ceremony, just not as fancy. Her mom and I'll fix it for her tomorrow."

Entering, Heather looked over at me smiling, and I gulped. She was lovely, not equal to my Anne, of course, but striking nonetheless. The hair on top seemed darker, more auburn than red and revealed her slender, white neck.

"Isn't she beautiful?" asked Anne.

"She's a fair sight," I whispered just loud enough to be overheard. "John might just need help standing up when he first sees her 'cause his knees will be shakin'."

Heather laughed and said, "No he won't, but in case he does, you'll steady him."

"Reckon so. It's one of my jobs as best man."

"What do you think of the dress?" asked Anne. "It was her mother's and with Martha's help it fits perfectly now."

Being a male Texan, I was lost for words, so I asked Anne to describe it for me. She did and in more detail than I needed or could ever remember. Pointing to the gown, Anne said, "Martha calls it the 'New Silhouette' because the style showcases the intricacies in her mother's light blue silk dress. Beginning with a champagne-colored lacey square neckline, a light gauze insert covers Heather's bodice. The sleeves are elbow length ending in a band of the same wide hand-made lace gotten from the hem. This same lace falls from each shoulder down to the tea-length hem. Being a truly modern woman, Heather has chosen to forego the hoops and petticoats which allows the skirt to fall softly around her slim figure."

It took me a moment to realize she had finished and I was expected to comment. I cleared my throat and said, "If John's legs ain't shakin' tomorrow, mine might be." Hopefully, the laughter that followed from the three ladies wasn't entirely at my expense.

We gathered early Friday evening for a buffet dinner that made it easier for the ladies to continue wedding preparations. To be exact, we were told to stay out of their way. About eight in the evening, we boys strolled over to the café where the men were gathering for the bachelor party. Fred and Mike were in a rollicking good mood. However, a light rain had begun to fall that both John and I took as a bad sign.

Another Texas buffet greeted us at the café: homemade bread and baking powder biscuits ready for stuffing with flank steak, steak tips, and creamed dried beef, plus plenty of fried chicken. That last was probably for the Yankees. There was a huge pot of mashed potatoes as well as strawberry shortcake and oatmeal cookies for the sweet tooth. But no salads or vegetables – a feast fit for Texan men. Helen Martin was the only female allowed and only because she, Burt, and Toby had done all the cooking and would be our servers for this event.

After seeing that spread, I looked around the room and observed the great decorations: surgical instruments were hanging on the walls, as were the flags or banners representing the Universities of Michigan and Houston. A Final touch were posters from Westerns starring Hart and Mix. *Where on earth had they gotten them?* Then I remembered Tony and figured he must have brought them with him from various Hollywood studios and left them behind as mementos. They were perfect. Everyone commented on them, egging John on a bit. He went along with the good-natured humor.

By nine p.m. nearly thirty men had shown up: Pastor Dan and several congregants, townsfolk, Decker and the two Rangers, Chief and Darius. I was glad to see Darius and fixed to talk Toby into taking off his apron later so he could join Darius and the rest of us in this shindig.

Someone had carted in a piano that the reverend attacked with gusto while one of his deacons played the guitar. Sometimes we listened, at other times joined in with familiar songs. Mostly we jawed with friends and made quite a few trips to the food and drinks tables.

Well into the evening, John leaned in and said, "I think my buddies are up to a prank or two."

"Figured as much. What have ya spotted?"

"Saw Fred pouring something into the punch bowl."

"Doctored it with some kind of booze, no doubt. I've had some and ain't tasted nuthin'."

"Think it's vodka. You can't taste it mixed with some other things."

"Gotta move fast, cousin. I'm on the wagon and Anne's countin' on me. Gave my word."

"I know and I'm proud of you, Ted."

"Also worried a mite 'bout the pastor and those other abstainin' Baptists. Reckon the prank won't sit well with 'em."

"Agreed. I'll tell my friends to knock it off. Then I'll tell Burt and we'll figure out something. In the meantime, steer people, especially the church folk, away from that doggone bowl."

I did my best until Burt had replaced the punch with what he called his "secret formula number two." Everyone enjoyed that concoction, even the Yankees, who looked a bit hang-dogged after their "talk" with John. To their credit, they showed "true Texan backbone" and admitted they would've done something else had they known about my problem. Maybe, maybe not. I was just glad they had come all the way to Texas to support their friend. They clinched it with me when Mike said, "No more pranks like that at tomorrow's reception."

It so happened most of Burt's first secret formula had been drunk before the prank was discovered. While Decker and the Rangers could hold their liquor, that was not the case with most of the teetotalers present at John's party. As the evening wore on, several men had become louder and brasher than normal. Pastor Dan didn't seem to notice, perhaps for obvious reasons. John called everyone together at midnight and thanked them for coming. Before heading out, I saw the three lawmen slap John's back and give him knowing smiles. He even got a wink from Springer. They had figured out John's friends' "secret" after all, I reckoned.

Walking back home, we both were relieved that the rain had stopped. Maybe this outdoor wedding would be a bang-up affair after all. With moods lifted, we quietly entered my house. Mine sank, though, when I remembered that three of us would be sleeping on the floor. Settling in, I could feel my muscles tightening up. The groom had been given the couch, which was entirely appropriate. Lucky man!

Still no rain Saturday morning and the final call was for the outdoor ceremony. Several of us men spent the morning making sure everything at the lake was ready. The women of the church were already setting up for the reception under the big tent. As a last minute favor, I asked John's buddies to help with parking wagons and cars on the other side of the bridge and assisting people over the bridge and down to the wedding area. And in case of a heavy downpour, they might best stay close to help guests back to their rides.

We came back into town at mid-morning and enjoyed a quick brunch with Uncle George and Aunt Mary and Susan. I hadn't seen them in quite a spell and had a lot of catching up to do myself. We shared fond memories of our summer visits together in Michigan and Texas. We were really getting wound up when my mom poked her head in and pointed to the clock. "Get a move on, young man," she said sternly. "John needs to dress up and get out there 'fore Heather. Give him a hand, Ted, now."

That last comment was a command and we all rushed to obey. Thirty minutes later, John had on his best suit and tie. He looked like an Eastern dandy. I quickly donned my best cowboy jacket, hung a new bolo tie around my neck, and yanked on my best, polished cowboy boots. No cowboy hat, though, that was a bit much. I didn't want to outshine the groom, ya know.

We gathered everyone together and made it to the lake at eleven-thirty. By eleven-forty-five the place was right quick filling up. Looking east several times, I didn't like the picture: unfriendly black clouds were forming. The wind was also picking up. *Why hadn't they planned an earlier wedding?*

I could see a car arriving with Heather and her wedding party. Her Uncle Howard was driving and would be giving her away in just a few minutes. Heather, her uncle, and Anne stayed in the background while the rest found seats in front of the platform where John and I, and Pastor Dan were waiting beneath the decorated arch. Off to my right I could see a piano resting on a smaller raised platform. We continued to wait. Why the delay?

The answer came when several women up front stood and climbed the platform, joined by a guitarist. Assembled, music began and they sang two secular songs and two hymns, all enjoyable. *But did they have to include all verses of each song?* Finishing, they returned to their seats. The pianist then began playing the traditional wedding march, the signal we'd been waiting for.

The maid of honor led the way, and I'd never seen Anne look lovelier. She was wearing a simple, yet stylish, jade green dress that was new to me. Must have bought it, I reckoned, on one of those female-only trips to Brownsville. She carried a bouquet of flowers and smiled left and right until she was halfway to the platform. Then she only had eyes for me. She broke eye contact momentarily as she accepted the pastor's help stepping onto the platform. She graced me with another heart-melting smile. I feared my own legs might start to tremble.

All eyes turned toward the bride and people stood to honor her. As she got closer, I thought I sensed a slight tremor in John's legs. I decided not to lay a hand on him. If he fell, I'd pick him up but right now he was on his own. He'd just have to buck up. Also me one day, I figured.

Heather's uncle handed her to John and returned to his seat in the front row beside Heather's mother. Heather and John shared a long lovers' smile only breaking eye contact when the pastor cleared his throat to assume command.

All four of us then turned to Pastor Dan as he prayed. It was a long prayer. *Was this a sign of something bad about to happen?* As he greeted the happy couple, I thought I heard a faint rumble of thunder in the distance. "Pick it up, pastor" I shouted to him in my mind. He started preaching and it was soon clear he hadn't heard my mental command. After about ten minutes, I figured he'd be recalling every single New Testament passage on marriage. It was getting darker and windier by the moment.

John poked me unexpectedly and nodded to the east as if I hadn't already figured it out. The pastor, astonishingly, still seemed to be spellbound by his own impassioned preaching. Finally, the best man couldn't take it any longer and reached out to yank his left sleeve, the one holding the Bible. It fell to the ground, and he looked at me with a shocked expression. I pointed with emphasis to the danger heading our way. He paused in mid-sentence, mouth still open, and stared at the approaching darkness. Suddenly, the trance was broken and he turned back to John and Heather mouthing, "I'm sorry," then turned to the audience and said, "I think it's time these two handsome young people got hitched. John, place the ring on Heather's finger."

I gave him the ring and he did as ordered. Then the pastor said what we'd all been waiting to hear, "I pronounce you man and wife. John, you may now kiss your bride." A big smooch and cheering broke out. We made our way to the tent to form a receiving line and the crowd lined up to offer their congratulations to the bride and groom. After a few agonizing minutes, only about a dozen people had passed by us. Why was the line moving so slowly? I peeked at Heather and watched her greet a man. It was quick. Then his wife and the procession stopped. The woman kissed her on the cheek and stepped back to get a full view of Heather's gown after which they made a gabfest about it.

This chit-chat with the ladies happened with the next couple and the next until it was darn plain that *the gown* was the hold-up to everything. It was a rare lady who did not praise Heather's choice. Heather graciously replied to each with much more than was necessary, I felt.

Some women even stepped off to one side to gather in a small group to continue whispering about Heather's gown. The men, on the other hand, had two things on their mind: the coming storm and food. Nervously looking up, they bolted for the tables piled high with food and drinks. A few men even abandoned their wives and joined others directly at the buffet.

It wasn't long before in rapid succession came lightning and rumbles of thunder. I reached over Anne's shoulder and tapped John, pointing to the heavens. We shot each other a knowing look and turned to our gals but were cut short by an enormous clap of thunder directly overhead. It began to rain, slowly at first, but I had a bad feeling as I looked at the sky. I feared we were about to receive a cloudburst, even worse than the storm we'd been caught up in during the earlier bandit raid.

The smart Texans were already making their way to the safety of the tent or running for the bridge. My dad and Heather's uncle came up and offered umbrellas and blankets to the four of us. We men instantly got our ladies protected and hurried them as fast as possible to Howard's car for the ride back home. They resisted at first but soon relented and were whisked away.

At first the rain came down in vertical sheets. Within moments it changed into blinding, sideways waves driven by the heavy, gusting wind. Even the tent provided little relief. Soon everyone was running for the bridge – already drenched and slipping, some occasionally falling on their way.

Fred and Mike were doing a bang-up job of hustling guests over the bridge, but the water was rising rapidly. Before everyone could make it across, water reached the walkway itself. The two creeks were spilling over their sides and changing the wedding area into that new lake I'd talked about with John. Water was already up to my foot and rising. Then we heard a loud cracking noise. I looked up in horror and saw one side of the bridge break from its foundation. The second break followed in seconds, and the bridge was swept away, with several people including one child still on it. Amidst the screams, I saw Mike leap to safety on the other side and Fred dive headlong into the raging stream, not a desperate dive but a controlled one a competitive swimmer would make. I straightaway knew what he was doing. He was fixing to rescue some of those who had been swept away. I saw Mike as well as several other men running alongside him close to the water.

"Help them God and us too," I prayed silently and earnestly.

There were about a dozen people trapped with us in the newly-forming lake. Feeling something strike my calf, I looked down to see a fish being swept away – a bass no less! A small group of four women and two children were among those marooned with us. I figured they would have trouble making it across even with the help of the men. Now what?

That question and my prayers were answered when two wagons pulled up perhaps thirty yards north, one driven by Toby and the other by Darius. With the help of several other men who had stayed behind, two rowboats were lifted out and dropped into the current. Darius jumped into one, Toby the other, and they started rowing toward us. Swept by the current, they were upon us in seconds. Someone yelled for us to grab the ropes and hold on for dear life. Catching hold, we pulled with all our strength and brought the boats closer. Handing the children and women in first, we got in and set off for the opposite side, pulling in some thirty yards south of where we had been stranded.

It was then that John and I saw a group of men hovering over some bodies. We dashed through the drenching rain to learn there were five victims, one a child. Glancing back at the creek, I spotted Fred carrying one more person toward us. Six injured; four groaning and showing signs of life, two lifeless or so it looked to me.

One unconscious adult, one child. Naturally John started with the child. Turning him over on his side, he checked his mouth for any blockage, rolled him back and began pumping the boy's chest. It worked. After some more chest thumpings, the child coughed up some water and looked around confused. His mother dropped to her knees beside him and cradled him in her arms. She gazed upon John as only a mother could in that situation: bottom-of-the-heart thankfulness.

Mike was also doing many of the same things to the other unconscious victim. His revived as well. The image of these future doctors already saving lives was heartwarming. All the injured needed to be taken to the clinic. "You guys ready to show me more of what you've learned up north?" John asked his buddies. They were and off we went.

John and I jumped into Howard's car that had arrived a few moments earlier. Our first thoughts were about our ladies. John beat me to the punch. "Did you get Heather and Anne back safely?" he asked anxiously.

"Sure did, though, there's a wrinkle," Dad said.

Faltering, John said, "What do you mean?"

"Well, your gals said they were changin' clothes in short order and headin' to the clinic in case they were needed. Demanded I stay and drive 'em. Sound 'bout right to you two fellas?"

Shaking my head, I said, "It dang sure 'nuff does."

CHAPTER TWENTY

TOGETHERNESS

Toby's first concern had been Martha and the girls. Fortunately, they'd been sitting near the bridge and were some of the first to escape. He'd plopped them into a wagon and driven off at a rapid pace to his home. He wondered how much trouble he was in since it wasn't his wagon. Family came first, he thought, as he pulled into the lake parking area – just in time to greet the wagon's owner rushing up with his family. He then chauffeured them home. Not a word was said about his previous trip.

F RED HAD COMMANDEERED A CAR which we used to speed to the clinic. During the brief ride, he told us that my lawmen friends had been a big help in the rescuing people. That was no surprise to me. We found them in the waiting room dripping wet and helping the two victims by getting blankets and towels for drying. Family members had arrived to provide further care and comfort. Springer caught my eye and pointed to the examining room and said, "The ladies are in there with the other injured. Some of 'em ain't doin' so good. Water and blood everywhere. Watch yer step."

As I was thanking the three of them, Mike Flynn burst through the door. Realizing that his two medical friends had arrived, John waved everyone to follow him into the examining room. "Glad you're here, fellas. Let's get to work." They grinned, rolled up their sleeves, and pushed past me into the room. Figuring they might need an extra hand, I brought up the rear.

I saw Nancy, Heather, and Anne already at work. They were wearing dry clothes and also had sleeves rolled up. One patient was lying on the regular examining table, the other was stretched out on a normal bed that had been borrowed from the patient's wing of the clinic. Two others, a man and a woman, were sitting on chairs against the wall, with pale faces and still wearing their sopping clothes. Despite the heat and humidity, they were shaking. I could even hear the lady's teeth chattering.

John hugged his bride, I, my future bride. Weak smiles were exchanged among us. No words were spoken. None were necessary. There was work to be done even on a wedding day.

John had Nancy work with his two buddies and chose Heather and Anne for his assistants. John took off his suit coat, tie, and shirt and tossed them into a corner. They fell on a pile of soaked clothes already stripped from the two patients. He then pulled shirts from the usual stockpile stored in the room. He tossed one to me along with a towel. I was thankful for small favors. Fred and Mike would labor in drenched clothes, slowly drying. John then ordered everyone to wash up in the corner sink and slip into surgical gloves.

Finally ready, the clinic's newly expanded medical staff went to work. John asked me to check on the other two victims. Checking the man, I couldn't find any obvious injury and figured it was probably just shock. Finished, I hesitated and looked around the room uncertainly. Anne noticed my delay in checking the woman and suggested a family member might be in the waiting room. I went and returned with a sister who was happy to lend a hand. The sister found nothing wrong with her, so I guessed it was another case of shock. I moved out of the way, wondering how I could help. In short order, John asked me to be the "errand" boy, the person to fetch extra equipment or supplies for either patient. I accepted and waited for instructions.

John soon took command of the operating room, naturally focusing on his own patient, but also answering questions from his friends when they got into a fix. The ladies also sometimes needed directions. At one point, it seemed everyone was speaking all at once. Everyone in the end yielded to my cousin, the chief surgeon, as the man in charge.

There was a lot of blood involved with his patient's injuries: facial cuts, broken and lacerated fingers, and a large gash on his belly. Many stitches were called for, and when he ran out of catgut, I had to find more. I did, but it was shortly not enough to meet his needs and those of his friends. I hunted again and found enough silk thread to keep them all sewing.

John and Heather worked well as a team, as did Heather and Anne. I knew Anne was taking to nursing but, watching Heather, I felt she also might be a good one, if a teaching position didn't turn up. It was really something special the way the three worked so well together.

The facial cuts were easy to fix but the delicate fingers and belly injury weren't. And the man was now conscious. That was good but things would be much easier for all if he wasn't. Ann volunteered to give him ether. I was impressed by how much medicine she had learned in the past few months. Once the patient went to sleep, John quickly snapped two fingers back into place, applied a few stitches, finishing with small splints to keep everything in place.

Turning to the stomach wound, John warned us that he'd have to probe fairly deep and wasn't sure what he'd find. As Heather removed the bandage, the wound began oozing blood. Anne had her hands full soaking it all up with gauze. John sewed up some external veins, which helped, but the blood kept coming. "Got to go a bit deeper," he said and began to when something really bad happened. A stream of blood shot up like when oil had been struck in the ground. No shouts of joy this time. It was arterial blood. The stream landed mostly on John and Heather. I felt like cussing; John merely said, "Darn, that may be my fault. Gotta move fast now." He was amazingly calm considering the situation.

He grabbed more gauze and applied pressure holding it for several seconds. Then he removed the gauze, peered into the opening and said, "I think I see it." As more blood spurted out, more pressure was applied. He quickly described the action Heather had to take. "Ready?" She nodded. "On three," and began the count. At three, with the gauze removed, she followed John's direction, found and pinched the artery between thumb and forefinger. "Great job, honey," he said as he reached in with needle and thread to tie off the bleeder. Finished, they both stepped back from the patient and waited. To everyone's relief, no more spurts. Anne offered a prayer right there on the spot. It spoke for all of us. John quickly tied off other smaller veins and closed the wound. "Biggest fear now is infection," he said. "So don't stop praying, any of you."

Fred must have heard John's infection comment and called over, "What are you using to clean the skin and other areas?"

John replied, "We only have mercurochrome and iodine. I'm using iodine today."

"You know that Professor Perkins uses Acriflavine and swears by it. Used it up North, haven't you?"

"I have. Wish I had some now."

"Gonna be more available soon and much cheaper 'cause of the war. Army is building up a huge stockpile to treat future wounded soldiers. Made from coal tar of all things."

"Already cheap and pretty effective. I'll have Nancy order some more."

They finished talking about antiseptics as John moved beside them to the second patient. He obviously wanted to check on the progress of his buddies. With a hint of alarm, he said, "Surprised you set that bone already. No swelling?"

"Not enough to worry about," answered Mike. "Once we got the leg cleaned up we decided to snap it back into place after the ether took hold. Nancy did a swell job of putting him under, by the way. Sleeping like a baby."

"She's the best," agreed John. Nancy smiled her thanks.

"We used a new technique taught us by a visiting professor from South Africa. Claims he set a whole bunch of bones during the Boer War back at the turn of the century. Bet you didn't hear a peep from him."

"No, not even a groan. But you'll need to make a cast. How much Plaster of Paris do we have on hand, Nancy?"

"'Nuff for the job. I'll fetch it. Give me a hand, Ted."

We left and soon returned with the container as well as a big roll of cotton wrapping. She mixed the plaster with the water, dipped a strip of cotton bandage into it, and handed it to Fred. Fred and Mike then took turns wrapping layer upon layer around the leg from ankle to thigh. They worked quickly but not very carefully, and I noticed plenty of gobs falling on the floor and bed as they made headway with the cast. I hoped they didn't expect Nancy or either of our gals to clean up after them.

John praised their work when the cast was complete. "Anything else besides closing up a few superficial wounds?" he asked.

"Nothing specific," Fred said. "They did cough up some nasty looking fluid a few times. No doubt from the creek. Might have a bellyache or the trots for a day or so. And you can bet they'll have nightmares."

"The two against the wall still have the shakes," I said.

"Let's check 'em over to rule out anything serious," said Fred. I kept silent about the exam already done by me and the sister.

He arrived at the same conclusion: mostly shock from what they'd just gone through. Both were still a bit shaky and only a little color had returned to their faces. Maybe observing several medical procedures had even delayed their recovery.

Knowing they needed to calm down before being released, John pulled his friends aside for a confab. No one crabbed when I joined. Four solutions were suggested: 1) something call Barbitol, a new sedative but none was available at the clinic; 2) marihuana, which Fred claimed one younger professor's research showed worked well at calming nerves but not "possible" in Los Indios according to John; 3) the old standby, alcohol, which John said was available in a small bottle of whiskey the clinic stored for several purposes; and 4) prayer, which was John's suggestion.

Our little group brought up three of the options to them. The man chose whiskey without a blink. Nancy left and in a jiffy came back with the partially used bottle. The man took a slug, gasping as the liquid burned all the way down. Looking up with moist eyes, he asked for a second shot. The second one almost made him slide off the chair. Recovering "miraculously," he sat up straight and held out one arm – steady as a rock. Not bad, I thought, for this old-fashioned way to calm one's nerves. I didn't dare glance Anne's way as this kind of traditional medicine was being used.

The woman chose prayer. Anne and Heather had been standing in the background, and when they heard her make her selection, they stepped forward and offered to pray with her. She accepted, along with her sister, and the rest of us pulled away to allow them some privacy. We took this opportunity to head for the sink and rid ourselves of dirt, blood, and spatters of plaster. At the sink, I glanced back to see that the prayer circle had increased to five; Nancy had joined them.

Prayer worked! After a few minutes, the woman's shaking had ended and more hints of color were returning to her face. *Was prayer the best medicine of all?*

John and his friends made one final check on their two original patients before being confident they could be released to Nancy's aftercare. While this was happening, the three women moved to the sink to clean up. John joined them for a quiet chat. I stood back and watched them talking quietly and calmly, as if this was a normal day. But it wasn't. It had been John and Heather's wedding day! And my Anne was the maid of honor. A thought rushed into my head and it humbled me to my core. I didn't deserve to have such wonderful people in my life: selfless, loving servants of God. Not one of them had even mentioned how the wedding had been "interrupted." All that concerned them was the welfare of others. Deserving or not, I sure was grateful to have them in my life.

After cleaning up, Anne walked over to me and placed her head on my chest. She sighed and relaxed into my embrace. Right then and there I promised myself that I would love and cherish Anne as John did his Heather. It was my solemn oath.

Our spiritual moment was interrupted by a noise and we saw Nancy filling up a bucket of soapy water at the sink. She took the bucket and a mop to the middle of the room, and with a watchful eye on her patients, began cleaning the floor. All four of us made a fuss about her doing it but she waved us away. "Y'all get into that waiting room. Lots of people stickin' 'round to see ya. Still pourin' outside and I reckon the room is 'bout jammed full by now."

"It's only fair that we help you," John protested.

"Nonsense. I'm better at this than nursin'. Besides, I wouldn't let y'all do this kinda work, 'specially not today. Get movin'." And that was that! Nancy was another person I didn't deserve in my life. "I'll take her, though," I said to God in my mind.

John lined us up for a once-over at the door. We both gave special attention to our gals, wiping off a final drop or two of blood and grime from a nose or forehead. Our clothes were a different matter. No chance for clean ones – so we were stuck. Heather and John, had fared the worst. Heather's white shirt still had blood smears on it. John said, "Honey, I can't let you go out there with that blouse. Especially not on your wedding day." Heather seemed unconcerned.

Nancy, of course, came to the rescue by offering her blouse for Heather to wear. Heather resisted at first but finally gave in. We men turned our backs and they swapped blouses. Opening the waiting room door, we looked at family members, wedding guests, patients, even a few people who were simply trying to get out of the rain. We filed out, inched our way along the wall, and leaned against it, the only space available. The crowd's first reaction to seeing us was silence, then they suddenly broke out in loud cheering and applause. Even Decker and the Rangers joined in. I got behind John and Heather to gently push them out into the middle of the adoring throng. Once again the center of attention, praise and love was showered on them from all in the room. Not having had a proper wedding reception, they truly deserved it.

The front door creaked open and a group of church ladies edged in carrying covered baskets of utensils, food, and hot coffee. Making their way to the reception desk, they spread everything on it leaving an empty spot in the center. Next came Pastor Dan with my mom and Heather's. The three carried a small bench covered with a tarp. It was the wedding cake. A bit squashed on top by the tarp, but otherwise it appeared to be in pretty good shape.

The pastor shouted to get everyone's attention, then requested that the new Mr. and Mrs. come forward. He handed them a knife and the two together cut the cake, fed each other the first bites, then started cutting for everyone else. Everyone got something to eat even if they had to eat standing up. The bride and groom sat because I had found two chairs and suggested they sit down behind the desk. They did, eating off their laps, smiling, waving, and talking with nearly everyone around them. I took over cutting the cake, with help from Anne. When I had time, I grabbed a slice for myself. The very moist cake tasted great.

Pastor Dan and his wife led us in singing several songs. Standing so they faced Heather and John, they sang two songs together: *Let Me Call You Sweetheart* and *Irish Eyes Are Smiling.* Heather sure was a sweetheart and her red hair perhaps hinted at some Irish blood, and both songs were applauded enthusiastically.

So John and Heather, after saving one life and patching up the wounds of several others, ended up having a second reception in the clinic's waiting room. I was sure that the unusual wedding and both receptions would never be forgotten. Looking at their smiling, happy faces, I realized this couple could handle anything thrown their way.

The rain became a drizzle and eventually stopped in late afternoon. Family members and a few close friends went back to my folks' house around dinnertime. We picked at some food brought along by my parents from the clinic but mostly we just sat around talking with the new couple. Heather was her radiant self. She'd slipped back into her gown. It looked pretty good despite some minor water damage around the neckline and sleeves. Once again, the ladies couldn't "ooh and ah" enough. I gave John one of my suit coats since his wasn't fit to wear. The fact that it was a Western styled coat didn't bother him at all.

I wondered how and when the honeymoon would be started. There were pools of water everywhere. I figured Main Street was a mess and dad said the trains wouldn't be operating for a day or so. While turning over that news, I saw mom huddled with Worth Henderson in the corner of the living room. What were they whispering about? Mom got everyone's attention and announced a plan. The couple would spend the night at Worth's house. Worth would bunk with a friend to give them some privacy. Further, the house was theirs as long as they needed it, as long as it took to get the train schedule back to normal. John and Heather gratefully accepted and said they hoped to be on their way no later than Monday. With more food and drink and a few more songs, our extended second reception broke up around nine p.m. While tired, everyone was thankful for the time spent together.

Alone with Anne and my family, dad pulled me aside and whispered, "Son, I got back here first from the clinic and this here telegram had been slipped under the front door. Don't know how it even got through. Didn't wanna interrupt the goin's-on so I held it back. Ain't looked at it. Appears to be from A & M." *Good news or bad?*

I tore it open and read it, first to myself, then to dad. "Looks like I'm headed fer college in the fall, Dad. They got exemptions fer all the students with B or above averages. Made it by a hair, thanks to those midnight study sessions. That's a relief." It was also a relief to dad, who playfully punched my shoulder, grabbed the telegram, and went to share the good news with others, starting with mom. I went to do the same with Anne.

Anne was delighted and kissed me on the lips right in front of Diane. She responded with a wink. Shortly later, I heard some noise from the living room and went to investigate. There I found mom, Anne, and Diane on the floor cleaning the mud away. Dad came in and we both stared, astonished. Couldn't this have waited until the morning? We sighed and got down to work beside them. Exhausted, we went to bed early. Sleep came right quick.

The Sunday service was changed at the last minute to one of song and prayer. John and Heather attended and were again the focus of everyone's attention at the close. While many people were around, John declared that he and Heather would stay another day in order to help in the town's cleanup. There was an awkward moment of silence as many glanced at each other in disbelief. Speaking for them, I said to John, "Cousin, that ain't gonna happen. It's Houston fer you two. If the trains ain't rollin', we'll drive ya north ourselves."

The newly married couple seemed a bit relieved by that announcement.

I spent Monday morning helping sweep mud and debris out of buildings. One branch of Wilson's creek had overflowed and washed through Main Street. It had even seeped into the bottom floors of buildings on one side of the road. Darius, Toby, and Chief joined us, and by noon we'd made substantial progress. Decker and the Rangers were elsewhere, probably hunting down bad guys.

John and Heather, along with John's two buddies, caught the early afternoon train north on Tuesday. All four would be traveling together as far as Houston. Family and friends had gathered for the happy couple's send-off. It was heartbreaking to everyone. Los Indios would miss them, terribly. The separation would be especially hard on Heather and Anne who'd grown so close in the past few months. Tears flowed. I turned away to hide the moisture in my own manly Texan eyes.

Monday afternoon I went to take up my patrolling duties again with Decker. Dad had decided Decker needed me more than he did since Toby was proving to be a valuable new clerk. I had prepared myself for another routine patrol. I was wrong. As we mounted up, Decker directed us to the house of the "vegetable" lady from last winter. "This time," he said, "She claims she's been robbed. Over $200 taken."

"That's a pile of money."

"Is 'round here. Had put it in a jar at home 'cause she don't trust banks. Crazy, huh?"

"Bit crazy. She know who done it?"

"Says she saw 'em runnin' away. Gave me a description of their clothes."

"Helpful?"

"Yeah. One of 'em was wearin' a hat that we've spotted 'fore. Got a couple of suspects in mind. Ready fer some investigatin' and interrogatin'?"

"At yer side, Captain." I used his former Ranger title and he didn't kick up a fuss. Besides, there was a fall election that he expected to win. We'd then all call him Sheriff, not Deputy. He'd like that.

So off we went to the old lady's house before hunting down some lawbreakers. I reckoned that my deputy work would keep me busy for the rest of the summer. I hoped I wouldn't be too busy with my duties, and pleasures in the case of Anne, because I wanted some free time before fall and college to think back on all the interesting and scary things that had happened to me. It was just last summer I'd begun working in those oil fields. The past fifteen months had been truly amazing. Adventure after adventure. I didn't want to forget a single experience, not even the bad ones. Perhaps I'd have to write it all down. When would I find the time?

CHAPTER TWENTY-ONE

TED

Toby sometimes took his family to Wilson's lake for a weekend picnic. This Saturday he was alone and saw Mr. Ted on the dock fishing and seemingly in deep thought. He wondered if he should leave him be. He knew from experience that at times a man just needed to be alone.

TED HAD FINALLY FOUND SOME time to himself to settle his thoughts. Until a couple days ago, the month since the wedding had been as busy as ever. By that late August Saturday, three goings-on had happened in the meantime. First, his dad had lightened his load at the store because college was around the corner. Second, Decker had hired Ted's replacement, a new deputy sheriff, and was busy training the new recruit. Though a bit miffed, he knew his days were numbered and tried not to be offended. Third, and most importantly, Anne had just left on the train heading north to visit her family in Pennsylvania. When they'd heard about Ted's marriage proposal and the trip to Brownsville to buy an engagement ring, they'd practically ordered her home. He smiled thinking she'd probably stare at the ring all the way back to mom and dad.

Anne had also taken along a photograph of the newly engaged couple, guessing her parents could barely wait to see what their future son-in-law looked like. He chose to wear his finest cowboy duds. No sense trying to hide the fact he was a true-blue Texan.

So on that Saturday afternoon, he'd borrowed dad's car, filled it with fishing equipment, a basket with sandwiches, and a jug of water and driven to the lake, mostly to think. It had been nearly fifteen months since he'd started working for Phil Archer on that oil rig outside Midland, and he had heaps to recall and think over. He carried everything to the dock, yanked off his boots and socks, and dangled his feet in the cool water. It was hotter than blazes and there was no shade anywhere near the dock. But he'd brought his broadest brimmed cowboy hat and worn a long sleeve shirt.

He was glad he'd talked to his mom about his plans for the afternoon because she'd suggested taking along pencil and paper to jot down memories. That way nothing would be forgotten. He baited his hook with worms collected Friday night and attached a bobber before casting out. He didn't really care if his splashing feet frightened the fish. Fishing was just an excuse for remembering.

He set down the pole on the dock and anchored it with his lunch and fishing baskets, picked up his writing materials and traveled back in time. He was one bass and many memories richer two hours later. He looked over the pages of scribbled notes and was astonished with all he'd written, the good and the bad, the uplifting times and the embarrassing ones. All of a sudden, his stomach grumbled reminding him of a hearty sandwich laying nearby. He took his notes and the food basket to the shade of a nearby cottonwood tree, leaving his pole on the dock on the off chance he might snag another fish.

A half-hour later, the list was longer and rearranged chronologically. It included: rowdy times during his last spring semester at A & M; hard work and exciting adventures on the oil field; John and Heather arriving under orders from his mom to straighten him out; his fascination with Anne Yoder, the young lady traveling with John and Heather; his friendship with Captain Decker of the Rangers and with the Indian, Chief Parker; all the medical adventures he'd shared with John around Midland; realizing Heather was perfect for John, and his falling in love with Anne; realizing reforming his loose ways was essential if he wanted a future with Anne; fighting to defend Anne's honor following a religious revival north of Midland; traveling with John, Decker, and Chief to El Paso to meet the movie director Tony Milano; John's narrow escape from the governor at a political rally; twice helping John and others rescue soldiers from Mexico; hunting, finding, and escaping from Pancho Villa in northern Mexico; Decker being wounded by Villa's men and nursing him back to health; sending John off to California and returning to Los Indios with Decker; becoming a deputy sheriff beside Decker; loving and almost losing Anne in west Texas; and finally, welcoming John back from California.

Finished, he leaned back against the tree and said to himself, "Thunderation! There's 'nuff adventures for four or five years all rolled into one, and that don't even include everything that's happened since John returned." As he was looking over his initial list one last time, he heard a splash from the dock. Uh-oh! He leaped to his feet and watched his pole being pulled out toward the middle of the lake. The one remaining anchor, the fishing basket, had been too lightweight to save the pole from another big strike.

Reaching the dock, he watched the pole sink to the bottom. The bobber reappeared a short time later and drifted slowly back toward him. The fish had plainly cut the line with its teeth. Well, he had one bass and a great list so he was satisfied.

Walking to the car, he stopped when he spied someone in the distance heading his way. He thought it was either Toby or Darius. Once in sharp focus, he recognized the familiar face of Toby Washington. He decided to wait and chat, if Toby was in the mood.

Thinking of Toby turned his mind to more recent events. He'd learned from Captain Springer that the two raiders sent to Laredo had been released, not in the usual way but in the Ranger way. The Rangers must have heard how the crazy young lieutenant on General Pershing's staff treated prisoners under his control. Following that soldier's example, according to Springer, the two men had been tied up to the waist, rowed over to Mexico, and set free with body paint to warn the drug traffickers to stay out of Texas. Springer had also brought up that King and his son were laying low and not bringing across any drugs. The law might be winning. Was drug smuggling finally dwindling? Ted also pictured in his mind Phil Archer, who'd boarded a train heading to the northeast corner of Texas where "gushers" were still common. Perhaps Archer's vast experience would quickly land him a job. He sure hoped so.

Lloyd Jenkins also came to mind as Toby got closer. Jenkins was still struggling to remember his recent past but was making progress. Mom still cared for him. She was a saint and Jenkins was a very lucky man.

Ted's final thoughts were a blur: back to college in days, a Christmas wedding for him and Anne, hopefully with John and Heather attending. There would be January military training for John. Anne wanted to have Heather live nearby while John was in basic training and overseas. Ted also had hopes of finishing college by the summer of 1918. What then? Would he be called into service before the war was over?

Another thought popped into his head at the very moment Toby walked up. What the heck, he'd bring up the crazy idea after greeting him. "Glad y'all are here, Toby. Want to run an idea past ya and get yer 'pinion."

"Sure, Mr. Ted. Saw ya back aways. Knew ya was thinkin' hard. Didn't want to interrupt. What d'ya got goin'?"

"I've had a heap of excitin' adventures past year or so. What 'bout a movie based on my life? Better yet, a book. Bet Steve Brundage would be interested. 'Specially after the studio changes the screenplay 'bout John's adventures. Heard that happens lots of times. My life would make a pretty good story, though. Don't ya think?"

Toby stared at Ted blankly. Ted waited. The answer came, and Ted knew it had the ring of truth.

"I can swear to yer excitin' life of late, Mr. Ted. But a movie or book? Y'all best check with Miss Anne. She'll know what to do." *Check with Anne!*

Sighing, Ted put both ideas out of his head and suggested they spend a few minutes on the dock, feet dangling in the cool water. While they relaxed, he turned to Toby and asked him to share his feelings about Los Indios, starting when he stepped off the train. Toby grinned and began to speak.

CHAPTER TWENTY-TWO

TOBY

TOBY WASHINGTON BEGAN BY REMINDING Ted why he'd moved to Los Indios: racism in his hometown. His distant cousin had been terribly abused and lynched and Toby feared for himself and his family. They'd found shelter and friendship in Ted's town and he was very grateful. There had been some difficult situations, as Ted well knew, but overall it had been a much friendlier town than he'd expected.

Ted interrupted him saying, "And it's all right, after we lawmen drew that line in the sand fer ya with those youngsters and the Kings?"

"Yessir, Mr. Ted. Ain't had no trouble fer weeks now. Never 'spected it to be perfect. No perfect place in the South fer us colored folks as ya rightly know."

"Sure do. John says it ain't perfect up North either. But it's gettin' better. And the kids? They havin' any trouble?"

"Had some at first but not much these days. Mostly a case of bein' ignored. They're fine young ladies, though, and are learnin' to deal with it."

Ted quizzed him about Martha and got the same answer: not perfect but improving. "Don't her bein' accepted have somethin' to do with her two jobs, sewin' and house cleanin'?"

"Sure think so. Probly mostly the sewin'. Got herself a fair middlin' of jobs as a seamstress 'cause of puttin' the finishin' touches on Miss Heather's gown."

"Mom's been talkin' up her talents too."

"Done heard as much and sure do 'preciate it."

"Mom says Heather wants Martha to take a peek at the gown when she's here fer Christmas. Says Heather's mom is upset about the condition it's in. Heather's not too worried. Just a little water damage at the edges."

"My Martha can save it and turn it into somethin' Miss Heather can use fer years to come. She's a mighty talented woman."

Ted agreed and praised Toby up and down for what he himself was doing. "Burt Martin claims y'all sure can cook and he'll be usin' ya more in the kitchen in the future. And my dad says next to mom, you're the best clerk he's ever had. Guess that means also better than me."

"Ain't so sure 'bout that, Mr. Ted, but I do work hard and try to do my best."

"Ya do, and I heard there's even a third job, right?"

"Yessir, but not many hours a week. Pastor Dan has me cleanin' the church on Saturdays. Best part of havin' three jobs is the extra money. 'Nuff to fix up some things in our new house, the one yer mom and dad found fer us."

"Been some talk 'bout Darius puttin' down roots in these parts."

"'Pears so. Clinched a deal on some land next to ours. Plans to put up a small house. It'll be the new last house at the edge of town."

"Y'all are good friends and that's probly why he's settlin' here."

"And there might be some other grounds fer settlin'. First, he's been spendin' a lot of time at the Indian reservation. Mr. Chief says he's makin' so many friends they're thinkin' of makin' him an honorary member of the tribe, just like Mr. Chief. Second, and it's sure the best one, I reckon, is 'cause of Miss Heather and Miss Anne."

"How's that?"

"Those two fine ladies found a gal fer Darius over in Brownsville. Seems to be swept off his feet by her. Think they might end up hitched. Pretty good matchmakers, those two ladies of yers."

"Funny, Anne hasn't said nuthin' 'bout it to me."

"Don't know 'bout that but that gal and Darius, they're a perfect pair to me. Darius better build more'n one room," Toby chuckled.

Making a spur of the moment decision, Ted hitched up his pants even farther and walked out into the lake. Toby quickly followed suit. They talked a spell longer before Toby brought up a more serious matter: the war in Europe.

"Think the draft'll catch hold of me, Mr. Ted?"

"Doubt it. Y'all fit under the headin' of Extreme Hardship, meanin' havin' a wife and young children to watch over."

"Heard that too, still worried. Have ya heard 'bout that ruckus in Houston little while ago?"

"Did read somethin' in the paper."

"It was Negro troops fightin' 'gainst the white police. Troops say the police was discriminatin' 'gainst 'em. Pretty bloody fight. Lots o' Negro soldiers arrested. Don't cotton to gettin' caught up in no race war."

"Don't blame ya, but y'all should be safe. One thing fer sure, if you're called up, this Christian community here in Los Indios will help out Martha and the kids."

"Thank ya kindly. Sure seems like I picked the right place to call home."

Both knew home and friendship were two of life's greatest blessings. Ted offered Toby a ride home. On the trip he said, "See my fishin' basket in the back seat? Take it with ya when we pull up. Caught a bass. 'Nuff to feed yer whole family."

"Mighty generous of ya, Mr. Ted. I'll get the basket back to ya right quick. Next time I have some luck fishin', I'll share the catch with you and yer family."

As they reached Toby's house, they talked about John and his future. "Where will Mr. John go when he's finished schoolin'?"

"Hopes he can do his basic trainin' here in Texas."

"That sure would please Miss Heather. Could stay close by, either here or with her mother."

"That's her hope, I'm sure."

"Where might the army be sendin' him, Mr. Ted?"

"No one knows. This war is now 'round the whole world. There's fightin' in Belgium, France, Russia, even in Africa. Reckon he could end up anywhere. Wherever he gets to go, there'll always be poor guys hurtin'."

"Tell him that me and Martha will be prayin' hard fer him."

"I will and thanks. See ya in church. Remember, y'all don't always have to sit in the back row."

"Best sit there fer now, Mr. Ted. Things are changin' all 'round us, but some comes harder than others."

Ted accepted the truth in Toby's comment. And it was uttered with a hint of sadness and pain.

As he turned for home, he wondered how long it would take for the nation, the South, and Texas to appreciate the "ordinary greatness" of a man like Toby Washington.

EPILOGUE

Summer 1918

THE LETTER ARRIVED IN MID-JULY and covered events from the previous month. It came from Italy where John had been placed in the Medical Corps. Strangely enough, Italy had begun the war on the German side but by 1918 was fighting with the Allies: England, France, and the United States. Heather had by this time returned to Texas to live with her mother not far from Anne. The two young women visited each other frequently to continue their friendship and discuss a situation they both had in common: pregnancy! Heather's baby was due in September, Anne's around Thanksgiving. They were overjoyed by their similar "condition" and talked tirelessly about what other wonders the future had in store for them.

On that particular day, Ted was out job hunting. His accelerated program in engineering would end in late fall and he was already getting interviews with oil riggers. When he returned to the new home he shared with his bride, Heather was there visiting. Anne asked about John and Heather produced a letter. As usual, Heather was concerned about the danger to John in a place of heavy fighting. Ted had assured her many times that John would be fine since

309

he wasn't infantry and only near the front after the shooting and shelling stopped. Ted could tell, as he accepted the letter, that more reassurance was needed.

He quickly read the brief letter and recognized immediately that it was the middle of three paragraphs that was troubling to Heather. It read:

> *In early June I was assigned to ride with a nurse in an ambulance carrying wounded men from the front. We are able to save many of the injured. One young driver is quite a character. He's from Michigan and we swap stories about hunting and fishing and life in that great state. Name's Ernie Hemingway. Drives like a mad man. Haven't crashed yet though. Sadly, just as I was getting to appreciate him, he was hit by a mortar shell not far from the truck. Did my best to patch him up but he suffered major damage to his legs. He won't see any more service, I'm sure. I'll be visiting him at the hospital in Milan in a few days. I hear he's writing up some of his war experiences. Probably good therapy for him. There will many stories of the horrors and heroes of this bloody conflict. Thankfully, it should all be over soon. At least that's the rumor here.*

To comfort both ladies, Ted said that shelling rarely hit medical workers. He was fairly certain about this. John was obviously out of harm's way because he was headed for the safe zone of Milan. Further, John was no doubt right when he said the war would soon be over. "All the papers at home are predictin' it'll be all over by fall, at the latest." He wasn't so sure about this but spoke with as much confidence as he could muster.

Both ladies seemed relieved, so he continued to distract them. "Say, John will have a heapin' load of great stories to share when he gets back. Let's get 'im to write 'em down. Might even get someone to write while he's a talkin'." Ted decided right then and there that preserving history through stories would be one of his goals in life.

Who among us gets tired of another good story?

THE END

I F YOU ENJOYED *COUSINS,* CONSIDER reading the first two books in the trilogy: *Tex Med,* and *Follow the Setting Sun.*

They can be ordered both as e-books and in cloth from any of the following: Authorhouse.com, Amazon.com, or BarnesandNoble.com

ACKNOWLEDGMENTS

T HANKS TO ALL THOSE WHO urged me to turn my efforts at historical fiction into a trilogy.

Special thanks to my typist, editor, and proof reader, Merrilee Skrocki, who labored many hours to hunt down typos and mistakes and whose suggestions for improvement were gratefully received.

Once again, Bethany Anderson's front and back covers are a major contribution to the book's appearance.

Finally, thanks to my wife, Janice, for the contributions she made to the style and content of this novel, especially the time she spent researching what a World War One wedding dress might look like.

Five years and nearly 300,000 words later and I'm finished. Perhaps I will return to pen and paper in the future to create more stories. And yes, I still write long hand.

ABOUT THE AUTHOR

I N ADDITION TO THIS THIRD volume of the Tex Med trilogy, Robert J. Eells has authored four other books, including two political biographies and two volumes of short stories about his father's sixty-year medical practice in a small town in New York State. He has also written several articles and numerous book reviews about contemporary political and cultural life in America. He earned a PhD in American Studies from the University of New Mexico in 1976. He has taught at four colleges and universities and is a retired Professor of History and Political Science from Spring Arbor University in Michigan. He and his family live in Jackson, Michigan.